PRIVATE RESERVE

BOOK 1
Desire & Luxury Wine

DIANA SOBOLEWSKI

Copyright © 2016 Diana Sobolewski
All rights reserved.
Cover photography © Kaspars Grinvalds / shutterstock
ISBN-13: 978-1523989799
ISBN-10: 1523989793

DEDICATION

To my real life hero, my brilliant husband, Georges, who understood that I just had to pursue my dream and encouraged me to do so. Thank you for your unconditional love and support, and for keeping me laughing throughout the process. Whenever I would recount some fantastical part of the story, we would always go through the same banter.

"What color is the sky in your world?"

"Blue. But it's *always* blue."

"So it never rains?"

"No. Never. It's *my* world."

You are my rock. Every woman should have a Georges in her life. She would be *richer* for it. I dedicate this book to you.

Deserving of special mention: GSD Daisy and GSD-Husky Kolten, my constant companions while I was writing; who alerted me when the city was stealing our garbage and when dogs passed the house. Mostly though, they motivated me to keep up our power walks, so that I would get my exercise and some fresh air.

DIANA SOBOLEWSKI

CHAPTER 1

Elżbieta Zalewski had cut it close. But Ela always cut it close at the airport; she didn't enjoy flying, and was never in a hurry to get on a plane. Ela dreaded takeoff and was uneasy the whole time that the plane was climbing to its intended altitude. She hated the descent just as much. When the plane banked, she instinctively shifted her weight in the seat to prevent the aircraft from spiraling out of control. Once the plane leveled off, she could relax … unless there was turbulence. Ela fought through it all though; she loved her work and in her business she was required to attend events an ocean away.

Ela Zalewski was the owner of Les Vins EZ Inc., an agency that represented producers of luxury wine in the Quebec market. This evening, she was flying to Bordeaux, via Paris, for a very important wine show that took place every two years: Vinexpo. She was also a regular at ProWein in Düsseldorf and Vinitaly in Verona. She had even attended Buy Wine in Florence a couple of times.

Robert Lecler, her director of sales, attended Les Grands Jours de Bourgogne in the Burgundy region of France, and Vinisud in Montpellier, France. Dividing the traveling helped, but any time in the air was too much time in the air for a wine agent with a fear of flying.

Since so much of her agency's business revolved around the wines of Bordeaux, Ela's trips to the wine producing region were not limited just to Vinexpo. This would be her sixteenth trip. Flying never got any easier.

Fellow passengers had no idea of the turmoil inside Ela's head. They only saw an attractive, self-assured professional, perhaps about thirty-five years of age, calmly boarding and then reading the airline's in-flight magazine while the plane taxied on the runway. Managing appearances was a coping mechanism.

Ela made a point of looking her best when she traveled. Robert had once asked her why she didn't just put on a nice pair of jeans, a casual top and some comfortable shoes to travel in. She had told him icily that if she were going to die on one of these flights, she would do so fashionably dressed.

This evening, Ela wore a cropped black zippered jacket over a black short-sleeve jersey top. The jacket cinched at her waist and flared out slightly to the top of her hips. Skinny pants in the same cotton blend, stretchy material stopped just above the fine bones of her ankles. Classic pointed pumps in buttery soft black leather, with a modest three and a half inch heel, were her idea of reasonable footwear. At five foot one, Ela had long ago adopted stilettos as part of her daily wardrobe, but the long airport corridors and wheeled luggage made certain concessions necessary.

There was a lot of black in Ela's suitcase. But then, when traveling, it was easy to mix and match black items. Should red wine get on her clothes at a tasting, the stain wouldn't show. She was also aware that she wore black well. Ela's attire was always polished and sophisticated, whatever the occasion. A wine agent had to look professional, of course, but it was also a glamorous business. Ela liked showing off her sense of style and her assets. She liked standing out.

Ela had a formula to help her look and feel her best on international flights. She dressed well and relied on CC cream for a healthy glow, and red lipstick, for a little color. Black mascara made her eyes look bigger when she was tired and squinting. A squirt of *eau de parfum* at the nape of the neck kept her feeling fresh. The custom-made diamond earrings were simply an indulgence she was never without.

Though Ela was not a fan of flying, she always looked forward to Vinexpo. Every two years over forty-five thousand wine and spirits professionals descended on Bordeaux to do business. It was an important event to be part of, whether you were selling or buying, and the atmosphere was electric.

On the buying side, there were importers, hotel and restaurant owners plus agents like herself. Wine journalists from all over the world gathered there as well. Yet it seemed that everyone knew everyone. You were always bumping into a familiar face.

During the day, Ela would meet with her existing producers to taste their new releases and plan strategy for the next two years. She would also meet with new producers whose wines she was interested in introducing into the Quebec market. That would entail understanding more fully what these producers could offer and an explanation of the buying practices in her home province. She would also take the opportunity to outline what she could do for them within this system, and what they needed to do on their ends. These were very productive appointments that almost always ended in a commitment.

The evenings were a different matter. Since her primary business was selling and promoting the wine produced by prominent Bordeaux châteaux, Ela was invited to parties and gala dinners that not many agents had the opportunity to attend. This was her big payoff for working so hard; this was where Ela got to really live it up.

Ela's week normally started on Saturday evening with La Jurade de Saint-

Émilion, a celebration of the wine and heritage of Saint-Émilion, dating back to the late twelfth century. The exclusive event took place in the heart of the medieval city. It was an occasion to induct new members who acted as ambassadors for these regional wines in their parts of the world. Ela herself had been inducted into this illustrious group several years earlier; she'd stood on stage in a red velvet cloak trimmed in white vermeil as her accomplishments were read out to the assembled guests.

The celebration always began with a cocktail period. The formally attired guests were served Champagne, as was the custom all over Bordeaux. A grand dinner that showcased the refined wines of Saint-Émilion followed, and then dancing into the wee hours.

Ela's week would end with La Fête de La Fleur on Thursday evening, a celebration of the wines of Medoc and Graves, and Sauternes and Barsac that was held on the grounds of a different château each time. It was a very prestigious event attended by over fifteen hundred elegantly clad guests from Bordeaux and other parts of the world. To receive an invitation was as rare as the wines that were served.

After the ceremony to induct new members, which might include famous personalities, cocktail period allowed guests to enjoy Champagne and white wine while mingling. Having never missed, Ela now knew a great many of the people who would be there.

The dinner tantalized the taste buds, but the wines were the stars of the evening. Guests who stayed beyond dinner were treated to fireworks and dancing.

All of this required numerous advance shopping excursions. Ela would figure out with pen and paper what she would need for what events, so as not to be seen in a dress or suit twice by the same people, but still get some of her clothes and accessories to do double duty.

She'd start planning in April and would only be done a week or so before Vinexpo, which was held the third week of June. Packing light was not an option in her business.

As a rule, Ela arrived the day before the hectic schedule got underway. She needed to rest and acclimate. She also flew out a day after everyone else, so she could recover after her last gala dinner and treat herself to a spa day.

A suite in the five-star Grand Hôtel de Bordeaux & Spa in the heart of historic Bordeaux would be home for the week. Just thinking about the luxury that awaited her did a remarkable job of lessening Ela's anxiety about flying. She thought only of her arrival now. A car would meet her at Merignac Airport, and transport her in comfort to the hotel that would take away her fatigue, restore her vitality and transform her back into the Ela that people expected.

She worked with some of the most renowned producers in the world ... their wines were legendary. It was only fitting that she stay in such a hotel. Besides, she deserved it. Ela had worked hard for this kind of life and she meant to enjoy her success.

While Ela was a woman who lived in the present and looked to the future, she did enjoy reliving some fond memories from the past ... like the last Vinexpo, two years earlier.

She had reserved a suite at Hôtel Burdigala, another beautiful five-star in the center of Bordeaux, with outstanding service. Nico Baggi had driven all the way from Tuscany to join her there for a couple of very memorable days.

Ela first met Nico Baggi in Florence at a wine salon intended to help stimulate sales for Tuscan wine producers.

Ela and Nico got to know each other over meals. Whenever another producer, an importer or journalist intended to sit next to Ela, Nico had made sure he got there first. At the end of dinner one night, after Ela mentioned how peacefully she'd slept in her room at the back of the hotel—unusual because she was someone who had difficulty sleeping well—Nico had complained that his room, which faced on to the street, was very noisy. He wasn't able to sleep. He had asked the hotel to find him another room, he claimed, but had been told it was impossible. All of the rooms had been taken. Could he sleep in her room ... on the sofa-bed, of course? Nico had asked Ela in his charmingly accented English. That was how Nico had come to be in her hotel room in Florence.

Once inside, Nico had deemed the sofa-bed inadequate.

Ela had agreed to let him share her bed and even pretended not to notice that he was naked when he got under the covers. While Nico kept to his side of the bed, trying to figure out how to bridge the space between them, she pressed her behind into his hip; feigning sleep. She moved against him over and over ... making Nico really horny and increasingly bold.

Then Ela turned onto her back in a position of proximity. Nico took that as an invitation. He turned on his left side and slid his hand under the flimsy nightgown to find her breasts. Ela had sighed but kept her eyes closed, even as he cupped one and rolled a finger over the nipple making it hard, then did the same with the other breast, caressing her until her nipples were tight with desire.

When he had started to stroke the thigh that was by then pressed against his, Ela had moaned, giving Nico the courage to take another chance.

He slowly inched his caresses up under the hem of her nightgown, sliding it higher and higher, until his fingers met the juncture between hip and thigh. Ela paralyzed with want, nearly melted with relief when Nico's fingers had begun stroking Ela between her legs. He had been surprised and delighted to find a bare pussy and even more surprised that she was so very wet. It was then that Ela opened her eyes and smiled at him. Nico smiled back as he bent his lips to hers and resumed his explorations of her body with renewed vigor.

When Ela had closed her eyes again, it had been out of ecstasy. She had raised her trembling thighs as Nico rolled a finger over her clit just as he had over her nipples. It had created a tension of unbelievable pleasure, and she had gasped at the electric shock that jolted through her when he slid that same finger into her pulsating, needy pussy. Ela remembered making an animal sound at the back of her throat as Nico had withdrawn his finger, teased it over her aching clit and reinserted it deeper. Again and again, he had penetrated her slowly, passing his finger over her clit with gentle pressure and then thrusting it deep inside her until Ela had raised her hips off the bed in an all-consuming orgasm.

Freed from any form of inhibition, when Ela had stopped trembling, she'd reached between Nico's legs to stroke a cock that was as hard as steel. He had moaned, uttering something in Italian as her fingertips had explored the length and width of him. Six inches with a width that was just right, a tight ball sac and short, fine pubic hair. She had pulled the foreskin over the head with her fingers. The tip had been wet with pre-come; his desire for her evident. Ela had wanted his pleasure to last, so she'd alternated between stroking his shaft slowly, using only her thumb, index and middle fingers, and tugging gently on his balls while delicately running a fingertip over the thickly lubricated head of his member.

Nico had been powerless to move. If the fire alarm had gone off, there wouldn't have been enough blood going to his brain to get him to safety.

When Ela had switched to sliding the foreskin of his cock over the tip, Nico had not been able to hold back. The first convulsion had gripped him from deep inside, passing through his balls, up the shaft, to the head and exploding outwards. He had made sounds that could have been pain, as spasm after spasm rocked his body.

Ela's hand, her thigh and his thighs had been covered in the sticky mess. Nico had been apologetic and a little embarrassed, but Ela had only laughed and suggested that it would be a good time for a shower.

To his delight, Nico had found Ela to be, as he put it, a hot-blooded woman; in the end, despite all his scheming, she had seduced *him*—something he had always fantasized about.

What Nico had not known, and Ela had not said, was that he'd played right into a sexual fantasy that Ela had entertained for years. It was a fantasy that helped Ela find her own release when there were no other hands around, which regrettably, was most of the time.

Eyes closed, Ela would conjure up a handsome man who found an excuse to be in her hotel room on one of her business trips. She would allow him to stay the night and to sleep in her bed. Then in the middle of the night, she would feel herself getting aroused. She would wonder if she was dreaming in her half sleep state, then fantasize that a strong hand was fondling her breasts, moving down to caress her inner thigh. Fingers would find her clit and tease her to a heightened state of arousal. Then when she was wet ... really, really wet, those fingers would enter the opening of her pussy, plunging deep inside her again and again, until the pleasure grew to unbearable heights and she was rocked to a long and satisfying orgasm.

So when Nico had provided her with a chance to see that fantasy realized, the temptation had been too great. Ela, who for many years had slept alone, consumed by her professional life, was glad that she had given into lust. Nico had not only performed just like her fantasy lover, but he had introduced Ela to other things that felt good. He had been quite adept at using his tongue on her clit, while simultaneously using his fingers inside her two other sensitive places. He had brought her to a ripping orgasm that way.

In the shower Ela and Nico had agreed that oral sex would be fine because there was no risk on either side, but lacking condoms, they had refrained from going further.

Nico, who had been deprived of the pleasures of lovemaking for far too long, found Ela to be an enthusiastic lover. The way she had used her hand to get him aroused and the way she had sucked on his balls and taken him deep into her mouth to make him come, had enslaved his body that night. He had never come so many times, with so short a break in between.

They'd had sex three times that night, three times the next night, and once on the morning that they parted. In between they had laughed and talked of their lives; both had known that this was only a very welcome diversion, not the start of a relationship. Before parting, they had made tentative plans to see each other again, the next time Ela was in Europe.

The next time had been Vinexpo two years ago. In Bordeaux, with a sufficient supply of condoms on hand, Ela and Nico had taken up where they'd left off in Florence. Ela's back to back appointments from Sunday through Tuesday, had given her two full days with Nico. They had barely gotten out of bed the first twenty-four hours, except to shower and eat what they had ordered from room service. It had been marathon sex for two people who were starved.

When Ela had thought she could not possibly have another orgasm, Nico would add something new to the repertoire. His tongue would weave in and out between her toes, and then he would suck on them as he thrust his steel cock into her drenched pussy sending her over the edge as she cried out in ecstasy. Under Nico's expert ministrations Ela came again and again. Only when *he* was satisfied that he had pleased her well enough, did Nico give in to his own orgasm.

On the second day, they had taken a drive around Bordeaux and walked along the Gironde River to get some fresh air and take advantage of the warm sunny day.

Hunger pangs had brought their stroll to an end. They'd returned to their hotel to eat lunch there. One appetite had been satiated, but another had started to build. They had kissed and groped each other in the elevator on the way up to their suite, shedding their clothes as soon as the door closed behind them. Nico had skillfully maneuvered her to a plush chaise longue, kissing his way down her body and plunging his tongue deep inside her aching, ready folds. She'd come almost immediately, her fingers tangled in his fair hair as she arched her back, calling his name, pulling his head in closer, shuddering with pleasure. Before Ela had been able to catch her breath, he'd lifted her and turned her around; she was kneeling on the chair, her hypersensitive breasts resting on the soft, rounded back. In an instant, Nico had knelt behind her, his hard chest to her back, his ready cock positioned between her legs. He'd kissed her neck and fondled her breasts as he entered her. The two of them had moved together, seeking release with uninhibited abandon. Ela had pushed back into his powerful thrusts as he squeezed her nipples and nipped her neck, bringing them both to the heights of passion until orgasm again overtook her and this time Nico had come with her, both surrendering to wave after wave of pleasure.

When they could finally move, they'd decided on a shower, soaping each other playfully until arousal again grew; Ela had dropped to her knees with a mischievous smile and took Nico's erect cock into her mouth. He'd groaned in pleasure as she'd expertly fondled his balls while sucking his length deep into her throat, rivulets of warm water flowing over them both as he found his release in her mouth.

With passion temporarily sated, they'd dressed for dinner at one of Ela's favorite spots, Bistro du Sommelier, barely five minutes' walking distance from Hôtel Burdigala.

At Bistro du Sommelier, the food was unpretentious and delicious. And the wines were fairly priced all year long. Ela had eaten there often. It was hard to get a reservation during Vinexpo, even when you called well in advance. Yet somehow the staff always seemed to remember her and managed to seat Ela at her favorite table in the courtyard, or as she called it in her flawless French "the room under the stars."

Ela and Nico had enjoyed a lusty romp in bed upon returning to their suite, and again the next morning. What better way to say goodbye. This time, they had not made any plans to meet up. It hadn't looked like they would have had any reason or excuse to for a while, or ever. Besides, they both had busy lives to get back to.

Ela would often think of their time together. When she thought about the sex, it would get her hot and wet, and the reality of her hotel encounters with Nico replaced the previous fantasies of a vaguely handsome man encountered during her travels. The images in her head were so vivid; her body seemed to remember them as well. She would climax to them. Still, Ela would think about the *man* as well. When they hadn't been enjoying each other's bodies, they had talked, so Ela had gotten to know a lot about Nico and his life. She would remember many things about him, but mainly that he had been affable, funny, warm and demonstrative. Most importantly, he had been himself.

On New Year's Eve, six months after their passionate farewell in Bordeaux, Ela had received a text message from Nico. It had said that he was thinking about her and how much their time together meant to him. A smiling Ela had expressed the same sentiment back to Nico.

CHAPTER 2

Ela slept in the Saturday morning after she arrived in Bordeaux. She had nothing scheduled until La Jurade de Saint-Émilion that evening and wanted some time to recover. Eventually hunger roused her from bed.

After a quick shower, Ela pulled her fingers through her hair and fluffed it, then applied matte red lipstick. She put out her traveling clothes for dry-cleaning, and dressed herself in a pair of white jeans, rolled up over her ankles, and a fine knit black top with three quarter sleeves. By the time Ela stepped into her black open-toed mesh booties and grabbed the bag she traveled with, her stomach was protesting loudly the lack of food.

Only minutes later, she was at the buffet table. This hotel had everything. She filled a bowl with that white cheese with the consistency of Greek yogurt that she always sought out when in France and fresh fruit. Then she piled a plate with smoked salmon and asparagus spears, ham, slices of cheese and scrambled eggs. She ordered a pot of American coffee with hot milk to wash it all down with. Ela didn't always eat like this, but today she had quite the appetite. Besides, all of these foods fit her eating habits.

Weighing just under a hundred pounds, the tiny woman with the overloaded breakfast plate attracted the attention of other guests. Ela had noticed the looks she was getting and figured out why. If they only knew. She had been fifty pounds heavier just a few years earlier. In her thirties, Ela had given her business everything she had with no time left to take care of herself. She ate anything and everything, not caring about the consequences, and packed on the pounds.

At that point, Ela hadn't exactly enjoyed fashion although she had always maintained a professional appearance. She had been self-conscious and done her best to hide her body with sliming undergarments and clothes that disguised her thickest parts.

In her mid-thirties, her business had hit its stride. Now well established, the agency allowed her to be her own boss and she had proven to herself and others that she had good entrepreneurial skills and instincts. Ela preferred to trust her own vision rather than someone else's and it had paid off.

One day, pleased with the way things were going in her professional life, Ela decided that it was time to take control of her body.

Once Ela had made up her mind, she never wavered from her goal. She eliminated carbs, processed foods, sugar and salt from her diet. She discovered that low fat proteins in the way of meats, poultry, fish and seafood gave her good muscle definition and revved up her metabolism. She found that vegetables, fruits, almonds, almond milk and low fat dairy could be tasty and satisfying for meals and snacks. Grilling, steaming and portion control helped reduce calories as well. Then she started working out and the results were noticeable; she adjusted her wardrobe to fit her newly honed body.

Soon Ela's only real indulgence was fine wine and the finest Champagne and she had no intention of depriving herself on that front. Bordeaux was what she liked most in the way of wine, as her palate was geared that way and she considered herself lucky to be able to spend so much time there—air travel aside.

Among her favorites were the Premier Grand Cru Classé A wines from the right bank, especially Château Ausone and Château Angélus, but she liked a great many of the Grand Cru Classé B wines from there as well; most notably Château Beau-Séjour Bécot. And who could resist Clos Saint Martin Grand Cru Classé.

Ela also enjoyed many of the wines of the left bank, including Château Haut Brion, among the first growths, Château Gruaud Larose Saint-Julien 4e Grand Cru Classé in the classification of 1855, Château Pontet-Canet Pauillac 5e Grand Cru Classé in the classification of 1855 and Château Malartic-Lagravière Pessac-Léognan, one of only six in the 1959 classification of Graves with a Grand Cru Classé white and red.

But she absolutely adored Champagne. Krug was one of her favorite brands. That made Ela a Krugist. However, she quite liked the Champagnes produced by the house of De Venoge as well. Their range of exceptional Champagnes could take you from aperitif to dessert.

Once Ela committed to her course of fine drink and healthy eating, cravings for foods that put the weight on disappeared because she did not see the logic in cheat nights. Cheat nights were supposed to reward you, so you would stay on the diet. She did not crave those foods, so why undermine her efforts by re-introducing them into her body. Besides, to her it was not a diet. It was a lifestyle change. Something she planned to do for the rest of her life.

The results were all the motivation Ela needed. Having gone from size 10 to 0, she began to again enjoy fashion. Rather than using clothes to hide her body, Ela sought clothes that would show it off. With that came a new attitude. She experienced self-confidence and discovered her sensuality and sex drive once again.

At the age of forty she now looked and felt better than she had at thirty-five. People who had not seen her since the transformation could not believe how good she looked.

The day that this handsome guy in his very early thirties, stopped his Lamborghini Gallardo convertible in the middle of the street as Ela came out of her Audi A4 and said, "Hi, gorgeous," she knew that she had turned a corner. Not long after, she had taken a chance with Nico.

Ela decided to take an even bolder approach to Vinexpo this year. She'd had enough of the conservative business clothes and modest evening dresses in muted colors. She gave all of her clothes away, save for a few dresses which her dressmaker altered to fit her new body and show off her now fabulously toned legs. Sometimes walking up stairs could be a bit of a challenge, but her dressmaker was not satisfied until everything was taken in and taken up.

This was when Ela discovered what Hervé Léger bandage dresses could do for her body. It was like they were made for her new figure and mind-set. They hugged her lean frame, but still managed to make her appear curvy and sexy. They made her feel feminine yet strong and confident.

Play big or stay home was her new mantra—corny but accurate. So the first dress she purchased was lipstick red, low cut, with small straps and a pencil skirt that showed off her flat stomach, firm behind and nicely rounded hips. It hugged her thighs and stopped just above her knees, bringing attention to shapely calves and delicate ankles. This was how she planned to introduce the newly sexy Ela at La Jurade de Saint-Émilion.

Ela thought out her accessories just as methodically: a red satin evening bag, a red silk and cashmere pashmina the exact color of her dress, her usual pear-shaped diamond earrings and neutral open-toed Stuart Weitzman patent leather platform pumps that made her legs look longer.

She would go with neutral eye makeup to accentuate her brilliant blue-green eyes. Of course, Ela would not be caught dead without her signature red lipstick. Since there was already a lot going on in the red department, Ela chose matte rather than high gloss, and she was glad that she had gone with a French manicure rather than red for her nails. It was enough that her toes were red.

While the lipstick was a staple, Ela changed perfumes often. She was trying a new one on this trip. To appreciate the fragrance, a man would have to be standing close. Then, it would draw him in, and on the practical side, not corrupt a tasting experience for another wine professional.

Émile Delacroix pulled up in front of Le Grand Hôtel promptly at five o'clock just as Ela Zalewski had requested when she'd called to book his chauffeuring services. She would be attending La Jurade de Saint-Émilion and needed to arrive in time for the reception, but after the induction ceremony. She would be in the lobby wearing a bright red dress. She had been very specific.

Émile chauffeured the wealthy around. Sometimes it was just driving ladies to cocktail parties and sometimes there was a need for his highly specialized skills, which included defensive driving and hand-to-hand combat. These skills had secured him a contract to drive the clients of an exclusive private club some nights, but most of the time, Emile took whatever business came his way, assuming the price was right.

Émile had plans to retire before he was fifty and he learned useful things driving rich and careless people. But Ela Zawelski's clear instructions and no-nonsense manner didn't seem to promise much more than a generous tip. He sighed as he closed the door behind her and returned to the driver's seat.

Ela caught the driver looking at her in his rearview mirror a couple of times as they drove away from Place de La Comédie. He was wearing tinted aviator sunglasses because the late afternoon sun was strong, but she knew he was looking into the backseat.

Émile was checking her out. He didn't often get clients that looked like this one.

When Émile delivered Ela to her destination, he removed his sunglasses and gave her his invoice, wondering whether or not she was wearing underwear. Ela was all business as she paid in cash, and added a respectable tip.

Emile thanked her and handed her his business card, so that she would have his number handy, he said. Émile made certain that his meaning was very clear when he told her that should she like to do some sightseeing, he would be very pleased to show her some places off the beaten path.

It was then that Ela noticed that his trousers were bulging in front. The driver was handsome in a tough-guy sort of way but she was not going to go there. That would be asking for a whole lot of trouble.

Ela curtly informed Émile that she had back to back appointments the whole week. There would be no free time.

"*Dommage,* too bad," he replied with a wicked grin. "Do keep the card, *Madame* Zalewski ... in case your plans change."

Ela nodded and walked away, relieved she hadn't booked him for the return trip. She had many business acquaintances who would be coming back into the city at the end of the festivities.

Émile took a moment to watch Ela as she walked away from the car and merged into a crowd of people lining up to get their seating card for dinner. He regretted that he would not have another chance to seduce her during the car ride back into Bordeaux, after she'd had a few glasses of wine. He did pride himself after all, on being quite good at getting women to do a lot of things.

Ela was looking forward to the evening ahead and sitting with Edmond Mallet. Though they were in contact several times a week, she had not seen him in person for over six months. Edmond was the Bordeaux négociant that Ela represented in Quebec.

Never had she known a man to work as hard as Edmond, but then he hadn't gotten to the top by sitting around twiddling his thumbs.

Edmond had been her conduit into the elusive world of luxury wine. Through him Ela had met some of the most memorable people she could have ever hoped to meet in Bordeaux. She used to read about these same people in wine magazines and then suddenly she was meeting them at the airport, setting up interviews for them, organizing events for them, taking them to meetings and getting to know them over lunch and dinner. They were the rock stars of the wine world, and they were taking advice from her. It was surreal. It was thrilling. She would always be grateful to Edmond.

For her part, Ela executed her responsibilities passionately and with precision. Edmond had opened the door to her but she contributed significantly to his reputation and that of his company, Mallet Bordeaux Société de Négoce, with châteaux owners. They always had high praise for her and her work and genuinely liked her. They found her real, without guile. She had a sense of humor and a way of making them feel comfortable on a human level. It was refreshing.

Edmond was thankful to have found someone as dedicated as Ela to work with in the important Quebec market. She helped Edmond and his employees navigate the system, and he knew he could trust her to look after his interests. They had accomplished much together over the years.

It was through their relationship that Ela developed an expertise in upscale wines. By definition, that meant smaller quantities, higher prices and a unique marketing, promotion and sales strategy. This was where she excelled and this was what she wanted to continue doing. Yet working direct for these particular wines was not possible in the Bordeaux system. It took an intermediary. It took a négociant, and a good one.

Over the years, Edmond had proven worthy of his results-oriented reputation and innovative methods. Ela too was well known in Bordeaux for her high level of service and professionalism. Producers had come to think of Edmond and Ela as a package deal.

Ela had been approached by five négociants since she started working with Edmond, but never once entertained any plans to move. She was loyal to Edmond. She believed that there wasn't anything they couldn't achieve together. Her positive attitude was her calling card … something else that Edmond liked about his agent.

Hong Kong billionaire Jianju Tcheng arrived in Bordeaux on the evening of La Jurade de Saint-Émilion on his personal plane accompanied by two male body guards and two male employees. The sixth passenger was not from Hong Kong, and Jianju treated him as an honored guest and deferred to him in all matters on this trip. The man who Jianju held in such high esteem, was none other than Aldrick Konig.

Aldrick Konig didn't have a specific job title. It was enough to be Aldrick Konig. He had been advising Jianju for years about Western business practices and brokered many a deal for the Hong Kong businessman. Each time Jianju branched out, Aldrick made a tidy commission. It was Aldrick who had found the three properties in Bordeaux that they would be looking at … Properties that the rest of the world didn't even know were for sale.

Aldrick Konig was probably the most unusual person that Ela had ever met in her business life. She was first introduced to him two years earlier by her négociant Edmond Mallet at La Fête de La Fleur. They were seated at the same table. He was there on some business that no one talked about.

Aldrick was physically unassuming, just under six feet with a slim physique, silver hair and conservative attire. Aldrick was known for his policy of not taking a drink except with people he liked, and he usually did not eat at the parties taking place during Vinexpo. Aldrick had indulged on that evening though, but Ela wasn't sure if it had been because he liked the people at the table, or he felt it would be too rude to refuse the astonishingly good wines that were being served, so expertly matched to the first-class cuisine. Aldrick did have good breeding, after all. He was an aristocrat.

At sixty-four, Aldrick wasn't impressed by much. His life was about high stake deals, complete control, recognition of his power and payment of his astronomical consulting fees.

Aldrick sized people up quickly and found most of them lacking. That was one of the major reasons that Aldrick was easily bored at social events. When he spoke with Ela at their table during the evening of Fête de La Fleur two years earlier, he found her to be suprisingly entertaining. She had called him out on his superior attitude. He liked that. She got his attention by telling him that she had never seen a person at one of these events that was so understimulated. They both knew she was right.

They'd talked for a while and it seemed Aldrick Konig knew everyone: world leaders, royalty, old money, new money. He kept many secrets too. He knew where all of the bodies were buried.

"If you ever wrote a book, Aldrick, some government would have you bumped off," Ela had told him with a saucy grin.

Aldrick decided that he liked Ela Zalewski and when he gave her his very plain business card with only his name and mobile number on it, she did not realize it made her a member of a very small and privileged group.

Aldrick Konig made his way to Edmond Mallet's table at La Jurade de Saint-Émilion after everyone else was already seated.

Edmond had been looking around every thirty seconds for the last half hour. He had sent a car for Konig and his high-profile Asian client Jianju Tcheng, but with Vinexpo on, the traffic was beyond bad, and Saint-Émilion was quite a drive. He should have sent a helicopter. *"Putain,"* Edmond said under his breath, using his favorite swear word. Why had he not sent a helicopter?

Ela had no inkling that Aldrick was one of the two invitees Edmond so eagerly awaited, but she recognized him immediately. He had not changed one bit in two years. And he wore the same expression of total boredom and complete disdain. Another one of *those* evenings that had to be endured.

When he spotted Ela, the smile on his lips was genuine, not the one he pulled out for everyone else.

Edmond also saw a look of interest in the eyes of the well-built, well-dressed, unusually tall Asian man in his early forties as he took in Edmond's Quebec agent in her red Hervé Léger dress. So, Edmond did not wait for Aldrick to introduce Jianju to Ela. He did it, and he also informed Jianju that she would be his dinner companion. Edmond went to switch the place cards around, and asked one of the other guests to move ... stating that the people who had set the table had made a mistake in the seating arrangements. Ela didn't think that this was true, but saw no harm in going along.

Jianju enjoyed himself that evening; more than he had expected to. Ela Zalewski was a good conversationalist and she became very animated when she talked about the wines that they were being served that evening. She was truly passionate about fine wine, but he sensed that she was a passionate woman in every way. She also made a point of saying some very complimentary things about their host, Edmond Mallet, and the excellent working relationship that she and Edmond had. Passionate and loyal ... trying to further Edmond's position with Jianju and asking nothing for herself.

Jianju pretended that his interest in his dinner companion was purely professional but in reality, he found himself physically attracted to this Western woman. She was appealing, feminine but also open, warm and engaging. He approved of the red dress that she had selected for this evening. In his culture, it symbolized good fortune and joy and he told her so. Ela smiled, charmed but not attracted to this interesting man.

When dinner ended, so did Jianju's time with Ela. He and Aldrick would be leaving as they had meetings early the next morning and their driver would be waiting.

Andris Gere stood out in the crowd but not because he was six feet tall. He was pretty much the same height as many of the other men, but still Ela found her eyes drawn to him. Perhaps it was that he had this clean shaven face and head which made him look just a bit dangerous, especially since he was wearing dark sunglasses.

A hit man, was the first thing that popped into Ela's head. The international kind that could use traveling for the wine business as a cover. Ela laughed to herself. She had an overactive imagination and she watched too many movies … telltale signs of a single woman.

When Ela had first arrived at the UNESCO World Heritage Site of Saint Émilion for the Jurade de Saint Émilion, the first person she had spoken with was Andris.

They were both in line for a glass of Champagne during the reception that preceded the dinner put on by the brotherhood of wine, which now included women, of course.

Ela had to get her own glass of Champagne because she was unescorted and she had not yet spotted Edmond Mallet. In line Ela overheard the big scary man in front of her complain to someone that he had been in Bordeaux for a day and a half, and had not had any wine yet. Ela's mischievous side came out and she spoke up.

"That's very sad."

Andris Gere turned to see who had mocked his plight and was delighted by what he found. She was easy on the eyes in that red dress that she wore more like a second skin than an article of clothing. She was going to attract a lot of attention this evening dressed like that, but he had a feeling that she knew this. No pretense. Just out to enjoy herself. They exchanged introductions and chatted flirtatiously as they waited for their Champagne.

Both Ela and Andris had plenty of opportunity to see each other during the course of the evening and when he said, "Hey, Montreal, why don't we meet up when the dancing starts," Ela had responded with, "Good people always find each other, New York."

Andris was a key player in U.S. wine and spirits distribution, so he was invited everywhere—like on this evening. He did not suffer fools gladly, lived to make deals, had no use for people who did not work for a living, took pride in renting an apartment in a rough part of the Bronx, visited wineries all over the world to satisfy his travel lust, liked to advertise that he had engaged in all types of deviant behavior so he could read shock on people's faces purely for his own entertainment and wore a custom-made tuxedo with complete irreverence.

It was pretty clear that people saw him as the bad boy of the wine and spirits industry in the U.S., and that was exactly the image he wanted to project. The fact that he was single did not surprise Ela one bit.

But it did interest her.

It was through Andris that Ela met Elden Ford that evening. Elden Ford was another American. He was at least two inches taller than Andris, with a full head of closely cropped hair, and he filled out his immaculate tuxedo quite well. Elden Ford, who looked like the actor Jeremy Renner to Ela, was all male.

His demeanor said it all. Ela recognized the type. He was confident, knew what he wanted when he saw it and he was very competitive.

Elden had been watching Andris and Ela on the dance floor. He was well acquainted with Andris, and he was curious about the woman in the red dress.

When Andris and Ela finally took a break, Elden made up the distance between himself and the couple in seconds, startling Ela, who was a little breathless from the dancing.

Elden's first words were, "Good to see you, Andris. You're obviously enjoying the evening. Why don't you introduce me to your lovely dance partner?"

Elden Ford ran a large wine importation and distribution business started by his father, "Out of some choice real estate in Miami," Andris added grudgingly. "He's almost as successful as I am."

The two men had not seen each other in some time, and as they chatted, their friendly rivalry became apparent.

For a while, they were a threesome, with Ela holding court. She unabashedly enjoyed the attention of the two handsome men vying for her affections.

When she finally excused herself to head for the ladies room, both men stood as well. When Ela returned, only Elden remained at their table.

Ela, slightly panicked that her ride back into Bordeaux had deserted her, scanned the crowd in search of him. "You seem very intent on finding Andris. Are the two of you involved?" Elden asked, not mentioning Andris had stepped away to greet a wine producer.

"I only met Andris this evening, but I am trying to keep track of him because he is driving me back to my hotel," Ela explained somewhat truthfully.

With Andris temporarily out of the way, Elden made his move. "I will drive you back to your hotel," he told Ela assertively.

"That's very kind of you. Thank you." She liked men who went after what they wanted, and apparently Elden wanted to get her away from Andris and Andris wasn't interested enough to stay on the offensive.

Elden then put a gentle hand around Ela's waist and pressed a fresh flute of Champagne into her hand.

At some point, much later than he expected, Andris returned to find that Ela was quite taken with Elden and Elden was being possessive about Ela. His body language said: *Too bad, buddy. You are the one who left us alone,* even as he politely explained he would be escorting Ela back to her hotel.

Andris felt strangely protective of the woman he had met only a few short hours earlier but he was a good sport in all things. He sought Ela's assurance she was fine with this change of plans and then took his leave.

Ela had had no reservations about Andris seeing her back to her hotel, nor Elden. Theirs was a small world and this was a very big event. People did not generally risk their professional reputations by behaving badly.

Elden did not often have the opportunity to be around an attractive unattached woman when traveling for the wine business, much less have an excuse for the kind of close physical contact that dancing provided. He had broken up with his long-term girlfriend over five months ago and had not even come close to anything remotely resembling sex with another person for a total of ten months.

Elden was especially grateful to have been invited to La Jurade de Saint-Émilion the moment he met Ela. He congratulated himself on being smart enough to stick around after the dinner and that he had put a few condoms in his wallet back at the hotel. To date he had not encountered many women like Ela, fascinating, fun loving and professional. He meant to make the most of whatever time she would spend with him.

Ela had not danced in years. With a second partner this evening, she was swaying to the music in perfect rhythm. Elden was doing a superb job of guiding her around the dance floor. She had no idea she could even move like this. They fit so well. She never tripped or stepped on his toes. She felt graceful in her high heels.

Elden spun Ela around, and she ended up with her back pressed against his front. She could feel his erection against the upper part of her backside as there was a significant height difference between them.

Ela swayed to the music in that position, enjoying the knowledge that there was indeed a big hard cock pressing into her. This was unexpected but certainly welcome. Anyone that would happen to be directing their gaze at his groin would not see the evidence because his tuxedo trousers were a classic cut and not so snug fitting. His jacket added further camouflage and presumably body hugging briefs were holding his member securely in place. Still, she knew and it gave her a surge of sexual pleasure; something she had not felt for a long time. Her appreciation of his aroused state was not lost on Elden.

Soon enough they made their excuses and went to retrieve his car. Spotting an opportunity, Elden ducked into an alcove hidden by shadow and potted tree and before Ela realized what was happening, his mouth was on hers. He kissed well … really, really well. His lips were soft and parted. His tongue was there between them, tasting her lips and gently probing for her tongue.

When Ela opened her mouth a little more in response, the tingling he felt on the tip of his tongue shot down to the tip of his hard cock. Elden attributed the level of excitement to being with a truly passionate partner.

A cream colored SUV passed them and Ela stiffened a little, wondering how much the occupants had seen and if she knew them. She knew a lot of people in Bordeaux and in the business in general. Shit, shit, shit. She had gotten carried away. She had been careless. It was possible that she had been recognized in her red dress, but hoped that through some miracle, she still had anonymity.

When Elden stated boldly that they might have to stop en route three or four times, pleasure stirred in her. To hell with anonymity.

Elden, very much the gentleman, opened the door of his rental car for Ela and closed it when she was seated. The nicely appointed French sedan was large and comfortable.

When Elden let himself in, he didn't start the ignition right away. Instead, he leaned in for a kiss. Ela met him halfway this time. She returned his kiss without reluctance, aroused by his forwardness.

Feeling sure of her invitation to continue, Elden caressed her knee and lower thigh. The tight Hervé Léger dress promised his eyes so much, but denied his fingers … a device of chastity for her and torture for him.

He decided to change strategy and caressed her breasts from the top, but that was also proving to be a challenge, at least at first.

Elden was finally rewarded when fingers met taut nipples. Ela ventured to caress the inside of his thigh and then took the initiative to squeeze his cock through his pants. He sighed. This was going to be a very long ride and he was not all that sure how it would all end. It had been a long time since he was last single and he'd been in situations before that looked promising and ended rather abruptly, without the kind of gratification he was now so desperately longing for.

He wanted so badly to unwrap this beautiful creature and explore every inch of her. To watch her face as he brought her to climax, heightening his own pleasure in the process. But first he needed to get them to Bordeaux.

They talked a little between bold caresses while he drove. She was intoxicating and he found it nearly impossible to concentrate on the road.

Good thing there wasn't a lot of traffic in the middle of the night.

Ela started to worry that her passion might very well be endangering their lives. She tried to distract both of them from their primal urges by occasionally asking questions about his business. She heard him responding, but did not register any of his answers. She was in a mental fog brought on by the physical ache building in her. Ela was a woman who knew what she wanted.

When he came to a stop at the barrier before her hotel and they were touching and exploring again, Ela said in a voice heavy with her need for him, "Why don't we finish this in my suite?"

Elden squeezed her inner thigh and quickly headed for the underground parking lot across the street before Ela changed her mind.

As it was three a.m. and the hotel was locked down, Ela had to ring for the man on duty to unlock one of the heavy front doors and let them in. She was a little self-conscious, but also very glad to know that they took the security of their guests seriously.

When they entered her lavishly decorated suite, verbal communication was replaced by instinct and body language. Elden found himself standing behind and to the side of Ela. The angle was perfect to kiss that side of her neck. He let his lips linger while his fingers caressed her bare shoulders. She was clearly lost in all of the sensations. His fingers found the zipper at the back of her dress and she did not resist when he started to work it down. She stood very still, enjoying the touch of his fingers against her spine. Elden pushed the straps off her shoulders, but she held the front of her dress over her breasts. Elden wondered if it was modesty or if she was she doing it on purpose to prolong the delicious agony he was experiencing at the desire to see her standing naked before him. The latter, he decided from the signals her body sent out. She held the dress seductively, not defensively. He took a moment to enjoy the view.

Ela's whole back and the upper part of her behind were already nicely exposed to his gaze and begging for his hand. She shivered when he brushed his fingers along her spine once again and rewarded him by letting go of the dress altogether. It fell away from her breasts and she wiggled her hips as she pushed the dress down until it wilted on the floor around her feet. Then she simply stepped out of it and turned to face him. She was totally naked except for her earrings and the neutral patent leather four-inch peep toe shoes that showed off her pedicure. She was sexy right down to her pretty red toes. He was still in his tux. There was something erotic about that.

Elden did not move towards her right away. He drank her in with his eyes … the way her chest was expanding from labored breathing and how her little breasts seemed fuller now that her nipples were hard.

Naturally his eyes found her flat, muscular stomach and the curve of her hips before landing on the V between her legs. He was transfixed. He realized that she was totally smooth where he expected to find a patch of hair. His lips parted slightly. The way he looked at her body was as arousing to Ela as if he were actually using his hands or his mouth on her. Every nerve ending was longing for him to do just that. This was a sensual man. But first she had to have him naked.

Ela did not have to wait long. His eyes never left her nude body as he undressed with haste and purpose. Ela's eyes followed his fingers as the black bow tie came off and landed on a chair followed by the jacket of his tuxedo. Then he was undoing his cufflinks and the buttons of his formal white shirt and stepping out of his shoes. She wondered if she should help, but since she was enjoying watching him disrobe, she decided against it, instead running her fingers lightly over her aching breasts, inviting him to hurry.

Elden met her gaze and purposefully unzipped his trousers. Ela could see white boxer briefs straining to hold back his ready cock. The package out front was conspicuously large.

Elden put four fingers inside the waistband on either side and freed himself, pausing a moment to run his hand over his enlarged member, teasing her just as Ela was teasing him. Then he pushed his pants away and stepped out of them, standing to his full height.

Ela did not look up into his eyes although she could feel the force of his gaze on her. She immediately looked down. She inhaled sharply, in awe of his substantial cock. At least eight inches fully erect, with an impressive thickness to match.

To complement this gift that nature had bestowed on him, was a large firm sac. Ela had a thing about balls and she longed to touch these. These were superb balls, perfectly suspended to add to the strong appeal of his beautiful cock.

His pubic hair was well trimmed. He was obviously proud of his genitals, and with good reason. She licked her lips.

Elden was amused at the expression on Ela's face. It was raw sex. He marveled at how at ease she was with her sexuality. He didn't move right away, so she could have a good look.

Desire was thick in the room.

Suddenly he covered the distance between them; his mouth was on her mouth and he was pressing her body into his. Ela bit his bottom lip gently and sucked on it at the same time. This sent him over the edge. In one effortless, fluid motion, Elden picked her up and carried her to the king-size bed that had been turned down by hotel staff earlier that night. Ela's left arm encircled his neck while her right hand rested on his chest.

Elden lay Ela down on her back against fresh cool bedding. He lay down to her left so he could devour her with his eyes as his hand was poised to explore every part of her ready body.

Dark loose waves framed her face and spilled onto the crisp white cotton sheets. This position emphasized her hip bones, making her shape seem even more waif-like. Elden started to trace that appealing curve and then moved lower. Ela responded by parting her legs a little, anticipating his next move, but not wanting to seem too desperate.

Elden bypassed where Ela had hoped his hand would land, and caressed the upper inside of her left thigh. He was driving her crazy—on purpose. After what seemed like an eternity of teasing and taunting, his fingers found her slick and swollen pussy. The middle finger of his right hand sought out her clit and he stroked her there lightly but persistently.

Ela was so wet ... so inviting. Elden could not help but slip that same finger inside. It had taken considerable self-control to have waited this long. She was open, and her body was telling him not to stop now. Elden moved his finger in and all the way out so as to engage her clit in the motion. Ela bucked against his hand, wild with the need to end this sweet torment.

Elden covered her mouth with his full lips and entered her mouth with his tongue, as he entered her below with his finger. His kiss was demanding and urgent; his finger sliding in and out of her and over her clit with relentless efficiency. Elden was going to give her the orgasm her body wanted so badly, but on his terms.

Beginning to feel the onset of a tremor, Ela prayed that Elden would not stop. Elden had no intention of stopping. He took her through wave after wave of pleasure, until the tension left her body and she fell against him limp. He felt her pussy pulsating with the aftermath of a very intense orgasm and he was pleased with himself.

As her breathing calmed, Ela appeared restless, something that had never happened with his girlfriend. Then it dawned on him. Ela was multi-orgasmic. He would have to do better, he decided.

Elden kissed the side of her neck, located a breast and sucked on the nipple until it was slightly reddened and swollen. His mouth moved to the second nipple and he flicked it repeatedly with his tongue.

Ela squirmed. Elden decided that he would just have to pin her hands to her sides to keep her still. Now he could go lower. Not free to use his hands, he had but one recourse. He kissed his way down, slowly using lips and tongue. This was such exquisite torture for Ela, but at that moment in time, she could not imagine a more pleasurable feeling. He stopped for a second and looked up.

"How do you feel about oral sex?"

"Yes, please ... I just want you to know that the last time I have been intimate that way was two years ago and I have been tested since then." Ela was glad he'd brought it up, she didn't want even a hint of practical concerns clouding their passion.

"I was in a monogamous relationship for six years and had myself tested when it ended five months ago, just to be sure. Everything is okay on my end."

No need to hold back now, the realization washed over them. So, Elden didn't.

His mouth covered her mound and his tongue searched out her clit. He licked her there with the dedication of a man who had a natural aptitude and was enjoying his work.

Elden's tongue found her center and he alternated his focus between licking, sucking and penetrating her there. The fact that she could not move and that he was in full control was such a turn-on, Ela could barely breathe. She was a prisoner of the tongue that he was now using like a penis. She knew she was close.

Elden did not relent. He concentrated on her clit now, intensifying her pleasure and bringing her toward the inevitable orgasm. Ela thrashed around, grasping at the sheets, turning her head from side to side as moans vibrated in her throat.

When it hit, she was transported by the orgasm's power to some other place. Elden would not let up, even when Ela was nearly at the end. She was a bit sensitive there and the exquisite pleasure bordered on pain for a fleeting instant, but soon the stirrings began again, and this orgasm blended into yet another. Then there was only the pulse between her legs.

Breathing regulated itself. She was back. Satisfied with the results, his lips wet from her, Elden smiled and released her hands.

Flushed and with a glow of light perspiration between her breasts, Ela was eager to be the one in charge now.

Ela pushed Elden onto his back to his amusement. He weighed almost twice what she did, but she had determination on her side. Lying beside him, she propped up her head with one hand while she traced his full lips with two fingers of her free hand.

She moved her hand to the base of his neck and caressed his broad shoulders and chest. He was slightly hairy … very masculine. With all of that testosterone, it was no wonder. When Ela arrived at Elden's torso, she could see that his already hard cock was stiffening even more. She avoided it on purpose. Two could play that game.

Elden pulled Ela's upper half onto his chest so he could enfold her in his arms. She raised her head off his chest, sought out his right hand and brought it up to her face. She kissed his palm slowly, sensually, deliberately, then isolated his middle finger and took it into her hot mouth.

She worked her tongue around it, advertising the pleasure yet to take place. By the time Ela slipped his finger out past her lips, only to maneuver it in much deeper, his breathing had changed.

What she was doing was so incredibly erotic, he worried that he would come the moment she touched him below, even if by accident. He had to stop her. It would be too embarrassing and he so wanted to prolong this ecstasy.

"Please stop," Elden pleaded. Ela released his finger and placed her head on his chest innocently, not moving for a full minute. When she felt that the danger had passed, Ela's hand started to travel south.

She stroked his strong thighs and stopped just below his balls. He sucked in his breath. Now he really wanted her hand on his shaft. As if she had read his mind, Ela reached to take hold of him gently with her fingers.

Ela's repetitive stroking had the tip of Elden's cock glistening. Encouraged, Ela switched the position of her body to nestle herself between his legs.

She used her tongue on his wonderful balls and then sucked on them. She licked up one side of his immense shaft and then the other, stopping just below the head. She licked the lubricated head almost like an ice cream cone with her flat relaxed tongue.

Elden was at a loss what to do with his hands, but when Ela took him into her mouth, or as much as she could fit into her mouth considering his size, he grabbed her head and raised his hips. She had to pull away a little. He was just too big. Realizing that she would choke if he continued, he released her head and gave her control.

There was just too much cock to do justice to by using only her mouth but Ela was not one to be deterred. She extended her reach by employing her right hand. With her index finger she traced the tip of his cock while it was still in her mouth. She lubricated the shaft of his cock so that she could glide her hand up and down while using her mouth over the sensitive head and giving him the chance to admire her French manicure.

Ela looked up at his facial expression to gage his level of arousal. Elden's attention was focused on her hand movement and how the head of his cock disappeared into her mouth. The visual was adding to the general stimulation in a big way.

She liked that he was watching her. She knew that there was only one way to please him beyond this point. "Do you want to come like this?" she whispered the question, her breath sliding across the head of his penis.

Self-control was well beyond the realm of possibility now. He was ready, so caught up in what she was doing to him that he could barely manage to form the word *yes* with his lips.

Ela needed no additional prompting and set to work on the head and shaft with a steady slow rhythm. Having propped herself up between his thighs, with her legs under her, she was able to bend right over his cock. From this angle she could move up and down over about two thirds of his large shaft quite effectively. The fingers of her right hand stroked the balance in unison.

The technique was tried and true, bringing about the expected reaction, but it was when she gently tugged on his sac with her other hand that Elden gave in to one of the most intense orgasm he had ever had.

He came in her mouth—the orgasm lasting longer than he could have ever imagined, the pleasure making coherent thought nearly impossible. He briefly wondered if it was okay to come in her mouth but he was powerless to do anything else. Ela did not show any aversion and swallowed. Elden was relieved.

This was the best blow job he had ever had. He would not forget it anytime soon and he silently thanked whatever forces had brought this marvelous creature into his life.

Ela was suddenly feeling very sleepy, and like a child up way past bedtime, crawled under the duvet prepared to be overtaken by sleep. Elden wrapped his arms around her and pressed a kiss to her forehead. "Please feel free to spend the night," she offered sleepily.

Neither Ela nor Elden broached the subject of going another round later. They were suffering from extreme exhaustion. Both had been up since early morning of the day before.

Thankfully Ela didn't have any appointments until the afternoon, but that was not the case for Elden. He suddenly realized the time, and that he had an early morning meeting—in just three hours. He explained to Ela he had to leave immediately.

Elden moved quickly to dress, so Ela resisted the desire to slip into restorative slumber. Instead, she sat up in bed cross-legged, holding a sheet over her breasts, a little shy now. Elden came to the edge of the bed when fully dressed and kissed her softly on the mouth.

"Do you have a business card?" was all he could think to ask. Ela reached for her evening bag on the nightstand, and fished out one of her agency cards. She held it out to him as if they had just been introduced.

Elden took it from her, looked at it quickly, as was the polite thing to do, and put it in the pocket of his tuxedo jacket. "I'll call you," was the only thing that would come to him.

Ela smiled, but said nothing. She blew him a kiss and he let himself out. Men always felt that they had to say things like that. To Ela it seemed silly. This had been a good night. Each had given the other much pleasure. That was enough. That was more than enough. That was absolutely great.

Ela dragged herself to the door to double-bolt it and then slid into the deep European bathtub. She would sleep well this night if she could manage to lift herself out of the bathtub.

DIANA SOBOLEWSKI

CHAPTER 3

Hugh Jordan ran a hand through his long wavy medium brown hair, his hazel eyes scanning the private party, looking for someone of interest. As head of his family's Bordeaux Supérior château he was obligated to attend these sorts of things and hobnob with certain people but nothing prevented him from having a bit of fun later in the evening. His brooding expression turned to a smile when he spotted Ela Zalewski … chatting with a group of producers.

Ela and Hugh had become acquainted a few years earlier when mutual friends had introduced them at a cocktail party. At the time Hugh's family was seeking to diversify their international dairy business by purchasing a productive château and Ela had given them some invaluable counsel on what agents looked for and which wines held her loyalty. Buoyed by her counsel Hugh had convinced the family to invest in a particular property whose clients even purchased the wines in the difficult vintages when the weather had played havoc with the grapes.

It was in those difficult years that the château had achieved its reputation for uncompromising quality. By harvesting only the very best of the fruit and working magic during the vinification process, the winemaking or production part, the château team assured their brand's ongoing success.

The yields were small in those years, but what they produced was surprisingly good and they had sold out.

The château had changed hands and Hugh found himself at the helm of a major operation.

Ela had worked closely with Hugh over the last two years and had seen how women threw themselves at him. That's not to say that she wasn't attracted to him herself. He did exude a certain aura to which she was not immune.

There had been some sexual tension between them each time they got together and they had had some pretty frank conversations about sex, love, relationships … but so far nothing more.

In those conversations, Ela had learned some things about Hugh that surprised her. Like most people, she had always thought of Hugh as a bad boy. Apparently he had earned that reputation in part because he was resisting his family's pressure to marry and present them with heirs. His parents reminded him constantly that it was his duty. Two sets of grandparents were just as adamant.

Hugh had told Ela that he loved his family, but he did not look forward to Sunday dinners and the procreation grilling. "What was he doing about it?"

they wanted to know. At least they didn't tell him who to marry.

Hugh had confided in Ela that the he could not imagine himself tied down with just anyone. He'd had a few long term relationships, some satisfying ... but he never found *the one*.

People would not have taken him for a romantic ... a man holding out for his soul mate. In truth, he was looking for the woman who would be his partner in life. The right woman would challenge and stimulate him intellectually, and captivate him in bed. Someone like Ela, he often thought, though he had no actual knowledge of what she was like in bed. She just seemed to have those qualities. That would explain why he was attracted to her.

Now standing between the white tents gracing the lawn in front of his friend Gaspar Haillet's château, Hugh contemplated his glass of Gaspar's white Bordeaux ... the 2010 vintage.

Holding his glass by the stem, he swirled the liquid to release its bouquet and was rewarded with aromas of exotic fruit backed by citrus fruit. The palate was equally pleasing, with citrus flavors coming to the forefront followed by white fruit and good minerality. Gaspar's Sauvignon-Semillon blend was well balanced. There was that long finish in the mouth. An elegant wine. The term seemed overused, but it was accurate when a wine had all this going for it. It was not that he hadn't had it before, it's just that he hadn't had it for a while.

Hugh remembered that the red from the same vintage was equally delightful. He'd enjoy it next. The evening looked promising.

Minutes later, Hugh noticed Ela making her entrance. Ela was now representing Gaspar's wines as well ... His friend mentioned that a couple of months ago. Hugh had mentally classified the information under *small world* and then completely wiped it from memory for some reason.

Ela looked particularly enticing this evening. Hugh didn't know one women's wear designer from another, but he did know that the white bandage dress with sweetheart neckline and cap sleeves that defined every curve of her body was amazing. Nude patent leather peep toe platform pumps lengthened her shapely legs.

Hugh observed Ela for a while from this vantage point. Unaware, she continued to make her way through the crowd, stopping for the obligatory two-cheek kiss almost every few feet. After all of her years in the business, she knew quite a few people at every gathering she attended. This evening was no exception and there would be a lot of greetings and a lot of kissing.

Business acquaintances would introduce her to their business acquaintances and there would be the perfunctory *enchanté* meaning "enchanted to meet you" and some small talk ... maybe a little business talk. It was how these things went. Everyone followed the same script.

As soon as there was a respite and before she could fully get her bearings, a good looking guy that Hugh judged to be only a couple of years older than himself made his way to Ela's side.

Hugh recognized him after searching his memory for a couple of seconds. Though he did not recall the name, the man was Gaspar's new *maître de chai,* or cellar master.

When Ela's self-appointed companion had gone off to fetch her a glass of white wine, Hugh walked over nonchalantly, as if he had only just spotted her.

After Ela and Hugh had engaged in the usual pleasantries for a few minutes, Ela was lured away by another producer friend of Gaspar's, Marceau Lyon. He did not do business with Ela at the present time, but was interested in such a collaboration.

Gaspar's employee looked confused when he returned to the spot where Ela should have been standing. He looked a little ridiculous with a glass in each hand and no one waiting. Hugh resisted the desire to laugh, turned and walked away.

Marceau did not sell his wines through négociants either. There would be no conflict for Ela so she seized this chance to chat with him. Ela had been interested by what he had told her. His wines had been winning medals in the big international competitions over the past few year and they had been awarded some impressive scores by several of the most reputable wine guides and magazines for three years in a row. Consistent quality was good. That would sell. Ela saw the potential right away and Ela always went with her instinct.

The icing on the cake was that Marceau had a pretty decent promotional budget to work with and was ready to support his wines in the market to attain his objective, establish brand and build sales. He seemed marketing oriented and highly motivated. Ela liked that. She would be able to work with him and felt confident about being able to sell his wines and promote them effectively.

If they worked together, he would attain his objective in a two-year time frame. Of that she was sure. She had the results to prove it.

It seemed that Marceau was aware of her excellent record and that she lived up to her producers' expectations. He had heard good things about her and was eager to work with Ela, even though he had been approached by other agents and would be approached by more this week. If she agreed to represent his wines, he would not take any other meetings.

So, they set up an appointment at the exposition site for a tasting of his full range of wines in the most recent vintage, but he promised to pull out some older ones, so that she could see that his well-priced wines were age-worthy, up to about ten years in a good vintage.

This was how it usually happened for Ela—word of mouth. You just never knew where you would meet the next supplier during Vinexpo. This was when strange and wonderful things happened and any one of them could change your life.

In the meantime, Hugh was being monopolized by an overeager couple in their early sixties, clients from Quebec City. They had insisted that the next time he presented his wines in Quebec City, and they hoped that it would be soon, he absolutely had to have dinner at their house.

They managed to mention at least three times that they had a well-educated daughter that had just turned thirty and happened to be single. He wasn't engaged by chance, was he?

Husband and wife were relieved when he replied politely that he was not, and were quick to inform him that as their only child, she would inherit their business, which they assured him was not so small—they both winked at that last statement to show that they had let him in on a valuable bit of information—if he caught their meaning.

Between the winking and the matchmaking, Hugh was in hell. He finally managed to extricate himself by holding up his empty glass to show that he was going for a refill. He had been drinking quickly, rather than taking the time to enjoy, just so that he would have a reason to get away from the couple without openly offending them.

Later that evening while still dodging the couple, Hugh noticed that Gaspar's cellar master, was pretty much stalking Ela. This annoyed him for some reason.

When her shadow went to the men's room, Hugh went to see Ela and asked how she was getting back to her hotel. Ela told Hugh that she had arrived by taxi and had planned to return the same way, but Gaspar's recent hire, Antoine Fortescue, had been nice enough to offer her a ride.

Hugh insisted that he be the one to drive her back to her hotel, saying that he had some business to discuss with her. Ela did not seem to mind the change in plans, so Hugh told her that he would explain everything to the chivalrous gentleman who had come to the aide of *his* agent.

The cellar master's fake smile and nod of understanding told Hugh everything. The man had had designs on Ela. Neutralizing Mr. Amorous gave Hugh a certain feeling of satisfaction.

As it turned out, Hugh never broached any kind of business topic with Ela throughout the whole car ride. Strange, but okay, she thought. Maybe he was no longer in the mood.

When they arrived in front of her hotel, Hugh asked, "What is your room like?"

"I'm staying in one of the suites. It's very comfortable, and there's a king-size bed."

Ela assumed that Hugh was just curious. The inhabitants of Bordeaux probably didn't have much opportunity to see the rooms or suites of this hotel or any other in their home city, only the restaurants and bars.

He followed with, "If I leave my car in front of the hotel, will the valet service take it from there?"

Ela decided not to play along right away; she wanted to draw it out of him.

"Nice car by the way," she said changing the subject. Well she did appreciate his newly acquired vehicle. She reminded Hugh that she had had a smaller model in blue gray for several years and announced that she had just changed it for a new one in black. It was a great car to drive any time of the year. She loved the styling, how it handled and how well it performed in Canadian winters.

She had driven producers from Bordeaux around in snowstorms, she informed Hugh, launching into a long tedious story. Hugh fidgeted in his seat but pretended to listen, so Ela kept making the story more pointless, trying to force him to stop her and ask for what he really wanted.

Finally Ela managed to bore herself and Hugh looked exasperated. She stopped and looked at him. "You could just ask." Hugh feigned indignation through body language and said nothing.

"Anyhow," she went on, "it is late. Are you in any shape …?"

"*Mechante*—you're mean," Hugh replied—more indignation. "Get out of my car."

"Oh, go on and give your keys to the valet."

Victorious, Hugh smirked and did as instructed. The cat and mouse game was just part of the foreplay.

"*Je vais accompagnier, madame,*" he told the attendant to indicate he was going to accompany Ela to her suite. Ela provided the young man with her suite number as Hugh handed over the keys.

Upon entering her luxurious suite, Ela offered to pour Hugh a glass of wine from the bottle that her négociant Edmond had sent over. Château Pontet-Canet Pauillac Grand Cru Classé 2001 was one of Ela's favorite wines from the left bank. The *assemblage*, or blend, was Cabernet Sauvignon, Merlot, Cabernet Franc and Petit Verdot. The nose of red and dark berries was complex and beguiling. The elegant tannins were testimony to great *terroir* that gave the wine its personality and the long finish indicated that this was a *vin de garde,* a wine to lay down. Fortunately the 2001 was already a great pleasure to drink and seemed fitting for what would likely be a particularly memorable evening.

Hugh was tempted, but declined, citing that he would have to drive himself back home at the end of the night.

"I have an early meeting tomorrow morning … so much going on this week … all of the importers in town," he continued apologetically.

Hugh decided to take up residency on the edge of the bed. So, Ela walked up to him to stand between his legs and offered her back to indicate that she needed help with the zipper of her summery white Hervé Léger number. Hugh was more than happy to oblige, fully aware that she did not really need his help. She was teasing him.

Unzipped but held in place by the cap sleeves, the dress only exposed Ela's back to his view. Damn sexy though ... no evidence of panties ... exactly where she intended for him to be looking.

Ela disappeared into the bathroom, closing the door behind her. A moment later, Hugh heard the sink and then the shower running.

Still fully clothed, Hugh reclined comfortably on the bed against a stack of pillows, hands behind his head. Not having come armed with a toothbrush, he had made do with breath mints he had taken from the car.

Ela emerged in a short white silk kimono robe and the same pumps with the four-inch heels she had been wearing at the party. The material of her robe looked fluid against her body in the soft lighting and threatened to reveal more skin with every movement.

She smelled delicious. Her skin was pink from the warm shower and a couple of wayward strands of damp hair were plastered to her neck.

Hugh asked if he could use the shower and detected minty breath when she responded to his request with, "Sure. There's a robe behind the door."

Hugh did not bother to close the door behind him, but Ela could not see a thing from where she positioned herself. Imitating Hugh, Ela occupied his former spot, legs crossed and hands behind her head. She meant to ogle him playfully when he came out of the bathroom.

Funny how natural all of this seemed. Ela was now eager with anticipation. Caressing yourself to get off was just not the same as a hot guy in your bed.

"I guess the drought is over." Ela's thoughts strayed to the last man to have shared her bed before this trip. It was Nico Baggi ... two years ago right here, in this same city.

She remembered how he would take his time to build her arousal and make her come, and how she found that she could not leave him alone for long. They didn't get much sleep. Well, sleep was overrated. Great sex was stress relieving and invigorating. Oh, yes, it had been both of those things, and euphoric.

It had been the first time that she had allowed physical desire to override her self-control on a business trip. Ela was glad she did. She could admit wholeheartedly now that it was one of the most pleasurable experiences ever. Nico had been a glorious lover. To think, she almost passed that up.

If she had, she probably would not have been receptive to Elden's seductive charms or Hugh's sexual prowess. In both cases that would have been a crime against nature.

These days, she couldn't imagine denying herself that kind of rare pleasure with such amazing lovers.

Thinking back she realized what the three men had in common. What must have always been noted on a subconscious level came to the surface. They had pursued her and, in each case, competed for her. She had been the prize they had walked away with after beating off the competition. Like episodes of *Wild Kingdom* with alpha males, but in evening wear and a little more subtlety…That was what she had responded to, if she were to be completely honest with herself.

Ela could not have predicted how her week would go, but after Nico, she always traveled with condoms … just in case.

In less than five minutes, Hugh walked out of the bathroom barefoot and wearing the white terry robe provided by this top hotel. Ela noticed droplets of water at the base of his neck and some wet tendrils of hair. He had not spent a lot of time drying himself off. He was impatient. Good. It would be sweet.

Hugh smelled of soap and was wearing a big smile that revealed straight white teeth. She noticed teeth because the wine business was not kind to teeth.

"Do you like what you see?"

"For now, but I need to see more before I can fully commit to an opinion."

Hugh reached for Ela, pulling her up and off the bed. He quickly sat himself at the edge of the bed once more and placed her in his lap with absolutely no effort. He marveled at how tiny she was, *"Tu es tout petit,"* he exclaimed in his mother tongue, then added, "Don't lose any more weight."

Seated on his lap, her head was level with his. Now he could brush back her hair and kiss that lovely neck. Ela absorbed the sensation of his warm breath and soft lips on her skin.

Hugh cupped her chin and turned her head to kiss her mouth. He had thought of doing this on more than one occasion over the last couple of years. She tasted good when he parted her lips with his tongue. Ela started to squirm in his lap and reached up behind his head to bring him in for a deeper kiss.

Well she was obviously not the passive type—and that was good, thought Hugh. He had no use for the passive type.

Hugh's hand slipped under the cool fabric of her robe to engage a warm breast. It gave Ela goose bumps all over. When he removed his hand, it was only to undo her robe so he could fondle the other breast while kissing her mouth again. This time the kiss was deeper and more demanding.

Eyes closed, Ela kissed him back with equal ardor. Her responsive nipples were making Hugh crazy with the desire to explore more of her body. If she reacted like this now when he was hardly doing anything, she had a great capacity for pleasure.

Hugh caressed the outside of Ela's thigh and moved all the way up her hip and down again; Ela felt that she might just pass out. An electric current was building up inside her body—certain parts of her body anyway.

"Open your legs for me, Ela."

Still on his lap, Ela opened her thighs to Hugh's touch. She was so hot and so wet when his fingers found the lips of her pussy that it took him a second to register that she was bare there.

Perfect... direct contact. His large hand wedged her thighs apart a little more, while his middle finger went in search of her clitoris. He rubbed that precious bit of her anatomy with such expert motions that Ela almost immediately felt herself building toward climax. She surrendered to his touch and came in a long, satisfying orgasm without ever touching him. Only once he felt her relaxing against him did he take his hand away.

"Wow, you're good."

"Ela, I want to use my tongue on you. As you know from the conversations we have had, I am the cautious type. I think I told you all of that because I always knew we were headed to bed one of these days. Would it be a safe thing to do?"

"Yes, but first I want to use my mouth on you."

Ela slipped off Hugh's lap to indicate that she was in charge. "Lie back," she ordered and lay to his right when he was on his back.

Ela undid Hugh's robe. Even before she had a chance to touch him, Ela found herself looking at a full-blown erection. Now she could confidently commit to an opinion. "I like," she said in admiration of his rigid cock. It was above average length and width and he was endowed with a nice set of balls to go with it. The manscaping just made his cock look that much longer.

As Ela leaned in and over to take him in her mouth, Hugh flipped her into a perfect 69 position without warning. Luckily Ela landed gracefully without taking out an eye with one of her stiletto heels.

Her robe remained relatively intact; having slipped down just one shoulder and risen up only high enough to expose the lower part of the cheeks of her cute ass.

There was little point in keeping the robe on, but it did not get in the way and Hugh was not exactly making it easy for her to maneuver herself out of it. Holding her behind in place under the robe with his hands, his mouth covered her entire pussy. He was now able to explore every inch of her with his tongue.

At this point, there was only one thing for Ela to do so she lowered her mouth onto his shaft.

Ela certainly liked to receive pleasure, but she was a considerate lover herself and it made her even hotter when her actions made her partner uncontrollably horny. Besides, it was all very normal for Ela. It's the way she was made.

Hugh took her a little by surprise at that moment by penetrating her very core with his tongue. He was clearly hell-bent on driving her to madness. The telltale wetness, the throbbing and the sound she made in the back of her throat, let him know she had reached another orgasm.

Ela stayed in that position so as not to interrupt the attention she was giving his cock. She had him deep in her mouth and had maintained a fairly even tempo of moving up and down right through her orgasm.

This made Hugh delirious, but he was going to have to put an end to such activity or he would come sooner than he wanted to. He was not quite done with the single-minded Ela and would have to dissuade her from her present course and quickly.

That's when Ela found her behind in the air and then the rest of her. She was being lifted out of her position. It was impossible for her to continue what she was doing. At first she wanted to ignore his rude interruption. Well that was the point, she realized, and looked to Hugh with interest.

Hugh got off the bed and walked over to the chair where he had laid out his tux. Reaching inside a pant pocket, he retrieved a foil packet and held it up to show Ela.

"STDs are not an issue between us obviously, but pregnancy is … Alright?"

"Perfectly alright."

Hugh sheathed himself in record time, and sat on the edge of the bed motioning for Ela to slide herself onto his ready cock.

It wasn't that he wanted her to do all of the work, but knowing the female body as well as he did, he knew that this position provided good contact between penis and clitoris for double stimulation and was known to produce some powerful orgasms in women.

This was his go-to position when he wanted to ensure that his partner experienced the ultimate in sexual fulfillment. He also liked the idea of playing with her breasts for her pleasure and his, and watching the expression on her face as she reached orgasm. It would be an additional stimulant for his own orgasm.

Ela had other ideas though. She was on the edge of the bed beside him … on all fours with arms down to brace herself, and her ass up in the air. The last time she got to enjoy this position was with Nico.

Hugh decided that the lady should have a say and immediately moved to his knees. Holding on to her hips, he penetrated her slowly from behind, easing himself in, a little at a time, while pulling her towards him. She was very wet, but she was also very tight. She was so tight in fact, that he was getting overstimulated even through the condom.

"Am I hurting you?"

"No, it feels really good." To demonstrate her sincerity, and allay his fear of hurting her, Ela moved against him and brought him deeper into her. With his whole length inside, she started to rotate her hips and rolled herself over his cock in a kind of corkscrew motion.

Ela did not know how she came by the idea, but when Hugh told her that he liked the way she moved and found the natural rhythm to go with the movement of her hips, it heightened her pleasure.

They were heading to the same place. Hugh wanted to last, but he was getting so close. He was tempted to slow down or stop altogether, but would not risk depriving Ela of what she needed from him now.

He tried thinking of other things instead … the meeting tomorrow … the couple who were trying to marry off their daughter with him as their prime candidate … what he had for breakfast …

Ela cried out that she was coming and he met her there with a deep final plunge … a guttural sound rising out of his throat as his head snapped back.

Hugh released his hold and saw that he had left white marks on slightly reddened skin where his fingers held her behind firmly. He withdrew. She flopped on to her stomach, exhausted.

He dropped the condom into the bin and flopped on his back beside her, trying to catch his breath. When they made eye contact, they both started to laugh.

Like riding a bicycle, Ela thought, *only a much more fun cardio activity.*

She would always think of him as an expert lover who was very considerate. What luck that it was he who had driven her back to her hotel this night.

They were content just to lie there like that for a long while. Both were slightly sore but utterly sated.

Reason eventually prevailed and Hugh got himself into a standing position. He pointed to the bathroom, too tired to speak. Ela nodded that she understood, too tired to say anything herself.

After a refreshing tepid shower to bring himself back to life, Hugh dressed himself and thought what a special woman that Ela was—warm, passionate, funny, *adorable* as the French say.

It was no longer Monday night. It was Tuesday morning. If he didn't have to be in business mode in the next few hours, he would have held her in his arms and they would have fallen asleep together. She would be fun to wake up to. Or maybe they would not have slept at all.

Well, he really didn't have a choice, so it would be best not to dwell on these things for the time being. He wondered if he could manage to keep certain images out of his mind during his business meeting. He hoped so. It wouldn't do to get a hard-on right in the middle.

When Hugh was gone, after kissing her affectionately with a, "See you soon," Ela forced herself into the shower. She had nothing until her lunch meeting. Thank goodness; otherwise she would have shown up wrecked.

CHAPTER 4

For the second morning in a row, Ela rode the elevator down with a tall broad shouldered man in a well-tailored Italian suit, polished shoes and luxe watch. He was freshly shaven, with an expensive haircut that was parted on the side in that sexy retro style.

From Milan, she had thought Tuesday morning. With the sandy blond hair and magnetic cobalt blue eyes, it was possible. He had a trace of boyish good looks to soften his handsome masculine features. Ela felt an instant physical attraction to him.

He had incredible presence, so he would have an important job, Ela had decided. She was drawn to power, so that made him doubly attractive.

"Good morning," he'd greeted her yesterday.

"Good morning," Ela had replied politely, then added, "Thank you." Not Italian. Though he spoke perfect English, she detected a very faint German accent.

This morning, it was she who held the elevator for him.

"Thank you."

"My pleasure. We have to stop meeting like this. People will talk."

The man smiled warmly at the petite brunette in the sleeveless lightweight black business dress that played up her feminine figure. The pointed-toe pumps did the same for her tanned legs.

She knew how to bring attention to her best features. Classic eye makeup made her gorgeous blue-green eyes pop, light coverage with little color for a flawless complexion ... classic matte red lips for a sophisticated smile, and a subtle fresh scent to make her memorable.

Her only adornment, exquisite diamond earrings. The bag over her shoulder was more briefcase than handbag.

"It seems we are on the same schedule."

"Normally, I would be at the exhibition site by now, but I didn't have any meetings this morning, so I decided to go for breakfast a little later and then return some emails in my suite." Ela talked a lot, and fast, when she felt this kind of nervous excitement. "And you?"

"I have been invited to a lunch in Saint-Émilion, and was also planning to work in my suite this morning."

"I know Saint-Émilion very well ... the producers, the wines ... I was inducted into La Jurade de Saint-Émilion a few years back."

"Then you would know Laurence Bonnet. I'm going to be her guest at her château."

"I was invited to that, but I have an appointment today at one o'clock and it was set months ago."

"That's too bad."

Ela blushed.

"My name is Torsten," said the good-looking man holding out his hand.

Ela took it. Firm grip.

"Ela."

"Would you care to join me for breakfast then, Ela?"

"I would be delighted."

Ela found that she wasn't as ravenous as she had thought. They were shown to a table for two by a window overlooking Place de La Comédie, and only made one trip to the buffet, together.

Torsten handed her a plate and let her in before him. Old World manners. She liked that.

They had the same eating habits, judging by what was in their respective plates, but did more talking than eating.

Ela told her new acquaintance about her work at his request, and learned in turn that Torsten wasn't actually in the wine business, so that was why he didn't go to the exhibition site.

She also discovered that his full name was Torsten Lucas Furst when he presented her with his business card. There was only his name on it, a mobile number and an email address. "This is my private contact information."

Ela gave him one of her business cards in return.

"Nice logo … I like the partial wineglass, and the card stock … A bold choice. The shade of gray is modern, but says: You need to take me seriously."

"A friend of mine designed it. He now refers to this shade as Les Vins EZ gray. You don't by any chance run a communications agency, do you?"

"As a matter of fact I do."

"So how is it that though you are not in the wine business, you are in Bordeaux during Vinexpo and have been invited to a lunch put on by Laurence for VIP importers?"

"Laurence and I are friends and I am a client. I buy through the négociants, but Laurence comes to Germany to do winemaker dinners for my corporate events and some charities that my organizations support. I have a similar relationship with some other châteaux owners, and I have been visiting them as well over the last few days."

"Will you be at Fête de La Fleur?"

"Will you?"

"I really look forward to Fête de La Fleur. I haven't missed since I started the agency. My négociant Edmond Mallet always buys a table for his top clients and invites me."

"Then I shall attend."

Ela had her doubts, but said nothing. Maybe he didn't realize that the fifteen hundred guests had confirmed months ago, and invitations were hard to come by, even if you did know someone. She didn't want to embarrass him, so she simply said, "I hope I'll see you there."

That was another strange thing about this particular wine event. You could run into the same people a couple of times during the evening and just as easily never come across someone else. Still Ela was flattered that this charming European wanted to go to the trouble of securing a place because she was going to be there.

"Are you free for dinner this evening?"

"I'm having dinner with my Chablis producer. We have dinner together at Bistro du Sommelier during Vinexpo. It's a tradition now. I should be back by eleven, though. A drink at the bar?"

"Rooftop at eleven fifteen, in case you are delayed. The Champagne will be chilling."

"How do you know that I even like Champagne?"

"You don't just like Champagne; it's your drink of choice."

"You're good."

"Dom Perignon 1971?"

"You do know how to live, Mr. Furst."

Ela had fun at dinner with her Chablis producer. They talked a little business, but since they had worked so well together over many years, a good part of the evening was devoted to finding out what was going on with the other personally.

He wanted to know if Ela's relationship status had changed. She gave him the same answer she always gave him. She was too busy, she hadn't found the right guy. Then she reminded him that *he* had taken *his* sweet time. He had scored big though. His wife was a prize ... Beauty and brains, and now they had this terrific family which included two kids, a boy and a girl.

At eleven fifteen p.m. Ela Zalewski made her appearance at Night Beach with its panoramic views of Bordeaux. The warm breeze caressed her shoulders. She had been in the hotel by eleven but decided to detour by the ladies room: pee, wash hands, brush, floss, blot the shine off face, re-apply lipstick, pose like a diva in front of the mirror and walk out confident.

She would after all, be matching wits and maybe even flirting a little with the attractive, self-assured, successful businessman who was springing for Dom Perignon 1971.

Torsten was already there and watching for her. He stood up, being a gentleman, so she could see him. The Champagne was chilling.

Torsten looked relaxed in an open neck white shirt, well cut summer jacket and trousers in navy blue, neutral footwear and that pricey watch.

Ela felt his eyes move over her. She was glad she had worn her color blocked black and white Hervé Léger dress. She knew it flattered her body.

Torsten was thinking the same thing. He was also thinking that he could probably get both hands around such a small waist. The scoop neckline showed a little cleavage, which wasn't a bad thing, but could be a somewhat distracting. Her black leather sandals with their high skinny heels, made her legs look sexy. She was wearing those diamond earrings again.

Torsten's guest placed her black leather clutch beside her as she sat down.

"Did you enjoy your dinner?"

"I had a great time. Thank you. How was your lunch?"

"Enjoyable. Laurence knows how to make her guests feel special. You did miss some good wines and delicious food. We talked about you. Were your ears burning?"

"Really?"

"She enjoys working with you."

"And, I with her. So what did you do this evening?"

"Since you were unavailable, I had a bite in the hotel and made some phone calls."

Torsten asked Ela about her ancestry, where she was born, what she had studied in school and how she came to her line of work.

"Ela is short for Elżbieta?"

"Yes. My parent were born in Poland, and even though I am Canadian by birth, they decided on a Polish name. It was the name of both of my grandmothers, so it was pre-destined. The funny thing is that they called me Ela since I can remember … even when they were speaking to me in Polish."

Ela asked Torsten where he was from, and found out that he was indeed German but spoke several languages due to his academic studies in different parts of the world.

"Which languages besides German, English and French?"

"Italian and Spanish."

"Fluently?"

"Yes."

"As well as you are speaking English?"

"Yes."

"That is quite a talent."

"It's practical."

"You're far too modest."

"I noticed that you speak North American English, but now and then, you throw in a word in British English."

"I know. I live in North America and work with Europeans. I say *cell phone* when I'm home and *mobile* when I'm in Europe, for example. I write that way too. What's more; I live in Quebec and work with people who live in France. In Quebec, as I'm sure you know, we have certain expressions in French that don't mean the same thing in France. Then there is the switching from English to French and vice versa. Sometimes I'm speaking the two to the same person in the same conversation."

"Do you speak Polish?"

"I'm rusty. You know, I understand a little Italian. I studied it in school, but it has been so long that I have lost any conversational ability that I once had. I love the way that Italian sounds to the ear, though."

Before the night was out, Ela just had to ask the question she always asked of all of her producers and anyone connected to the wine industry. "Torsten, if you were stranded on a deserted island, and you could only have a case of one wine to sustain you for a while, what wine would you choose?"

"It would be a Bordeaux with Merlot as the primary grape."

"You could narrow it down."

"I like to leave my options open."

Ela and Torsten enjoyed the 1971 vintage of the legendary Champagne as they talked. It was remarkable how it still retained a certain freshness, while the color had turned golden. They both adored the notes of pear, caramel, baked apple, toasted brioche and nutty flavor. They agreed that minerality was present, and that it was rich and round in the mouth. It was a shame that they were taking their last sips, marking an end to their time together.

When Torsten walked Ela to her door, she wondered if he would ask to come in, but he didn't. She kissed him on both cheeks and thanked him for the exquisite Champagne and stimulating conversation.

"Thank you for the pleasure of your company. I look forward to seeing you tomorrow evening."

"So, you did manage to snag yourself an invitation?"

"I was motivated. It will be delivered tomorrow morning."

"Until tomorrow evening, then."

It would be too bad, if they missed each other at Fête de La Fleur after all of the trouble he must have gone through, but he did have her business card. He could always call her mobile and they could meet up somewhere on the grounds. He was obviously a resourceful man.

CHAPTER 5

Thursday morning was hectic. Ela took a taxi to the exhibition site, mostly to say goodbye to producers she worked with and those she would be working with. They probably wouldn't see each other for a while.

Exhibitors would be packing up that afternoon, as another edition of Vinexpo came to a close. Those that would have to get ready for Fête de La Fleur, usually left the site a little earlier. Ela wanted to avoid the long line at the taxi stand on that last day, and waiting in the traffic going back into Bordeaux, so she was out of there by twelve thirty.

Arriving at the hotel, Ela walked directly into L'Orangerie, the inviting bar off the lobby with its glass roof and orange trees. The bar menu was much to Ela's liking. Lunch would have to get her through the afternoon and into the evening, so she ordered a ham omelet, a salad as a side dish and non-sparkling bottled water to keep from getting dehydrated.

Ela had taken a seat where she could better see some of the comings and goings in the lobby and be seen … in case Torsten should be around.

There was no sight of Torsten and she had taken her last bite, sighing with contentment. It was a well-known fact that omelets tasted that much better in France.

Ela headed back to her suite. She wanted to have some time to return emails, rest, then get up and lay out her toiletries, makeup, dress and accessories for the evening. She didn't want to rush too much in the shower either or while drying and styling her hair.

Edmond would be sending a driver to pick her up. She wouldn't have to do anything more taxing than wait in the lobby.

As Torsten came out of the elevator, a couple of women of different ages wearing floor length evening dresses cast admiring glances in his direction. When they saw that he was holding the same invitation as they, they raised theirs and smiled. Without using words, the ladies were saying *We're part of the same exclusive club.* Torsten smiled back and nodded in acknowledgement.

It was Ela that drew his full attention though. To find her, all he had to do was look in the direction that a group of formally dressed men was looking.

Ela hadn't seen him because she was focused on the doors of the lobby. He took a moment to enjoy the way she looked in profile. There was time. It's not like she was going anywhere.

This evening, Ela was wearing another bandage dress that fit her body like it was spray painted on, but didn't look the least bit uncomfortable. It showed off her great figure. This one was black, strapless with a sweetheart neckline partially adorned with silver sequins. It was cocktail length and Torsten wholeheartedly approved. It would be a shame to cover up those legs.

Her black platform evening sandals with bandage detail on the crisscross straps and four-inch cigarette heels were very sexy. He hoped she wouldn't hurt herself, but if she happened to fall into his arms … In any case, it would give him an excuse to offer her his arm and help her to maneuver the steps out front, while she hung on to her evening bag with the other hand.

Once again, the only jewelry that the wine agent had on were the distinctive looking earrings with their pear shaped diamonds. She wore her hair in loose waves to her shoulders, but he could see them when she moved her head. They suited the shape of her face.

Ela only saw Torsten from the corner of her eye at first.

"Good evening, Ela. You look very beautiful."

"And you cut a fine figure in that tuxedo or should I say *smoking,* since we are in France."

"Thank you. Are you waiting for a ride?"

"I think Edmond's driver was delayed."

"He's not coming … because, you're going with me. The car should be here any minute."

"Edmond's driver was to bring my invitation. Security is very tight. No one gets in without showing an invitation."

"I have it, right here. It was delivered with mine, this morning."

"Edmond?"

"He was very accommodating."

"That would mean he would have had to ask his wife to sit this one out. She couldn't have been very happy."

"She forgave him when the three dozen roses arrived this afternoon, along with the invitation to spend a long weekend on a private yacht, and the telephone number and email address of the travel agent that would arrange airline tickets in first class."

"All this to be at Edmond's table?"

"Of course. That's where you'll be sitting."

"I presume that Edmond is already there changing the place cards around?"

"It seems that we are going to be dinner companions."

"I hope that I can keep you entertained after all of this effort."

To this, Ela got a cryptic smile. "I see the car. Shall we?" Torsten guided her out of the hotel with a light touch to the middle of her back. She liked the feel of his hand there.

The car was like others Ela had seen around the hotel except that when the driver got out to hold the back door on his side open, another man got out from the right front seat to hold the back door open on that side.

Ela didn't want to look like she was new to such things, so she didn't ask. By the way that this other man was acting, paying more attention to people around the car than the passengers, he had to be with some protection service.

During their drive, Torsten listened attentively to Ela's summary of all of the Fête de La Fleur evenings she had attended. She was most animated when she told him about her very first Fête de La Fleur at Château du Tertre.

"I didn't know what to expect … only that it was going to be a very special evening, and I was one of very few people in Bordeaux to have this privilege.

"At six p.m., the sun was beating down on us. I had not thought to wear sunglasses, so I was squinting a lot. On top of that, I was wearing black. It was boiling hot in the shade.

"Thankfully the long evening dress had a side slit for ventilation, and we were given a fan and cold water to sip when we arrived. In some of the years that followed, the weather was drastically different. It was gray, cold and raining. I was chilled to the bone even with a silk and cashmere Pashmina over my shoulders. I yearned for the heat of my first Fête de La Fleur."

"Anyhow, something else I remember is that we boarded one of these mini trains that evening, and it took us from the parking area right up to the manicured grounds of the magnificent Margaux château. It was so the ladies in their heels would not have to walk the distance on the cobblestones. I had entered another world. I was already on a high before the Champagne."

"When we arrived, there were these well-groomed young men in black trousers and pristine white jackets done up at the neck, with beads of perspiration on their foreheads holding trays heavy with flutes of Champagne at the correct serving temperature. I don't know how they managed that."

"When it was time for dinner, we found our table under this huge spectacular peach tent. Inside, suspended from the ceiling, or whatever the term is when you're sitting in a tent, were these large chandeliers. It was so beautiful, but it was uncomfortably hot in there. The men asked the ladies for permission to remove their jackets and we gave it unanimously. If I could have, I would have put ice cubes down the front of my evening dress and in my panties."

Torsten laughed at her bluntness.

"The way they serve wine ... well you'll see ... music cues this parade and then there is this person at your table, pouring one of the most coveted wines in the world into one of your glasses ...

Dinner blew me away and to this day, when I think about the wines, I get goose bumps. After dinner, we enjoyed Armagnac while watching fireworks. I remember a band that looked more like an orchestra, a pool with floating candles and dancing until early morning. I was living a dream. I will never forget that feeling."

Torsten was trying to remember if he had ever come across a woman who was so alive. She was contagious. She was like a tonic for his weary spirit.

"By the time we take our first sip of Champagne, you'll feel it, Torsten. There is this electricity in the air."

Ela and Torsten arrived undetected, but by the time they had toasted with their first glass of Champagne, Edmond found them. He kissed Ela on both cheeks, and turned into the consummate PR man with Torsten.

Torsten had been enjoying his time alone with Ela and didn't care for the intrusion, but Ela represented Edmond. He couldn't forget that. She seemed fond of him too and he was one of the reasons that they were here together this evening, so Torsten decided to be polite to their host.

Ela wouldn't have minded having Torsten all to herself, but she understood how things worked. She was just happy to be at Fête de La Fleur and if not for Edmond, she would have never attended this time nor any of the previous times.

Edmond left them for a while to continue with his PR activities. He was there to work. He sought out clients, *courtiers,* or brokers, and important château owners.

Ela and Torsten were not alone for long. They were joined by the owners of châteaux that they both knew and were stuck chatting right up until it was time to sit for dinner.

They were the last to arrive, and when they did, Edmond made the introductions. Edmond's best clients and a couple of wives were his guests this evening.

Edmond had placed Ela between himself and Torsten. It was wise to be in the good graces of a man like Torsten Lucas Furst.

The Asian lady on Torsten's left didn't speak any one of the languages that Torsten was fluent in, so he just smiled at her now and then. She was the wife of the gentleman to her left. Her husband and Torsten exchanged a few words in

English, but there was no steady stream of conversation.

Halfway through dinner, Torsten excused himself, presumably to find the mens room, and Edmond took the opportunity to speak to Ela without the others at the table overhearing.

"How do you know one of the richest and most influential men in Europe?"

"What?"

"You don't know?"

"We only just met."

"Torsten Lucas Furst is worth billions of euros."

"I guess I'm just not up on the billionaires of Europe."

"He went to a lot of trouble to be here as your dinner companion. It's obvious that he's interested in you."

"You're reading too much into this, Edmond," Ela said nonchalantly, but secretly she was pleased by what Edmond had said.

Ela and Torsten exchanged comments about the dishes that had been created by the Michelin Star chef for the wines being served. They also expressed their impression of the wines.

Edmond noticed that whenever Ela had high praise for a wine, Torsten made a note in the margins of the menu. Ela had clearly some influence over this man and Edmond would love his business.

Ela excused herself to join a short line for the ladies room. Edmond took advantage of her absence to speak with Torsten.

"If there's anything that I can do for you, please let me know," he said courteously as he handed Torsten his *carte de visite,* expecting one in return.

"I don't have any business cards with me, but I have yours." With that Torsten tucked the card into this pocket.

When dinner came to an end, and the other guests said their goodbyes to Ela and Torsten, Edmond wanted to know if they would be staying for after dinner drinks, entertainment, fireworks and dancing.

Ela had not thought to ask Torsten.

"Torsten, all I planned for tomorrow is a spa day, but if you would like to get back, it's fine with me." She wouldn't have minded the close contact of a dance with this man, but it would have to come from him.

"I'm afraid that I have an early flight tomorrow and I'll be going straight into a board meeting when I arrive."

"Of course."

A two-cheek kiss for Edmond from Ela and firm handshake from Torsten to express their thanks, and they were on their way.

The car was waiting for them.

When they were on the road, the sky was pitch black and filled with stars. It was peaceful. Ela was getting sleepy from the wine and the excitement. It was late enough. She tilted her head back and closed her eyes to rest them for a bit. Ela never felt her head land on Torsten's shoulder. Neither was Ela aware that Torsten had turned his head slightly so as to look at her, but not enough to disrupt her slumber. She certainly didn't know that he was smiling.

When the car pulled up in front of the hotel, Torsten woke Ela gently, and for a second she didn't know where she was. It came to her slowly, and then she realized that she had been sleeping on Torsten's shoulder the whole way.

"This is embarrassing ... falling asleep like that. Thank you for the use of your shoulder."

"You are tired. It's understandable. I closed my eyes too."

"So we slept together?" Ela asked mischievously.

Torsten laughed. "It would seem so."

When Torsten walked Ela to her door, she wondered nervously what would happen next.

"I can't remember enjoying an evening so much," he said, "You're very good company."

"I had a great time, and not only because of Fête de La Fleur."

"I'll take that as a compliment."

Should she ask him if he would like to come in, she wondered.

"I guess this is good night." Torsten spoke firmly.

Ela was a little disappointed. He did have that early flight, but ...

"And, goodbye."

"Not necessarily. I have a meeting in Montreal a week from today, since technically it's Friday morning. If you're free next Friday evening, would you have dinner with me?"

Ela wasn't ... but she would be.

"Yes. I'd like that."

"Wonderful."

"Where are you staying?"

"It's a last minute thing. I'm not sure that all of the arrangements have been made. Could you recommend a hotel with meeting services and a very good restaurant with a very good wine list close by?"

"You have all of that at the Ritz Carlton. The restaurant is Maison Boulud and it's outstanding."

"I'll inform my office tomorrow morning and confirm with you in a couple of days. I have your coordinates. Sleep well, Ela, and enjoy your spa day."

This time, it was Torsten who kissed Ela on both cheeks.

"Good night, Torsten."

Torsten was smiling as he walked into his suite. He did have a meeting ... only it was to be held two weeks from today and in New York. He had never even been to Montreal. He certainly didn't have any business dealings there.

Tomorrow the executives involved would find out there had been a change in venue and the meeting moved up by a week. They'd be scrambling if they weren't already well prepared by now. It would keep them on their toes for next time. It was good to be the boss.

Ela felt separation anxiety in her room. This was crazy. They had just met. In any case, she would be seeing him again. She was excited about that. Then what? She was already dreading those goodbyes.

DIANA SOBOLEWSKI

CHAPTER 6

Ela had been back in Montreal for four days and there was still no news from Torsten about his trip to her city and their dinner at the end of the week. Should she try to contact him, she had asked herself. No, that wasn't really her style. She'd just have to wait it out … but God was it frustrating.

The normally industrious wine agent got little done workwise after her return, but she did do a fair amount of pacing in her two bedroom apartment in Old Montreal.

It was nothing like the luxurious suite in the Grand Hôtel de Bordeaux, and it was sparsely decorated. Still, it was comfortable enough.

The open layout and minimalistic style of her furniture made the place feel airy and spacious. Besides, Ela's apartment had been a wise investment. She bought it when people were just starting to move into the area, so she managed to get it for a pretty good price, indoor parking included.

Ela's parents had left her their house in Notre-Dame-de-Grâce, or N.D.G. as it was locally known, which she was able to sell in a sellers' market. She had invested the money while continuing to live in her modest N.D.G. apartment. When it became a buyers' market, she bought her apartment in Old Montreal, cash.

The apartment was more than just her home. It was the nerve center of her small but very productive company. She found it conducive to working with producers by email and telephone in a variety of different time zones. She could get up in the morning and start working right away. She could work late into the night. It gave her yet another leg up on her competition. She provided solutions in a timely manner. She saved all kinds of travel time, especially in bad weather, and was able to get a lot of work done by nine a.m. when other agents were just getting into the office.

If she had to meet with her director of sales, Robert, who had worked out of his downtown apartment only a few blocks away before he had gotten married, the large dining table doubled as a work table.

These days though, Ela and Robert did a lot more work via video call on Skype, because he and his new wife had moved to N.D.G.

Nevertheless, Ela and Robert still got together once a week at her apartment, to finish off the week and set up the following week. Robert would take a taxi into Old Montreal and back home, so that that they could go out for a nice long lunch that included wine.

It was an efficient and practical use of space. Ela defined the living room part with a large, deep sectional sofa, ottoman, stereo, side tables and a large storage-like piece of furniture that framed her flat screen television. It was actually a Murphy Power Wall Bed. A remote would open and close it, and an overnight guest would have a built in television to watch.

Ela never actually had an overnight guest, but she was ready should the need arise. The area rug further defined the space and gave the subdued decor that pop of color for contrast. The artwork was limited to two large contemporary paintings she found in one of the galleries that Old Montreal was known for and a huge heavy framed mirror that reflected light and gave the place a touch of glam.

Her light fixtures and lamps did as well. She didn't bother with plants, but ordered flowers every week to make up a big arrangement for her dining room table.

Ela dedicated a corner of her living area to a treadmill, mat, exercise ball and weights. Her personal trainer came by once a month and changed her program. Thankfully with a couple of days' notice, he was usually able to accommodate Ela's schedule.

Ela did not entertain in her apartment. She preferred to go out to eat when with other people. She did occasionally prepare a simple healthy meal for herself, and the Atwater market and large Metro store nearby provided her with all of the ingredients she could possibly desire.

For a wine agent, Ela's wine collection was abysmally small and fit into a one hundred-bottle humidity and temperature controlled unit. It was filled with older vintages ready to drink. She was not much of a collector of wines that needed time. She bought older vintages when they were available.

Her office was very functional with the usual high tech office equipment, but it could only be described as organized chaos. That suited Ela just fine. She once read something about a number of successful well respected people who she shared this trait with. Ela had felt vindicated. She had to plead with her cleaning lady almost every week to leave everything where it was. Her cleaner had obviously not read the article. There was a lot of rolling of the eyes.

Ela put a lot of effort into her bedroom. She outfitted it with a comfortable king size bed. The eight-hundred-thread-count sheets had cost a fortune, but they made her bed so welcoming she never regretted the splurge. And, anything that would give her a little uninterrupted sleep was worth the money. Ela Zalewski was an insomniac. She had been since she was a child.

Ela was aware that while she knew a lot of people and attended a lot of social events, it was mostly for business, she had no real friends, other than Robert and his wife. Diane was her first female friend since Ela was in her early teens. She had always had more in common with males than females.

Even the relationship with Robert's wife was recent. Diane had only come into Robert's life a year earlier.

Ela sometimes thought that maybe she should make more of an effort to get to know more members of her own sex but she really wouldn't even know where to begin. Aside from work and work-related events, Ela's social life was nonexistent.

Ela made herself believe that she liked her privacy. In her heart of hearts though, she really did not like living alone all of the time. It was not that she wanted a roommate or a cat, she wanted more. Ela suppressed the thought adequately enough most of the time, but once in a while, she would find herself daydreaming.

There would be a lover … He would come through the door in the evenings or she would come in to find him already there when she came home. They would prepare a meal together. He'd have to cook. She was more the type to buy ready-to-eat foods, like smoked salmon, or rotisserie chicken. They'd tell each other about their days. They would select a wine together, maybe two. They would finish their last glass cuddled up on the couch. One would get up and the meaning would be clear … They would head to the bedroom to make love on that huge bed. She would sleep well. They would wake up together.

When Ela had been a girl, like so many young girls, she dreamed that she would one day marry her Prince Charming. By the time she reached thirty, the memory of that dream grew fainter and fainter, displaced by her professional hopes and goals.

Ela had mastered immersing herself in the physical act of sex, while remaining emotionally detached during her carefree college days, consequently, she'd never had to deal with a broken heart. She considered herself lucky. Pleasure with no messy breakups and there was no pinning after someone. Her way was best, Ela often told herself.

Ela's mind wasn't on work, but she couldn't just sit around waiting for a call, text or email from Torsten either. She'd drive herself crazy. If he did get in touch last minute to confirm his arrival, she wouldn't have the time to get done what she'd need to get done. So, Ela made an appointment for her nails and a pedicure for Thursday afternoon. Friday morning she'd get her hair colored and styled. If he didn't call, she'd treat herself to a night out.

Wednesday morning, Ela finally received a text from Torsten confirming their dinner at Maison Boulud, Friday evening at eight p.m. and politely asking if she would meet him there.

Ela replied that she would see him at the restaurant.

Looking forward to our evening, Ela.
So am I, Torsten.

Ela hoped that Torsten would be punctual, so that he would already be at their table when she arrived. She planned to make an entrance.

Ela was on cloud nine and filled with nervous energy. She went into her walk-in closet and rifled through the boxes that contained her Hervé Léger dresses. She would know which dress was the right dress when she saw it.

After Ela put aside what she considered to be the perfect number along with the accessories she would wear, she got on her computer to check out the suites at the Ritz Carlton Montreal. She was acquainted with Maison Boulud, the opulent Palm Court lobby that paid homage to the hotel's historically significant past and the sleek Dom Pérignon Bar that was a modern addition, but not the rooms or suites, as she had never visited a guest.

Ela had read that recent renovations had cost 200 million dollars and that elements of the hotel's glamorous past combined with elegant modern décor and newest technology made for an unforgettable stay even for those who were used to five-star hotels.

Ela wouldn't stay over because she wouldn't have a change of clothes with her but she felt confident he'd invite her to his suite even though he had not hinted at an overnight bag. There was something she would come equipped with, however; a few condoms tucked into the little pocket on the inside of her evening clutch.

The doorman of any great hotel is the first indication of what the hotel stands for, so when the doorman at the Ritz Carlton Montreal opened the back passenger door of Ela's taxi and welcomed her, she knew that she had recommended the right hotel for Torsten and his people.

Ela had entered through the hotel rather than the outside entrance of Maison Boulud, so she could check her appearance in the ladies room before entering the restaurant. She wanted to come across poised and attractive, not someone who was trying too hard, and she needed a minute.

The mirror reassured her, and the smiles of a couple of good looking men in the lobby did so even more.

The young woman in black that greeted Ela in her perfect Parisian accent when Ela came through the door between the hotel and Maison Boulud confirmed that the gentleman was waiting at their table.

"But, I didn't give you my name."

"The gentleman described you. Please follow me."

Ela followed the beautiful dark-haired woman through the lounge, past the open kitchen to the green house that opened out onto the terrace overlooking the garden complete with duck pond.

The way these cute feathery white creatures frolicked about entertaining the patrons had always fascinated Ela. It's like they knew they were the big attraction at this valuable piece of downtown real estate.

Torsten noticed that something or someone caught the attention of several men at a nearby table, and smiled when he saw Ela. He was not surprised to see her wearing still another bandage dress—nor was he disappointed.

This one was nude, sleeveless, with a v-neckline and cross-over detail bodice. It hit just above the knee. She wore platform sandals in the same hue and carried an evening clutch. There were those diamond earrings he had gotten used to seeing, the familiar red lips, and that infectious smile. His heart rate sped up.

Ela had watched Torsten rise to his feet and she liked the way he was looking at her. Dressed in a navy blue suit, white shirt, navy tie with red pin dots, white pocket square and black oxfords, he looked like the captain of industry that he was.

"Good evening, Ela. You're a vision."

"Good evening, Torsten." He kissed her on both cheeks enjoying her delicate fresh scent.

"You look pretty great yourself, for a man who must have had an arduous day."

Torsten helped Ela with her chair. The light colored heavy wood frame of the chairs in this part of the restaurant matched the wood of the tables. Big cushions in a resilient fabric gave the chairs an outdoorsy feel. The attentive, good-natured staff, open kitchen and charming decor conspired to create an ambiance conducive to relaxation.

"How was your day, Ela?"

"Not very taxing. A better question is how was yours?"

"Quite productive. Everyone earned a nice relaxing weekend, and they are on their way home."

"When did you arrive?"

"Yesterday … late afternoon. We met up for dinner here, and took advantage of their private dining service. We made an early night of it, though. Everyone was tired from their flights and aware that we'd be going non-stop from eight this morning until five this afternoon, with only a couple breaks. You were right about the hotel. Meeting Services did an exemplary job."

"How is your suite?"

"Very comfortable."

No mention of showing it to her later, Ela noted. She had given him the perfect opportunity. Perhaps during their dinner.

"Will you be staying in Montreal over the weekend?"

"I'm afraid not. I must leave tomorrow. On Monday, I start out on a tour of the businesses that I run and I have called some meetings. I'll be traveling for three weeks. If I could have extended my stay, I would have inquired if you were free."

Ela acknowledged the compliment with a smile, and her heart skipped a beat.

They started the evening with the bottle of Champagne Salon Grand Cru Le Mesnil Brut Blanc de Blanc 2002 that Torsten had ordered before her arrival.

"What shall we toast to, Torsten?"

"To the absolutely best part of my trip to Montreal and the woman that has made it so."

"I am humbled by your graciousness."

"Humble does not suit you."

"Agreed." Ela shot him a wicked smile. "Here's to you, Mr. Furst, and your excellent choice of dinner companions."

"That's more like it."

"Please let me add: And your exquisite taste in Champagnes. Look at this lovely light yellow color and those tiny racy non-stop bubbles. I love the acidity and minerality, and the pear and almond with a touch of lemon. What a long finish. I'm going to be thinking about this Champagne tomorrow, the next day, next week… A great Champagne stays with you."

"I am glad that you approve. It's not every day that I dine with a wine agent specializing in luxury wine. I made my selection very carefully. Shall we order some oysters, and then you can tell me the significance of those earrings."

"These earrings were my first frivolous purchase. After putting a roof over my head, clothing myself and getting my business up and running without incurring debt, the earrings were my reward. They were a gift to myself for hard work, sacrifice and determination. It was the first time that I ever indulged myself like that."

"I understand completely. When I reached a certain milestone, I did the same. I promised myself that when I achieved certain goals, this was the watch that I would acquire." Torsten pointed to the platinum timepiece with a black alligator strap on his wrist. "It was made by one single watchmaker and it took a whole year to complete. I flew to Switzerland to meet the watchmaker that had crafted my watch, because we were connected through it. This unique timepiece is not about bling," Torsten emphasized. "As you can see, it's actually rather understated. When you buy this watch, you are paying for mechanical excellence."

Ela could not even imagine what it must have cost. "It speaks volumes about who you are, Mr. Furst."

The conversation flowed easily. Torsten wanted to know all about Ela's business … the role of a wine agent and how she came to represent the most coveted wines in the world. He kept her talking and barely gave her any time to ask him about the businesses he was involved in.

Torsten seemed to prefer talking about her more than himself, so Ela let him steer the conversation.

"I think we should have a look at the menu, now that we have devoured those oysters. Never let it be said that I let a lady starve."

Ela decided on the chilled pea soup with smoked mozzarella emulsion and Parma ham, followed by Mediterranean sea bass, green asparagus, truffle butter, chanterelle mushrooms and walnuts.

Torsten didn't see any reason not to order the same.

"What would you suggest from the wine list, Ms. Zalewski?"

"Really, Mr. Furst, you're quite capable of choosing, as you've just demonstrated with the Champagne."

"After a whole day of decision-making, it would be a pleasure to have you select for us this time."

"You're relinquishing control? Has that ever happened before?"

"Infrequently."

"Very well. Sauvignon Blanc from upper Loire, I think. Domaine Didier Dagueneau Pouilly Fumé Silex 2002 should do nicely."

"So, how do you find the wine, Torsten?"

"Are you fishing for a compliment?"

"Definitely. I like the wine, otherwise I wouldn't have ordered it, but I want to know what you think."

"Concentrated … I had heard that the wines from this estate are quite muscular. It's fresh, structured with a hint of spice and I like that it is flinty."

"Silex … flinty. It stands to reason."

"Well done, Ela."

"Thank you, Torsten."

Their meal was outstanding. Ela's taste buds had been activated and dialed up to maximum pleasure by the inventive creations served. Now they cried out for one of those unbelievably delicious sounding deserts on the restaurant's dessert list that fit Ela's regimen, but her full stomach vetoed the action. So Ela declined, but told Torsten to go ahead.

"No, I'm fine as well. Would you care for a dessert wine or coffee?"

"I really couldn't, but I don't want you to be deprived."

"I'm very satisfied with our dinner and the wines. Perhaps on another occasion."

That sounded promising, Ela thought.

Ela and Torsten left the restaurant the way she had come in. Now that they were in the hotel lobby, Ela was nervous and excited. Surely he would invite her to his suite.

She was about to head in the direction of the elevators, when Torsten stopped abruptly in front of the set of doors that led out onto the street. He kissed Ela on both cheeks.

"Thank you for a delightful evening."

"But …"

"Yes?"

"Nothing. The evening was very enjoyable. Thank you."

Torsten guided Ela towards the main entrance and the ever attentive door man opened a door for them.

"Would you like a taxi, sir?"

"For the lady."

"Until next time. I'll be in touch very soon. Good night, Ela."

When Ela was comfortably seated in the back of the taxi, Torsten handed the driver some bills and said, "Please see that the lady has entered her building safely before driving away." The taxi driver nodded.

Ela was dumbfounded. Torsten was sending her home. Things had gone so well over dinner. This wasn't how the night was supposed to end.

Torsten Lucas Furst had exercised a great deal of self-control. He did the opposite of what he wanted to do; which was to take the wine agent up to his suite and have sex with her until the morning light intruded on them.

He wondered how it would have felt to kiss her deeply … passionately. How would her breasts and the curve of her hip feel to his palm? What would she taste like when he cupped the cheeks of her sweet ass in his hands and used his tongue on her? How would she feel under him when he was inside of her? What kind of motion would give her the most pleasure?

He knew that she had wanted him tonight, but if he played it right … she would want him even more.

CHAPTER 7

"You're going to Rome ... just like that, Ela? You usually need weeks to prepare for a trip. If it was for business, you would have said so. You have been very secretive lately."

Robert had noticed that Ela was getting texts all of the time these last few weeks and she was responding quickly and with accuracy. She had even mastered the keys with one finger, and she was always in a good mood these days. Robert knew something was up with his boss.

"Okay, it's pleasure. I was invited."

"Aha! You've met someone ... Who? When? Where?"

"Bordeaux during Vinexpo. We had breakfast together one morning, a bottle of Champagne in the bar of the Grand Hotel that evening, and we spent some time together again at Fête de La Fleur." Ela didn't say anything about sitting together at Edmond's table. It would be too easy for Robert to find out the rest. "Then he had some business in Montreal and we had dinner together."

"You're flying to Rome at the invitation of a man you spent a few hours with in Bordeaux and a couple of hours with in Montreal? Have you lost your mind?"

"Probably ... But I'm beginning to think that sanity is highly overrated. Life is short."

"I hope you know what you are doing," said Robert, shaking his head.

Robert, although several years younger than Ela, saw himself in the role of older brother ... He made sure she would take time for lunch when she was running on nothing than adrenaline, that she relaxed when she worked for too many hours on too many days in a row and cautioned her if he felt she was taking unnecessary chances that might harm her in some way—like now. It was the nature of their relationship almost from the very beginning.

"Where will you be staying?"

"In a suite in a five-star hotel."

"Which hotel? In case I need to reach you."

"My cell will work just fine in Rome."

If you aren't going to tell me the name of the hotel, I guess you're not going to tell me the name of this man."

"No."

"Is he in the wine business?"

"No."

"But he was in Bordeaux during Vinexpo?"

"Yes."

"Is he from Bordeaux?"

"No."

Robert frowned. "You're flying to Rome … So he must be Italian then?"

"He's German and he lives in Germany, but he has lived in Rome, among other cities in Europe and the U.S."

"How do you know he's not some fugitive from the law, wanted by Interpol … moving around like that? I don't want to have to go to Rome to identify your body."

"He's not a criminal. I Googled him."

"Well you're a grown woman … Am I taking you to the airport?"

"No, a limousine is picking me up."

"A limousine … a five-star hotel … Are you flying business class too?"

"First class."

"A man of means."

"It would appear so."

"Men like that … Well you may just be a plaything to him. I don't want you getting hurt."

"I know you mean well, so I am going to overlook the chauvinistic remark. How do you know that he's not *my* plaything?"

"I give up."

"Finally. Now what did you find out about the estate in Languedoc?"

"As you know, Sylvain and his wife honeymooned in the area and brought back some wine. Diane and I joined them for dinner when they got back. We had two wines from the same producer. The estate is called Domaine Guizard. They are not presently selling their wines in Quebec, but they are working with an agent here to get them in. It's too bad because the wines are top notch, and Sylvain tells me that they are really great people with over four hundred years of family history in the region. Wine is in their blood."

"That is too bad … for us. What did you taste?"

"Domaine Guizard Tradition 2010 is a blend of Syrah, Grenache and Carignan. It has a deep color, is full-bodied with pretty good tannins and red fruit on the long finish. Domaine Guizard Grés de Montpelier 2010 is Syrah and Grenache. It also has that deep color and is full-bodied. The tannins are present but don't dominate. It too has a long finish. This one though, has chocolate on the finish. I like both."

CHAPTER 8

Ela wanted to know all about the man she would be seeing in Rome in a few days, so she decided to do what she already told Robert she had done: Google him. She should know his business history, so she wouldn't be ignorant about what he did for a living. She should have done this weeks ago.

Torsten's name came up in connection with dozens of companies in Germany, other parts of Europe and North America: pharmaceuticals, computer software, furniture manufacturing, chain stores, transportation, publishing, insurance, food, breweries, real estate, communication … In addition he sat on twenty boards, five of which were formed for companies belonging to a Jonas Koertig. He was estimated to be worth seventeen billion euros and with recent acquisitions, it was very likely that he would exceed his present worth in a few years.

His education was listed too. He had studied at the best schools in Germany and also in London, Paris, Rome and Madrid.

He was married to Lara Adler Furst, now forty-seven. They had no children.

"That can't be right," Ela said out loud, but there it was, the photo and the date that photo had been taken—last year.

Nico had been married … but there were extenuating circumstances. Perhaps it was like that between Torsten and his wife. Or perhaps they had an *understanding* … as long as everyone was discreet. What did it matter anyway? It would be a casual thing because there was so much geographical distance between Torsten and her, and their lives were vastly different. Ela knew she would be content to see him if he came to Montreal or if he passed through Montreal on his way to the U.S. a couple of time per year, or if he joined her in France or Italy when she travelled there on business once every few months. She would never make any demands on him. She would never ask about other women. Obviously the understanding would be that it worked like that both ways.

What threw Ela off a bit was her feeling that he wanted something more from her, but she couldn't quite pinpoint what. He called her several times every week and texted her at all hours of the day and night, from his home, office or the back of his chauffeur-driven car. Even when he was away on business, or on his yacht somewhere in the Mediterranean, he kept the communication going. It had never occurred to her that there would be a Mrs. Furst.

Maybe he was just into her a lot. It was pretty hot between them. Regardless, Ela would find out what Torsten was all about in a few days and maybe he himself would even tell her about his wife and whatever their deal was.

In the meantime, it wouldn't hurt to look her up too, so Ela Googled Lara Adler Furst. The photos kept on coming, with headlines and captions that placed a handsome but reserved woman at the head of numerous charities. It seemed she loved being in the spotlight.

There were a couple of photos of her and Torsten. He didn't seem particularly happy in them. Then there was an article on the lifestyles of the rich and famous, and photos of her christening the yacht that was named for her.

The online publication gave out the technical specifications and there were photos of the interior. Mrs. Furst was credited with decorating the whole yacht. Ela cringed. This woman had awful taste.

Ela snapped her laptop shut. Between finishing up with some professional obligations and shopping for the trip … she had enough to think about, so that was as much time as she intended to spend on her investigation.

Whatever this thing was with Torsten, it was a great adventure.

It had only been three weeks ago that Torsten came to Montreal. Last week he'd invited her to Rome and Ela had been quick to accept. It looked like she was finally going to have a proper outlet for her pent-up sexual energy.

In the first texts, Torsten had seemed interested in her work and her life. She was flattered that someone of his stature would care. In turn, he told her some things about his work and his life. If people only knew … jaws would drop. Yet she never mentioned Torsten to anyone, she just didn't think it would be right, at least for now.

He gave her compliments that were more personal in nature in some of the texts that followed. That took Ela by surprise, but she discovered that she liked intimate compliments from Torsten. Emboldened, she replied in kind.

Then the *sexting* started; Torsten was seducing her through her smartphone and very effectively. Ela gave as good as she got. She hadn't even known that she had it in her. *He* brought out this eroticism in her—and she liked it.

Ela came to rely on their sexting. She was more sex obsessed now than in her twenties—but sex obsessed with Torsten and exclusively Torsten. It didn't matter that he wasn't in the same room, or on the same continent.

The first time that Torsten sent Ela a risqué text was from his yacht. He had some business people on board and broke away to go for an afternoon nap in the master suite. At first he mentioned that while he had been enjoying a glass of wine on the main deck, he was imagining her sitting in his lap.

Torsten told Ela that he would find that so arousing it would be difficult to hide his arousal in swimming trunks. Ela responded instantly with, "I can imagine sitting in your lap like that, but I would probably have to find the most comfortable position, so I would be moving around … a lot."

When Torsten texted Ela next, he told her about a dream he had had. They were having dinner in a restaurant overlooking his favorite city, Rome.

"You were very forward. You removed one of your shoes and placed your toes on my crotch under the long tablecloth. You began rubbing me there. You kept rubbing even when the sommelier came to take our wine order. He couldn't see what you were doing because the tablecloth went right to the floor and he stood across from you. I had to tell him what we had decided with a hard-on. I thought I might come right there and then."

"You stopped when he returned with our wine, but once he departed and we were alone in our dimly lit corner of the dining room, you slid off your chair with a naughty smile and you were under the table undoing the zipper of my trousers.

"I felt your hand around my cock, then your lips and tongue. You took me deep into your mouth over and over … and I was coming. I gripped the sides of the table until my fingers hurt, trying not to make a sound."

"I shall have to remember that. Sounds like fun."

A couple of days later, Ela texted Torsten, "Did you have any erotic dreams last night?"

"Yes, as a matter of fact. We were lying together by the pool on the grounds of a luxury hotel and I slipped my hand down your bathing suit top to cup and caress a breast. We were being observed by a couple of disapproving older ladies, but we paid them no mind.

"When I slipped my hand down the front of your bikini bottom and between your legs, they called for an attendant. This was just too much for them. We were asked to leave—politely."

The following day, Ela received a text that asked, "Can I tell you something wicked?"

"Yes, I like wicked," she texted back.

"I want to have sex with you all night long."

"Why limit yourself like that, Mr. Furst?"

Ela was becoming very good at inflaming Torsten's desire.

The next night, Torsten read, "It's ten p.m. and I can't sleep. Any suggestions?"

"I'm in bed with you …" He proceeded to describe what he was doing to her. It involved penetrating her with his tongue and Ela found the scenario intriguing enough to play along with her own hand.

"When it comes to pussies, I hope you like Brazilian."

"I am going to show you just how much one day very soon."

The next time that the phone vibrated, Ela read, "I can't sleep. Any suggestions?"

"I'm lying in bed beside you …"

The next day, Torsten asked, "What do you like in bed, Ela?"

"It doesn't always have to be *in* bed, but I like everything. Sometimes I want it slow and tender and other times I want to give in to urgency. Sometimes, I'll want to take control, but there are also times when I won't want to be in control. I'll want my arms pinned over my head and to be taken ... hard. I have never said this to any other man."

"You are making this man *so* horny, right now."

"Me? I'll have you know that you are responsible for three orgasms today."

"I hope you are not being driven into the bed of the closest available man."

"I don't sub-contract. I take care of it myself."

"You'll have to show me how you make yourself come, Ela."

"I've never done that before, but if it would please you ..."

"It would more than please me. Have you ever had sex with another woman?"

"I don't think that there is anything wrong with it, but it just isn't something that I have ever been aroused by. I'm all about men ... always have been. So what do you like in bed besides watching a woman play with her pussy?"

"A passionate, uninhibited partner ... then the possibilities are endless."

"So a bad girl would not scare you off?"

"Women deserve the same pleasure that men have always thought was their right."

"I like that you're such a modern thinker."

"I'm looking forward to meeting this bad girl. Really I am looking forward to having a wild night of sex with this bad girl ... in a variety of positions and not always *in* bed."

There was more sexting over the next two weeks, and Torsten told Ela that he couldn't bear it anymore. Could she get away the following week?

"I'll rearrange my schedule. Where am I going?"

"My favorite city ... Rome."

"Mine too, though I have not been in a very long time. I would love to see it through your eyes."

"You're wonderful. My personal travel agent will send you an itinerary and let you know what information she will need from you. Just tell her what you want and she'll handle it. A driver will meet your plane. I'll fly in later and we will meet up at the hotel."

Ela learned that Torsten usually stayed at Rome's Hassler Hotel at the top of the Spanish Steps. He had told her that the suites were very luxurious, the views nothing less than spectacular, the Michelin-starred restaurant, Imàgo, was one of the best in the world and the spa was renowned.

This time, however, on the recommendation of a close friend, he had his travel agent make a reservation for them at the Rome Cavalieri Hotel overlooking the Eternal City with an unforgettable view of the Dome of St. Peter. Ela looked up the Rome Cavalieri and found she concurred with the friend's recommendation.

She saw photos of the grounds, expansive and breathtaking. There was an outdoor pool, something not all that common in Rome but most welcome in the heat of an Italian summer. Among the things that the Rome Cavalieri was famous for was its three Michelin star restaurant, the only one in Rome. The wine cellar stored sixty thousand bottles, thirty-five hundred labels … winners of the Wine Spectator Grand Award since 2004, she read. Over the years, many of the important gastronomy guides touted it to be the "Best Restaurant in Rome." The famous chef was German; Ela wondered if there was a connection. She came to her own conclusion about the spa. It re-defined pampering.

Torsten had told her that the name of their suite was the Vista Suite. Ela devoured the photo and description. The neutral tones looked rich because of how texture was used in the design. There were some pretty dramatic elements too, including a dark carpet, four large pillars at the entrance, a beautiful marble fireplace and a king-size bed where they could lie and look out the balcony windows at the panoramic view. If that wasn't enough, the suite held an additional surprise: original art and antiques. So, this was how Torsten lived.

"How would you like to spend our first evening?" Torsten asked in phone call. "The hotel boasts a fabulous restaurant. I think you told me that you read about it on the hotel website."

"Several times. I have a very sexy red Hervé Léger cocktail dress …"

"That will make it very *hard* at dinner."

"Funny you should say that. I was just thinking that we may never make it out of our suite. I saw there is a nice big balcony with an unbelievable view. Why don't we meet on our private balcony and I'll wear *fewer* clothes? We might as well take the edge off as soon as you arrive. It's all we've been thinking about … Why not enjoy a romantic dinner for two afterwards in our suite. I don't think I want to share you with a dining room full of people on the first evening. Perhaps we will get inspired again after dinner. It will only be a few steps to our bed."

"I like the way you think, Ela. We'll have dinner in the hotel's restaurant the following night."

"I'm going to have to do a little shopping for some Agent Provocateur lingerie."

"Why don't I take you shopping for lingerie in Rome when we go sightseeing? We can pick out some things together. … and shop on Via Candiotti for other things you might like."

"I don't want to spend the whole trip shopping, but picking out lingerie together sounds like a very stimulating activity."

"Exactly."

"Can we include the Pantheon in our sightseeing, even if I have been there before?"

"Certainly."

"Can we walk down the Spanish Steps? There's such a nice view of Piazza di Spagna from up top."

"If you like. And now I have to broach a delicate subject … I have had a vasectomy and have not been intimate with anyone without protection for several years. Perhaps your situation is different or you would just feel better if we used protection?"

"I haven't engaged in any activity that would present a danger to you; I think it's important to know your partner's sexual history and to discuss these matters beforehand. I am at ease with what you have told me, but if you prefer to use protection, that is also okay."

"No. That's fine."

Later, Ela wondered why Torsten would have used protection with his wife. Maybe because he'd had sex with someone other than her. Were they separated? Torsten was very good looking and evidently highly sexual. Even if he was not exactly an eligible bachelor, he would have no trouble attracting beautiful, successful women.

The day of Ela's flight, she received a text from Torsten asking how she pictured their first time.

"I'm going to be conventional about our first time. Missionary position and in bed. In between a few hard thrusts, you should withdraw slowly until you are almost all the way out. Repeat, repeat, repeat. I'm getting so aroused just thinking about it. It's like we're having sex before we have sex."

"I can do that. Anything else?"

"I want you to take me from behind. I want to straddle you reverse cowboy on the terrace, so you can enjoy the view, while I enjoy the view. I want to get dirty with you in the shower and make you come in my mouth."

"You forgot the part where I eat your pussy a dozen times or so … But what will we do the next day?"

"So ambitious, Mr. Furst. I'll try to keep up."

CHAPTER 9

Ela had never flown first class before. It was quite a treat, the Champagne, the wine, the food, the service ... Even though Ela was afraid of flying, she was loving this experience. She was stepping into Torsten's world.

Ela's driver was holding a sign with her name on it as promised and introduced himself as Sebastiano Byron Barsetti. His mother had had a thing for Lord Byron and decided that Byron would be part of his official name, much to the disapproval of the priest who baptized him. The good looking young Italian drove a big black late model German car—something Ela was getting used to in Europe, but this one had windows you could not see anything through. She imagined that he must drive celebrities; who else would demand this kind of privacy.

Ela was thrilled and excited as she texted Torsten about her arrival and to inform him that she was in the back of Sebastiano's car and they were on their way into the city.

On impulse she decided to mention in the text that she would be sending him an email to his private email address, but that he should not read it until he was alone.

Torsten texted back that he was in a meeting, but couldn't wait to see her that evening.

So Ela proceeded with her email. "Subject: Warning very hot. Do not read in the presence of others or risk exposure." She had had an extremely erotic dream the night before the flight, and hadn't had the chance to tell him about it.

"We were coming out of a shop in Rome, and you decided that we should take a short cut back to the car. We were walking through a narrow alleyway and suddenly you pushed me into a very deep doorway. You pressed me against the heavy old wood door and kissed me roughly, and I liked it. You had your hand down the front of my dress caressing my breasts roughly and squeezing my nipples between your fingers, and I liked that too. My jersey sundress had a tight bodice, so I hadn't worn a bra. I hadn't worn panties either for that matter. The skirt of my dress flared away from my body. Your hand slipped under the hem and you realized that I was completely nude under the dress.

"Your fingers were between the lips of my slick pussy. I was so ready for you by then. You were using your fingers on me, moving from clit to the opening of my pussy, relentlessly back and forth until you made me come, burying my screams in your neck, as people went about their business only steps away. Then you kissed me deeply and told me we had to hurry back to our suite ... but I had other ideas.

"When we got back to the car, I told our driver that Mr. Furst and I had some things to talk over privately. Was there any way that he could drive us to some secluded spot ... somewhere he could leave us for about thirty minutes.

"Our driver knew just the spot, and it was even in the shade. He left the car running and looked at his watch, promising to be back in half an hour. Then he was gone.

Well, you locked the doors as he suggested and turned to me with a look that asked, *and now what?* I had formulated a plan in that alley. I undid your belt and the button of your pants. I undid the zipper. Who knew you weren't wearing your boxer briefs? You were taking a big chance walking around all aroused. So, that was why you were holding the shopping bags in front of you. You were fully erect and I hadn't even touched you. I thought, I am still nowhere near satisfied and so wet, and he looks very horny.

"So I just mounted your cock and rode it until I had the orgasm that would keep me going until the hotel. You didn't mind the lack of foreplay at all. You grabbed my hips and moved me up and down, finally lifting me almost off your shaft then slamming me down all the way to the base of your cock when you were about to come. I could feel your release even as my own orgasm had me shuddering and grinding against you as we clutched each other in the car.

"I woke up aroused and alone. It was so real, that I actually came in my sleep.

"That was my first time ever. I never knew that women could have wet dreams. And ... then I made myself come on purpose."

Torsten had made the mistake of telling everyone in the conference room to break for coffee. It was not a logical time to break, but he was the boss so they did.

When his department heads filed back into the conference room, he was trapped in his seat. Whenever he finally thought he had his arousal under control and there was no risk of being found out, the images returned.

What was the matter with him? The micromanaging Torsten was sabotaging the Torsten that wanted nothing more than to have Ela in his arms right now ... and she was waiting for him.

"Ladies and gentlemen, I have been called away on an important matter. We will pick up where we left off next week. My assistant will take care of the re-scheduling." With that he dismissed the perplexed executives and called for his driver.

Torsten texted Ela, "Read your email. Cut meeting short. On my way to the airport. Taking an earlier flight. Desperately need to have sex with you."

Ela smiled when she received the text just as the limo stopped in front of the hotel. She answered with, "That's one of the most arousing things you ever wrote. What is your ETA?"

The Rome Cavalieri Hotel was stupendous. It surpassed all of Ela's expectations. She felt like royalty.

Sebastiano brought her luggage to the check-in desk and gave her name. They told her that as soon as the suite she would be sharing with Mr. Furst, was ready, her luggage would be brought up. Ela was reminded about the massage at the spa and the concierge explained about the Imperial Club—it was restricted to guests with *those* privileges—as he discreetly handed her a special card.

After visually feasting on the priceless art collection, Ela went about exploring the grounds. The Rome Cavalieri Hotel was the *grande dame* of Rome, and the fifteen acre private Mediterranean park was her boudoir. The vegetation was lush. The pool was inviting ... and it beckoned. Ela's senses were overwhelmed. So much beauty.

There was an indoor pool ... practical for cooler weather or if one forgot to pack sunblock. Ela used the excuse of coming down to confirm the time of her massage to visit the spa. By now, she was suffering from sensory overload. She was worried that she would not be able to absorb everything. "In the great tradition of Roman baths ..." she had read in the Cavalieri Grand Spa Club brochure, which also described lavish decor and various treatments to promote well-being.

Feeling hungry now, Ela considered where to have lunch. Why not something light and tasty in the Imperial Club. She did not want to eat heavy before her massage and she was one of the guests that was entitled to access this exclusive space. She was curious about the view anyway. It would be part of her exploration.

When the elevator doors opened to the seventh floor, Ela got goose bumps. As she walked through the glass doors, the first person she saw was a polished looking young woman with attire befitting an employee of the five-star hotel who was entrusted with the responsibility of welcoming elite clients with Imperial Club access. She greeted Ela pleasantly from behind an impressive desk.

Is it possible to actually get physically stimulated by the amenities of a luxury hotel? Ela decided she must be strange because it would appear that this was what was happening to her. Her heart was racing ... as if she had overdosed on caffeine. Her senses were at a heightened level. Every time she looked at another part of the Imperial Club, she felt a new sense of euphoria.

Ela Zalewski had been invited to the most exclusive events in Bordeaux. She knew the owners of mythic Bordeaux châteaux. She had their private mobile telephone numbers programmed into her cell phone for Pete's sake … *Sorry, Saint Peter,* she said to herself when her eyes found the dome of Saint Peter's from her perch.

This was different somehow. She had never flown to another continent on the whim of a billionaire before. Was it the experience that made her feel intoxicated or the man? Was she starting to feel something more for Torsten than she had expected? How was that possible? They barely even knew each other.

The well-dressed above average looking man with the good physique observed the attractive petite brunette reading a magazine at a small table overlooking the historical city. He had been watching her since she arrived. She had taken a couple of minutes to appreciate the way that Rome looked from up high before getting up to fill a plate with some delicacies. She was not wearing a ring.

He had seen her go to the self-serve bar, look at labels of the wines that were being chilled and decide on one. When she came back to her table, he told her that she had made a good choice.

Ela told him that she liked to try new wines because she drank for a living. That took the man by surprise and he told her that she would have to explain. When Ela told him that she was a wine agent, he laughed. The statement made sense. Ela seemed happy and animated. She was. She would be meeting up with Torsten soon and her imagination was running wild.

The man and Ela struck up a conversation. Wine as a subject was always a good ice-breaker. The man introduced himself as David Vaughn from Toronto and Ela told him her name and that she was from Montreal.

David was there on holiday for a week, with his two college-age daughters. He managed to mention that he had been divorced for a while. The Rome Cavalieri was one of his most favorite hotels in the world. Ela told him that it was her first time and she was waiting to get into her suite. He assured her that she would love her accommodations. He never asked what brought her to Rome; she was relieved because she did not know what to say. Ela guessed he probably thought that she was here on business.

He knew his wines, was partial to Bordeaux, but liked good white Burgundies. This was all right up her alley. They found that they had things in common.

David volunteered that he was a structural engineer and commuted between his offices in Toronto and Montreal. He had a home in the Bridal Path area of Toronto. Ela told him that she had visited the small exclusive community on a couple of occasions.

She told him about her work as a wine agent and he told her about his companies. Groupe LVL in Quebec and LVL Group in Toronto were involved with many of the large building projects in the two cities.

When Ela would Google him later, she would see that he was written up frequently in various business, architectural and engineering publications. He made the news often because he had received many awards and he was a financial success story in a weaker economy. The media hinted that his net worth was over two hundred million dollars.

The media had also called him a very good catch and referred to him as an eligible bachelor because he did not seem to have someone permanent in his life.

David Vaughn had a quiet strength about him and Ela liked him right away. He was assertive, but did not act entitled. He was also a *bon vivant*—he enjoyed the good things in life.

On the day Ela and David met, he was going to be taking his daughters sightseeing and asked if she had planned to do so as well. Ela told him that she had a massage booked at the Cavalieri Grand Spa Club and was really looking forward to it.

"Will I see you in the bar this evening? I would like to buy you a drink."

"That's very kind, but I'm afraid that I'm going to be busy."

"My loss. Do you have a business card? Perhaps I could buy you that drink in Montreal?"

Out of reflex Ela pulled out one of her business cards. She always kept them handy; one never knew.

"Les Vins EZ Inc."

David gave her his in return. One side was the English version for the Toronto office and the other was the French version for the Montreal office.

"Groupe LVL Inc. and LVL Group Inc."

"All my numbers are there. I hope to see you soon."

Ela didn't quite know what to say, but suddenly felt a little guilty given that she was involved with Torsten. She felt as if she had somehow just betrayed Torsten.

That was ridiculous, she wasn't really actually involved with him—he was, in fact, married to someone else. They met, there was a crazy attraction, they sexted and he had invited her to Rome for sex. She shouldn't try to read more into it and she had no reason to feel guilty. She also had no reason not to see David in Montreal if he called her up.

Their suite was to die for. Ela's eye went directly to the king-size bed that she and Torsten would be putting to good use in a few hours. She wasn't used to spending the night or having a man spend the night. She thought that with Torsten beside her she might sleep better and not the reverse. The bed was even big enough so that they wouldn't roll into each other—unless they wanted to, obviously.

Then Ela took in the rest. The marble bathroom had a separate bathtub and shower and a bidet, of course. Why didn't North Americans put in bidets? They were so useful after sex. The suite was all about giving the guest the highest quality of everything imaginable.

It was the balcony, however, that was the biggest draw for Ela. She had told Torsten that she would see him there when he arrived, and that she expected their first kiss to take place on that balcony.

She assured him that Rome would never be the same after that. What she meant was that he'd never be the same and that whenever he travelled there in the future, he would always think of her. Why was that so important to her?

Then Ela went about the business of installing herself in their suite, but taking into consideration what Torsten's needs might be.

When she was done, she put her hair up changed into a loose fitting off the shoulder summer dress and sandals and headed to the spa.

The spa atmosphere was calming. People spoke in hushed voices. As soon as she had that white terry robe on, Ela started to relax.

With the massage her nervous energy was transformed into a peaceful state of mind. Jet lag vanished. The hands that worked the oils into her skin and kneaded her tired muscles were soothing to the body, mind and spirit.

Ela returned to the suite floating on a cloud, but a nap was out of the question; she was too aware that Torsten would walk through the door in a couple of hours. On the other hand, she would have more time to prepare. She would dry and style her hair, now wet from the shower she had enjoyed after the massage.

She'd apply evening makeup for their first night together, complete with red lipstick and sealer, so that she wouldn't leave lipstick marks on Torsten. Ela had told Torsten that she would be wearing red lipstick when she took him in her mouth. It hit the right chord evidently.

The fragrance this evening would be summery, sexy and feminine. The woody floral Paradiso by Roberto Cavalli went with her mood. The scent of a modern woman. What was she if not modern … flying all the way over here for a booty call. Ela picked a fragrance the way she picked wine. It had to speak to her. Ela usually bought a scent to please herself. This time, she hoped it would please Torsten as well.

Ela wore her signature diamond earrings. The black silk kimono with sash would be the only fabric between Torsten's exploring hands and her body. She planned to keep her black four-inch silk mules with the cigarette heels on even when the robe came off. There was nothing that made her feel sexier in bed. She had packed them in her carry-on especially for this evening.

It was past dusk. Ela could still see the rooftops, but lights were coming on all over the city and on the hotel grounds. There was a magical quality about the whole thing … magical and memorable. Ela heard soft music playing. It was a perfect auditory interpretation of the scene before her. She had dimmed the lights in the suite to better appreciate the view and to create a romantic atmosphere. Ela got goose bumps again. The night, the city, the suite, it all held so much promise.

Ela had been clutching her cell phone for the last thirty minutes. She didn't want to miss the text from Torsten that would tell her he was on his way up. When it came, she responded that she was out on their balcony waiting for him as planned. She clicked send and her heart started to beat wildly in her chest. She swore she could hear it.

It was beating like that for five minutes and then Torsten came through the door.

Ela didn't move. She waited for the man in the well-tailored dark blue suit, blue check shirt and dark blue striped tie to come to her.

He had brought up his own travel bag and briefcase—probably so she wouldn't feel uncomfortable about an intrusion from hotel personnel at a time like this.

Torsten had had his reasons, but mainly wasn't prepared to share this vision of loveliness with anyone.

He walked up to Ela, took her face in his hands and stared into her eyes.

"You take my breath away."

"Shhh … Just kiss me."

Torsten's lips found Ela's. He pressed them open and his tongue sought out hers. The kiss went from sweet and tender to demanding. It communicated the need he was feeling for her. Ela met his passion in that kiss. They stayed locked in their first kiss with Rome below for a long time before Torsten let go, reluctantly.

"I'm going to slip into something more suited to the occasion. Don't go anywhere … and don't cool off."

"Be quick, Mr. Furst. I don't like to be kept waiting."

Torsten got out of his clothes and into one of the white hotel robes as if someone was timing him with a stopwatch, but it seemed to Ela that he had been in there for an hour. She was pacing the length of the balcony when he came out.

Torsten came back to the same exact spot. "You are so sexy in that short robe … great legs. I can't take my eyes off you."

"Thank you, Torsten. You look pretty irresistible yourself. Maybe you can take your eyes off me for thirty seconds—not that I'm complaining, mind you, I love it—but the view from here is pretty spectacular."

"For thirty seconds, then." He quickly cast his eyes over the shimmering city lights below. "Very beautiful. I have a feeling that I am going to find it even more wonderous with you here," and with that Torsten took Ela in his arms and kissed her deeply and a little possessively … Or at least that was how it felt to Ela. She had slipped her arms under his and around his back. There was nowhere she would rather be.

Torsten kissed Ela for the second time that evening. She bit his lower lip gently and sucked on it. The kiss was stirring the same ache in them as before. This time they would not stop. Torsten's hands were caressing her body through the silk. He was taking his time. He was teasing both of them by avoiding her breasts and ass.

Ela could feel his erection and she doubted that he was going to keep her waiting much longer. To give him some incentive, she pushed herself into him. Torsten kissed her hard and his hand sought out a breast over the fabric. He liked that her nipple was so responsive to his touch. He moved to the other breast, filling his hand with it and giving it a gentle squeeze until this nipple too hardened against his palm. He let go only to place his hand on her tight little behind while holding her close with other hand. He was getting harder.

Ela did some exploring of her own. She boldly squeezed his ass with both hands through the terry robe. He was muscular there. A good sign … thrusting power. Then she brought her arms around his neck for a bit.

Torsten's large strong hand went in search of soft skin. He touched the back of her neck lightly, slid his hand around her neck and down her clavicle, slipping it under her robe on one side and then the other. The silky material slid from Ela's shoulders, baring the tops of her breasts as Torsten continued his explorations. This was so much better. She could have purred like a kitten.

Ela's new lover separated the lower part of her robe to caress an outer thigh and reach around to her ass. He squeezed a little again and pressed her towards him and his hard-on. She liked that.

Torsten loosened his hold so that he could reach between her legs from the front. He found a very wet pussy that was *all* delicate skin. He had not forgotten that she'd mentioned Brazilian.

He caressed her down there and she went weak in the knees. One finger danced along the edge of her folds, preparing to slide inside her.

"You had better stop, or I am going to come."

"You told me you can have many orgasms."

"I can. It's just that I want the first one to be with you inside of me."

Torsten disengaged from his seductive partner and went back to kissing her.

Ela, however, was a naughty girl. She took advantage of the change in position to separate the heavier material of Torsten's robe and traced the outside of one of his thighs with her fingers, before moving lower and cupping his balls with her hand. His arousal was fully detectable, so she boldly encompassed the shaft of his very impressive cock with her hand and started to work it with a deliberate and steady motion.

Torsten forced himself to let go of Ela and step away. "If you keep that up, I'm going to come right here and now and we'll have to wait another fifteen minutes."

Only fifteen minutes? thought Ela. Good to know, but she didn't try to stir things up again.

"Take off your robe, Ela, and let me look at you."

Ela obediently turned away from Torsten and walked a few steps. She undid the sash of her robe with her back to Torsten. She slipped the black silk further off her shoulders, held it in place for a few seconds then allowed it to glide down her arms and onto the floor of the balcony. She stood like that; her back exposed to Torsten's gaze for a few seconds more, before turning to face him. Then she stepped over the puddle of silk and took the same few steps forward to stand right in front of him. Torsten had noticed that her skin glowed in this light against the backdrop of Rome. His eyes followed the contours of her body and he made a mental note of all of the places he would be exploring with his hands, lips and tongue.

Oh, the way she walked over to him … So proud and completely confident that he would like what he saw. He didn't recall any former lover having that kind of aura about her.

Without breaking eye contact, Ela reached for the sash of his robe and undid it. She pushed the fabric back and off his shoulders with that same kind of confidence.

When Torsten was naked too, Ela craned her head to kiss him lightly on the lips while resting her palms on his hairless chest. Then she pulled away, taking in the full length and width of him with hungry eyes.

His pinkish cock was well above average length and girth, and he had been circumcised. His ball sac was tight and uniform. The blond pubic hair was neatly trimmed. This was a cock that would give her much pleasure, Ela decided, stroking it in admiration.

Torsten reached for her hand and pulled her along in the direction of their bed.

He had Ela lie back at the edge of the bed, and began removing her mules.

Ela started to protest, but Torsten was insistent. "They're very sexy, but they're getting in the way."

Before she could argue with him, Torsten bent over her to kiss her lips and her neck, and then used his lips and tongue on each sensitive nipple causing her to wiggle her hips in pleasure. He kissed his way down her stomach where she was ticklish and to her mound. His tongue played with her clit and he was licking the opening of her pussy just right. He sucked on her clit with soft lips, then went back to using his tongue. His tempo was perfect and continuous. The man knew how to eat pussy. He was bringing her to the edge … too close to the edge. Ela maneuvered herself backwards on her elbows while pushing off with her feet.

With Ela out of range, Torsten stood up. He was in the optimum position for Ela to slide back down and raise herself into a sitting position, with her feet planted on the floor between his legs. She stroked the shaft of his straight, long, thick pink cock and then put the tip in her mouth. He was breathing hard. Ela experimented with how deeply she could take him in. She worked his shaft with her mouth slowly, while she placed her hands on his ass to hold him in that position. Torsten told her that it felt good, really good, but she had to stop. He was about to reach the point of no return.

Ela stopped, moved into the center of the enormous bed and lay down waiting. Torsten followed and lay on top of her, his cock resting at the opening to her pussy. Ela guided the tip in and Torsten raised his upper body off her, afraid that she would be crushed under his weight.

Torsten took his time so that he would not hurt her, gently easing in and out, playing with the lips of her pussy before thrusting his full length inside. Ela was much tighter than he had expected.

With some space between them, Ela did something she had never done before. She reached down to play with her pussy while Torsten moved inside her. She liked the sensation of her hand on herself and the shaft of his cock inside her pussy. She became bolder as his moan told her he liked it too. This additional source of stimulation opened her up a little more to him and started a high octane arousal that spread outwards and came back at her.

It was having the same effect on Torsten. He thrust hard now, plunging deep inside her then withdrawing slowly right up to the tip of his cock. He plunged himself back in … There were more thrusts and withdrawals. He buried himself deep inside her then pulled back again … Slowly. Then Torsten switched to a steady rhythmic thrust and Ela pulled Torsten down to lie on her with his upper body. She wanted to feel his weight on her as she was coming. She wanted him to pin her to the bed and placed her arms up over her head. He read the signals. When he did as she wanted, Ela started breathing heavily and making a throaty sound. Her orgasm was intense and long. It had built and built, over the miles of separation, the weeks of sexting, the hours of waiting. She felt it rise up in her and then roll out into little tremors that faded away slowly and left her pussy a little sensitive.

Ela was sure that Torsten wouldn't be far behind, but he was somehow managing to hold back his orgasm, though he had not really slowed the pace.

She matched his rhythm with her hips for his pleasure and he slipped an arm under her and around her waist, pressing her lower body up towards him. This was even more arousing than before. Ela couldn't help herself. She wanted him deep inside her and she wanted it hard. She didn't want him to stop.

With a few more of Torsten's deep thrusts, she was climaxing again. Only then did Torsten give his cock permission to explode in unrestrained pleasure. Ela felt his body tense up and release. He let out his breath and it was mingled with a throaty sound of ultimate satisfaction. Then there was an intake of breath and Torsten collapsed on top of Ela.

"Oh my God, Torsten, can you die from too much pleasure?"

"I knew it would be good between us, but I had no idea it would be this good."

Neither of them was the cuddling type, so Ela went about freshening up and when she came out of the bathroom in her kimono and heels, Torsten, now back in his white terry robe, was going through the wine list and menu for their dinner *in*.

"I'm starved. I have barely eaten anything all day. I wanted to get away as early as possible. My assistant had a soup sent up and grilled chicken over salad. I got as far as the soup."

"You performed quite well … considering your lack of nourishment."

"You performed quite well … considering you must be seriously jet lagged."

"I caught my second wind."

"That may be, but you need sustenance as well. What are some of your preferences?"

"Lean protein and anything resembling a vegetable. Would you please order for me? I have to be honest … I am starting to fade a little. Oh and when I am overly tired, I can't eat a lot. I don't mean to disappoint you, but I don't think that I will be able to go another round tonight. Tomorrow morning?"

"You're not disappointing me. I would have understood if you had been too exhausted from the trip to do anything more than kiss me on the balcony. This has already been a very special evening. We'll wind down with a good dinner. Wine?"

"Always."

"When I am in a country known for producing exceptional wines, I drink those wines. Is that alright with you?"

"I leave the wine selection to your discretion, Mr. Furst."

"Shall we eat on the balcony?"

"I would love that. I'll have you all to myself and we'll have Rome all to ourselves."

"I could get very attached to you, Ms. Zalewski, if say things like that."

"Why, Mr. Furst, I do believe that you have an Italian soul … more specifically … a Roman soul."

"And, you think that there is a difference?"

"I know that there is."

"I'm impressed."

"I hope that you do not mind if I am still very enthralled with Florence, though. My first time in Florence, I was travelling with some friends and something extraordinary happened. We were walking around at night and we heard a violinist play outside the Uffizi museum. We stopped to listen and could not make ourselves leave. I cried … openly … I'm not ashamed to tell you that I was that moved … Florence captured my heart that night. It has an artistic sensibility. Florence revealed more of her secrets and wonders to me in the days that followed."

"Admirable. I understand. I am going to call down for our wine and dinner, and take a couple of minutes to freshen up. While we are waiting, I would really like to know what other parts of Italy you have toured and why Rome is your favorite city."

"Let's see … I've been to Verona on business, but I did a little sightseeing too. In Tuscany I visited Siena and San Gimignano … really charming … And, then there was Montepulciano.

"When I was there, I tasted a couple of very memorable wines. One was Contucci Vino Nobile di Montepulciano DOCG 2009. When Wine Enthusiast Best of 2013 came out, this particular Vino Nobile had been awarded 94 points and it was #16 out of the top 100 wines. What an elegant wine … cherry and plum with fine tannins as you would expect, but also so well balanced, with good length and freshness.

"It was also a pleasure to taste the Contucci Vino Nobile di Montepulciano DOCG Mulinvecchio 2009 with its ruby red color and aromas of red fruit and tobacco. I distinctly remember ripe cherry and plum flavors as well a pleasing acidity and a nice long finish."

"The family must have been making wine for many generations. The estates tend to be quite old."

"The Contucci family history goes back a thousand years. They still live in their ancestral home, Palazzo Contucci. They were one of the founders of Vino Nobile. Isn't that fascinating?"

"So they know a little something about producing Vino Nobile. Are you going to be representing them in Quebec, perhaps?"

"I'd love to, but they already have an agent in Quebec who is going to be proposing their wines. I think the wine writers in Quebec are really going to like the style of these wines.

"To continue; I have vacationed on the Amalfi Coast, Positano specifically. I have also spent a couple of days on Capri."

"What about the north of Italy?"

"I have yet to experience the northern part of Italy, other than Verona."

"Perhaps we can experience Venice together soon."

Torsten was planning ahead. So this was not going to be a one-time thing. That gave Ela a warm feeling all over. She smiled shyly at her lover. "That would be very nice. Have you been there before?"

"Many times. So, Rome in comparison to your beloved Florence?"

"I am seduced by the beauty of Florence, but I am awestruck by the grandeur of Rome. Sometimes it is almost too much to take in. Florence whispers and persuades. Rome demands your attention and conquers your senses."

"And you believe that I have a Roman soul … That's telling."

"I stand by my initial observation, Mr. Furst."

Dining-in at the Rome Cavalieri Hotel was not a service of convenience. It was designed to be an experience in fine dining. People made a point of intimate dinners on their private balconies at this hotel.

The Franciacorta was brought up only moments after Torsten had called for the sparkling wine made from Chardonnay and Pinot Noir grapes, as was a bottle of non-sparkling water. The dinner would be brought up a little while later.

Clad only in bathrobes and seated on the balcony, Torsten was soon raising his glass to toast his lovely companion on the occasion of their first dinner in Rome. Ela reminded him that they had to look into each other's eyes …

Otherwise they would be risking seven years of bad sex.

That evening, they dined on delicious lobster medallions with a citrus sauce and sea bass and grilled vegetables. The wine that Torsten had selected to go with their meal was a blend of Chardonnay and Sauvignon Blanc. This was a blend that Ela had never come across before, but she found herself liking it a lot.

While they were still eating their dinner, a gentle breeze wafted the sound of very sensual music up to their balcony.

"Would you dance with me after dinner on our private balcony, Mr. Furst?"

"I thought you were fading out."

"I definitely am, but I can manage one slow dance."

"I don't dance."

"Why in heaven's name not?"

"Don't pretend you didn't notice my limp, Ela," Torsten said self-consciously.

"I noticed your gait was a little uneven without the shoes, but I would hardly call it a limp."

"One leg is shorter ... due to an accident when I was a child. I wear a special insole, so it is less noticeable when I am wearing shoes and concentrating on how I walk. It's different with dancing. Dancing brings attention to my deformity regardless of the insole ... So, I don't dance."

"It's just you and me here, Torsten."

"It's something I wouldn't be comfortable with, Ela. I have been trying to overcome this physical defect since I was a boy. A very good friend of mine has a theory: That I may owe some of my success to the problem with my leg. He thinks I overcompensated in school and in business. He thinks I still do; and that is why I work so hard. I am sure he is right. Now you know. Can we please leave it at that?"

"I didn't realize, Torsten. I'm sorry if I was being insensitive."

"You have nothing to apologize for."

The fresh night air atop their haven, the soothing music from below, the pleasant aftermath of satisfying sex, delectable dishes that appeased hunger, the effect of the delicious wines and jet lag, hit Ela all of a sudden. The insomniac was falling asleep in her chair.

"You're about to collapse. I think it's time that you got ready for bed. I'll call down to have everything taken away."

"That sounds like a good idea. I'm so sleepy."

When you wake up in Rome, all things are possible, Ela thought as she stretched and looked over at the naked man beside her, remembering the kind of night they'd had.

Torsten was still sleeping. How to wake him? Ela moved a pillow to the foot of the bed and lay her head on it.

Torsten woke to the sound of Ela in pleasure mode. Her eyes were partially closed; her lips were partially open. She let out her breath in shorter and shorter spurts. Her knees were almost at a forty-five degree angle and part of the top sheet was balled up in a clenched left fist. Her right hand was between her legs.

Torsten positioned the pillow under his head for a better view and said nothing. His hard-on was saying it for him.

He watched her dexterous middle finger work in a repetitive circular motion over her clit then enter her wet pussy as she arched her back.

Ela brought herself to orgasm in front of Torsten the way she had many times since their sexting. She liked that he was watching her and that his cock appreciated the performance. It had made it hotter and more erotic for her, and she didn't stop at one orgasm. She had two more. Torsten was horny as hell.

"I believe that was on the to-do list?"

"I recall."

"There was something else on the to-do list. If you would care to join me in the shower, Mr. Furst? It looks as if you're in need of my attention."

With warm water sluicing down her back, Ela slid to her knees and took Torsten's balls between her lips, teasing with her tongue. While he steadied himself with one hand on the shower wall, Ela closed her hand fist-like around the shaft of the cock now slippery with water and worked the whole length of him slowly and consistently. He liked it, he said. He liked it even more when she took the head of his cock into her mouth and then nearly the whole cock down her throat. With hands on the clenched cheeks of his muscular ass, Ela used only her mouth and throat to take him the rest of the way.

Torsten didn't have command of his body at that point. For Ela it was a great big turn-on to be in control; to have this billionaire at her mercy. She applied herself diligently to the task that she was so enjoying and Torsten's head went back in surrender. He closed his eyes, not aware of the sounds coming from the back of his throat. Liquid pleasure rose up from his balls and spilled out of the engorged tip of his cock into Ela's hot mouth and down her throat. The long fulfilling orgasm left him weak in the knees as she sucked out every drop of his pleasure.

Though not yet recovered, Torsten helped Ela to her feet and saw that she was pleased with herself. Ela Zalewski knew she had delivered on the world class blow job she had bragged about in one of her texts.

"Well that was an eye-opener. You're very talented, Ms. Zalewski."

Ela responded with, "I'm well rested, Mr. Furst," then demanded breakfast.

Having toweled themselves off they consulted the in-room dining menu. Ela asked Torsten if he would be so kind as to order her plain yogurt with fruit, two scrambled eggs and American coffee with hot milk.

Would she like to have breakfast on the balcony, Torsten had inquired. The sun was already quite strong.

She would put on her silk robe and sunglasses, Ela had assured him, but if he found it too hot in his terry robe, they could eat inside in air-conditioned comfort.

Torsten could see that Ela was all excited about eating breakfast overlooking the magnificent grounds and enjoying the view of Rome.

"Nonsense. I'll put on my swimming trunks, a polo and my sunglasses. I'll order some cold water, as well."

Torsten ordered their breakfast in perfect Italian. The words came to him easily. He did not have to search his memory for them.

Soon they were ensconced on their private balcony, coffees in hand, Rome at their feet.

Ela had changed into her swimsuit in the bathroom while the in-room dining person was removing their trays, and came out with a black tight mesh cover-up tied up at the waist, leaving what was underneath to Torsten's imagination … for now, and her hair in a ponytail. She was in heels, as usual. These platform sandals had thicker heels though, and wider ankle straps, than what he had seen her in. They were black too.

Ela stuffed a good size silver metallic beach bag with everything imaginable, as an amused Torsten looked on.

Torsten, who had been dressed in his gray swimming trunks, white cotton piqué polo and gray canvas slip-ons since before breakfast, had his few personal items in a small gray nylon bag that looked pitifully underutilized by comparison.

"I'd like to see what you'd pack in an overnight bag."

"See, now you sound just like my director of sales, Robert."

"I'm looking forward to seeing what's under your cover-up."

Torsten selected sun loungers as close to the pool as possible, and Ela realized that this was so he wouldn't have to walk more than a few steps without shoes and his special insole.

As they put down their bags, Ela told Torsten that she had a confession to make.

"I like water, but I'm not a good swimmer."

"We'll get you one of those foam noodles, and I'll keep an eye on you."

Torsten didn't seem too disappointed. She could cool off and he wouldn't be expecting her to do the *butterfly stroke*. Actually she did the *side stroke* okay for about a minute, but her best was the *dog paddle*. No need for him to see that.

Torsten wasn't thinking about whether Ela could swim well or not. He was looking forward to the unveiling, as he got comfortably settled in his white lounger.

When Ela removed her cover-up, she was in a black two-piece. The top was a halter with triangular cups. At the upper part of each cup, there was a ribbon of very fine black mesh. The bottom went up to her belly button, but the upper two thirds was sheer black mesh as well.

Torsten thought that the high-fashion two-piece was even sexier than a string bikini. It seemed that some of the men at the pool thought so too.

"You look like a Bond girl."

"Would she be a good Bond girl or a bad Bond girl?"

"Bad ... I hope."

"Would she have one of those double entendre names?"

"Let's see ... Ina ... Ina Satiable?"

"Hmm."

Sebastiano, their driver, had someone in the front passenger seat of his car when he pulled up in front of the hotel to take Ela and Torsten to lunch. When the two got out, Ela noticed that the passenger had that certain elegance Ela associated with Roman men. He was about the same height as Sebastiano, but very muscular in build.

Like Sebastiano, this man had a full head of thick wavy dark brown hair and an olive complexion. While Sebastiano was wearing the dark suit and white shirt of a driver, this man was in a medium-blue linen, silk and cotton blend jacket and pants. His dark blue crewneck knit was fine gauge cotton, and he was wearing a pair of those vintage inspired dark blue leather trainers. He wore a pair of black sunglasses which he removed when Ela and Torsten approached the car.

Sebastiano came around to the same side.

"Good afternoon, sir, Miss Ela," Sebastiano greeted them with a smile.

"Good afternoon," Torsten replied pleasantly, echoed by Ela.

The other man didn't smile, but followed with a *good afternoon* and introduced himself as Bruno Cassano. He informed them that he would be looking after their safety that afternoon.

"Thank you, Mr. Cassano."

Torsten had not told her anything about this, so it must be routine, Ela decided.

Sebastiano was able to park the car close by, and at Torsten's insistence, he and Mr. Cassano would have lunch at the same restaurant. Though they seated themselves at the opposite end, Mr. Cassano had an unobstructed view of Mr. Furst and his guest.

"Why Trastevere? Don't get me wrong. I like it. It's very picturesque."

"It reminds me of when I was studying in Rome. I used to come to this working class neighborhood with its narrow cobbled streets and medieval houses. It was away from the beaten path and the tourists, at that time. If you were a foreigner but lived in Rome even for a short time, you quickly learned that this was the place to come to on the weekends. You got to mix with the locals, which was always a good time. The food was always great. It was pretty lively in the evening, and it still is."

The trattoria in Trastevere was definitely on the rustic side. The food was something that Grandmother would make, if Grandmother was an Italian *nonna*. The owner himself served them and there was no doubt that this was a family affair.

"Why this particular restaurant?"

"Because of the fried Jerusalem artichokes and the osso bucco."

"It's not exactly a light lunch; especially in warm weather, but I could go for that."

"A bottle of Barbaresco?"

"Definitely."

"Good, and I'll order a bottle of sparkling water."

"You didn't tease me about wearing sandals to walk on the cobblestones. I'm surprised."

"Well, you told me that you have been to Rome and to this neighborhood, so I felt that you knew what you were in for. Plus, Sebastiano knows that we're not doing a walking tour, and he did see your footwear. Besides, I'm starting to get the picture. You're all about heels. You wanted to wear the slip-ons to bed and you wore these to the pool. Since you told me last night that you had emptied your luggage, from what I saw, all of your footwear is like that. The sandals look good with the green, blue and black print of your sexy jersey summer dress, and you negotiated those cobblestones quite well. I'm impressed actually. The Spanish Steps might present a bit of a challenge though."

Ela didn't regret the sandals or the dress one bit. She wanted to be well dressed beside Torsten who was wearing a light blue cotton chambray suit, navy polo and dark blue lace-up shoes with crepe soles. She knew he wasn't the type to wear a tank top, cargo shorts and sandals. It just wasn't his look. She wasn't intimidated by the prospect of walking down the Spanish Steps.

Thinking about walking down the Spanish Steps in high heels, was a different matter from actually doing it.

"I had forgotten that this is one of the longest and widest staircases in all of Europe."

"I think I have to take little breaks. Just how many steps are there?"

"A hundred and thirty-five, if memory serves. Take your time. The shops are open till seven," Torsten teased, then added thoughtfully, "You just have to make it down. Sebastiano will be meet us down there after we're done shopping."

At least Torsten hadn't reminded her that this had been her idea.

Mr. Cassano, who was keeping his distance but never letting Ela and Torsten out of his sight, moved at their pace.

With Mr. Cassano satisfied that the shop Ela and Torsten would be entering was secure, he waited outside with Sebastiano.

The manager had admired the look of the stern man who entered the establishment and had readily answered his questions, as did the saleswoman.

When the man exited and his client and companion entered, the saleslady was certain that she would be moving a lot of inventory from the new collection.

Shopping for lingerie with Torsten was an event. An event that turned into foreplay. It had started innocently enough. At first, Ela perused the merchandise, then Torsten made some suggestions. Ela was glad to have his input, but it wasn't long before Torsten was out of control, selecting a bra and panty set in silk, and another in lace. They would need the suspenders to go with these he had informed the saleswoman.

"Or garters, as you call them," he clarified to Ela. Then the stockings. It wouldn't look good if she didn't have the right shoes he concluded, so he tasked the saleslady with finding something suitable. After that came a corset and matching panties, a black lace kimono, a sexy black silk slip, thongs and hold-ups.

When Ela found the right fit in the items chosen for her, Torsten would come into the fitting room to give his approval. She would pose for him more suggestively each time. They were already behind in their schedule with the lunch and shopping lasting longer than foreseen, so Torsten informed the saleswoman that they would not be waiting around while she wrapped everything. He asked her to have their purchases delivered to the hotel in about an hour.

"Certainly, sir."

"Torsten, it's so extravagant. I can't possibly wear every piece for you before tomorrow morning."

"You just did, and it was worth it. You'll have other occasions ... like under a cocktail dress when we go out to dinner. I'll know you're wearing something very special and secret, for my eyes only. Or to entice me when we stay in. I saw the size of your travel bag, there's plenty of room, so I knew that I did not have to curb my pleasure."

He was saying that they would be seeing each other again … maybe many more times. Ela was ecstatic.

"I couldn't help but notice that everything you picked out, Torsten, in the way of risqué lingerie, was in black."

"Ina Satiable only wears black when she's in the mood to play."

Visiting the Pantheon with Mr. Cassano trailing behind was a stark contrast to the way they had spent the last couple of hours.

This well preserved ancient Roman building of temple design, may have been part of pagan history, but it had also been part of the history of Christianity in Rome, and was still being used as a Catholic Church.

"After what we've been doing …you don't think we'll get struck by lightning do you?"

"Of course not. It's not Saint Peter's Basilica," Torsten replied jokingly.

So Ela and Torsten toured the Pantheon with its portico of massive Corinthian columns under a pediment, and rectangular vestibule that linked the porch to the rotunda with its famous dome, without incident.

Ela was just as in awe of the oculus, or eye, on this visit as the last. She marveled that it not only provided natural light, but also ventilation, which was very welcome on hot days like today. She had learned on her previous visit that a drainage system under the floor handled the rain that came in through the oculus.

Since the Renaissance the Pantheon had been used as a tomb and was the resting place for two kings and a queen, in addition to architects, painters and a composer, all revered in their day.

With a last look around, and a minute to admire the original marble floor, Ela and Torsten concluded the sightseeing part of their day.

CHAPTER 10

With the lingerie already in their suite when they arrived, Torsten thought it might be fun if she modeled something for him again.

Ela had felt so sexy when she was trying on the items in the changing room that she was dying to put something on again and required no convincing.

She moved all of the bags into the bathroom, so Torsten wouldn't see what she had picked to wear. The bathroom was certainly big enough to be her dressing room, but before that, she'd pop into the shower to freshen up, and apply a little perfume in strategic places.

When Torsten looked up from his smartphone, Ela was standing there in the lace bra and matching bikini with hold-ups and the patent leather pointed toe platform pumps with bad girl heels. Hands on hips, head tilted, legs together and right foot raised off the floor except for the toes, she posed for him suggestively.

"Come here," he said from the divan facing the large marble fireplace.

"Ina Satiable doesn't take orders. She gives them."

"Does she have anything in mind?"

"She's going to walk over to you, and you're to remove her panties. Nothing more."

Ela walked slowly and seductively to the divan and waited. Torsten slipped his fingers into her black lace panties on either side, taking his time.

"Ina should feel free to use my shoulders to steady herself."

Ela did when the panties were around her ankles, so she wouldn't catch her heels when she stepped out of them. She even found a way to "accidentally" brush her breasts across his cheek.

Torsten waited to see what was next.

Ela walked to the other side of the divan and sat on the armrest, put her hands behind her to brace herself and parted her legs, giving Torsten a clue into what was expected of him.

"You're going to sit there." She indicated to the ottoman with her eyes. "And you're going to go down on Ina. If you do a good job, and remember her full name; she will reward you."

Torsten smiled. Ela was really getting into the role. He sat himself on the ottoman, but didn't exactly approach her timidly. That wasn't the role he was prepared to play. She wanted him to eat her pussy? He'd eat her pussy until she begged him to stop.

Torsten spread her legs further apart and went to work on her clit with his tongue. She had been only slightly aroused. Now she was really wet from her own juices and his saliva. Ela had a feeling that it was he who was in control, not she, as she gave in to one shuddering orgasm after another. He was up to three when she ordered him to stop. Her poor pussy was swollen and sensitive.

Torsten did, but only long enough to say, "I don't think so." Another orgasm in, and she pleaded with him to stop.

"Say please."

"Please stop."

"After the next one."

He was up to five orgasms before releasing her in a boneless heap.

"It's time we both started to get ready. I feel like having a drink at the Tiepolo Lounge before dinner. Maybe after dinner, you can reward me. Don't forget your panties."

Torsten had turned the tables on her. The Ina Satiable persona needed some fine-tuning.

After freshening up, Ela went around their suite in the black lace kimono, with nothing under it, and black silk mules. She found all kind of reasons to bend over in front of Torsten, tiding up, rummaging through an empty suitcase …

Once Torsten had ample time to enjoy the provocative view, she asked, "Aren't you supposed to be getting ready?"

When Torsten came out of the bathroom in a towel, clean shaven and smelling great, Ela was already made up and dressed in her red sleeveless V-neck peplum, knee-length bandage dress and neutral platform sandals.

"Would those be *glad-he-ate-her* sandals?"

Ela threw him a look of indignation.

Torsten's towel ended up on the bed and he proceeded to walk around their suite stark naked in search of the pieces of clothing that he would need for the evening. He seemed to have problems locating what he wanted and he changed his mind a lot, before finally donning navy cotton pants, a light blue cotton shirt, a light blue wool, silk and cotton houndstooth jacket accented by a navy blue tie and light blue pocket square. He wore his black lace-ups with socks this evening.

Ela had been doing her best to pretend that she hadn't noticed his show, but when Torsten had caught her looking, she raised an eyebrow suggestively.

Ela and Torsten stopped at the bar on their way to dinner. The barman asked what signora would like to drink.

"Whatever the gentleman orders will be fine."

So, the barman asked if signore had a preference.

"It was just on the tip of my *tongue*. Never mind. We'll have a glass of Franciacorta out on the terrace."

"You're not going to do that the whole evening, are you?"

Torsten just shrugged his shoulders.

"I thought Ina Satiable was the type of woman who took charge."

"She's more of a seductress. Besides, Ina Satiable actually has a weakness for alpha males … men she can't dominate. Didn't I tell you?"

Seated at a fine table overlooking Rome at night, and surrounded by art treasures, Ela and Torsten went about the serious business of studying the menu at La Pergola.

Their selection was identical. Food compatibility was important to Ela, she realized. They would be having the scampi tartar with coconut cream and dehydrated lime, the deep-fried zucchini flower with caviar on shellfish and saffron consommé, then the lobster and John Dory with Chinese cabbage and aromatic smoky black tea infusion. It would make the wine pairing that much easier too.

With so many complex flavors, they had decided to leave the wine selection to the supremely knowledgeable sommelier, and were thrilled with the suggestions.

La Pergola's handsome and extraordinarily talented chef came by their table, to make it the perfect dining experience.

Back in their suite, Torsten asked, "Didn't you say something earlier about rewarding me?"

"Did I?"

"Perhaps if we retrace our steps it'll *come* to you?"

"You're such an overachiever. Oh, I remember now … I was thinking that you could go into the bathroom and get into your bathrobe. I can put on that lace kimono out here. We can close the lights in our suite and go out on our *private* balcony … to enjoy the lights of Rome and the stars. It would be such a shame not to take *full* advantage of that *exciting* view on our last night in Rome … If that meets with your approval?"

"As a matter of fact, it does. When I come out, I'll take care of the lights. See you out on the balcony?"

With Ela in his lap out on the balcony, Rome never seemed more spectactacular to Torsten. Ela nuzzled his neck while caressing his chest inside of the bathrobe. He put his hand behind her neck and brought her in for a kiss Torsten style. It was demanding, suggestive, possessive and passionate … the way women dream of being kissed by a man like Torsten.

Ela's juices were flowing from the way he had been kissing her, and it was time to give him his reward. She stood and reached down to untie his robe, then dropped her own robe to the ground. She had his full attention. He was already hard. Apparently kissing her the way he had been was equally arousing for him.

Ela spun around on her heels and straddled him backwards. She rode his cock in that position for a couple of minutes, before bending forwards so that he could watch. He wrapped his hands around her waist to lift her higher, but even so she wouldn't have had the staying power if not for all of those squats she had added to her workouts. It wasn't easy to stay in this position for the duration though, and Ela suggested that they go inside, so that she could try something different.

Torsten was happy with the reprieve, because he wanted to last. It may have been his reward, but he had no intention of being the only one to reach orgasm.

The inventive Ela had him sit on the divan, close to the armrest, but not right against it. She was not ordering him like earlier, but asking in a voice heavy with promise.

When Torsten was seated, Ela placed her knees on either side of his thighs. She lifted her right leg into a forty-five degree angle with her right foot flat on the seat cushion. Ela took hold of his shaft and when he was in position, she lowered herself onto his cock. It felt good for both of them. Ela placed her hands behind Torsten on the back support of the divan. She started slowly, up and down, building momentum, then she added hip rotation.

The penetration and the stimulation she was getting from the friction of her clit against his cock was bringing on arousal big time. Then Torsten started to play with her sensitive breasts, and she was done for. She came in one long multi-layered orgasm.

Ela really wanted to give Torsten pleasure this way, so she continued in this position. It was working. She was so turned on by watching him getting close, that she worked herself into a second orgasm and then a third.

Even though Ela was tiring, she wouldn't let up. Just when she thought her body might give out though, Torsten came deep inside her. When the orgasm subsided, he rolled his head back on to the backrest, and let out his breath.

"That was some reward. You're an amazing woman, Ela, and very creative."

"I was making it up as I went along. I may have been channeling my inner Ina Satiable. Or maybe you just bring it out in me."

The next morning Ela woke in a spooning position. Torsten was on his left side, caressing her breasts with his right hand while kissing her neck and shoulder. His erection was pressed against her bottom. It may have started as morning wood, but it was now directly linked to the foreplay.

Ela stayed still, pretending to be asleep, but when Torsten caressed her between her legs with slow, teasing strokes and clever fingers, she gave herself away by coming.

Torsten then lifted her right leg in the air from behind the knee and asked her to hold it like that for a second, which she did, knowing what would happen next.

He moved into position and slipped into her wet pussy. While holding her leg up again, he used his hips to satisfy her with another two orgasms. After her second, he satisfied himself with a final deep thrust, and kissed her shoulder one more time.

"You are habit forming, Ms. Zalewski."

"You're saying that, as if it's a bad thing, Mr. Furst."

"On the contrary."

The conversation over breakfast on their terrace after the vigorous lovemaking session was not something Ela saw coming.

"Ela, this is going to sound crazy: We don't even really know each other, but, I can't bear the thought of parting in a few hours. Darling, tell me you'll be mine, and I'll be yours till the end of time."

"I think I already am. That's what scares me."

"Why, darling?"

"Because nothing like this has ever happened to me before. It's overwhelming."

"I have to be in New York next week. I'll fly into Montreal first. We'll have dinner, and we can talk about our future then. I know it's a lot to take in, so let's just leave it until Montreal. This way, by the time I get there, you will have had a chance to live with this for a few days. I'll let you know about the restaurant and details in a couple of days."

Ela was distraught when it was time to say goodbye to Torsten at the airport, but reminded herself that it was only for a few days. She consoled herself with the knowledge that she would be seeing him very soon for that important talk.

An excitement was building within her at the realization that she was in love with Torsten Lucas Furst. He must love her too, to speak of a future together.

Ela decided that she would let Robert know that things had gone very well in Rome and all of his concerns were unfounded. She'd promise to tell him more in a few days because the man was coming to Montreal for a heart-to-heart.

DIANA SOBOLEWSKI

CHAPTER 11

"Darling, I want you to move to Germany."

"Torsten, I never said anything in Rome, but I looked you up on the internet, and I read that you were married. I guess since you came here to talk about our future, you are recently divorced?"

"No, but my wife and I have not lived together for some time, so that's not an issue."

"You're legally separated then, and planning on getting a divorce?"

"We're separated, but very few people know this. We keep up appearances for business functions and social functions."

"So, you don't fuck her?"

"I haven't for a long time."

"I'm still trying to get my head around this. So you're this power couple and you, Torsten, are planning to continue with this deception. What about her? Doesn't she want more out of life?"

"Neither one of us wants a divorce."

"Does she have a lover?"

"No. She wouldn't risk it."

"Really?"

"That's just the way it is. Our world is very different, Ela. My wife has survived one divorce, and though it hasn't worked out for us, it wouldn't look good for her in our social circles if she was a divorcée for the second time."

"Won't it get out when you and I are living together, traveling together and being seen together?"

"We won't be living together. I have an estate outside of Munich, but I just bought a building in the city with four apartments. Two on the ground floor and two on the second floor. I bought it as an investment and to house some of my executives that fly into Munich for extended periods of time from other cities or countries, or people from out of town that I do business with. The idea was to provide the feeling of a home, but with a hotel next door, they could take their meals there. They would also have access to hotel facilities such as the pool, the gym, the spa and the hair salon."

"So, that is where you expect me to live?"

"You would be very comfortable. Each unit would sell for close to eight million in your Canadian dollars. The apartments are very luxurious. They are fully furnished and decorated with collectible art pieces. They are even stocked with Champagne and fine wine and spirits. There are two master suites with en-suite bathrooms and there's a powder room. There's a good size office and a large open plan kitchen, dining and living area with fireplace. There is also a large private balcony off the living part, but you will have the rooftop terrace to yourself because you will be the only tenant.

"There is underground parking. I will provide you with a car, or you can use a limousine service. There's a cleaning service that would come by weekly and you can order meals and snacks from the hotel if you feel like staying in. You will have the hotel's twenty-four-hour concierge service for sightseeing, shopping, and to replenish the wine cellar, or even to gas up the car. There's virtually no limit. The building has a state-of-the-art security system. You'll be well cared for. I haven't forgotten about your living and entertainment expenses either. You'll be well cared for in that respect as well. There will be gifts too. I'm a generous man."

"I see. So you would be staying with me in this apartment from time to time?'

"I would be staying in the other apartment on that floor. It would be better that way, should anyone come by from the hotel, for example. They are very discreet, but this provides another level of discretion. We would have the floor to ourselves. My security person and driver would stay in the apartments on the ground floor."

"So we couldn't be seen dining out together?"

"There's a restaurant nearby, where the staff accommodates this kind of situation. We'd arrive separately and at different times. You could come through the front door, and I would come up the elevator from the indoor garage."

"You mean that's where rich powerful men dine with their mistresses."

"You could put it that way."

"I suppose traveling together would be out of the question."

"We wouldn't be traveling together when I'm traveling on business, but we could vacation together three or four times per year. There are resorts with private villas that cater to people like us."

"We were together in Rome. We dined out, we went sightseeing and shopping together."

"Yes, but it was a risk. If it's a one-off thing, I can roll the dice. But to consistently rub my wife's face in the fact that I have someone new in my life would be disrespectful to her."

"That's why you never held my hand in public or kissed me … in case someone recognized you."

"It's best to take precautions. In Munich we'd have to be that much more careful. There is another type of vacation we could take, that I am sure you would find very pleasurable ... on my yacht. All of the members of the crew, like all of my employees, were required to sign a confidentiality agreement when they were hired. They would never divulge such information, but my lawyer doesn't believe in taking any chances."

"The *Lara* ... named for your wife and decorated by her. I saw the photos online. I don't think so."

"Now you're being childish. She doesn't come on board anymore."

"Well you've thought of everything, haven't you?"

"There are only two details left. My lawyer is looking into ways to have you stay in the country, and there is the confidentiality agreement, of course."

Ela looked down at the table, crestfallen.

"You don't look very happy."

"Let's review. I give up my home, my work, my friends, my whole life to, humm, let's see ... wait for you to drop in when you're not working, entertaining businesspeople, traveling on business, or attending events with your wife. I wouldn't even be able to tell anyone back home what I was doing in Germany. I don't like lying to the people who care about me. Say I did make friends in Germany, which seems highly unlikely, I wouldn't be able to say anything to them either."

"I'm proposing a perfectly logical adult arrangement."

"As you said in Rome, we don't really know each other. If you knew me at all, you would know that I would wither away in this *arrangement.* We could have kept it to meeting up a couple of times a year, discreetly as you mentioned, for sex ... since we're very compatible that way. I would not have asked you about your wife or other women. I would have expected the same of you, of course."

"That would be unacceptable. I would always want to be your only lover and I would be completely faithful to you. I couldn't do with a couple of times a year. That's why I need you close by."

"I haven't finished. Instead you brought emotions into it. Strong emotions. I began feeling things I have never felt. You didn't say the words *I love you,* but they were implied, or so I thought since you were adamant about making plans for our future. What was I to think? I started believing that we were going to be a couple. What you're proposing is something entirely different. It's one-sided."

"I wouldn't call living in the lap of luxury one-sided."

"Yeah, well I wouldn't call it living. It's more like existing. Hey, maybe I could get to know the other mistresses that frequent this restaurant with their benefactors. We could start an association. I could run for president; because you're probably the richest and most powerful of those men. We could organize lunches, shopping and other such stimulating and enriching activities.

"By the way, are there health benefits and is there dental coverage? What about a retirement plan? Oh, and what is the age of retirement for a mistress? For that matter, where do mistresses go once they retire? Is there a special retirement home or community?"

"I don't appreciate the sarcasm, Ela."

"I have worked too hard to get to where I am today to sit around letting my brain atrophy and hoping you stop by. I would have to be a total dimwit to accept your offer. Here's my counteroffer: It would be far more *discreet*—your favorite word—if we lived on different continents, and never saw each other. That way, you can go on with your ridiculous marriage without worry of discovery. Or, maybe you should work on getting back together. She's probably more your type anyway. I think I prefer recreational sex, where I don't have to uproot my present life to go live under your stifling conditions. Excuse me ... *exist* under stifling conditions."

Torsten didn't say a word, but his eyes grew cold and his expression hard. He was angry. He stood up, reached into his inside jacket pocket, pulled out his wallet and removed several large bills. He placed them on the table without looking at Ela, and walked out the door of the restaurant. He was heading for the limousine that was waiting to take him to his hotel *alone*.

Ela was starting to shake from the realization that it was over. She needed to get out of there. She steadied herself to wait out the couple of minutes that it would take not to run into Torsten.

Seeing the cash on the table, the waiter looked confused.

"*Monsieur* is not coming back?"

"He had to leave."

"Will *Madame* be leaving as well?"

"Yes."

Getting a taxi didn't take long, thankfully.

Ela gave out her address, and hoped the tears wouldn't come until she could get into her apartment.

Just before they got underway, the driver noticed that there was something wrong with his passenger.

"*Madame,* are you alright?"

"I'm sorry ... I just received some bad news."

"A death?"

"Yes."

"It was sudden?"

"It was unexpected."

"My condolences. There are some tissues behind my seat."

"Thank you."

The doorman was surprised to see Ms. Zalewski back so soon. She had looked jubilant when she left, but now she didn't look very well.

"Are you ill, Ms. Zalewski?"

"I'm afraid so, Howard. It just hit me. It's nothing serious. Don't worry."

Alone in the dark in her apartment, tears turned into uncontrollable sobbing. Hours went by and Ela had not moved from her spot on the sectional.

The old Ela would not have been in this position. This Ela grieved the loss of what could have been. She had changed too much in a very short period of time. She had not protected herself.

Ela had never understood the meaning of a *broken heart.* People talked about it as if it was a medical condition. Now for the first time in her life, she felt a non-relenting pain in her chest. It was not a stabbing pain. It was oppressive and it made her feel weak and physically ill. She was lost in unfamiliar territory. She wondered how long it was supposed to take to recover from this condition. Was recovery even possible? She hoped she could believe in the saying, "Time heals all wounds," but, what did one do in the meantime?

"You should have fought for me, darling," she told the man who wasn't there to hear her. "I was ready to love you. One day, you will realize that a life of wealth, power, position and success can be empty without love."

Ela eventually fell asleep in a fetal position on the sectional, but awoke intermittently from bad dreams that frightened her to the point of nausea. In one, she was trapped. In another, she was lost. By morning, Ela was a total disaster. She looked at herself in the bathroom mirror through eyes that were swollen slits. The lids were a purple red with only traces of eye shadow, barely any eyeliner and some clumpy mascara. Whatever makeup had not rubbed off on the pillow that she had slept on was smeared all over her face. Her hair was plastered to the sides of her face from dried tears and hair spray, and felt matted in the back. She didn't exactly feel fresh, and she was woozy from a drop in blood sugar. Her stomach was making sounds to protest the fact that she hadn't eaten since lunch the previous day.

Ela sliced up an orange and sucked in the juice from the segments to bring up her blood sugar, though she had no appetite. It didn't satisfy her thirst though, so she drained a half liter bottle of spring water.

Having no strength to stand up in the shower, Ela let the water run to fill up the bathtub. Her shampoo, conditioner, moisturizing wash, razor and shaving cream were within reach, but she added her makeup remover and facial cleanser. She would brush her teeth later. Doing so after just eating acidy fruit would harm the enamel. Weird, it was like she was on auto-pilot.

It took a lot of effort for Ela to get out of her bath, dry herself, put on the fluffy white bathrobe that hung behind the bathroom door and locate a pair of reasonably comfortable slippers.

She didn't have it in her to dry and style her hair. Looking in the mirror through purple red slits, she reassessed the damage. She'd have to apply cold compresses to her eyes to try to get the swelling down, but miraculously she hadn't broken out from sleeping in her makeup. Now what?

It was Saturday morning and she'd have today and the next day to get it together before throwing herself back into work, but she had a feeling that she wouldn't be able to concentrate and deliver her best. It would be better to forward her emails to Robert, and just to sit it out for the next week. She'd pull herself together in that time. A week was all she could spare to get Torsten out of her system, before real life would come knocking.

Ela had enough in the fridge to get by on for a couple of days. She'd have groceries delivered after that. She could watch television. She had missed many episodes of *Penny Dreadful* and *Game of Thrones* and there were some new movies out. She'd be careful not to land on a film with a romantic theme, and a travelog about Rome was to be avoided at all costs. With her luck, they would be playing *Three Coins in A Fountain*, *Roman Holiday* or *La Dolce Vita* on one of the channels.

Robert read the strange text: "Taking next week off. Not feeling well. Will forward all emails to you. Have no meetings, but if anything comes up, can you please put it off or handle it yourself. Don't come over, I'm contagious and the whole agency can't shut down."

Robert didn't believe any of it, except the part that she was not feeling great. Contagious? What a load of crap. Something was wrong and he just knew it had to do with the mystery man.

First things, first. Ela was probably not going to feed herself adequately and would make herself sick for real. He had made several containers of a low fat version of cream of carrot and ginger soup. He'd pack that up. Robert's fridge was well stocked. He had all of the ingredients for a cheesy cauliflower crust pizza with artichokes, olives and sundried tomatoes. He added fresh salmon and *jambon maison* from Maître Boucher in his neighborhood. She was fussy about ham, but this ham, she'd like. He threw in the ingredients for a hardy Greek salad and some apples, pears and walnuts. She'd likely be low on her favorite coffee, so Lavazza went into the bag.

The doorman was used to Robert coming and going, as he and Ela worked in her apartment, so he didn't bother to announce him. Robert had never used his key, but this time, he would. If he knocked, she might not let him in.

Robert was so quiet that she never heard him turn the key. He didn't want to startle her, so Robert knocked on the door once it was open and he had stepped into her apartment.

Ela sat up on the sectional with a wet face cloth in her hand, trying to focus. Her vision was blurry after the cold compress, so it took a couple of seconds to make out her visitor.

"What did I tell you?"

"Lies."

"I don't have the strength to do this."

"That's obvious. You look like hell."

"Thanks."

"Tell you what: I'll feed you and when you have regained some strength, you can tell me off."

"I don't feel like eating."

"Yeah well, maybe you should consult with your body. I don't want you to keel over. Then I'd have to call 911 and wait with you in emergency. It would ruin my weekend."

"Fine."

"Good. I'll just put a couple of things in your fridge first."

Robert heated up his tempting first course and prepared the second course. He ate with Ela, because he adhered to the hypothesis that if she saw him enjoying his food, it would make her hungry. They ate in silence.

When Robert cleared the table and put the dishes and pans into the dishwasher, he took Ela by the hand and walked her over to the sectional. She didn't resist.

"Feeling better?"

"Some. You're a good cook."

"Want to talk about it?"

"Not really."

"It's not healthy to keep your feelings bottled up when you're this upset."

"If you must know, things did not go well on my date."

"I figured. He ended it?"

"It depends on your point of view. He offered me the sun, the moon and the stars."

"And what's wrong with that?"

"There were certain conditions. For one thing, I would have to live on the space station alone. So, I passed. Guess you're stuck with me."

"Ela, can't you speak plainly for once?"

"No. Especially not now, or I will sound like a blithering idiot. Allow me to keep some shred of dignity, please. Why haven't you said it?"

"Said what?"

"I told you so."

"What purpose would that serve?"

Robert was about to put his arms around Ela but she backed away.

"If you do that, I'm going to bawl my eyes out. It's all just below the surface. I'm dealing with emotions that I can't control right now. What you did was nice, and don't take this the wrong way, but could you please go now."

"I'll go, but I'm cooking you dinner for the next few evenings, and I'll do some grocery shopping for you as well … nutritious food, easy to prepare or ready to eat."

"You don't have to babysit me. You have a wife. You can't neglect her."

"I'll make dinner early and have a glass of wine with you—I'll take a taxi—don't stress … then I'll go home and have dinner with my wife. Okay?"

"That sounds nice. I don't deserve your friendship."

"You do and a lot more, but I think you know that. I think you made a very important decision based on that. If only your mystery man could have seen it too."

"Robert, if I tell you who he is, will you promise never to tell anyone … except for Diane because I know the two of you don't keep secrets from each other, and I don't want this to spoil it. Then I would feel really horrible. Can you ask her to keep it just between us, though?"

"You have my word, and Diane will never say anything. She cares about you, as much as I do."

"I know I can trust the both of you. I'm just not thinking clearly. His name is Torsten Lucas Furst. He's one of the richest men in Europe. He's reported to be worth seventeen billion euros and his fortune is still growing. He's legally married, but he says it's in name only, and he will not be getting a divorce. I would not have had a problem with that under different circumstances, but he introduced an emotional component into the equation in Rome which gave me a different impression. In Montreal, he spelled out conditions that were impossible. So it's for the best."

"Ela I didn't understand anything you just said."

"I know, but it's the only way that I can tell you, without losing it completely."

"That I can understand."

"Thank you. Can you go back home now … please."

Thirty minutes after Robert left on Tuesday, Ela heard the text notification on her cell. He must have forgotten to tell her something.

"I'm not willing to give you up. Tell me your conditions. I'm certain we come to an agreement."

Ela's heart was pounding wildly, like she had just done her forty-five minutes on the treadmill. A part of her was happy to hear from him, but after she read his text over three more times, there was disbelief. No apology for the way he left. No remorse about how he led her to believe that he wanted to be with her … *really* be with her. No change of heart now, either.

"Are you negotiating with me?"

"I'm open to the idea that my first proposal might need to be amended to better meet your needs."

"I'm not a business acquisition, Torsten."

"Just tell me your terms and we'll go from there."

"I'm not doing this."

"Alright, then I'll put this on the table: You live in Montreal and keep your agency. When you travel on business, I'll arrange to be there. Twice a month, I'll fly to Montreal for a long weekend on a private plane and I'll buy us a home where we can meet up when I'm in town. We can have meals there, but occasionally go out for dinner. Montreal isn't Munich. We can still vacation together as I had suggested. We'd be exclusive. That's non-negotiable."

"So, basically the same deal?"

"You're not understanding the spirit of the gesture."

"Again … I'm not a business acquisition."

"You're being unreasonable."

"I'm sure you're not used to hearing this, but the answer is still no and that's non-negotiable."

No return text. She had just barely started to cope and he disrupted the equilibrium she was working so hard towards.

Wednesday evening, Ela opened the door to Robert in her bathrobe.

"So you've given up bathing and dressing. What happened?"

"Torsten. Read for yourself."

Ela picked up her cell from the kitchen counter and showed Robert the texts.

"Okay, now I think I can piece some things together."

"So, I had a little relapse."

"Do I need to take your cell phone away from you?"

"No. I don't expect to hear from him again, and if I do, I am better prepared. By tomorrow, I'll be bathed and dressed."

"How about this evening while I'm cooking … the bathing part?"

"You're a hard task master. What are you making?"

"A steak, mushroom, red pepper, onion and cheese sub dressed with chopped lettuce, thinly sliced tomatoes and marinated hot peppers, minus the submarine bun."

"Sounds delicious. I'll be out of the shower in ten minutes."

CHAPTER 12

The beautiful, statuesque, fair-skinned ash blonde that Torsten was so often photographed with was Lara Adler Furst, his wife.

She did not work for a living; in fact, she had never worked a day in her life. She was a socialite who frequently appeared in the society pages because of the charities and cultural events she chaired.

In business, Torsten overcompensated for his perceived deformity to win acceptance and succeeded in turning a weakness into a strength. Consequently he became one of Europe's wealthiest and most influential men.

People were so mesmerized by his good looks, commanding presence and long list of accomplishments that they didn't even notice his slightly uneven gait.

As with many powerful men, Torsten had a healthy sexual appetite and he had not lived a chaste life, but for all the traveling he did and for all of the people that he was surrounded by, he was living a pretty isolated life as he neared forty. He began to wish for someone to share his life with, but dating is no easy matter for a workaholic billionaire.

His contact with the opposite sex was limited to the few single women in his inner circle of the same social economic standing, a small group of women he did business with and female employees, so in fact he was a pretty lonely man.

Initially Torsten had been attracted to Lara because of her old money social standing which further legitimized him in a very elite circle, but he came to think of Lara as someone that he could have a permanent relationship with. She understood his busy schedule and fit well into his life. Lara had been attracted to Torsten because of his drive, wealth and influence. Together, they would be the ultimate power couple, a very comfortable arrangement.

Six years earlier, Torsten had believed himself in love with Lara and had had honest intentions of being a devoted and loving husband. He'd waited a long time to marry—to find the right partner. He had been forty-four and she forty-one and newly divorced. Now he recognized the reality of their situation. Theirs would always be a business arrangement and not a romantic partnership. In public they appeared to be a unified couple. They traveled separately, but people just assumed that this was the way of wealthy, powerful people who had a lot of demands on their time. In truth, they actually lived apart, but no one except those very close to them was aware.

One day, Torsten realized that there was something missing in his life that he could not seem to fill with business or objects of wealth. He was always surrounded by people, but Torsten Lucas Furst was experiencing a very human emotion and he was not used to that. He was lonely and longing for *the* woman in his life, and not just a woman.

While he could acquire just about anything and control any situation in the business arena, true love and companionship had eluded him.

As far as he knew, Lara was not seeing anyone and seemed quite content to keep up appearances. If he were to get involved with another woman, it might get out, and she would be subject of gossip and innuendo, and it would be his fault. He should never have married her, but he had. Even though she had a personality that most people didn't exactly warm up to right away, he couldn't just turn his back on her. Torsten had boxed himself into this less than satisfying life and saw no honorable way out.

Lara *was* seeing someone, in fact—or rather discreetly fucking someone. She had no intention of letting anyone find out, least of all Torsten, that she was enjoying the hard body of her much younger, fair-haired, blue-eyed personal assistant.

At Émile Delacroix's suggestion, Amand Peters had presented his credentials to her in Bordeaux. Lara had been impressed by his marketing and computer skills, knowledge of wine and fluency in English and French in addition to his native German. Plus he looked at her in a certain way, and Émile had not been returning her phone calls lately.

Amand had not been in her employment for very long when he took her on the desk of her home office one evening. They were working late on seating arrangements for a charity dinner. She might have been his employer, but there was no doubt as to who was the boss in bed. From then on, they worked late a lot.

CHAPTER 13

David Vaughn came to Montreal a month after they had met in Rome, and three weeks after Ela and Torsten had broken up.

As promised, David called Ela and asked her out for a drink. They got together at the wine bar in the Crystal Hotel.

That led to dinner in the adjoining dining room, La Coupole. Their conversation was going so well, that they did not wish to jeopardize the flow by switching venues. Their meal would be everything they could possibly want; the chef was renowned, the wine list superb.

Over dinner Ela told him that she had been in a relationship as recently as Rome. That it had been quick and intense, but was now ended. Still, she confessed, she felt that she was not quite over this man and would need some time for life to resume as normal. David smiled at her to let her know that he understood and touched her cheek so gently she thought she had imagined it. "I am a patient man," he had told her, and she knew he was being truthful.

David had a knack for calling her or emailing her just when she was at her lowest and she started to depend on him to lift her spirits. Ela would blame her mood on work, though she suspected that he had a pretty good idea that it was not work related at all. She had not divulged who it was that she'd had this relationship with … or how badly it hurt when Torsten had walked out on her.

They had dinner several times over the next few months. Sometimes they even worked lunch into their busy schedules or took a couple of hours to go shopping—for David. They even looked at a luxury apartment downtown one afternoon and made plans to see a building in Westmount.

David leaned towards contemporary with some traditional architectural detail. He wanted a grand home suitable for entertaining, but one that was comfortable and livable as well.

Apartment living suited him well, but he had come across a recently built château style home that met his criteria and had space he could grow into, should his personal life require it.

He seemed to be finding reasons why he needed to come to Montreal more often as autumn wore on. He would tell his staff that he had to oversee certain projects personally. Some of the key people that had been with him a long time, would exchange knowing looks, but no one dared comment on his personal life, or his ever-improving wardrobe.

He was, after all, the boss. It was his company, and he could do whatever he wanted regardless of the motivation. They respected the hierarchy.

David would have liked to shower Ela with gifts by now, but knew that it would scare her off. Everything in its own time, he convinced himself. So, dinner it was. At least he got to spend time with her.

David continued to call Ela, email her or text her when she was down and needed a boost of confidence. He seemed to have time for her no matter how busy his day.

She wondered if the universe was trying to tell her something. Could she have been wrong to have pinned all of her hopes on Torsten? Here was this eligible and attentive man—who incidentally was very attractive as well—just waiting for her to give him a chance at romancing her.

Ela had rushed into a relationship with Torsten and was keeping David at arm's length. What was wrong with her?

Physically, apart from being approximately the same height with the same well-proportioned body, there were notable differences between the two men. David had a head of short unruly dark brown hair and dark brown eyes. His complexion was also naturally darker.

What appealed to Ela beyond David's good looks was that he had an easy smile, a relaxed expression, and a wicked sense of humor. He was easy to be around.

Ela was becoming very fond of him. She could admit that she even held some affection for him. But she was not hot for him.

David was having more than a little difficulty keeping his hands to himself these days. One evening he invited Ela for a bottle of Champagne in the suite of a hotel where he was staying for the very first time. They had a reservation at Europa later that evening. It had become their favorite restaurant. He was surprised she had accepted and hopeful.

Ela arrived a little breathless because she had to rush to make their date, but as lovely as ever. She loved dressing for dinner, and though he would rather wear a Hugo Boss leather jacket and blue jeans when he was not working, he dressed in the suits that she had helped him pick out when they went out for dinner. She liked Brioni and Armani on him and he had a body that was easy to fit. She took him out of his comfort zone and introduced him to some slick brands. "Why not? You have the body." That was all he needed to hear. No salesperson could have persuaded him the way Ela did. He wanted to please her.

When Ela arrived at his door, she found him dressed in one of the suits she had helped him choose. It was the gray Brioni and it fit beautifully. He was wearing all of the accessories they had selected together.

He was also wearing the Patek Philippe pink gold perpetual chronograph wristwatch with moon phases and Bordeaux crocodile strap. It was the current favorite among all of the moon phase watches of his ever expanding collection. It was also the most expensive, worth the price of a luxury home in a very good neighborhood.

David's father had introduced him to the idea of investing in vintage collectible moon phase wristwatches and left him his collection. David had developed a real passion for these expensive timepieces. The passion was the reason why he made it a point to get a manicure regularly no matter how busy his schedule. Ela took in his appearance now and decided he looked really handsome.

David's first instinct was to carry her off into the bedroom. He took command of his senses and showed her around the suite, before walking over to the ice bucket where the bottle was chilling. He poured the one hundred percent Chardonnay Champagne, Krug Clos du Mesnil Blanc de Blanc 2000, knowing how much Ela loved Krug.

It would have been fresh and focused a few years earlier. Now Ela was anticipating lovely layers of flavors like shortbread biscuits, nuts and spice, as well as a floral quality, good minerality, fine acidity and a long finish. This was a complex and very special Champagne from one of the greatest houses in existence. David had chosen well.

"Are we celebrating something?" Ela walked over to the window to take in the view. Montreal was spectacular in the evening from this high up. After David's toast, "To the most intriguing and uncommonly attractive woman I have the pleasure of spending time with," they looked into each other's eyes so as not to invite bad luck, or as Ela would tell it, seven years of bad sex—not that they were having sex.

David was acutely aware of how close they were standing to each other. His expression barely hid how much he wanted her. He was pretty sure that Ela was attracted to him and decided to test the theory with a passionate kiss. David was thrilled when Ela's lips met his and she was responsive. She kissed him back; there was no mistake. Then she took a step back. He was confused.

"David, I have to tell you something," she got out reluctantly, as she tried to rub her red lipstick from his lips with her thumb.

"You can tell me anything, baby."

It was the first time that he used the term of endearment. This was going to be more difficult than she had thought.

"I have been offered a one-year contract by a wine importer-distributor in Vienna. I'm seriously considering taking the offer. I have to let them know by the end of this month. If I agree, the president, who is also the owner, will fly to Montreal personally to meet with me and go over the contract with me and my lawyer. I would have to move in two months. They need me to start as soon as possible, so I can be at Prowein and Vinitaly and then in Bordeaux for *en primeur* week to check out the best of the production and then work on the offers with the Koch group."

To say the announcement hit him like a ton of bricks would be an understatement. She had not shared this piece of news with him until now and lately she shared a lot about her work. She made no secret of the fact that she had found parts of her job less than exciting these days, but she gave nothing away about another option.

David regained enough of his composure to ask, "When did all of this happen?"

"At the beginning of the week, actually. I didn't say anything over the phone, because I thought that I should tell you this evening in person. When you asked me up here, I thought this would be the right time. You must think that this is crazy, but I checked the company out. They are on the up and up. Koch Wein has been around for over thirty years. I'm going to have an acquaintance of mine look into them, but if he's satisfied, it looks like I'll be moving there."

"Ela, I know you are very capable and have a tremendous work ethic, but surely they could have found someone in Europe?"

"Apparently, I am their first choice. I was told that I came highly recommended, but Mr. Koch insisted that this part was confidential. I put some conditions in front of him including getting two weeks off every three months to come home and attend to my agency. It's not the kind of business were I would have weekends off. I could be travelling or working on a time-sensitive project. So Mr. Koch accepted my terms. But I'd still get the usual holidays off and a few weeks of vacation time.

"When I didn't agree immediately, he sweetened the deal. He would be putting me up in a furnished luxury apartment, which would allow me to keep my place here. I would have the use of a car and driver. I would have a generous expense account. I would fly first class and stay in five-star hotels. The offer is very generous. I would be allowed to also represent my own agency when I travel for them, as long as there is no conflict of interest. It's difficult to turn down.

"Anyways, David, it's not about whether they can find someone else. It's about the fact that I would welcome a new challenge. It's an opportunity to approach the wine business from a different angle but I don't have to give up everything I've worked for. I am not feeling very stimulated these days. I believe I could be quite effective there."

"How does Robert feel about all of this?"

"He's on board. Robert would keep things running on this end and he would get more responsibility and hopefully I would be able to procure some new producers from my base in Vienna. After the year is up, I have the option to renew, but knowing me, I'll probably be homesick. You can always come visit … when you can spare the time."

Outwardly David appeared calm, giving nothing away. He had perfected this technique over the many years of facing crises in his work life such as the threat of a strike, cost overruns, delivery delays… the list was long. To his employees, suppliers and clients, he was unflappable. He relied on this technique to prevent the escalation of undesirable situations, diffuse antagonistic attitudes and bring about conciliation. It was a skill that served him well in business negotiations and in poker.

What was presently going on in David's head was a different matter. He wanted to keep her local and in his life, or better yet, make her a bigger part of life. David Vaughn was starting to have some very deep feelings for Ela Zalewski.

David had been contemplating selling his house in Toronto lately. It was Ela that had him thinking that it was time to move on. The girls were away in university and though they would come to visit some weekends and holidays, they usually stayed at their mother's house. As it happened, even though David had not put his house on the market, he had been contacted by a real estate broker the previous week with an offer that he knew he should probably take.

David was sure his daughters would understand. They had lives of their own. He intended to continue their tradition of having dinner together whenever they came home from university and they would still travel together when possible. He could buy an apartment with a couple of extra bedrooms in case the girls decided to stay over. He had already looked at a luxury penthouse apartment near the Yorkville neighborhood. It would more than suit his needs. There were four bedrooms with en-suite washrooms, hardwood floors, a ten foot ceiling and eight foot high windows. It came with two indoor parking spots and there was a fitness room in the building. It was not far from his office, but he would turn one of the bedrooms into a home office. He worked odd hours like Ela but not because he had to contend with different time zones like she did. It was because he was very hands-on and when inspiration came to him or when he wanted to respond to emails quickly, or take action quickly, he needed a comfortable place to work wherever he was at the time. He had wondered if Ela would like this apartment.

He had also wondered if Ela and the girls would like each other. He took the girls away a couple of times a year … Rome, Paris, London, New York … it was how they remained close. Perhaps if everyone got along, Ela could join them on some of their holidays and they could get to know each other. But that would be impossible if she moved to Vienna.

CHAPTER 14

The day after Ela's conversation with David about the offer she had received from Koch Wein, Aldrick Konig, the important contact she had made in Bordeaux, called her with the information she had requested.

"The company is legitimate, but it is no longer owned by Mr. Koch. Torsten Lucas Furst has acquired Koch Wein very recently, but the acquisition is not public knowledge. I guess he didn't own enough of Europe already."

"That can't be. Aldrick, are you sure?"

"Ela, my sources are not always high profile, but they are invariably accurate. I take it this news is not welcome." Aldrick could tell by her reaction that Ela knew who Torsten was. The fact that Torsten kept it secret most likely meant that it was personal on his end. Aldrick wondered what explanation Torsten had given to the president of the company he now owned to keep his name out of it. Then Aldrick remembered that in matters of business, Torsten Lucas Furst did not give explanations. He gave orders and expected them to be followed to the letter. Aldrick sensed there was more to this story and suspected it involved Ela.

She thanked him for the valuable service he had rendered her and explained she needed to contact them and refuse the position. Ela promised not to tell of his involvement.

"You would be doing me a big favor, my dear, if you would use my name in this particular situation. I have my reasons."

The favor Aldrick had asked of Ela would demonstrate to Torsten how valuable an asset Aldrick was to his friends. To Ela he added, "Torsten should have hired me to broker the deal, when he decided to purchase Koch. Then he would have been in the position to ask that I sign a confidentiality agreement." He was only half joking.

Ela had written an email to the president of the Vienna based wine import-distribution company of the same name right away.

> *Dear Mr. Koch,*
> *Mr. Aldrick Konig assisted me in some research about your company.*
> *Please inform Mr. Furst that I am declining his offer.*
> *Sincerely,*
> *Ela Zalewski*

DIANA SOBOLEWSKI

CHAPTER 15

Pierre Joubert was the unlikely owner of a very exclusive private club. Happily married to his wife of twenty years whose traditional cooking he loved more than he should, according to his doctor, the middle-aged man with the portly physique was indispensable to clients seeking a special sort of entertainment.

Pierre ran the kind of salon that rotated between several locations at different times of the month. His club catered to a particular group with very specific tastes. They thought of themselves the New Libertines.

The term Libertines came from a notorious tradition that dated back centuries in France and Britain. It referred to those devoid of moral restraints who placed a great deal of value on the pursuit of physical pleasure.

It was rumored that the original movement still existed, but the members of Pierre's private club didn't adhere to all of the dubious old ways. They considered themselves to be highly evolved and their pursuits highly refined.

One thing that was as true today as in the seventeenth, eighteenth and nineteenth centuries: the New Libertines consisted of the wealthy and the privileged class, but this new version of the secret organization under Pierre's trusteeship had embraced politicians, actors, businessmen and the owners of some very prestigious wine producing châteaux—all male, however, as had been the custom. And membership was by invitation only; you had to be recommended.

Pierre accepted members from abroad as well. With a downturn in the economy worldwide, multi-millionaires and billionaires weren't what they used to be. Pierre had had the foresight to court potential members from other countries from the very beginning.

So, an old way of life was revived and the pursuit of sexual pleasure was at the center of this lifestyle. It was a lucrative business.

The end of an evening at The Club marked the beginning of one of the salons. Pierre provided discreet drivers to take his clients to a location where they could indulge in their desire for ultimate pleasure in luxury and total privacy, unless they wanted to be watched that is.

Pierre had a few rules though. No one could be forced. All had to be willing participants. No one could have pain inflicted on them, unless they specifically desired it and then a safe word was mandatory. There would be no underaged participants and obviously no bestiality.

Everything else in all configurations could be made available to satiate various appetites. He had his own security people who made sure that no terms were violated upon the threat of a lifetime ban. Secrecy was also paramount. The Club was too exclusive to even speak of in public.

One would think that in Bordeaux, the comings and goings would attract attention and that the New Libertines would be better served if the establishment was located in Paris, but this was not the case.

Bordeaux was, in fact, the ideal setting. The salons were held in remotely located châteaux, away from prying eyes, but in luxurious surroundings where the on-site staff was in Pierre's employment.

The talent came to work in conservative street clothes, with little makeup for the women.

It was a formula that worked. Pierre had enough on everyone to ensure that this secret society remained so.

Though Pierre never attended these salons, as he preferred to be in his wife's loving arms, he was no fool when it came to fully appreciating how financially rewarding his services could be.

Torsten Lucas Furst and Jonas Koertig resembled each other physically. Both men, friends since their university days, were tall, athelic, blond and blue-eyed. Both were exceptionally good looking, but Jonas did better with women because he was the more outgoing of the two.

After completing their undergraduate studies in Germany, they went on to study in London, Rome, Paris, Madrid and finally New York together to get a well-rounded education and hone their linguistic skills, then both returned to Germany to take over their families' businesses.

Now years later, they still lived only a few kilometers from each other, made a point of playing golf and having dinner together as often as time constraints would allow. Between them they owned some of the largest and most profitable corporations in Europe … transportation, hotels, software development, security systems, telecommunications, pharmaceuticals, insurance, publishing, high performance plastics and automotive plastics, just to name a few; they also had their fingers in a lot of pies on an international level.

While Torsten was hands-on, Jonas appointed the best people for each job and maintained a certain distance. That gave him a lot more time to pursue other *interests*, but he still knew exactly what was going on with every single one of his companies at all times.

Torsten enjoyed Jonas's company and Jonas enjoyed Torsten's company, but had long thought that Torsten worked too hard and did not play hard enough.

Jonas was the only person that Torsten confided in about anything of importance in his life and this thing with Ela was monumental.

At first, when Torsten had told Jonas about the breakup, Jonas tried to find ways to distract Torsten. Women came in and out of Jonas's life with regularity, and he was glad that Torsten was finally looking beyond his indifferent wife for companionship. It was simply a matter of finding a woman more flexible than Ela.

At Jonas's prompting, Torsten had attempted to get involved with a couple of women that Jonas introduced him to. These particular women understood the need for secrecy, so Torsten wouldn't have to worry about news of such a liaison leaking out. He did so only halfheartedly, hoping to get Ela out of his system.

Torsten had a high sex drive when properly stimulated, but these women just didn't inspire the level of passion that the billionaire had felt for Ela.

Though they seemed to find him attractive, he had the distinct impression that the ladies he hoped to find solace with were attracted to his affluence and what he could provide materialistically, more than to the man.

Ela had never given him the impression that she wanted anything from him. On the other hand, she wanted everything from him.

The beautiful women that should have helped Torsten forget Ela only served to remind him of how special she was and how much he missed her.

Before long Jonas realized that Torsten was head over heels in love with this woman. Jonas, a stranger to both love and long-term relationships, had no notion about how to handle this kind of situation. So Jonas decided to do what he knew best. He would speak to Pierre Joubert on his next visit to Bordeaux.

A reservation at The Club had to be the solution to Torsten's frame of mind. It would take some convincing to get Torsten there, but eventually he'd give in … if only to get Jonas off his back.

There were no markings on the Beaux Arts building to indicate that The Club even existed behind the ornate façade. That was just how the members who paid out a million euros annually in membership fees liked it. The fee covered multi-course gourmet dinners prepared by an *étoilé* chef and his staff. Wines selected by the in-house sommelier from the extensive wine cellar to complement the dishes were part of the fee structure as were the services of a driver to pick up members and their guests at their hotel and return them after a long evening of debauchery.

The rare wines in the best vintages were not covered by the membership fee. It was understandable as there were very few of these wines in existence. Such wines were listed on a separate *carte des vins:* One with the gold key symbol that was the logo for The Club.

Members of The Club were offered two menus in addition to the special wine list, once they were comfortably seated at their table. One menu presented the member with the cuisine that the chef was known for, to which a couple of options were added each day based on seasonal availability and the chef's inspiration. The wine pairings for each dish were also there.

The second menu was the one that differentiated The Club from every other private club: it had a picture of "the dish." No explanation. Just a photo of what was invariably a rare and wondrous delicacy with limited availability. So exclusive not even all the billionaires could have it.

Calling it The Club was a nod to the private clubs in England where membership denoted a certain rank in society and wealth … where male gentry went to gamble, smoke cigars, drink fine port, discuss politics and escape their wives.

Members of Pierre Joubert's private club had their own key card to let themselves in. A member could invite another male guest if properly vetted for suitable social standing in advance.

Members were given four guest passes annually—no repetitions. A member could sponsor such a guest for membership.

German billionaire Jonas Koertig had such a key to The Club and this evening, Torsten Lucas Furst would be his guest. Pierre Joubert liked Germans. They were no nonsense and practical, much like himself.

Pierre hoped that Torsten Lucas Furst would be so impressed that he would soon be able to add his name to the list of prominent members and another million euros annually to the coffers.

Pierre Joubert was far too clever to leave anything to chance. He did not get this far without knowing how to fix the odds in his favor. When Jonas Koertig made the reservation in person on his last visit, Pierre had asked if his guest had any special requests.

"Just the usual service, *Monsieur* Joubert." Jonas did, however, indicate that his billionaire industrialist friend had a type. "She should be a petite brunette, well-toned, with green eyes. Her hair should be about shoulder length with bangs and worn in loose waves. Oh … and soft red lips and neutral eye makeup. She must be feminine, sexy without flaunting it, and no hard edges." Jonas was going from memory. Torsten has showed him photos from Rome on his mobile.

Pierre's people searched high and low for over a week for a reliable and professional woman who would appeal to Torsten. Amateurs were not welcome at The Club.

A woman by the name of Clémence Bandeau fit the description, but she was no longer in Pierre's employment. So, Pierre had his people find a replacement.

She was sent to have her hair cut and styled, fitted with green contact lenses and provided with luxurious lingerie that was slightly provocative, but left some things to the imagination. He would pay her well over what she was earning as an independent.

Jonas and Torsten flew into Bordeaux from Munich on Jonas's private jet. Torsten worked the whole way. He nodded his approval when being served a glass of Bollinger Vielles Vignes Brut 2004 Champagne, but didn't pay any attention to the leggy blond flight attendant serving it.

"Heathen," said Jonas under his breath.

Jonas has been noticing that the only time Torsten looked in the direction of the fairer sex was if the woman was petite with shoulder length, dark brown hair. When that was the case, Torsten seemed to have some weird kind of radar. While normally oblivious to the beauties around him, he could spot a woman with these physical characteristics in his peripheral vision.

Hopefully, Torsten would get out of this mood that was plaguing him and putting a damper on their friendship, once they got to The Club. A couple of bottles from the exquisite wine list should put Torsten in a more appropriate frame of mind, thought Jonas optimistically. The cellar at The Club was even better than Jonas's, and that was saying something.

After getting Torsten to relax, they would depart for the evening's festivities—the real reason for the exorbitant membership fees.

They rode in the back in silence. Torsten did not feel like talking. He barely said two words over dinner. Jonas had to keep the conversation going. He wasn't entirely sure that Torsten heard half of what he was saying.

This time the salon was being held in the Libourne region. When they arrived, the château turned out to be a well restored, eighteenth-century, wine producing château. This was new to the roster. Torsten could not know that, but Jonas did.

As they entered the château, their hostess showed them to a grand room. *Madame* Emmanuelle Dufort had been running these salons for Pierre for a number of years. Pierre knew she ruled with a silk glove over an iron fist and that he could trust her completely.

She had the benefit of breeding and a fine education, knew how to dress and how to carry herself, but her family's money had evaporated a long time ago. She earned a very good living with Pierre. He was generous and treated her with respect. She would always be loyal to him for those reasons.

Jonas nodded to a tall, distinguished, gentleman with silver gray hair and no visible wrinkles to belie his age. He was standing by the fireplace, cognac snifter in one hand and his arm around the waist of a tall, very slim redhead in fine lingerie. Torsten started to ask, "Isn't that ...?"

"It certainly is," replied Jonas with a conspiratorial grin. "And that woman is a model. I saw her on the runway during fashion week in Paris. I guess moonlighting for Pierre must be worthwhile financially. She's wearing lingerie from my favorite shop, the recent collection. I took a friend shopping there last week."

He was incorrigible, thought Torsten shaking his head.

Jonas liked to take his pleasure with two women at the same time, always young, tall and well endowed. It was intimate and impersonal at the same time. Just the way that Jonas liked it.

The ladies were there for him and not the other way around. Even though they were well compensated by the house, they would expect a big tip from him. This was the understanding and Jonas was more than happy to oblige. They were not going to expect him to call the next day or whisper sweet nothings. It was a business transaction and everyone went home *satisfied.*

Jonas brought Torsten there to get him into a better frame of mind. If the lovely young women so versed in the art of pleasure at this salon could not engage Torsten, then he was doomed.

Jonas watched as Torsten looked around the room. He noticed that his friend's gaze fell on a pretty petite brunette about twenty-five years of age. He was taking in how she looked in her blush silk robe, wearing an expression of that perfect dichotomy—innocence and sexual allure.

Torsten walked towards her. Her eyes made him think of another time and another place when he had been deliriously happy. Her look of innocence was heightened by the way she smiled shyly. He told himself it didn't matter that it was a practiced innocence.

Torsten extended his hand to this pretty little thing and she rose out of her chair in compliance. The top of her head reached his chin. Torsten reluctantly disengaged and indicated with his hand that she should lead the way. He was confirming that he had made his selection for the night. Some of the other ladies seemed disappointed, not to mention a couple of the young men.

Ensconced in a luxurious bedroom, this lovely thing was trying her best to arouse Torsten, using every trick she could think of. Though she performed well, it was but an illusion. Her eyes were green, not the blue-green Torsten had lost himself in. They were not expressive in the way that Ela's eyes were expressive. There was no depth, no longing and no passion in them. Torsten had deceived himself. He had wanted to recapture a feeling and now the distance only felt greater. *Damn it. Why did that woman hold dominion over his every thought?* He should have kept his eyes closed instead of searching this girl's face for Ela's expressions. At least then, he could have relied on his memories. No, the rest of it did not feel right either.

By the time the young woman reached for a condom, Torsten had lost his erection. Embarrassed and apologetic, he dressed quickly and before leaving the room, fished a number of large bills from the pocket of his trousers then placed them on the dresser on the way out. The young woman was bewildered, though she had sensed that something was wrong almost from the beginning. He had not responded the way her clients usually did. Actually he seemed a bit tortured. She had liked him though. Not all of her clients were so well mannered and considerate. And it went beyond so called good breeding. It was the way he touched her. Pierre was waiting for a full report. He was not going to like it.

When Jonas finally emerged from his lair with his two feline-like partners, he looked disheveled but quite pleased with himself. He found Torsten in the sitting room impatient and looking anything but relaxed.

"Good God, man." Torsten could not hide his irritation. "I thought you would never come out." Jonas first assumed that having been deprived for so long and then administered to by the Ela look-alike, Torsten must have come quickly and been done early. No…something was not quite right. He should have been in a much better mood. Jonas smiled sheepishly. "The ladies were especially needy tonight."

A signal to the hostess that they were ready to depart was acknowledged with a nod of her elegantly coifed head. She got on the phone with their driver and instructed Émile to bring the car around to the front. They would be the first to leave the premises that night, much to Jonas's disappointment. He could have gone another round after a brief respite, but it would be pointless to try to persuade Torsten. He was already making his way down the hall to the front door. A tall broad shouldered man in a black suit and absolutely no expression on his face was reaching to open the heavy wood and wrought iron door.

To call Torsten's mood disagreeable on the ride back into Bordeaux would be an understatement. Foul was more accurate.

DIANA SOBOLEWSKI

CHAPTER 16

Lara Adler Furst had been coming to Bordeaux regularly for several years. She had travelled there with her first husband and later with her second husband. There were times, when she had even come on her own. It was always to persuade châteaux owners to support her various charity events.

Lara liked doing this kind of work, but not because she was philanthropic. She could care less about most of the causes, except maybe the arts. What she did like was press coverage and being photographed.

She also liked telling people what to do and knew that most people were afraid to displease her. If she banished someone from her circle, they would be a pariah forever in high society. This was a tactic she frequently employed to stay on top. She would sacrifice someone now and then, and the rest would fall in line.

The first time Émile Delacroix drove her, she was barely civil to him, though he was aware that she noticed his physical attributes. Throughout that week, Émile had adequate time to study Lara Adler Furst, without her being aware that she was under scrutiny.

Émile overhead many a conversation she'd had over her mobile from the backseat of his BMW. She spoke in German, of course. She spoke quite freely, having absolutely no idea that he understood every word she was saying. That's how he discovered that she was separated from Torsten Lucas Furst.

He also understood the sarcasm and venomous comments. This woman seemed to take great pleasure in ordering people around and manipulating them. She resorted to a variety of methods of intimidation. She liked having control. She was positively drunk on power. He'd seen this type before.

Émile did not approach her in the way he had approached other rich women. With them, it was relatively easy and straightforward. He would lay the trap and they always took the bait.

This one was different. She would require different stimuli. He would have to act quickly because he was scheduled to take her back to Merignac airport in just two days' time.

Émile knew that with what he was planning, if he misjudged, he would get in a lot of trouble. If he was right about Lara Adler Furst though … He had always been one to trust his instincts. They had never let him down before.

As a precaution, he wouldn't actually lay a hand on Mrs. Furst. He would find another way.

Now, to lock in the perfect accomplice.

When Émile was to return Lara to her hotel at the end of the day, less than eighteen hours before her flight out, he told her that he had a surprise for her, his way of showing appreciation for her business.

Lara told Émile curtly that it was not necessary and that he could proceed straight to her hotel. Émile insisted and assured Lara that she would not be delayed by more than an hour.

People were always trying to do nice things for her and it usually annoyed Lara Furst. What could a chauffeur possibly have in mind? Lara agreed with an annoyed sigh but she could not say whether it was out of curiosity or boredom.

Émile parked in front of a building with Beaux Art architectural details, like so many of the buildings in that part of Bordeaux. He held the car door open for her and extended his hand to help her out of the backseat.

Lara was beginning to have misgivings. This was not exactly a seedy part of town, but it was not what she was used to. To her it was like finding herself in a third world country. She wanted to get back into the limousine and be out of there.

"Please, Mrs. Furst, you won't regret it." Émile encouraged her to walk through the front door into the building. They had to walk up a flight of stairs. Was she in danger, she wondered. She quickly dismissed that concern. There were too many people that knew he had been driving her all week, including today, the hotel, the wine producers.

Émile let Lara into a spacious eclectically furnished apartment. It was mostly modern, done in masculine neutral tones with a few antiques thrown in for contrast. It looked like the work of a professional designer.

Émile excused himself for a minute. When he came back, he was not alone.

The look on Lara's face was not shock or revulsion. It was fascination. It was honest and primal. She was transfixed and she was licking her lips, but did not seem to be aware of it.

Lara never saw Émile smile because she was not looking at him now … Émile had been right about Lara Adler Furst, probably soon to be Lara Adler.

The young woman accompanying him was in her mid-twenties, about five four without heels, pretty, with high cheekbones and silky hair that was such a dark espresso brown, it was almost black. She had the faintest olive tone to her skin, pink glossed lips and though she was slender, gentle curves promised a womanly body under the simple cotton sundress. The pale turquoise material flared out from the waist and ended just above her knees. She wore strappy sandals with a kitten heel in the same hue and no jewelry. Instead, her accessories were a blindfold of heavy quilted black material and padded black leather restraints that immobilized her dainty wrists behind her back.

Émile stopped right in front of Lara Adler Furst and stood behind the young woman. His hands began to explore the front of her sundress, tracing and cupping her breasts. Lara's heart started pounding, her breathing deepened and her face became flushed.

Émile let his hands slide down the outside of the beauty's body, tracing their way to the hem of her dress. His fingers crept under her dress, bringing the material with them as they slowly moved up her thighs, exposing soft perfect skin, inch by inch. She stood very still, but she appeared to be trembling. He was rubbing her between her legs … exploring, teasing. He stretched it out long enough to create the desired response, Lara Adler Furst moaned with arousal.

When he knelt in front of his lovely captive and reached up under the fabric of her dress to slide her white lace panties down her thighs Lara was acutely aware of how wet she was between her own legs.

Émile ordered the young woman to step out of her panties while he held on to her so she would not lose her balance. He called her Inès. Inès did as she was told. Lara liked how authoritative Émile was with her.

He led Inès over to the divan across from where Lara was seated. Émile sat on it first and pulled her onto his lap. She sat prim and proper and bound, ladylike, legs closed, sitting up straight as if her mother had reprimanded her for slouching when she was a child.

Lara would not have been able to take her eyes off this scene if the building was on fire.

Émile unzipped the dress from the back, fingers lingering on the soft young skin. He undid the back of the white lace bra that matched the panties on the floor. He pushed dress straps and bra straps over her arms, further restricting her movement. Her breasts were now fully exposed and mere feet away from Lara's hungry gaze.

Émile cupped one breast and then the other. They fit perfectly into his palm. He squeezed one dark hued nipple and rolled it between thumb and fingers until slightly swollen and erect. Then he moved to the second nipple and did the same to it.

Émile pulled Inès's hair back forcing her into an arch. Her breasts protruded making them even more accessible to Émile. This time he used his lips and teeth along with his hand to grip them and suck on them—hard. Inès winced even as she began to breathe faster.

Émile had started to caress the top of her thighs under the material of her dress. Lara wished she could see where his fingers made contact with skin.

"Open your legs. I want to touch every part of you."

Inès defied him.

"If you do not obey, you will leave me no choice but to discipline you."

Inès remained resistant.

"Very well. You have brought this on yourself." With that, he pulled her over his knees effortlessly. She was facedown with her ass in the air and Émile was fully in control.

He took his time, letting both Lara and Inès squirm. Lara swallowed hard, wondering what he intended to do now. She had moved up to the edge of the divan in eager anticipation, wanting a better view.

Émile slid the bottom half of the dress all the way up exposing her splendid little round ass.

Émile played with his prey, squeezing the cheeks and eliciting a little whimper as he scolded her for her naughtiness. Then he raised his hand and brought it down on quivering flesh. Inès's back came up and Émile pushed her down and chastised her. One cheek of her ass was suitably red. The other one got the same treatment. Inès struggled again.

"You will not withhold yourself from me."

Inès did not listen. *Good,* thought Lara, *don't listen. Goad him with your insolence...* She did not want this to be over too quickly.

Émile responded by smacking and squeezing until both cheeks bore his handprints to Lara's carnal delight. She just about slid right off the divan when Émile switched to caressing each buttock now that he had shown Inès who was boss. She was delirious when Émile said, "I'll take what I want, when I want it," addressing the young woman as if Lara wasn't in the room.

Then Émile shoved his hand between her legs, spreading them enough for Lara to see that the young woman was smooth down there, and began caressing her pussy until Inès moaned with the onset of a powerful orgasm.

"There. Doesn't that feel good?"

Lara was experiencing the kind of sexual excitement she had not known since she had turned eighteen. It was then that she realized that several of her father's male friends and a couple of his business associates had begun to notice her when they came to the house.

She had fantasized about sitting in their laps. She had imagined these powerful men, captains of industry, undoing her blouse to fondle her breasts and pinch her nipples. She thought about them reaching up under her skirt and into her white cotton panties to probe her pussy with its silky blond fuzz. It wouldn't be like with the fumbling boys her age. They were men ... who knew what they wanted from her and how to take it. All her life, she had always been the untouchable, privileged princess. Lara longed for someone to put her in her place.

She had masturbated many times to a picture in her head of one of them giving her a good spanking because she had bent over in his presence while not wearing any underwear. Whenever she pleasured herself to this fantasy young Lara would come so hard she had to stifle her screams in a pillow.

If only these men weren't afraid that she would tell. If only they weren't afraid of her father. If only they would show her who was boss.

Lara's induldgent father had noticed the way she flirted with these men that were his own age and did not know what to say. He promptly shipped her off to an all-girl boarding school in Switzerland to finish out the year. There the virgin Lara had been taught by an all-female staff and was kept far away from the only two male employees, the groundskeeper and the janitor. Lara Adler was very frustrated and came to rely on her fantasies even more.

Today, now, those same feelings and desires rose up within her again and this time to fever pitch. She was totally consumed as she reached up under her own dress and inside the bikini panties to caress herself with demanding fingers. She had been imagining Émile's fingers stroking her pussy and her juices were flowing.

Lara Adler was likely ruining her dress by masturbating in front of a driver and his hostage and she didn't care at this particular moment in time. She moaned and then … the ubiquitous wetness as pleasure overtook her. Lara's orgasm shook her whole body and she was seeing stars.

Émile helped Inès to her feet, adjusted her bra and dress, picked up her panties and made his way to the hall with her. Just before closing the door that separated the living space from a hallway, Émile made a helpful suggestion to Lara.

"Perhaps you would care to freshen up. The washroom is just off the entrance."

Lara was a little wobbly on her legs, but had a strong desire to wash away the stickiness and process what just happened.

Meanwhile at the back door, Émile removed the young woman's blindfold. She smiled and with one quick maneuver of her wrists, she popped the restraints right off … trick restraints.

The trick restaints weren't part of Isabel Vega's usual arsenal. They were a prop that Émile had provided, knowing full well that she would never consent to real restraints. She wasn't a submissive. Her clients were.

Isabel Vega was a professional dominatrix. That meant that she didn't live the lifestyle. Rather, she was very well compensated for her highly specialized knowledge of particular equipment and insight into her clients' psychological needs, be it bondage, performing humiliating tasks, servitude or discipline. What she didn't do was have sex with them.

By specializing, Isabel could command higher fees. There was no shortage of clients for her services. It would astound people if they knew how many men of means and position came seeking to be dominated.

Isabel's clients never knew what she really looked like. She dressed the part and she wore wigs and costumes and applied makeup to play up her dominant sexualized persona. Isabel had discovered a retired theater costume maker from London who supplemented his meager pension by making custom pieces for the BDSM community … a cottage industry, he told Isabel jokingly, because he actually worked out of his cottage in the suburbs.

The gentleman enjoyed working with Isabel because she had a lot of original ideas and could pull off his more elaborate creations. Isabel liked working with him because she got to input and he interpreted her ideas very well.

She now had a trunk full of pieces, including corsets that would breathe, not cause any chaffing and were easy to clean. She looked like a modern version of a medieval warrior princess. At five foot four, she was no Amazon, so the illusion of height came from gladiator type footwear with five-inch heels.

Isabel even changed her perfume for the role. She wore a heavier spicier scent that hung in the air like sex. It was custom made for her and cost a small fortune. The perfume maker kept the formula in a library of scents. It was actually a vault. Isabel took great pains to enhance the experience for her clients. On her days off, she wore a fresh, clean citrusy store-bought scent that was to her taste.

Clients who made an appointment for a session, asked for Sabine, a cat-like woman with claws—metaphorically and figuratively speaking. During their sessions, they addressed her as Mistress, if and only if, she gave them permission to speak.

In everyday life, Isabel looked like any other young woman her age. She was prettier than most, but did not attract a lot of male attention unless a man would take the time to really look at her features … eyes that were almost onyx black, the glowing Mediterranean complexion, healthy thick hair that was nearly black and full naturally pink lips.

Though Isabel liked to dress up in sexy feminine clothing when she was going out for drinks or dinner, during the day, she would most likely be running around in a loose fitting white cotton T-shirt, boyfriend jeans turned up at the ankles and sneakers. Thus her body, made for worship, was not something that a man would notice right away. Émile, however, thought she looked sexy in anything.

Isabel never wore any jewelry when she was working. She was not one for jewelry. It would get in the way when she was working and it might identify her if she kept it on when she went out in public.

During personal time, Isabel wore a vintage 14K gold pear shaped Longines watch when she needed to keep an appointment. She had inherited it from her birth mother. At one time in her life she had been struggling financially and was about to sell the only object that connected her to the woman who brought her into the world. If not for a man named Xander who changed the course of her life at that most opportune moment, she would have had no other option.

When her birth mother had signed the adoption papers, she had asked if the couple who would adopt her baby, could give her the watch on her eighteenth birthday, so that she would have something of hers.

The couple that raised Isabel were kind, loving, decent people. They had never kept the fact that she was adopted from her, but made sure that she understood that they were very grateful to have had the privilege of raising her as their own. She was the greatest blessing in their lives. So, when she turned eighteen, they presented her with a gift from the woman who given birth to their daughter.

They did not know who she was, but she must have loved her baby very much. Whatever circumstances led her to give up her beautiful child, they never knew.

The one piece of jewelry that Isabel wore regularly when she wasn't working was an 18K gold initial pendant with cable link chain. The initial was a stylized letter X. It had been a graduation present from the only man she had ever given herself to completely, the only man who knew her better than she knew herself, the only man she had ever loved.

Isabel could have bumped into any one of her clients from The Club in a café and they would never have a clue that this was the woman who disciplined them. Only the staff knew and they kept each other's secrets. It was a code they lived by in that world of theirs.

What the staff didn't know was that Isabel had studied to become a schoolteacher in her native Spain before she found her true calling. She never once regretted the re-orientation.

Pierre Joubert had received a lot of requests for her particular talents and it had been financially rewarding for both parties. He liked that she was professional and very discreet. He had never pried into her personal life.

When Isabel was not working for Pierre, she taught self-defense courses to women at a local community center … something else that no one knew anything about, except for her neighbor Émile Delacroix because they worked out together sometimes.

Isabel had been working for Pierre for three years now. Originally, she'd had a five-year plan, but attained her financial goals two years ahead of schedule.

Émile Delacroix, the chauffeur with an advanced degree in economics, had given her some very good investment advice. With enough put away to live on comfortably for several years, Isabel had some choices to make. She could stick to her timeline and continue working for Pierre, this path guaranteed she would come out ahead financially. Or, she could go back to school and start a new life that much sooner.

Ultimately, Isabel thought she might want to earn a degree in sexology, open her own practice and lead a quiet life. Some additional courses in accounting, tax law, small business management, marketing and investment building wouldn't hurt.

She had looked into the schools that offered the required curriculum. That path would take her away from Bordeaux.

Émile had been trying to talk her into enrolling in a program in Bordeaux to acquire the technical and business knowledge to eventually work her way up to director of sales for a large société de négoce, or director of export for one of the important châteaux.

Both would involve traveling to visit clients all over the world, representing producers at shows and attending promotional events. She already had a good working knowledge of several languages, and the ability to handle herself around the wealthy and powerful. She would just have to learn the wine terminology in those languages.

Émile reminded her of her passion for fine wine and how she had told him about the enjoyment she got out of traveling. As a sexologist, travel would be limited to a professional conference now and then, and vacations, he pointed out.

Another good argument was that when it was time to do an apprenticeship, or *stage* as the French called it, she could do it at the wine producing château that Pierre owned. Everything was aboveground and totally legit. The people that tended the vines and worked in the cellar during the day, had no knowledge of what went on at night. Their offices were not in the château, but in a separate building with tasting rooms.

The employees had heard that the owner put on elaborate evenings for important people. They assumed that he was courting clients at the top level.

Pierre would have her gladly, and she would not have to explain what she had done in previous years. She could stay on for a while and gain some work experience for her C.V.

Isabel had to agree that it did sound good. It made sense to at least investigate this option, even if she had the feeling that Émile was trying to keep her in Bordeaux. They had a good thing ... for now.

When she was well set up in her new life, should the right guy come along— an accountant, lawyer, doctor, pharmacist or dentist, someone reliable, kind and affectionate—she might even consider settling down and starting a family.

Isabel was thinking that it would be nice to adopt. There were so many children that needed a family.

Her adoptive parents were not young when they had welcomed her into their lives as a baby, and had long since passed. She knew nothing about her biological parents beyond the watch and had no interest in trying to find them. She had always considered her adoptive parents to be her real parents.

If she married, it would be to have a more traditional life. Traditional to Isabel would be exotic, as she had yet to experience it.

The girls at work teased with, "If you should ever get married, you'll know exactly how to *whip* your husband into shape." But that was confusing Isabel's profession with her preferences. Once out of the business, she would retire the tools of the trade.

Isabel had no illusions about Émile. He was not the type that she would be involved with on any meaningful level, nor would he want that. She sensed that he had a plan of his own that he was following, one that he was not prepared to share with anyone.

Isabel's instincts told her that Émile genuinely cared about her, and that she was probably one of very few people he had ever felt that way about. They would go out for dinner at least once a week, pick up groceries for each other, cook together or stay in to watch a film together.

Émile introduced Isabel to some of his favorite French wines and Isabel introduced Émile to some of her favorite Spanish wines.

Émile added some techniques to Isabel's self-defense workouts, specialized moves beyond what she was already very adept at. Neither one asked the other how they came to have that kind of training in the first place.

Neither did they talk about why Isabel wore a pendant with the initial X around her neck.

Their easy relationship had eventually extended to sex. They had become friends with benefits. The arrangement suited both of them for the time being. They trusted each other for one thing, and they both needed sex with partners that were on par, as much as they needed the nourishment of food.

Isabel rubbed her wrists and stretched the muscles in her arms, shoulders and back. Émile handed her the envelope she was waiting for with the agreed upon amount, along with her panties.

"Who's your alpha female submissive?"

"What makes you think she's an alpha?"

"I know my business, Émile."

"I can't tell you. You know better than to ask. Suffice it to say that you have had the pleasure of dominating her first husband."

How come chauffeurs know everything? Isabel knew there was no point in asking any more questions.

"Émile, I'm not working tonight. If you do not have any plans later, send me a text and I'll come down. I would like a proper fucking this evening. I was really getting into it by the end."

"And you shall have it, Isa dear."

"I have a couple of bottles of Clos Martinet 2009 from Mas Martinet. I am looking forward to finding out what you think about my favorite Priorat wine."

"Mas Martinet sounds familiar."

"Remember the Cami Pesseroles 2008 and Els Escurçons Grenache 2008 we had?"

"Exceptional wines … world class."

"Same producer. The Clos Martinet 2009 is a blend of hot climate grapes … Carignan, Grenache and Syrah with a smaller percentage of Cabernet Sauvignon."

"Food wine."

"Definitely. Pick up some things for tapas, will you? We might as well make an evening of it; you know, eat, drink and fuck."

"Not necessarily in that order, Isa. I'm horny as hell from our little performance, even if it was for the benefit of the alpha female submissive."

Isabel's flat was at the back of the building. No street noise. It was conducive to falling asleep and staying asleep, she had told him many times. She would not be able to see who would be getting into the back of Émile's car in the next few minutes. It was best for everyone.

While Isabel Vega was relaxing in her tub and enjoying the soothing effects of lavender scented bubbles on her skin, Lara Adler was in a state of utter panic. Inside the pristine washroom, Lara stared at the woman in the mirror. She didn't recognize herself … all flushed, disheveled, with beads of perspiration on her lipstick-smeared upper lip. *What the hell just happened?* She wondered if she should say something to her driver. Or should she pull herself together and say nothing?

After making use of the bidet, repairing her makeup and pulling a comb through her hair, the outwardly composed Lara Furst walked out of the bathroom, anxious to be on her way. The outer Lara didn't work with the inner Lara, but it was the best she could do.

The driver was already waiting for her. Without a word, he held the front door open. She walked through it, equally silent and making no eye contact.

Lara felt like the twenty-minute drive to her hotel lasted for days. When finally the car pulled up and her driver opened the door, he spoke to her for the first time since offering her the use of his bathroom. "Until tomorrow, Mrs. Furst."

Lara panicked. "No. Never mind about tomorrow. I have made other arrangements." She knew she didn't sound very convincing, but she went on. There was no other way to handle this—whatever this was. "I would like to settle up with you right now ... for your services ... umm, for driving me today and for the time that you would have been working tomorrow. Oh, and here is something extra for you. I don't need an invoice. I can't wait."

She didn't wait, not for the invoice and not for Émile to help her out of the car. She flung some bills at Émile and pushed past him as the doorman rushed forward to intercept her.

Émile looked down at his tip. Five hundred euros, in addition to her overpaying his fee. But was the money to keep his mouth shut or to thank him for tapping into the real Lara Furst and showing her her own truth, without even fucking her? Émile decided it didn't matter. "Hard to put the genie back in the bottle ..."

What Émile was banking on, literally, was that once Lara got over the shock, she would be back ... and asking for more. He would give her more, but only in increments. Lara Adler Furst needed to be trained.

Entering the hotel lobby, Lara felt more naked than if she had walked in without a stitch of clothing. Should she feel shame? Should she be frightened that the driver knew this thing about her? Or should there be a sense of freedom, that a man should finally guess her secret desire?

Lara had married her much older first husband, Rainer Walther, for all the trappings of wealth first and foremost, but she had hoped that as an influential man in the world of business, he would have it in him to put her in her place, to dominate her sexually with masculine strength. How she had longed for that.

Lara had challenged him at every turn, hoping to provoke him. She had ridiculed him, hoping to rouse him to corrective action. What she did not see coming was that he liked it. Instead of pinning her to the wall and fucking her into submission, he wanted *her* to punish *him* for making her angry.

Rainer even suggested she walk on his back and bare buttocks in her black leather boots, the ones with the spike heels. If they punctured the skin and drew blood, well that was what he deserved, he told her. She mustn't hold back, he added with feverish excitement.

Lara was revolted. She told Rainer that she was divorcing him and threatened to expose his perversion if he did not give her the divorce right away. She also told him what she wanted in the way of a settlement and that he had better agree regardless of what his legal counsel advised … or else.

Rainer agreed not only to avoid the scandal that could ruin his name, but also because it felt good. She was being so forceful.

Lara chose her second husband, Torsten Lucas Furst, with greater care. He would elevate her position because of who he was. He could lavish her with pretty much everything she could possibly imagine. He was all male. He had a strong sexual presence. He had a dominant personality; she was certain he was an alpha male. Torsten would be the one to give her what she wanted … what she needed.

What a disappointment the marriage turned out to be. The more dejected she became, the more understanding he tried to be. The more demanding and belligerent she became, the more patient he tried to be. The more distant she became, the more supportive he tried to be. The more loving he tried to be, the more she grew to hate him.

If only he had understood that she wanted him to tear off her clothes, bend her over the dining room table and use her roughly … if only. She had thought that he would be the one and been bitterly disappointed.

CHAPTER 17

One day it just hit Torsten. He had lost Ela because of his marriage to Lara, a woman who preferred to maintain a completely separate existence.

Divorce had seemed inconceivable when Torsten had been trying to protect her from being ostericized by the snooty circles she ran in. Even now when Torsten wanted a divorce from Lara more than anything, he didn't want her downfall. He would work it out with her, so that wouldn't happen. The divorce would be the first step in reversing a terrible mistake.

On the day that Torsten decided, he went to see his personal lawyer to go over the pre-nuptial agreement that he and his wife signed six years earlier. It had been Lara father's idea; in fact, he'd insisted. He'd been very ill at the time and she was his sole beneficiary. Lara also had a substantial settlement from Rainer Walther, her previous husband, which was a bit strange. They were married only a short time yet the man had parted with a substantial portion of his wealth without a fight.

Though their pre-nuptial agreement specified the division of Torsten's money and assets if she asked him for a divorce, it allowed Lara to negotiate if he was the one who wanted the divorce. She had invested her money with the help of some very savvy financial advisors and was an incredibly wealthy woman in her own right. She would be able to live out her life in the style she was accustomed to and with millions to spare even if she never received a euro from Torsten, but Torsten knew she was demanding. Lara always pushed for more, never happy with what she had.

Torsten decided that he would concede some additional property and assets to get out of the marriage quickly. It would be an incentive for her not to drag things out. He briefly wondered if that was what had motivated her first husband to offer such a generous settlement.

There would be a certain amount of social stigma for her after her second divorce in a decade. If she made out well in the settlement, it would win her some admiration in her social circle. If her socialite friends felt that Torsten had paid for his disloyalty in terms that were near and dear to their own hearts, namely money and assets, she could still hold her head high.

Walking out of the lawyer's office, Torsten called his soon-to-be-ex-wife to find out when he could see her. He wanted this done as soon as possible but she did not answer her phone.

Torsten planned to announce his decision in person, hopefully in the next day or two, and then he would start the proceedings to file for divorce. Unless she preferred to file for appearance's sake. He would give her a few days to rearrange her schedule so she could meet with her lawyer and then they could fix a date for a meeting with the two lawyers and begin the formal proceedings.

He had tried calling late in the afternoon and early that evening. Though her mobile phone had not immediately gone to voice mail, Lara had not answered and she had not called him back. He knew she'd recently hired an assistant but he didn't have the man's contact information and no one answered at the house, which was odd.

Now that he had made up his mind, Torsten was anxious to speak to Lara. There was no point in delaying this any longer. He wanted to get on with his life. His life with Ela. Torsten felt tremendous relief and knew that it was the right decision.

At half past eight Torsten could stand it no longer. He called his longtime driver Tavin Vogt and told him to bring the car around. He announced they were adding a stop before his ten o'clock dinner reservation. The normal protocol was for Tavin to then alert his security team, so whoever was on duty would accompany them. Tavin did so, explaining the change in itinerary.

They would be picking up Mr. Koertig at his home at a quarter to nine and then they would be stopping by the other Furst residence at a quarter past nine, staying for about fifteen minutes before taking Torsten to a late dinner at his favorite Italian cantina, a small rustic looking place with no signage.

Torsten climbed into the car, looking forward to getting this business with Lara out of the way and then celebrating at one of his favorite restaurants. The chef prepared delicious regional Italian dishes. The wine cellar was one of the best in the country.

The owner stocked superior Barolo and Brunello, but lately he had been amusing himself with world class wines from indigenous grapes like Nero d'Avola from Sicily. His favorite Sicilian producer was Gulfi. The wines were superb. Such wines he served blind. If clients liked the wine and could identify the region and grape varietal or blend, he would offer them a bottle without charge that evening.

Torsten normally enjoyed matching wits with Jonas at the wine game, but first he needed to clear the air with Lara. Now that a decision had been made he was eager to act. Once again Torsten pulled out his mobile phone and once again, there was no answer.

When Torsten's driver opened the door for Jonas, Jonas saw an expression of concern mixed with irritation on Torsten's face. Torsten explained that he had been trying to make an appointment with Lara to discuss an important matter. Torsten admitted that he was worried because Lara was not answering her mobile phone nor calling him back after he had left her half a dozen messages. That was not like her.

Torsten told his friend that he would like to drive by the house on their way to the restaurant, and Jonas readily agreed. If she was home, then he would take the opportunity to confirm a day and time for their appointment on the spot, and put the matter to rest.

Tavin waited for Torsten to enter the code, then drove through the massive, state-of-the-art security gates with their garish iron scrollwork featuring an elaborate letter *F*. He stopped in front of the palatial five-story mansion, parking in one of the ten spots surrounding the pink marble fountain out front, rather than pulling into the underground garage.

As always, Torsten shuddered when he took in the façade of this gilded monstrosity that Lara had insisted he buy for them before they were married. He chided himself for not recognizing the signs they were incompatible sooner.

Glancing around, Torsten saw the stately British luxury car that Lara was chauffeured around in in its usual parking spot. The car had been a gift from him that she had picked out for herself just before they separated. Next to it was a German-made silver all-wheel drive convertible sports car that he did not remember ever seeing before. The latter was parked haphazardly at an awkward angle, the driver's side door still open.

Torsten let himself out of his German luxury sedan, asking his driver and security person to wait there, though neither one liked the idea.

Something felt off to Torsten as well, but he did not want to be an alarmist, so he walked up to the massive front door alone. He rang the door chimes but no one answered. He punched his code into the keypad. The lights were on but there was no staff. Looking back at Jonas with an expression that suggested something was definitely not right, Torsten let himself into the house, leaving the front door ajar.

Jonas quietly left the car and stealthily followed after Torsten, just in case his friend would need him.

As Torsten made his way to the back of the house on the first floor, he heard muffled voices coming from the indoor pool and spa area that opened up on to the terrace. The disembodied voices sounded raised and agitated, causing him to quicken his pace. When Torsten heard the unmistakable sound of flesh smacking flesh followed by a woman's loud cry, he broke into a run.

"Fuck me now in the ass … please … I can't stand it any longer. I've been so very bad!" Lara, naked and wet, was desperate to get what she knew was coming to her. On all fours on a thick mat at the edge of the spa, she presented her ass to the young man on his knees between her legs. Naked and wet himself, he grabbed her hips and entered her roughly. Lara moaned in satisfaction, lost in the throes of passion. He then grabbed a fistful of her damp hair with one hand and brutishly pulled her head back while keeping her hip in place with the other and ramming his large cock deeper.

"So you need to be taught a lesson, is that it?"

"Yes, yes, like that. Don't stop," Lara whimpered, pushing back into him.

Her assistant rammed his cock into her ass again, harder this time. "You don't tell me how to fuck you. I do to you what I want, when I want. You will not come until I give you permission."

Torsten stopped so quickly he almost tripped. It had suddenly dawned on him that this was a scene of consensual pleasure and not something more sinister. His concern for his wife vanished and he almost laughed out loud.

Torsten cleared his throat loudly and announced, "Well, this is quite a sight."

Lara removed her assistant's cock from her ass, got to her feet and turned around with as much dignity as she could muster. Without something to cover herself with, she was at a disadvantage in this situation but Lara was never one to cower. So she did what she always did and went on the offensive. "How dare you barge into my house," she thundered, lips still swollen with desire.

"You really should answer your mobile or at least check your messages. By the way, my dear, this is *my* house."

"What do you want?"

"I've been calling you for hours to set up an appointment; we have an important matter to discuss."

"My personal assistant, Amand, will get back to you." Lara looked in the direction of her lover who was now sprawled on a chaise longue, idly stroking his still-erect cock.

"No need. My lawyer will contact your lawyer tomorrow. I am filing for divorce. I have had enough of this sham of a marriage, as it seems, have you. When we first separated, I thought if I gave you some space, you would miss me and we would start over. Months turned into years and it became obvious to me that you never had any intention of reconciling. Though I really should have done this a long time ago, perhaps it was meant to happen now, like this. So glad you did not answer your phone or return your calls. What a perfect opportunity for your concerned husband to have come by to make sure you that you were alright—only to find you otherwise occupied. So nice to see that you have found companionship, by the way. Congratulations. I wish you both every happiness."

"I will not give you a divorce that easily, Torsten." Lara, although not actually opposed to a divorce, was fervently against being told what to do.

"Oh, I think you will for obvious reasons. I will give you a generous settlement just the same … to make it look good for your friends. I will even allow you to keep this monstrosity you like living in and all of the art and belongings in it. You can have the vacation home in the South of France as well. I don't have particularly good memories of our time there."

"I want the yacht." Instinctively Lara demanded the thing she knew he treasured most.

"No. Not the yacht."

"My lawyer will make you see things differently."

"Your lawyer will want to keep the taint of scandal away from you—as well he should."

"It's your word against mine."

"And mine, actually, Lara dear. Plus what my phone saw." Jonas stepped from the shadows, filming on his smartphone.

Sensing defeat, Lara changed tactics. "How dare you! Torsten, I have had it with your manipulative and intrusive ways. How dare you have your friend secretly film me in my own home? I want a divorce. As soon as possible. Get out of my home immediately; my lawyer will contact yours in the morning to work out the details."

Torsten felt as light as air, soon he would be free. He turned to leave and Jonas fell in step beside him. Then Jonas turned back, offering a parting shot to the indignant and still nude Lara. "As you were."

Back in the car Torsten didn't bother to conceal his relief. "Tavin, please take us to Sergio's; I feel like celebrating."

"Congratulations, old friend. That went particularly well." Jonas's smile was blinding. "I won't show the video around obviously, but I will enjoy watching it from time to time. I did not know she had it in her. She came across like the original ice princess."

"Frigid bitch is what you meant to say. You never did like her, did you, Jonas?"

"I have to tell the truth, my friend. I couldn't stand to be in the same room with her. She was never any fun and she has this mean streak. Now I know I should have taken Lara aside and given her a good spanking." Both men exchanged amused glances.

DIANA SOBOLEWSKI

CHAPTER 18

Without Ela, there had been no joy in Torsten's life and he knew that he would never be complete without her. His divorce in motion, Torsten turned his attention to winning back his true love. He enlisted the help of château owner and mutual friend Laurence Bonnet in an elaborate ruse to lure Ela to her château at the end of *en primeur* week.

Laurence got in touch with Ela right away. She explained that she would be hosting an evening at her château for the négociants, brokers, importers and distributors she worked with and she really wanted Ela to come.

Ela had planned to be in Bordeaux to taste the *futures,* anyway, so she accepted the invitation gladly. Laurence then convinced Ela to stay overnight in one of the château's guest suites afterwards.

"I could get you limousine service back to your hotel, but I'd have to reserve a car and driver for a specific time. If you stay at the château, you could cut out early if you're tired or if you're having a good time; you don't have leave because the car is waiting."

Laurence had a point, so Ela said that she would, and thanked one of her favorite producers for her thoughtfulness.

Ela had been told that a cocktail dress would be appropriate, so she pulled out a black Hervé Léger bandage dress with plunging neckline embellished with jet beading … the kind of dress that only a woman with tremendous confidence could pull off. That's not how Ela saw it, though. When she put on a Hervé Léger dress, the self-confidence just kicked in.

Ela had filled her black satin evening clutch with the usual … cash, lipstick, tissue, reading glasses, and a key card to her hotel room. Her only jewelry was the diamond earrings she wore with everything. The dress called for a pair of black pointed patent leather pumps from the Saint-Laurent Paris collection; a black silk and cashmere pashmina would do, as long as she didn't spend any significant time out doors at this time of the year.

The overnight bag was her carry-on. She packed it with the essentials and a change of clothes for the following day.

When Laurence's car pulled up to the Chateau in Saint-Émilion, Ela did not see any other cars in the gravel parking area. She assumed that she must be the first to arrive or perhaps everyone was being driven, but surely she would find Laurence inside supervising final preparations for her guests. The driver opened her door, let her out and promptly got back in and drove off before she could tip him.

The large heavy wood and wrought iron doors of the château were open. Ela entered the foyer, and heard soft music playing but could not identify the source.

A crystal Baccarat Eurydice vase on a small round antique table with inlay just outside the sitting room drew her attention. She was unable to place the period of this particular piece of furniture, but thought it pretty and kind of feminine, like Laurence. The tight bouquet of white roses, her favorite, made her smile. How perfect … that such gorgeous flowers be matched to such a stunning vase.

Laurence must be in the kitchen, Ela thought, but decided she would wait in the sitting room rather than disrupt what was going on back there.

Antique silver candlesticks on the mantel of the fireplace reflected their flame in the antique mirror and provided a warm inviting ambiance just like the fire that someone had considerately lit in the fireplace that was original to the château. The sun would be going down in a little while and she was grateful for the warmth. It was a chilly evening, but then it was April.

Someone had laid out a tray of hors d'œuvres, napkins cutlery, bottled water and water glasses on another antique table that matched the first one, only bigger. Next to the tray of bite size delicacies, Ela spied a Cristofle Malmaison silver plate ice bucket containing half ice and half water, recently filled obviously, but already cold enough for an excellent bottle of Champagne. And excellent it was. Lifting the bottle out of its ice bath, the label confirmed it.

Costing almost three thousand dollars a bottle, this cuvée in this vintage was known for its fine mousse, rapier sharp acidity requiring cellaring, and layers of nutty flavors as well as strawberry and citrus notes and long finish. She noticed that there were only two crystal Baccarat Clair De Lune Champagne flutes right next to the ice bucket.

At that moment, Torsten walked in, dressed in a perfectly tailored tuxedo, immaculate white evening shirt and black bow tie in a thick black brushed silk satin that matched the lapels of the jacket and evening shoes. He was wearing platinum cufflinks she had never seen before, and the limited edition watch he had worn every time they had been together.

His limp was evident this evening, Ela noticed. It was because he was not concentrating on his walk, though she did know that. His whole focus was on Ela as he tried to read her expression.

Torsten was smiling, but behind that smile there was some anxiety about how she would react next. He was having a great deal of trouble reading her all of a sudden.

Had she lost faith? Had he moved too slow … taken too much time to come to his senses? Had she met someone else? Had he lost her forever?

He had even resorted to looking her up on the internet. He had looked for any sign of another man in her life. At first, he could not find anything, then one day she popped up in connection with a prestigious winemaker dinner. Ela had been photographed with a glass of Champagne in her hand at the cocktail preceding the dinner.

Two men were on her right and one on her left. It was the man on her left that had irked him. His right hand rested on the small of her back in a somewhat familiar and possessive manner. It was indisputable. While all eyes were looking into the camera, he was looking at her. He was claiming her as his prize … warning all others who may have had designs on her to keep their distance.

Torsten had been able to tell from Ela's body language that she was totally relaxed. She even seemed happy. It had been obvious to him that the man with his hand on her was no casual acquaintance.

Ela had looked amazing in that photograph and even more so this evening. She was poised, sexy and so desirable. He just wanted to kiss that mouth.

He also remembered the look of disappointment and hurt in her eyes when he had told her that he wanted her to move to Munich where they would see each other in secret. She had been crushed. He had put an abrupt end to her hopes and dreams for them. In the process, he had sabotaged his own happiness.

Torsten realized that if ever he were to have a chance with Ela, he would have to repair all of the damage he had done. Her feelings had been genuine and they had run deep. She had not wanted his money. She had not wanted him to give up any part of himself … she had wanted him to claim her for his own and to do this openly without subterfuge. He had not fought for her when he should have. He had thought more of Lara's feelings and his selfish desire than of her proud, independent nature. He understood all of that now.

Ela had not moved since first seeing Torsten come into the room. Outwardly she appeared composed, but in reality she was having trouble breathing. He was magnificent. She was still attracted to him physically. He had that strong male presence and it was creating an ache in her body, but it was what she was feeling emotionally that had her overwhelmed with need for him. Ela was still in love with Torsten. It had been bearable when he was out of sight, out of mind. With him just steps away, it was agony.

Ela was sure that he did love her, in his own way. She had only to look to the effort he had made to be alone with her here. Unfortunately, it was not enough.

He didn't love her the way she needed to be loved.

Now here they were together in the same room.

"I hope you're not too upset with Laurence; I put her on the spot."

"As you once told me, she's a friend. I'm sure she thought she was doing the right thing."

"I've missed you … so much. I haven't been able to stop thinking about you."

Ela was hoping that the next thing he would tell her is that he wanted to work on a different kind of a relationship than he had proposed. She was willing to give him the time to get out of his marriage, but she needed to know it was happening.

"Ela, I apologize for tricking you like this. But I had to see you; I had to be near you. I've been missing you terribly. I just want to explain some things …"

"Excuse me. I have to go to the washroom."

Torsten nodded; he knew his ambush had been unfair.

"I'll pour us some Champagne and we can talk when you get back."

Ela took more time than Torsten had expected, but when she returned, she looked more at ease. She accepted the glass of Champagne from Torsten, and commented on how he had gone all out.

Torsten saw it as a good sign, and offered a toast, "To new beginnings."

Ela acknowledged his words with a nod and took a sip, saying nothing herself.

"Ela, about the job offer in Vienna with the Koch group …"

"Don't you think we should talk about how we left it between us?"

"Alright."

"I was shaken to my very core that you didn't want a real relationship after how well things went in Rome."

"That was a misjudgment on my part. In my world, those kinds of arrangements are entered into all of the time. You compartmentalize."

"And the way you left me sitting there in that restaurant. It was unbelievably hurtful and I was so humiliated."

"I was angry."

"*I* was angry."

"When you texted me after that, you really believed that you had come up with the solution. You were just bringing the same relationship to my door, instead of your door. The problem was with the nature of the relationship."

"And then Koch. That was so underhanded, Torsten."

"I wanted you close by. I thought that if you were already living in Europe, I could find a way to show you that we could have a life together."

"You mean in the arrangement you had planned out?"

"Yes."

"That's what I thought."

"I've been used to getting my way in most things, most of my adult life. I had come to believe that if you can't achieve something, but you want it badly enough, you come at it from a different angle, and you chip away."

"Not everyone thinks that way, Torsten," Ela pointed out. Why was he not saying something different that would move her? This was the same spiel, different venue. "Some men are decent and without subterfuge."

"Ela, is there someone special in your life?"

"As a matter of fact there is. His name is David Vaughn. Uncomplicated is nice sometimes, Torsten. Having someone care about you that does not have a hidden agenda, doesn't try to possess you and is considerate of your feelings, is nice."

Mad that this was more of the old Torsten, she added, "David has been nothing but kind to me. He's been there when I was down ... because of you."

"So, you've been seeing this David Vaughn for a while then ... romantically?" Torsten's tone of voice had changed reminding Ela of the scene in the restaurant in Montreal.

"If you're going to ask me if we've been to bed next? Don't. It seems that I have to go to the washroom again."

Torsten had wanted to know if David was a friend or more than that for a reason. It had come out wrong. Part of him didn't want to stand in the way of Ela's happiness if she was truly in love with David, after he had caused her such heartache. This David was coming off as a pretty decent man, who seemed to have her best interests at heart. What right did he have to upset Ela all over again?

On the other hand, even if he risked rejection, didn't he owe it to her to let her know that she had gotten through to him? He would be direct. When Ela returned, he would tell her that his divorce had been finalized and that he was deeply in love with her. He would then ask her to be his wife, and promise never to try to control her again.

Torsten pulled the ring out of his jacket pocket. It sparkled with possibility.

Ela had gone into the bathroom to make a decision.

It seemed that her being at the château was just another attempt on Torsten's part to negotiate a relationship between them. Never once had he said he loved her, that he was ready to give her what she needed. That he understood what she'd told him. And that he had been wrong. He did seem to regret his actions in some way though, before she had brought David up. That was something positive. But was it enough?

The first time Ela had excused herself, she had made a call to a car service on her cell phone. She had given her address and asked the driver to park outside the gate at the end of the driveway. She had been assured a driver would arrive in less than twenty minutes.

Ela contemplated what she would do. She could go back to Torsten and tell him about the driver. They could walk down the driveway together, pay the driver his fare and return to the château to try to talk things out. Or, she could place the note on the console table outside of the washroom for Torsten to find when he came looking for her. She'd already be on her way to Bordeaux by then; having snuck out the back door.

He would read: *This is what it feels like to be walked out on.*

Ela looked at the time on her cell phone. Now was the moment of truth.

She sighed and went into Laurence's office looking for writing paper and a pen.

Torsten took a sip of Champagne and looked at his watch. This time Ela was taking more time than before. He decided to go looking for her, remembering where the downstairs washroom was located.

Torsten was about to knock on the door and ask if she was alright, when he saw the note on the console table against the wall. Taken aback by what he read, the billionaire slumped into the upholstered armless chair against the opposite wall, deflated, hopes dashed and feeling a new level of emotional pain.

CHAPTER 19

What did Jonas want to talk him into now? Torsten knew that when Jonas adopted a certain tone in his voice he was scheming something. Though they were having the conversation over their mobile phones and Torsten could not see Jonas, Torsten knew exactly the facial expression that went along with that tone in his voice.

"You know that my birthday is next month."

"How could I ever forget? You would never let me."

"Right you are, Torsten. So, I was thinking … how about throwing me a party on the *Second Chance?* By the way, have I mentioned how much more I like the yacht's name now that you've rechristened her and how happy I am that you decided to take her out of moth balls?"

"I made a few changes to the interior design as well."

"Good. Your ex-wife had ghastly taste … all of that giltwork … on a yacht … frightful. The crew must have been nauseated all of the time. You probably acted just in time, to prevent blindness. Where is the yacht now?"

"Anchored off Greece. What arrangements shall I make?"

"No need. Just advise the captain that I will be flying out there to set everything up for a one week cruise around the islands."

"Do I want to know who's on the guest list?"

"Leave it to me. I promise you won't be bored or arrested. All I need for you to do is pay the bills. And do not even think of telling your sommelier to order reasonably priced wines or limit the number of bottles of Champagne. My people have a list and instructions. I'm going to have everything flown in, all kinds of delicacies, wines, Champagnes, flowers." Jonas was positively giddy.

Torsten knew that there would be no point in trying to talk Jonas out of something when he got like this. He was hell-bent. Torsten wished he could just work like everyone else. That would leave less time for him to plot these adventures of his.

Torsten would need to free up his schedule. He did have a complete office on board just off his master stateroom and could theoretically work there but birthday celebrations in progress would likely make that difficult."

If truth be told, Torsten was looking forward to being on board again and was grateful Jonas had given him a push to get away from work. It would be the inaugural voyage of the *Second Chance*. This was the one place where he felt happy and somewhat carefree and it was now purged of all traces of his ex-wife. Though he kept in touch with his office while out at sea, most of the things he was usually preoccupied with miraculously melted away about the time the shoreline was no longer visible.

His mind uncluttered, the warmth of the sun on his skin, surrounded by water, islands in different shapes and sizes out in the distance, Torsten was truly able to relax. He had always been able to relax on his yacht—except for those times when Lara had been with him. She had terrorized the crew and second-guessed the captain; mealtimes were spent waiting for her to blow up over some imagined inadequacy.

Even when Lara was out of his life permanently, he had had to contend with the ugly interior design that so reminded him of her. As soon as the uncontested divorce was finalized and he had made room in his schedule, Torsten met with the designers. An auction house sold off the artwork and furnishings and he donated the proceeds to charity. At least something good had come out of it.

Torsten kept the same crew employed full-time, whether the yacht was docked or in use. They were free to go home and see their families when they were not needed. He had a trusted crew and they had steady employment. It was an ideal arrangement and his crew was intensely loyal to the man who treated them well, paid them handsomely and asked only for a signed confidentiality agreement in return.

The yacht was usually docked in the South of France and never rented out with the exception of the Cannes Film Festival, if he was not using it. Torsten did that mainly to please the crew, who enjoyed having celebrities on board for a week or two. It kept them in anecdotes the rest of the year.

CHAPTER 20

Jonas Koertig watched the doors of the elevator close behind the petite redhead with the vintage Claddagh ring and the big attitude. He couldn't believe he had just asked her to dinner. He couldn't believe she had refused his invitation.

If he wasn't already late, he might have followed her into the crowd that had swallowed her. But that would have been a mistake. She'd made herself clear. Besides, he didn't stalk women. They stalked him.

She wore the Claddagh ring on her right hand facing outwards. That indicated that she was unattached and receptive. Jonas grimaced, no wonder she was still single, with *that* temper.

Jonas put the woman out of his mind now and quickened his step. He was in a hurry because he was meeting Robert Leclerc for lunch. The wine list at the restaurant he had selected would impress Ela's second in command and he did mean to impress Robert. It would be the first step in gaining his cooperation.

Robert had been shown to their table and was looking around nervously when Jonas walked up and introduced himself.

"Thank you for agreeing to meet with me, Robert. May I call you Robert?" Jonas's handshake was firm, as was Robert's.

"Please do. Nice to meet you, Mr. Koertig."

"I insist that you call me Jonas. Everyone does. I think we should order something special from the wine list don't you? Why don't you do the honors, Robert? It is *your* line of work."

Robert was a little confused about why he had been summoned like this but exhilarated at the same time. He'd never been invited to lunch by a billionaire playboy before and Diane had insisted he accept. As soon as he relaxed a little, professionalism and years of experience took over. He approached the task with an expertise that won the approval of the man across the table.

Jonas noticed that Robert was starting to relax. He made small talk and let the opulent atmosphere and wine do its work before broaching the subject of Ela and Torsten.

"Robert, you must have some idea why I asked for this meeting?" It would be best to ease into it. Robert still looked a little skittish.

"You mentioned that you are a friend of Mr. Furst. That is why I feel disloyal to Ela; I did not tell her I was meeting you."

"I can appreciate your concerns, Robert. They speak to your good character. Do you know anything about their relationship and what transpired?"

"Ela didn't tell me a great deal. She's kind of private that way. At first she wouldn't even tell me Mr. Furst's name. Eventually she did, though … after swearing me to secrecy. I knew something was up because she was preoccupied but in a good mood, and not stressing over work. Then after Mr. Furst came to Montreal the second time, something went wrong between them. I was able to figure some things out for myself. I do believe that she was in love with Mr. Furst and that she had her heart broken. He seemed to have tried with her afterwards and when that didn't work, he resorted to other methods. He bought a company secretly and had the president offer Ela a contract. She found out. She usually finds things out. That is why I hesitated coming here.

"Finally, Mr. Furst lured her to a chateau in Bordeaux under false pretenses. I don't know what transpired between them, but it was clear that they hadn't resolved their issues. You probably know all of this though."

"Well you're right. I do know all about it. It took me a while to get it out of Torsten, but it matches up with what you have told me. You must care about Ela very much Robert, to be so concerned about upsetting her."

"I do care about Ela a great deal, as does my wife."

Jonas heard the affection in Robert's voice.

"Ours is not just a working relationship. It's a true friendship. Ela is very loyal and she does these heartwarming things for the people she is close to. She tells me off sometimes for treating her like my little sister, which I am probably guilty of. Don't get me wrong, Jonas, Ela is a self-made success and she usually exercises very good judgment. I admire her business acumen and marketing skills very much. She can take care of herself, for the most part, but once in a while, she needs someone to look out for her. Don't we all though?"

"Robert, what would you say, if I told you that I am working on a plan to re-unite Ela and Torsten, but that I need your help to do it?"

"She would kill me if she ever found out."

"She will probably find out in time, since she's obviously very perceptive, but for now we'll just have to make sure that she doesn't. Torsten knows nothing about this. Torsten is very capable when it comes to business—almost as capable as I am." Jonas tried levity. "But when it comes to his personal life, he is hopeless. This time, I think that their reconciliation should be handled by someone else. Someone with more experience."

"Well, Jonas, Ela is seeing someone. He's a really nice guy."

"Yes, I know: David Vaughn, a very upstanding gentleman."

Robert nearly aspirated his next sip of wine. *Was Jonas having someone spy on Ela?*

Jonas smiled to ease the other man's fears. "I know about David Vaughn because Ela told Torsten about him and then I Googled them both. There were photos of them together at some winemaker dinner and one where he received an award."

Robert visibly relaxed.

"You remember what she was like when she started to get involved with Torsten— when she was at her happiest. Is she like that now with David Vaughn in her life?"

Robert hesitated. He didn't want to betray any confidences, particularly not to this strange man, but he knew what Jonas was getting at. Ela had been blissfully happy when she'd returned from Rome. With David she seemed merely content. "If she hadn't gotten involved with Mr. Furst, maybe David would have stood a chance."

"Then we're not too late, Robert. This can be fixed. You know, I have never met Ela, but I know Torsten very well. I have never seen him so miserable. Believe me, I have tried everything to snap him out of it. Nothing has worked. There is only one solution. Are you with me, Robert? You would be helping two people who will flounder for the rest of their lives if we don't step in."

Robert found himself nodding; he was going through the same thing with Ela and agreed with Jonas's assessment. Suddenly it was all so much more palatable; this meeting didn't seem like a betrayal, more of an intervention.

"What would you want me to do, Jonas?" Robert was still cautious but more willing.

"For now, I would just like to know a few things about Ela. What are her plans for the business in the near future? What kind of food and wine is she passionate about—you know, her dream meal if she were stuck on a deserted island. If there is anything else you would feel comfortable telling me, please do, anything that you think might help me to understand Ela Zalewski the wine agent and the woman."

Robert was surprised at how little Jonas was asking of him. He could answer those kinds of questions effortlessly and without guilt. Anyone who knew Ela would know these things. But how this would be of any real help to Jonas, Robert could not figure out.

Robert, feeling free from any sense of disloyalty, started by telling Jonas that Ela was currently interested in high quality wines from Greece. She felt this was the next big thing and wanted to add some top producers to their portfolio before the competition got there.

"Ela's latest obsession is Champagne de Venoge ... especially the Cordon Bleu Extra Brut which she would one day like to have with the wild flat Cancale oyster of Brittany. She talked about going to the source armed with a cooler full of Cordon Bleu Extra Brut so she could eat her fill with the appropriate Champagne. Apparently they are very much in demand and the restaurants in France snap up everything they can. But Ela's not one to be deterred so easily; she told me she plans to wait on shore for the boats to come in next time she's in France—and she'd do it too.

"She also loves the Louis XV Brut 1996 and thinks it would be ideal with a lobster dish that has a hint of vanilla in the sauce. The funny part is that with her complex palate, she doesn't cook. Ela can only prepare one dish, osso buco, but it's amazing. Anyways, she likes Sauterne at the end of dinner, instead of dessert, but thinks it would be wonderful to do a Champagne-with-every-course dinner and if she were to stretch it out to dessert, her choice would be Champagne de Venoge Vin de Paradis with strawberries dipped in dark chocolate or somehow filled with fresh cream and anointed with dark chocolate shavings, as she put it. I would have to say that this would be her dream meal."

But Robert didn't stop there. He told Jonas all about Ela's background and how she got into the business. He told Jonas about what she liked, including her favorite film, what she did with her days off, where she traveled to, who were the producers they worked with, her personal philosophy … and that she had an opinion about everything.

Robert proved very helpful and Jonas now knew that he could rely on Ela's director of sales if he needed something more. Yes, this had been a good move, Jonas commended himself. He had been right to have come to Montreal.

CHAPTER 21

Ela was excited. This would be her first time on a yacht, and since it was for a wine event, she felt completely justified taking the time off. She had planned to look into the wines of Greece in a serious way, so the invitation couldn't have come at a better time. Plus she had been restless and needed some new challenges.

The invitation had come by email as an attachment with a compelling personally addressed letter. It was from a newly formed international promotional agency based in Düsseldorf.

The agency specialized in event planning for the wine industry and had been hired by a group of wine producers in Greece to promote their wines to an exclusive group of importers.

The event would take place on a private yacht off Greece over the course of five days, allowing for two days' additional traveling time.

The first week was dedicated to the European market and the second week to the North American market.

The group of producers would be joining them for the duration of the cruise.

Mr. Karsten Reimann, owner of the Reimann Agency, went on to explain that for the North American part, two buyers with distribution channels in the United States, one covering the Western States and the other covering the Eastern ones, had already confirmed their presence, as did the two agents from Ontario and British Columbia.

Mr. Reimann acknowledged that Quebec would be an important market for the group, but confessed that he and his events coordinator had not known which agent to invite as they were limited to one.

They had done some research through contacts in Quebec as well as Europe and Ela's agency came highly recommended and her abilities much praised. Mr. Reimann apologized for the last minute invitation, but hoped that she would understand that it was very important to his agency and the group that they committed to the right agent. She had been worth the effort, he pointed out, exceeding their criteria with her credentials and excellent reputation.

Ela wondered who had recommended her, so she could thank them. Mr. Reimann never said but of course he wouldn't in an invitation. Oh well, she made a mental note to inquire at some point during the cruise. She would have plenty of time as Mr. Reimann would be on board the whole time to greet the importers and act as host, translator and moderator.

Further in the letter, Mr. Reimann expressed the hope that the lateness of this invitation would not inconvenience her too much and that she would be able to join them on the cruise in three weeks' time. It would be greatly appreciated if she could confirm immediately, since they had little time to arrange for her business class ticket for the flight to Athens. He reminded her to make sure that her passport was up to date.

Business class? They did think well of her. Then again, she did deliver. Still, that almost never happened when an association of wine producers had to shell out for a group like this all in one shot. It was a treat and dispelled any doubts Ela might have had. Business class to Greece, to do some research she'd been planning to do on her own dime.

Mr. Reimann had written a brief description of his newly founded agency because their website was not yet up, nor were they yet availing themselves of social media. He assured her that though his company was in the development stage, the employees had had extensive experience in this area. Before coming to work for him, they had organized the annual ProWein salon in Düsseldorf. He went on to say that the agency was fortunate to have such a strong start with this lucrative piece of business and one that would help make their name.

Mr. Reimann's letter outlined the itinerary. The day of boarding would be free time, as everyone would be arriving on different flights. They would cast off late afternoon and everyone would meet up on deck at a designated time for an intimate "getting to know each other dinner." Local caterers would set up before sunset on a small private island. The evening would have an authentically Greek theme to put everyone in the right mood. All amenities had been considered, naturally.

The following day, importers would present their companies, markets and buying practices. The next days would be allotted to the producers. They would present their properties and each producer would conduct a tasting with a series of their wines. A brief question period would follow.

Lunches and dinners would highlight wine and food pairings. Lunches would feature traditional and modern Greek themes and dinners would feature traditional and modern cuisine based on the high culinary standards of France and Italy. The idea was to show off the diversity of the excellent wines being produced in Greece.

Dinner would be served a little earlier than what European guests would be used to, out of deference for North American habits.

Mr. Reimann assured Ms. Zalewski that because they would make an early start of it each morning, there would be time in the afternoon for relaxation on deck … sunning, swimming. It would also give everyone an opportunity for informal chats with time enough for a brief rest below deck, prior to dinner.

Dinner would be preceded by a chilled white on deck with everyone able to move about freely and continue the exchange of information and ideas.

There would be a rotation in the seating arrangements at lunch and dinner to give everyone ample opportunity to converse with different people.

Ela was asked if she could let them know of any food allergies and to be kind enough to prepare a presentation for the first day. Mr. Reimann hoped that she wouldn't mind doing it in English. He was aware that most of the time she worked in French in Quebec, but had heard that she was bilingual.

Mr. Reimann explained that the dress code would be casual clothing during the day, but that the other guests had indicated they would enjoy dressing up a little in the evening. He filled her in on the weather conditions for the time of the year, and what to expect on the open sea. He mentioned that the sun would be strong and it could get quite windy on deck when they were out on open water.

There was also a gym in case she wanted to pack some workout clothes, and he reminded her to bring along a bathing suit. Bathing suit definitely, Ela told herself. She could skip the workout for those days. She would be extra careful about what she ate.

Unfortunately only soft, rubber-soled footwear was allowed on deck so as not to scuff the wood and to prevent accidents. The floor could get slippery. If she did not have anything appropriate, the crew would provide her with a pair of custom white cotton moccasins they stocked in all sizes on board.

At the end of his letter, Mr. Reimann indicated that there were several photos of the inside and outside of the vessel attached. Ela clicked eagerly and was awed by the opulence of the yacht. Then she had a strange sense of déjà-vu; there was something very familiar about that white hull, the white upper structure, the decks, the location of the pool and the position of the helipad; it looked a lot like like Torsten's yacht. Ela scrutinized the photos.

No, she was wrong. The common areas and staterooms where drastically different. Torsten's yacht was over the top. Every inch gilded and filled with stuff that belonged in a museum … It didn't reflect who he was. His wife, Lara, had been responsible for that. These photos showed subdued colors and sleek lines. This yacht was tasteful, modern, comfortable and inviting.

Relief washed over her when she remembered Mr. Reimann referred to this yacht as the *Second Chance* in his email. Ela told herself it was probably just the same builder or something; it's not like she was a yacht expert. She was ashamed that she saw conspiracy at every turn. Well after the job offer from Koch and the thing at Laurence's château, who could blame her?

Mr. Reimann may not have given her the names of the people who recommended her, the producers, or the other importers, but she attributed that to the fact that this important event was almost upon them. He wasn't being deliberately evasive. He was scrambling. Perhaps she wasn't even his first choice; that would be understandable. Ela felt compassion for Mr. Reimann. She herself had been thrust into the position of having to pull off the impossible when she was in marketing communications and a few times as the owner of a wine agency. She did not want to add to Mr. Reimann's stress and she did want to go to Greece. Besides, Ela reasoned, there was a free afternoon first. If she truly wasn't completely comfortable with the event, she would simply invent some sort of emergency and beg off the cruise.

It all sounded very plausible and Mr. Reimann could not have been more accommodating. He had even given her his private mobile number and said she should contact him personally if she needed anything for her trip.

More out of curiosity than suspicion, she Googled Karsten Reimann, but came up with nothing. Ela considered getting in touch with Aldrick again, but decided against it.

Any favor solicited from Aldrick, she now realized, would have to be repaid. She didn't like being indebted like that and really it didn't seem necessary.

She would get to know Mr. Reimann soon anyway, Ela told herself. Why not accept that this turn of events was due to the fine reputation that she had earned and a sprinkling of luck … and leave it at that. She should just enjoy it. Anyhow, it would offer the kind of diversion that she needed.

Minutes later she was typing her confirmation:

"Dear Mr. Reimann,

Thank you for your email. I am happy to accept your invitation and look forward to meeting you in person …"

Jonas grinned over his glass of Krug Grand Cuvée Brut 1998 Champagne, then congratulated himself. He'd known she would accept but this made it official. His plan was in motion. The captain and crew had been briefed and sworn to secrecy. The only two people that would be kept in the dark were Ela and Torsten.

What made it particularly delightful was that Jonas knew that Torsten had only himself to blame. His friend had called the captain of his yacht, instructing him to give Mr. Koertig everything he asked for as he planned his birthday cruise. Torsten further requested he not be bothered with the details.

Jonas sipped his Champagne and imagined the looks on their faces when Torsten and Ela would first lay eyes on each other. There were bound to be fireworks—and not in a good way at first. She would accuse him of deception.

He would swear that he too had been duped.

Jonas would put an end to that quickly enough though and soon they could get on with other things, namely, finding their way back to each other; which was the whole point. …

Jonas knew he would have to explain why he'd had to intervene, but he doubted they'd welcome the knowledge that they were screwing up their lives when left to their own devices. He couldn't very well tell them in person. It wouldn't do to tell them over a communication device where he could not see their reaction, either. Jonas would have to solve that problem, but first he needed to call the company that designed those custom tents for luxury safaris and all of the components that went with them. He would have some special requests and it would be a rush job. And … he was going to need a barge. More Champagne was in order.

Then another outlandish idea popped into his head. A friend of his had told him that the owners of a couple of châteaux in Bordeaux were using drone technology to survey their vineyards. Had he not himself recently bought a large amount of stock in a company that had a subsidiary that was about to put a new advanced model out on the market for non-military use? *Oh, yes, this would be perfect,* Jonas thought gleefully. This would solve the communications problem. Another phone call to make.

There were several more phone calls to follow, each vital to the plan. The first of the next series of phone calls was to his good friend Alister Tobbias Grey; ex-MI6 and now running his own security agency. Alister employed only the very best and hired only the very best independents.

"Hello, Jonas. What can I do for you?"

"Is this a secure line?"

"Naturally."

"I need one of your best people with the proper skills to break into a safe belonging to Torsten Lucas Furst. It's located in his home, more specifically his home office. There is something in there that I need."

"Is that all? Isn't Torsten your best friend?"

"He is. That's why this is imperative."

"I'm not following."

"If this is not done, my best friend is going to be unhappy for the rest of his life and a pain to be around. The person you send won't exactly be breaking in. Torsten's housekeeper will open the door and escort your operative to the safe."

"You have the housekeeper in on this?"

"She knows that it is for a good cause. I will send you the schematics for the model."

"And, what would this operative do with the contents of this safe?"

"There is only one item in there that I am interested in. I hope your person won't be tempted by anything else that might be in there. Mrs. Vogt, the housekeeper, will be watching like a hawk."

"Come on, Jonas. How long have you known me? I only work with the most professional people."

"Yes, you're right. Then … Torsten's driver, Tavin Vogt, will take your person to a private airfield."

"And, the driver is going to be involved in this as well … oh good. It's not the way we usually work, Jonas."

"They are husband and wife and I have known them long enough to know that neither one keeps secrets from the other, so why not work it this way? Anyway, my private jet will be waiting."

"And where will it be landing?"

"On a small landing strip in Greece. Your person will be escorted onto a helicopter that will deliver him or her onto Torsten's yacht, the *Second Chance*. I need for this person to break into Torsten's safe in his office on board, and place the item in it, locking it up obviously."

"Obviously."

"You'll receive the schematics for that safe as well. Oh, by the way, the captain, first mate and head stewart are expecting your person. The others will be told that he or she is a computer specialist coming on board to update some software."

"So a total of five people in addition to the pilots will have firsthand knowledge?"

"And, one flight attendant. Think of them as accomplices …"

"Fine. I'll need a schedule and all of the particulars. Next time why not just ask me to rob a bank."

"Bill me in advance, Alister, and I'm not even going to ask you about the amount."

"This one is on the house, Jonas. You helped me to start the firm—put me in touch with some people, backed me financially. I owe you."

"I lent you some money and you paid it back in three months with interest. Excellent return on investment I'd say, and just good business."

"Then next time you pay the full hourly fee plus expenses."

The devil is in the details, Jonas thought with satisfaction. All of this was so entertaining. Jonas was having the best time. Operation Reconciliation was underway.

CHAPTER 22

Émile Delacroix was on his way to meet his upstairs neighbor Isabel Vega at a local café. He was almost in front of the coffee place when he spotted Isa across the street ducking into an alley. Émile assessed the situation. She had done so on purpose. Then he saw why. She was being followed by a burly man and she knew it.

The man following the dark haired beauty would be thinking what luck, about now, Émile thought wryly. He'd be sure that Isa would be trapped in that alley. It was a dead end. The reality was that Isabel would be waiting for him.

The man pounced and pushed her against a wall. She didn't cower or beg, even as he squeezed a breast, before undoing his zipper.

"Get on your knees, bitch."

"You should leave, before you get hurt."

Isabel's aggressor never noticed that Émile had entered the alley until he spoke.

"Shall I wait for you at the café?" "Émile addressed Isabel.

"I won't be long. Be a love and order me the usual?"

The man seemed stunned for a minute.

Émile's parting words were, "You're lucky it's her and not me." He didn't have to look back to know what was happening next.

He heard the sound of a man going down in a lot of pain.

Pierre Joubert's people would be there in a couple of minutes to pick up the trash. Émile had called as soon as he saw Isabel turn into the alley.

"Isa, I won't be able to make dinner next week," Émile told Isabel over coffee.

"A friend of mine is moving to town. His name is Alexander Konig. We used to work together. I thought I would help him find a place and show him around. It has been a long time since we have seen each other and we have a lot of catching up to do."

What Émile Delacroix did not tell his Isabel was that Xander had been his handler in another life and the one who had trained him. He was also the one that had saved Émile's life on their final mission.

"There is an apartment on the top floor that just became available ... maybe your friend would like it."

"Our building is very nice, Isa, but Alexander has swanky tastes from what I remember, and he can well afford to indulge himself."

Isabel shrugged indifferently.

CHAPTER 23

Thrown into a frenzy of shopping to prepare for her upcoming yacht-based wine event, Ela had impulsively grabbed a novel as she browsed a bookstore for reading material. She had purchased this particular novel because the author was a local woman and she had been quite successful in this genre over the years. She was somewhat of a local celebrity, and was invited to almost every social event in the city. She was a Montreal A-lister, but was becoming a sensation in other parts of Canada, some parts of the U.S. and even a few European countries.

Once Ela got into the first few pages, she found the novel impossible to put down—the mark of a good story. She would never have guessed that a book in this genre could be so well written, so intriguing, so consuming.

The characters were vivid, the plot had a number of twists and the descriptions were so complete. It was really well researched too. The cover was luxurious. There was nothing tawdry about this erotic novel, which Ela appreciated. Plus, it was really, really *hot*. She was hooked.

What she liked about this author was that her main characters had life experience and still had potential for growth. They weren't perfect, they had flaws and problems, but they were captivating. You wanted to know them.

The part she found truly outstanding was that the author celebrated men and women in their forties and fifties … And they were just on the verge of their most satisfying relationship.

Unfortunately Ela did not have the time to keep reading. She had only gotten halfway through the book, and was forced to put it aside because of time constraints. So, she got into the habit of carrying it around, reading a couple of pages when she could. It was considered to be the author's best work yet, Ela had heard.

One day when Ela had a free Friday, which happened rarely, she contemplated curling up with her book. What a treat that would have been. She put everything into perspective and recognized that she needed some pieces to add to her wardrobe. It was more about necessity than anything else. Ela did not shop to entertain herself. She only shopped when she absolutely needed a piece of clothing or an accessory for a business function or a business trip. She was probably the most efficient shopper that salespeople would ever encounter. She knew what she was looking for and she made up her mind very quickly. Either the item was perfect or it would not do. No half measures with this client. She did not shop around either. She did not compare prices. If something was right, it would end up in a shopping bag and she would be heading out the door. Holt Renfrew on Rue Sherbrooke Ouest was one of Ela's favorite shopping destinations because of the selection of designers and the very professional sales staff.

This day, as she was going through one of the size 0 racks on the second floor at Holt's, she literally bumped into a woman with a similar body type and of about the same height, who was also looking in the same size 0 section.

Ela sported bangs because they made her look younger. Today she wore them swept to the side. Her gleaming dark brown hair fell in loose waves to her shoulders. The other woman's hair was a deep copper. It was a couple of inches longer than Ela's, with bangs, and she wore it straight and parted to the side.

Their styles were similar to a point. Ela's fashion style was sophisticated-sexy. The redhead was a touch edgier in her fashion choices.

Both women seemed to like good jewelry, but Ela was partial to white gold and silver and today she had opted to wear her silver Tiffany charm bracelet with a very unique watch charm. It served dual purposes: it adorned her wrist and kept her punctual. A pear shaped diamond surrounded by smaller pear shaped diamonds in a white gold setting was suspended from each earlobe.

She probably wore those earrings with cocktail dresses as well as jeans, and made them work, thought the redhead nodding at her fellow shopper.

The redhead wore gold jewelry, which made sense considering her coloring. Ela liked the gold Oyster Perpetual Rolex on her left wrist, particularly because it was gold all over … Gold face and gold Roman numerals. The earrings made quite a statement. H. Stern earrings, Ela was certain. 18K yellow gold, matte finish, and what looked like five tiny diamonds. So modern. All of this was balanced out by the ring on her right hand. Two rock crystals and diamonds with a wide gold band. Very bold. It had to be H. Stern as well. From Ogilvy perhaps. Ogilvy was Ela's other favorite store and just down the street.

Ela wore a white body con BCBG skirt with frill just above the knees and a fitted off the shoulder black jersey top with three quarter sleeves from Marciano over it. A thin black braided Judith & Charles belt emphasized her tiny waist and pulled the whole look together. Her super lightweight medium-sized black Longchamp Derby shoulder tote bag had been a deliberate choice for today's outing, so as not to interfere with the shopping experience. It allowed Ela to use both hands to part the garments on the rack for a good view. A pair of feminine cutout black Nine West sandals with four-inch heels brought attention to shapely ankles and fresh pedicure—glossy red almost the shade of her lipstick. Though the redhead didn't know what labels the brunette was wearing, she obviously knew how to highlight her best features.

While the redhead was doing a head to toe assessment of Ela in only seconds and without visibly moving her eyes, Ela was doing the same. This woman did "casual chic" very well. Skinny white jeans were tightly rolled up over her ankles. The loose fitting long sleeved linen V-neck sweater in warm beige matched the color of her sandals with the impossibly high heels. And to go shopping. *A woman after my own heart,* thought Ela. Opaque neutral color on her toes matched the shade of her long almond shaped nails. She looked effortlessly pulled together, fresh and summery. Ela admired the metallic beige SoHo Gucci shoulder bag with intertwined G, tassel and light gold hardware. Right on trend.

What they both had in common at that moment in time ... Red lips ... A bold statement. Each recognized that important fact about the other immediately.

"Nice shade of lipstick."

"Thank you. Yours too."

"It appears that we are women of considerable taste and style ..."

"I would be forced to agree. You look very familiar, but I know we have never met."

"Isla Duncan. Pleased to meet you."

Isla put out her hand and Ela shook it. Both women had an honest and forceful handshake.

"'Isla Duncan, the writer?"

"Yes, if you like the books. No, if you do not."

"I'm about halfway into your latest, *The Claddagh Ring*. I picked it up a couple of weeks ago; right after it came out. I find it difficult to put down even though I haven't much leisure time at the moment. It's in my bag. Look." Ela yanked the thick hardcover book out of her tote to prove it. "I take it with me everywhere. I had not read anything just for the pleasure of reading since my early twenties. With your book, I rediscovered reading. Getting lost in a good story is wonderful. The fact that it is written in the erotic romance genre, well, even better. This kind of escapism is therapeutic after an exhausting day ... along with a couple of glasses of good wine. Doctors should write the combination as a prescription. It would work on so many different ailments."

"You're a wine agent, aren't you?"

"How on earth would you know that?"

"I was invited to the Montréal Passion Vin banquet last year ... I was admiring your Hervé Léger dress and someone told me what you did for a living, but not your name."

"Ela Zalewski. So you like fine wine, then?"

"It's one of my major weaknesses. Clothes and shoes would be another. My father was Scottish and Irish, but more Scottish I always say because he was somewhat conservative in his spending habits, stereotypical, I know. But my mother came over from France. She had a love of fashion, cosmetics, perfume, wine, food. How they ever got together, I will never understand. I inherited her spending gene."

"It seems we have the same weaknesses. Do you think we should explore this further over lunch at Le Pois Penché?"

"Just on the strength of the lipsticks, Hervé Léger dresses and fine wine I feel we must."

"I really like your nails, Isla, but how on earth do you type with them?"

"They aren't my nails. I indulge myself in between books … while I'm doing promotional appearances. When I get back to the keyboard, I trade them in for a shorter rounded version."

"These aren't mine either." Ela referred to her French manicure. "In my case I alternate between, French, neutral and red. I write and answer a lot of emails daily, so I get them done on the shorter side. Then I'm good for three weeks."

"They look very natural. So what do you think of this season's Hervé Léger collection?"

As it turned out Ela and Isla had a great deal more in common. There was only a year difference in their ages. Ela had turned forty-one and Isla was forty-two. They both ate the same way: lean protein and no carbs. They agreed that lunch without wine was uncivilized. They were both single and alone in the world, the only children of deceased immigrant parents who met and married in Montreal. Neither had ever done the girlfriend thing, in their adult lives anyway, and both had wondered if that was weird. They also had a common philosophy about life, careers, men and sex. Love was not mentioned. They found it very easy to talk to each other.

Ela grew up in Notre-Dame-de-Grace, Isla grew up in Outremont. When Ela was studying marketing communications and languages, Isla was studying literature, history and psychology. They had both studied Shakespeare in university. Ela became fascinated with the bard's work through film, while Isla read the plays and sonnets as class assignments.

"Isla Duncan is your actual name and not a *nom de plume,* right?"

"People always ask that. That's what's on my driver's permit and credit cards. I know, it sounds like a pen name. My father was a Duncan from a long line of Duncans. I was named Isla after my aunt. It was her middle name, but that's what her family called her as a girl. That's how I come by my red hair and this funky turquoise eye color … family genes. My father always said that this particular shade of copper reminded him of his older sister, as did my eyes. The only photos I have of her are black and white, but he was adamant. I thought that when he looked at me he was reminded of how much he missed her. It made me sad. But my father told me that it actually comforted him. It was like he still had her in his life because of me. He acted like I had given him a gift. That made me feel a lot better. I rely on a gifted hairstylist at a salon downtown to return me to my natural color every three weeks these days though. Unfortunately she is going to be moving to Australia. She went there to visit a friend and fell in love with the friend's brother. He came to Montreal to visit her for a month and a couple days before he was due to go back, he bought a ring and asked her to marry him. She told me that if he hadn't, she would have. The wedding will take place in Australia. I'm happy for her, but it's damn inconvenient. I can always move to someone else at the salon, but I was going there because of her. She's going to give me the name of the products and formula, should I decide to switch salons."

"I happen to have a very talented hairstylist by the name of Alain, who mixes up the right shade of dark brown for me these days. The women in my family all went gray prematurely. For some reason, my hair grows so fast that I can't imagine waiting it out for three weeks. I would look like a skunk. I experimented with various shades of auburn … and copper, by the way. I even went blond before coming back to my own shade when I switched to Alain—though slightly enhanced. I always said that I had no intention of aging gracefully. I'm going kicking and screaming."

"Since you are obviously of Polish ancestry, why are you not blond or is that a myth?"

"My parents were both Polish. There were blonds in my family, I have been told, but we seem to have had brunettes on both sides as well. My mother had dark hair and blue eyes. My father's hair was medium brown and it had a reddish cast. He had green eyes. He looked like Willem Dafoe, incidentally."

"Is Alain also responsible for the tousled, just out of bed waves? I'm not talking about after a good night's sleep."

"It seems that over the years Alain has come to know the *wicked* inner me and thought the outside should match," Ela answered with a half-smile and sparkle in her eyes. "I now wear it the way he styles it, except that when he does it, it looks even better."

"I think we are going to get along very well."

"I know we are. If you would like, I could make an appointment for you with Alain. I could even let him know about the products and formula and he would be able to order what you need ahead of time. He's warm and funny … a great human being. And he listens to what you want. You leave with great color, a perfect cut and a hairstyle that is really you. You would like him. We have the most interesting conversations. I know that he would like you. You would be his first erotic romance novelist client. But if you would like to keep it downtown, I have heard from several people that Platine on Rue Sherbrooke Ouest is the place to go for color. Their clients are the who's who of Montreal, so it would be right up your alley."

"This morning I had no real options, and by lunch, I have two. Thank you."

"On a different topic … didn't you do some kind of Lunch with the Author thing downtown a couple of weeks ago, about the time that I picked up your book?"

"We tried something different for the launch of *The Claddagh Ring,* tied it in with a reading, book signing and photos with fans … It was a lot of fun. In addition to the fans, some journalists came out to do interviews afterwards. It was a good event. It would have been perfect in fact, if not for this irritating man that I ran into in the elevator before we got started. The elevator got stuck just after the doors closed. This man used the telephone in the elevator to call the front desk. The front desk knew about the problem, apologized profusely for the inconvenience and assured him that it would be operational in about five minutes. At first we were having a rather pleasant chat. I made a comment about being very familiar with the hotel and this was the first time time anything like this had happened to me. He noticed the top of a book sticking out of my bag and asked about it; presumably to keep the conversation going. He was quite good looking, tall, well built, blond with just a touch of silver at the temples, tanned and extremely well dressed. And he had these piercing blue eyes. I could have thought of worse ways to spend a few minutes, so I started telling him about the book; that it was an erotic romance, but the sex was pertinent to the story line and it was really about love found, love lost and the heartache that came with it, and of course redemption through love. Then it seemed as if I had said something wrong. I must have, though for the life of me I don't know what. He became somewhat antagonistic. And said something about fluff to entertain bored housewives."

"You didn't tell him you were the author?"

"We never introduced ourselves and by then it was pointless. I'm not sure he ever worked a day in his life. He had that look of having been born with a silver spoon in his mouth, to use a tired expression … you know, a look of entitlement. Clearly he had disdain for the working class, and I told him so to his face. He really rubbed me the wrong way. Strange man. I had just insulted him and the next thing out of his mouth was an invitation to have dinner with him."

"And what did you say?"

"I told him that I would rather stick a fork in my eye."

Ela laughed at her new friend's indignation. "His reaction?"

"I really don't know. The elevator had started up by then. The front door opened on the floor where we were holding the lunch. I got out, was mobbed by fans, thankfully, and pushed all of that unpleasantness out of my mind. I had forgotten about it actually, until just now."

"So you never saw him around the hotel for the rest of the day?"

"Lucky for him. I would have called security on him if he had taken even one step in my direction."

That lunch was the beginning of a friendship that grew quickly over the next couple of weeks to the delight of both Ela and Isla. It was like they had known each other their whole lives. They discovered that neither was the kind of woman that enjoyed calling the other to go shopping, get a pedicure or catch a movie. They preferred nice long dinners with a couple of exceptional wines and good conversation. There was no question of cooking when Montreal had so many good restaurants that were only minutes away by cab or within walking distance of their apartments. Like Ela, Isla lived in Old Montreal … something else they had in common.

They were each other's biggest fans and loved sharing good things that were happening in their careers. Someone else might call it bragging, but neither was the type to envy the other. They were both accomplished in their own rights, so who better to cheer the other on.

They vowed that even with a man in their lives, they would always make time for each other.

During their very first dinner Ela Zalewski, wine agent, could not stifle the impulse to ask Isla Duncan, author, how she became a writer of erotic romance novels and had she made any life changing observations on her journey.

"Let me answer your second question first. My motto is: That which is deemed impossible and fosters purpose anyway, concludes in the greatest success and most profound statement of self-expression. That statement is the framework for my career and my life. It's my version of the well-known saying: *Whatever doesn't kill you makes you stronger.*"

"Awe-inspiring."

"About my career … when I turned nineteen, most of the girls in my classes in college were already having sex. I was curious of course, but still a virgin. Mid-term, all of the girls were talking about this book that had come out. I was totally clued out. Well, I was too embarrassed to buy a copy, so one of the girls lent me her book. The characters in the novel were doing all kinds of things that I didn't really know about. I wondered if the girls in my class had experimented beyond the basics. Anyhow, I found myself getting really aroused as I was reading and I discovered what I could do about it." Isla winked and then cracked a smile. "I discovered that I liked this feeling and I got to know my body really well. Then I methodically sought out a partner that I was sure would show me the rest. I found a willing candidate. He was good looking and he was several years older, experienced. Or at least, I thought he was. It was a total failure. It didn't turn out the way it was described in the book. Not even close."

"Well, you did not give up on sex evidently."

"A few months later, when I least expected it, I met someone and let's just say, we were very compatible. I finally discovered what the fuss was all about—beyond self-gratification, that is. It was a long distance relationship and it didn't last, but after that I knew from that experience that I liked sex—a lot—and it taught me that the right chemistry made all of the difference."

"Kind of like the perfect wine and food pairing."

"Exactly." Isla grinned. "In school, I read the classics and at night I read erotic romance. I found both to be educational. Then I took a writing course and another and another. I think that to express yourself through the written word is either inside you or it's not. And for fiction, you need a good imagination and to be able to organize your thoughts. It helps if you are curious and dedicated and disciplined of course. The classes I was taking gave me the technical strengths. The assignments became more and more challenging and some of my classmates dropped the last of the three courses. I held on. I really loved writing. My professors and I didn't always agree on what kind of writer I should become. One in particular thought that I should pursue a second degree in journalism. I opted for contemporary fiction—erotic romance. I heard he wanted to cry when he found out … and they would not have been tears of joy."

"Were other people supportive?"

"There were a few people in my immediate circle that I told about my budding career. Some were very supportive and shared my vision. Others were skeptical or pessimistic. Instead of embracing the possibilities, they led with a negative comment."

"What happened when you became a celebrated novelist?"

"I was asked to speak on campus for one thing. That was quite satisfying. Then one of the *less than supportive* people that I mentioned, told me about a book that everyone was reading. She was dying to get her hands on a copy. She knew the title, but not the name of the author, so I asked her if she would mind Googling it on her smartphone, because my battery was low."

"You didn't?"

"I most definitely did. You should have seen the look on her face when the author's name and bio came up. I did a mental victory lap."

"It looks like you never regretted your decision."

"Never. I got to write what I enjoyed reading, I got to entertain myself in the process and I got to find out who I was as a sexual being. It was a journey of discovery that led to a career that pays well. I get to dine in the best places, buy nice things ... clothes, fine wine ... I get to travel for my work and take some pretty nice vacations. I make my own decisions and I have already achieved financial independence. I don't need a man to take care of me. I like companionship, if it is not too cloying, and I miss sex if I go without for too long, but I don't want to be with a man for financial reasons or emotional security. I want to be with someone because we enjoy each other. My parents, God bless them, left me a little, but it would not have gone far. I needed to make my own money in order to have the kind of freedom that I always wanted. Sure I have deadlines and I have to meet my obligations on the business end, but I am pretty much my own boss. Since I'm super motivated and well organized, that's not a problem. I can truly say that I'm living my dream."

"Isla, I am completely fascinated. Where does your inspiration come from, for the characters, for the sex, for the love story?"

"My inspiration comes from everywhere. People are interesting to study. When I come across a person who has a unique quality or a particular negative trait—something that makes them stand out, I can work with the essence of that person, add something from another person that is interesting, and pull the rest out of my imagination; that's how I bring a character to life. I can write their belief system, motivation, experiences, background and interactions with other characters. My aunt Isla, who I never met, was the inspiration for *The Claddagh Ring*. I wanted to visit her overseas when I was in college, but I just never got around to it. I attended classes and studied for exams during the year. When summer rolled around, I worked as a server in an Irish pub to pay my tuition. Then she passed. I have always regretted it. I should have found a way. My father would talk about her from time to time and she seemed like a remarkable woman. Years later, the main female character in *The Claddagh Ring* would emerge and I knew exactly who she was and where she had come from. It isn't my aunt's life story. Far from it. In any case, I don't really know that much about her actual life. But it is a tribute to her and her strength.

"So, you see, I generally don't lack for ideas. And I work extensively on back stories and character development, I usually overwrite and have to edit, and then my editor tells me that I have to edit some more. It works out in the end though. Things always fall into place."

"Although I am only about halfway into *The Claddagh Ring*, the elaborate back stories make your characters' actions easy to understand and the character development is what gives your work weight."

"Thank you. It is kind of you to say so. That is how I begin the process anyway. These characters sometimes take on a life of their own and they surprise even me. Sometimes I feel like they are taking over my life, each one clamoring to tell me his or her story …"

"No lawsuits to date?"

"None, I am happy to report."

"As for the sex and love … It is easier for me to write about sex than love. Sex does not have to be complicated. Love is usually very complicated. I think my readers believe the reverse. Personally I have done just fine without that kind of entanglement. Why does one have to subject oneself to potential heartache anyway? I find sex is necessary, love is not. But, my readers expect a great love story and a happy ending, so … this is where my imagination has to work overtime."

"You may not want to share that sentiment. Your readers would never recover."

"I know. I am telling you this in confidence. When I am asked these questions publicly, I just make it seem as if I am waiting for this great stuff to happen to me in real life and people usually back off and wish me well. They prefer to believe that I genuinely want to end up like one of my main female characters. I think they believe that I'm projecting when I am telling the story. There are times when I feel like such a fraud, but honestly it's fiction. Nobody thought Shakespeare was projecting onto Juliet."

"Maybe they did; back then men played all the stage roles so perhaps it was a given. Life imitating art. Speaking of, any chance that some aspect of the annoying man you met in the elevator will show up in the personality of one of your characters?"

"That's an awfully good idea."

"It won't be a flattering representatation, I take it."

"I think that I would have great difficulty attributing any positive qualities to that kind of man—apart from his good looks. But even then, I got the impression that he was far too aware of how good looking he was. Like wherever he went, there would be a slew of women lining up for his attention."

"I look forward to reading what you have planned for him."

"You can be one of my beta readers for the next book and let me know what you think."

"It would be my pleasure.

"Have you ever scared a man off because he was afraid that he would end up as a character in one of your books?"

"Oh probably, though no one has ever admitted it to me. I wouldn't write about an actual person that I was involved with or had been involved with or any part of our actual sex life. The characters are a hundred percent fictional.

The female characters are not me and the male characters are not men I have been involved with. I only wish that I could have had sex with the men that my female characters have sex with. I get these sly smiles sometimes at book signings. Like people are thinking that I'm having sex all of the time with a host of amazing men. If only ... Anyway, there's no point in denying anything. People are going to think what people are going to think. Some people would like to believe that a certain character is out there somewhere in real life. It's good for book sales. I get the feeling now and again from men I meet, that they are curious about what sex with the author of erotic romance novels would be like, but they don't often act on it. I wouldn't be surprised if some men were a little reluctant to pursue a relationship with a woman who writes in the genre I write in."

"Especially if they thought they might not live up to the sexual abilities of your alpha males."

"You may be right. I honestly can't tell if being this kind of novelist is good for my sex life or bad for it."

"Isla, I have to confess that I have felt the same way about sex and love as you. I told myself that the term *falling in love* said it all. When can *falling* ever be a good thing? It implies having no control and a painful landing. I never liked the term *settling down* either. It made me think of going through life, having a good time and then its full stop. I swore that this would never be me. I never shared my reservations about love with anyone—before now—for fear of being labeled a freak. I don't know where I got it from; my parents were very loving towards each other and towards me."

"Me too, Ela. My parents were very much in love their whole lives. I also grew up witnessing their affection for each other and they always made me feel much loved. I don't know where I get it from either."

"I wish I had stuck to my resolve, but that's a topic for another time."

"Ah, I see. Have you gotten over this man?"

"I'm working on it."

"So you haven't been seeing anyone since?"

"I have. He's a great person, but I am reluctant to get involved beyond where we are at now. He's been very patient. I don't how long that will last. I just don't think that it is fair to use him to try to forget another man. On top of it all, he doesn't seem like the type who would be satisfied with a casual relationship and I am nowhere near ready for any kind of committed relationship."

"It sounds like you haven't been to bed?"

"No. That would change things between us."

"Are you sexually attracted to him?"

"Yes, but not in that burning kind of way. Are you involved with anyone,

Isla?"

"Not at the moment."

"There is something I'm curious about and it's not because you write erotic romance novels. It's because you are the quintessential independent modern woman."

"Go on."

"What is the thing that turns you on the most about a man?"

"That's easy. His ability to seduce me. Seduction really is an art. If done right, seduction takes place in the brain long before there's a kiss or a caress. By the time the kiss or caress happens, I'm about ready to … well … you know. He has to be self-confident, witty and creative in how he goes about it. He has to take his time, prolong it."

"The man I used to see had mastered what you just mentioned, Isla. That's what got me into my predicament."

"You don't say? We are going to make time for a long conversation about that … very soon. In the meantime it is only fair that you tell me what turns *you* on most about a man. I'm always looking for material for my books …"

"Don't you dare."

"I'm joking … sort of. You don't have to go into details, Ela. Although if you would like to, that would be fine," Isla assured Ela with a naughty smile.

"Like you, I believe that the brain is the most important sex organ. I like to be pursued—even if it is only over the course of an evening. There is nothing worse than a man making a halfhearted attempt and then wandering off when it doesn't work immediately. It shows me that it was never about me. If a man really wants *me,* he will focus on me and me alone. He will stay by my side, compete for my attention if other men are around and no other woman in the place will distract him. *That* is terribly sexy. Anything worth having is worth working for, right?"

"Can I steal all of that—as an idea? Seriously."

"I was kidding before. Yes, sure. I should add that I like an assertive man who is a little territorial, not to be confused with a controlling man, which is a *big* turnoff. … *Huge* turnoff. It's not that I don't enjoy taking the reins. I really do, and I so appreciate a man who enjoys it when I do, but the first move has to be his. Obviously when we do become intimate, he has to be a generous and imaginative lover. I like to give pleasure as much as I like to receive it, so a like-minded partner is a must."

"Everything you're saying is perfect for a strong main female character who really knows herself."

"I'm flattered."

"I should hope so. I write all of my main female characters that way. Something happens to them, it's different each time, I don't want to be too repetitive, but they all have some kind of revelation, and then find their inner strength. When I was starting out, I met a man who was well off. He lived in London and I was really attracted to him. He invited me to visit him and offered to pay for my flight. If I could have, I would have paid my own way. Unfortunately I was not in the position to do so. I hadn't asked and I knew that the cost of the ticket in *economy* wouldn't be financially taxing on him, so I expressed my gratitude for his consideration and accepted. Things seemed to be going well the first couple of days… and then, out of the blue, he equated paying for the airfare with paying to have sex with me. He reproached me because he had paid for me to fly over to London and I wasn't putting out on request. It made me feel awful and very disillusioned. My pride took quite a beating from those words. So, the relationship ended before it really started. The experience reinforced what I had wanted anyway, to have my own money. It's not that I haven't accepted a present from a lover since, or been whisked away on a dream vacation. It's just that I became very cautious about where the grand gesture was coming from."

"That sense of self-worth comes across in your book very effectively. I may be overstepping, but has anyone ever told *you* they were in love with you?"

"There was this one man, but I didn't feel the same way and we were in different places in our lives anyway. Long story short, I felt that it didn't make sense to keep seeing each other at the time. Enough about me. How did you become a wine agent?"

"When I was eighteen, a family friend gave me a job as hostess in her trendy little restaurant. I worked there on weekends and during summer break. That's where I was first exposed to wine. She kept things simple, but the customers seemed to like the wine list and kept coming back. So I became curious about what made wine part of a pleasurable dining experience.

"I come from humble beginnings, so the idea of fine food in fancy restaurants held a lot of appeal for me, and it seemed that fine wine enhanced fine dining. Such things were out of reach for me, but a modestly priced bottle of wine was a little more attainable. While my classmates were drinking beer, I was tasting wine … whatever I could afford. I also spent a lot of time reading anything and everything I could find. I learned about different wines, the grapes, the regions, the appellations, the *terroir,* the winemaking process and also about established as well as up and coming wine producers. Wine captured my imagination. It was a pathway to a world of luxury that was filled with glamorous people— people who lived and worked in châteaux, produced some of the rarest and most prestigious wines on the planet, ate in Michelin Star restaurants, flew first class, stayed in five-star hotels, took expensive vacations, drove top of the line European sports sedans and exotics and were featured in wine magazines. I wanted to be part of that world. Wine was my ticket."

"You're very honest."

"By the way, the theme of naysayers, skeptics and people who do not give you enough credit seems to be universal. I encountered that too ... on the personal side *and* professional side. Even when my wines were *everywhere,* they didn't get it. Even when my wines were written up by respected wine writers and were highly recommended, they didn't *really* get it. Even when I made a commission in the six figures, which for a tiny agency was something, they still didn't see it. Thankfully, there were accomplished people who I respected in my personal life and in the wine business that really believed in me. I just told myself that I wasn't going to listen to negative people or buy into their limited perspectives. I categorized that group as *masters of inadequacy.*

"Every year that I was in the business, something would happen to top all of the wonderful things that had happened before; the people I used to read about in *Wine Spectator* were suddenly in my car and we were on the way to a meeting or a promotional event or interview with a journalist that I had given the exclusive to, or on our way to dinner, and these famous wine producers were interested in what I had to say. They asked me about the market and sales and we discussed marketing strategy. I built relationships with people who are icons of the industry. And, they would invite me to stay at their châteaux or domaines so that I could see their operations in person. Obviously there were exclusive gala dinners with older vintages. I learned how young wines would develop by drinking older vintages at lunch and dinner. Dishes would be matched to the wines and not the other way around. Since then, I tend to do that right here in Montreal. I'm kind of anal about it—and not in the fun way."

"That's right ... make fun of the erotic romance writer." Isla grinned. "I noticed how pushy you were about being the one to choose our wine this evening. Seriously though, you won't hear me complain. I love it. I followed your lead when selecting from the menu because I knew that whatever dishes you ordered would enhance the wine and vice versa. I had no intention of depriving my taste buds."

"Are you sure that you don't want an appetizer? Just because I'm not having one, doesn't mean you have to abstain."

"I had a three-course business lunch. I'm not super hungry. I am, however, parched. Can you tell me about the wine you ordered for us?"

"This restaurant has three wines from Domaine Henri Darnat on their *carte des vins.* This evening we'll be having a bottle of Meursault Premier Cru Clos Richemont Monopole 2010."

"Monopole? As in Monopoly?"

"Exactly. This wine is Chardonnay at its best. And, with this vintage you get apple with lemony accents. It's elegant, complex and round in the mouth. The oak is well integrated. It is already very lovely to drink today, but it has the potential to age for a few years yet. This estate produces good wines consistently. I tasted the 2012 vintage not long ago. There was the minerality and freshness that I had hoped for, but also a richness on the palate that made me think of pastry cream. And there were these delightful almond and pear notes that rose to the surface. I placed an order for some. I also ordered the Meursault 1er Cru Goutte d'Or 2012 from the same estate because I tasted that one at the same time. It too was rich in texture with good acidity, so you get volume *and* freshness on the palate. It had a pleasing nose of almonds and white flowers. On the palate … almond paste. And it has a long toasty finish. Both wines are great to drink now, but will drink well for several years. The Meursault Clos du Domaine 2011 is the third wine from this producer on the *carte des vins* here. You would think that you're drinking a 1er Cru. Obviously all vintages are distinctive, but I have come across spice and floral notes and white fruit predominately in this wine, and there is always a good minerality to back it all up."

"How would you bring these wines together with food?"

"I'm just scratching the surface here and all vintages are different, but the Meursault Clos du Domaine is the kind of wine that would usually work well with something like baked salmon or grilled lobster. For the Meursault Premier Cru Goutte d'Or 2012, I would want to be eating something like chicken in a light tarragon cream sauce. For the Meursault Premier Cru Clos Richemont Monopole 2012, I can just see Robert, my director of sales, doing something with a soft cheese that has a slight bite to it, broiled over a caramelized pear and toasted nut mixture, all golden and oozing. It's just his kind of thing."

"Sounds delectable."

"The Meursault Premier Cru Clos Richemont Monopole 2010, however, is going to be great with our seared sea scallops in lemon cream sauce."

"My taste buds thank you in advance."

"Your taste buds are quite welcome. By the way, I have been informed by a very reliable source, Robert, that this producer is now brewing an upmarket beer. It's a blond beer, La Jumalie. It's not available in Quebec yet, but Robert tasted it in France on his last trip there. According to him it's a very tasty beer and it's to be enjoyed like a food-friendly wine. Robert is always on the lookout for a *gourmet* beer, as he puts it. I can tell when Robert has stumbled across something that he is really impressed with by how much detail he goes into."

"What did he say?"

"That La Jumalie is crafted without additives: no sugar or acid. It's pure and the ingredients are organic. Plus the producer uses the same kind of new oak barrels for his beer as for his Meursaults. Also, the best before date is two years from the date that the beer is bottled. So La Jumalie doesn't have to be consumed right away. In fact, it actually improves along the way just like fine wines do. Robert tells me that although taste is paramount to importers, shelf life is very important too."

"Luxury beer that acts like wine, from a well-known producer of luxury wine."

"That pretty much sums it up. Anyhow, the next time we dine here, we'll have to select something very special to go with a red Burgundy that they have on this wine list, Clos de Vougeot Grand Cru 2009 from Domaine Armelle et Bernard Rion. We'll have to make it soon; they don't have many bottles left."

"Is that wine really so in demand?"

"Pinot Noir is considered a difficult grape to grow," explained Ela. "It is unforgiving. The conditions have to be just right. But, it produces some of the most majestic wines in the world."

Ela told Isla that while she could appreciate Clos de Vougeot Grand Cru wines in their youth when they were intense red in color and fruit forward with berry and raspberry in abundance, this wine would develop other desirable characteristics in the years to come. The color would deepen to garnet and one could sometimes detect a hint of leather and a faint trace of truffle. That took cellaring. That took patience.

"So, by the passion in your voice and the way you light up, you never regretted your career choice either, obviously?"

"Never. Everything turned out as I had hoped. I knew from the beginning exactly what kind of wine agent I wanted to be. I decided to specialize. I wanted to offer my services to the producers of luxury wine. I had no intention of building a large agency and working on volume sales. It just isn't my style, and there were already numerous agencies doing that, and doing it well. I wanted my agency to be the kind of business where I worked closely with people that I liked and got to represent wines that I liked—small quantities of high-end, sought-after wines. The promotional work is somewhat different too. I do more work with journalists and authors of wine guides, as well as VIP client events. Relationships are important. Personalized service is important. I managed to carve out a niche for myself and I now have a lucrative business on my terms. I had to hire a director of sales five years ago and now I couldn't do without Robert. I'm even thinking of making him my partner. He's earned it. He has wanted to expand the agency and I've resisted. If we can come up with something that is still fairly exclusive but gives him an expanded role, I'd consider it. He's also a really good friend, as is his wife, Diane. We should go out for dinner, the four of us. You'd all get along very well."

"That would be great. My mouth is already watering. Plus I'd get a glimpse of the glamorous life of wine agents."

"Your senses won't be disappointed but perhaps your sensibilities would be. Robert and I do a lot of paperwork. Identifying the wines we want to represent is only a small part of the big picture. When Robert and I dine together, we carefully choose the food and wine, then we wade through the details of getting wine profitably across an ocean. I cannot lie, though. I live for the glam. Still, no hard work, no sales, no happy producers—no glam. You can't exactly rest on your laurels. People have a short memory and wine is produced every year and has to be sold over and over. It's a fact of life. Anyhow I like my work. I particularly like to tell people that I do not drink fine wine and Champagne to celebrate … I celebrate every time I drink fine wine and Champagne. Sometimes, I just like to tell them that I drink for a living. Once someone asked me if I had been tasting some wines for business or pleasure. I just automatically answered with *Pleasure is my business.*"

"When people say something to me like: A penny for your thoughts … I usually respond with *I'm pondering sexual positions.*"

This statement, Ela would come to realize, was typical Isla. She liked to push the boundaries. She was laughing out loud at her friend's bluntness. "But what if it is a man who asks you about your books, Isla?"

"Oh, I say the same, I'm a big believer in the equality of the sexes. I have been trying to incorporate more of the male perspective into my books these days. I have a confession too … I lost my *wine virginity* only at the time that I started to write my first novel. I was a late bloomer. My characters introduced me to wine. When I did the research for the book, I felt I had to taste the wines I was writing about. I started with New World wines, but eventually got back to the *roots* … oh look, wine humor. Okay, you barely cracked a smile. Moving right along … I discovered wines from Italy and Spain and France; I could actually live on Champagne."

"If you say Champagne and oysters, I am going to kiss you, right here in the restaurant. It will be girl on girl love …"

"Of course Champagne *and* oysters. I'll skip the kiss though, even though you are a very attractive, and might I add, well dressed woman, I'm all about men."

"I think I'm hurt." Both women dissolved into gales of laughter.

DIANA SOBOLEWSKI

CHAPTER 24

Ela and Isla had become accustomed to attracting attention when they walked into a restaurant. Both women liked to dress for dinner to heighten the pleasure of the experience, and usually drew glances of admiration from the men at the bar and adjoining tables.

More than a few times, a man out on his own or with a buddy had contemplated sending over a bottle of wine, but when they overheard Ela making her wine selection and getting a look of approval from the sommelier, they were usually too intimidated to go further.

Whenever Isla was recognized, it was the same. A man would summon the courage to walk over to their table, but inevitably some bit of information would crawl up out of his memory—something that a girlfriend or a female co-worker said about one of the books—and he would make a hasty retreat.

Ela and Isla covered a number of different subjects during their conversations, but inevitably there was the mention of wine. Ela let Isla in on her discoveries and Isla was happy to listen, but would stop Ela each time to write down the wines so she could remember later.

Ela naturally told Isla about the producers that her agency represented and their superb wines, but considered it part of her education to taste interesting wines represented by other agents as well, so Ela let Isla in on those too.

Recently Ela had tasted wines from another property that was owned by the producer of the Château Malartic-Lagravière wines in Pessac-Léognan. These Bordeaux wines were a big hit in Quebec and one of only six châteaux in the appellation that produced *classé* wines in both red and white.

The same team produced a red and white from an adjacent property. Ela had thought that Château Gazin-Rocquencourt red 2010, which was available in Quebec, to be an ideal *vin de garde* the first time she tasted it. It received recognition from several wine critics and Ela considered it to be a great wine to lay down for an unbelievably good price.

While Ela drank red wines a little earlier these days, she explained it was to appreciate the fruit, she still liked to taste older vintages. The beauty of an age worthy red that went from purple to a scarlet red and eventually a garnet red, was that it took on mushroom and leather notes, as it evolved.

Ela loved the red and dark fruit on the nose and palate, and she perceived a smokiness in this extraordinary vintage of Château Gazin-Rocquencourt. The tannins were velvety, the oak well integrated and the finish fruity and long. One had to include the word elegant when describing this red.

"By the way, the 2013 white from this producer is spectacular ... I tasted it in Bordeaux. The 100% Sauvignon Blanc white was fresh, elegant and very dry." In addition to grapefruit, which was typical for the grape, Ela found that pineapple came through nicely, as did white peach. She wondered aloud if it would take on some honey notes as it gained a progressively richer golden color in the years to come. No wonder that Wine Advocate awarded Château Gazin-Roquencourt white 2013 91-93 points.

Another excellent find which Ela shared with Isla was a Burgundy estate by the name of Domaine Millet. The wines available in Quebec were Petit-Chablis, Chablis and Chablis 1er Cru Vaucoupin. They got great write-ups in the local press year after year, and Ela became curious about putting them to the test with her own nose and palate. She had tasted several vintages of each over the years. She had to admit the positive reviews were justified. As she went from the Petit Chablis to the Chablis and then to the Chablis 1er Cru Vaucoupin, Ela pointed out, the wines became richer and rounder, which was expected, but the fruit and minerality was always present, as was the fine acidic spine that gave these wines a very desirable freshness. Depending on which appellation you were tasting, the vintage and whether you were tasting the wine young or after a couple of years, you could come across a flinty minerality, citrus fruit, pear, white peach, exotic fruit, green apples, baked apples, raw crunchy almonds or almond paste. The Petit Chablis was a fairly crisp Chardonnay and ideal as an aperitif or with oysters. The Chablis, a slightly rounder Chardonnay, could be served with white fish, and the Chablis 1er Cru Vaucoupin was a perfect Chardonnay for salmon and lobster.

Then there were the wines of Château de La Dauphine from the appellation of Fronsac in Bordeaux. She had the pleasure of tasting several vintages of Château de La Dauphine over the years, going back to 2001, Ela stated. Each vintage she had tasted stood out in her mind, but there was always an elegant feminine quality to the wine. There were so many reasons to celebrate the differences between the vintages and how they paired with different dishes. Ela remembered when she first found out about the producer through the Quebec wine writers, which in her opinion, were among the best in the world. Depending on the vintage and whether you tasted it young or after a few years of cellaring, Château de La Dauphine could be paired with a tender rare piece of beef in a red wine sauce, sometimes a dish with truffles ... Or it could be game with a berry sauce ... And, it was well suited to a modern interpretation of many a classic French dish, Ela had discovered. Like Château de La Dauphine, Delphis de La Dauphine was 90% Merlot and 10% Cabernet Franc and was another revelation from this producer. Delphis de La Dauphine, however, was meant to be enjoyed earlier and its freshness was a delight. It was one of those purchases, you didn't even have to think about.

Ela had seen photos of the property and noted that it was one of the most beautiful in the region. The painstakingly restored château was situated in a well-tended park complete with its own pond. The château was becoming well known on the wine tourism scene, unsurprising for such a romantic setting. Too bad that she had not thought of telling Robert and his wife, Diane, when they were planning their destination wedding, Ela confessed. The photos would have been something really special, the meal a treat for the finickiest foodie and the wines would have impressed the most discerning of wine lovers.

Ela admitted that she was not easily impressed by just any sparkling wine. Then she came across one from Australia with the characteristics of a well-made Champagne. Cuvée Midnight from *World Champion Sparkling Winemaker,* Blue Pyrenees Estate Vineyards, opened her mind and changed her thinking. By the time she got her hands on it, it was one of the last few bottles still available in Quebec … Probably because it had gotten great write-ups from several Quebec journalists. This *Méthode Traditionnelle* wine, made the same way as Champagne, was elegant and complex with fine acidity and persistent bubbles. The 2004 had evolved beautifully, but there was still a certain freshness about it. Apparently, Midnight Cuvée was only produced in the best years and the grapes were harvested by hand at night under lights instead of under the hot sun. The result was a crisper wine. Ela was looking forward to whatever vintage would be next, and hoped that their highly awarded red wines would come to Quebec.

"If we are talking about the Champagne that I would want to drink with oysters, my go-to would have to be Champagne de Venoge Cordon Bleu Extra Brut. It has this fine, acidic spine, beautiful minerality and fine persistent bubbles. Though there are so many varieties of oysters … each with a unique taste profile, they generally have a certain rich texture or mouth feel and that clean mineral taste. What is really special about the De Venoge Cordon Bleu Extra Brut is that it is aged for three years rather than the fifteen months that is required. The additional aging time means that they can't put it out on the market and turn a profit as quickly, but they produce a Champagne that is complex on the nose and on the palate. The man who is in charge of this Champagne house is brilliant as far as I am concerned. He is completely dedicated to the highest quality when it comes to the reputation of the house. It's one of the best Champagnes I have ever tasted as an aperitif, with oysters it is absolutely divine. I am obsessed with it. It scored 91 points with Wine Spectator and was awarded the Grand Médaille d'Or at the Concours Mondial de Bruxelles, so there are obviously others who agree that it is a very special extra brut Champagne. By the way, it is very rare for a non-vintage Champagne to receive a score like that or that kind of top honor."

"I don't know anything about this house."

"Not to worry. That's what you have me for. The house of De Venoge has been around since 1837 and throughout history has been a favorite of European royalty and aristocracy as well as celebrities and politicians on two continents. Sarah Bernhardt, the stage and early film actress, was a customer in her day."

"Sarah Bernhardt is said to be one of the finest actors of the nineteenth century. You do know that the bar at the Intercontinental is named after her?"

"The Sarah B."

"Have you been?"

"Not yet, but we should definitely go."

"I wonder if they serve Champagne de Venoge?"

"It would be a logical tie-in, and several labels are available in Quebec."

"We'll go find out, when you're back from your wine event in Greece and I from my vacation on the Almalfi Coast."

"It's a date."

"Oh, we could make it a working lunch. How would you like to be technical advisor for wine in my books? I would give you professional credit. Unless you think that your wine producers might pull their business because you're consulting for the author of erotic romance novels."

"My producers are really great people—and they're mostly French. More likely, they would want to meet you. You know, if you were to incorporate luxury wine into your books in a big way, you might end up being a celebrity in the wine world as well. The perfect blend: erotic romance and luxury wine. I can see you getting invited to all of the exclusive events, with the French leading the way with La Jurade de Saint Émilion and Fête de La Fleur." Ela explained the significance of these two gala evenings during Vinexpo while Isla listened intently.

"I'm restricted to the producers that I work with, but when it comes to a famous author of erotic romance books that incorporate luxury wines into the story, the invitations could come from anywhere. I bet a lot of very famous estates will want you to taste their prestigious cuvées and describe them in your novels."

"I could only write about wines that I would not hesitate to recommend in real life."

"Well, of course. As your technical advisor I insist upon it. Integrity is important. It would give you more credibility anyway."

"And I would need your help to do the wines justice."

"It would be fun to work together like that, but I suspect you'll pick things up very quickly. While you would be doing the producers of these wines a tremendous service, on the flip side, you may even sell more books."

"My agent is going to love you."

CHAPTER 25

Ela had just finished *The Claddagh Ring* and would be meeting up with Isla for dinner at Holder on McGill College Avenue. Both women could walk to the European style brasserie from their respective apartments, so it was an easy choice. The sound level was high, but that was part of its dynamic atmosphere. It was a fun place to go when you wanted to have a couple of dishes made with fresh ingredients that were presented in an appetizing way, and could be matched to a decent wine.

Ela was looking forward to discussing various parts of the book with Isla over the salmon tartare. It would be their version of a book club get-together.

"Your ending was beautiful, I get goose bumps just thinking about it. It was so romantic, tender and very hot. And, they lived happily ever after. Very convincing for a woman who does not believe in love."

"I'm a good writer of fiction. What can I say?"

"I particularly liked the little mystical detail of the ring bringing them together. So in fact it could be called an erotic paranormal romance novel."

"The idea came from my aunt. No, she did not speak to me from the dead, if that is what you were hoping to hear. There is an actual Claddagh ring. It once belonged to her. My uncle did not have the money to buy Aunt Isla an engagement ring, so his mother, who was in fact Irish, gave him her engagement ring. All my aunt ever wanted was that ring. She saw no need for a wedding band because the Claddagh ring could serve as either. It was how you wore it on your left hand that made the difference. It's all about the direction of the heart. It had been worn by three generations, I was told, prior to when my aunt received it, so it is quite old. All of the women who wore it at one time or another were deeply in love and had successful marriages—so the legend goes. My aunt became convinced that with so much love flowing through this ring, it had to have magical qualities; she felt that it was a talisman of sorts. Aunt Isla was sure that if a single lady wore it, the ring would act as a beacon and her true love would find her, the man that she was meant to be with. She actually left a note behind, saying so and bequeathing me the ring. My uncle died tragically while she was still a relatively young woman, but she wore it until her death—and never remarried. You would think that my aunt would have wanted to be buried with it, but no. She had no children so she had it sent to my father for me. I was touched but didn't consider it a very attractive piece of jewelry. So, it stayed in a drawer until novel inspiration hit."

"I have never seen you wear it."

"I wore it for Lunch with the Author, on my right hand with the point of the heart facing outward, which is the correct way to wear it, to show that you are a single woman and open to finding love. It was my publicist's idea. He was right, of course. It went over very well with the fans. One group of ladies wanted to touch it, for luck. It's on my finger in the photo on the back of the book too. My publicist, who can be rather smug, told me that he knows for a fact, that Claddagh rings are coming back in fashion in many countries now because of the book. Women are wearing them to advertise that they are single *and* looking.

"I hope I don't have to keep wearing it for all of the upcoming promotional events, but knowing my publicist, he will insist on it. By the next book, people will have forgotten all about it though, and they will move on to the next thing."

"Does that mean you have a title for your next novel?"

"I was thinking *Lavender Roses*."

"I didn't know that roses came in lavender."

"They are not very common, which is part of the appeal for me. I became aware of lavender roses when I was researching for another book. They represent love at first sight. Obviously that's what I'm going for. And they are vintage and modern at the same time. So at my next Lunch with the Author, we will have vases of lavender roses and hand them out to the fans on the way out. My publicist loves the idea. We already have one of the top flower shops in the city ready to sponsor the event."

"Then, lavender roses will be all the rage."

"I'll drink to that." Both women took a sip of wine as a companionable silence settled over them.

"Isla, wouldn't you love to test the theory?"

"What theory?"

"That your aunt's Claddagh ring might hold some magical power."

"I know that my father's people believed in things like that, but I am French on my Mother's side …"

"I dare you to wear it for one month. You'll be making your publicist happy and the fans too. It's built-in credibility. And just to make things interesting, how about a little wager? If you don't meet a man of substance by then, I'll buy the Champagne and oysters. If you do; you buy."

"Fine, if only to prove to you how ridiculous this idea is."

By the end of day three, Isla almost forgot about the Claddagh ring on the fourth finger of her right hand. She was used to chunkier rings, so this little piece of vintage jewelry didn't feel like much of anything. It was neither too loose nor too tight, so it wasn't uncomfortable. It fit her as perfectly as if it had been sized for her hand. It certainly did not have any kind of supernatural glow emanating from it though. In fact the gold was somewhat dull from years of wear. It could be dipped of course, but if she had it restored, it would lose that antique quality that the fans were looking for. It went a long way in stimulating their imaginations about the ring as talisman. Besides, why bother. She wasn't planning to wear it for long.

That night Isla forgot to take the ring off before bed. She fell asleep in minutes and slept well through most of the night. It wasn't until dawn that she started dreaming.

Where was she? There was a woman just several feet away from where Isla was standing. She was familiar. How did she know her? Why was she dressed so strangely? The woman was holding the hand of a little blond boy in short pants who was laughing, and Isla clearly heard the laughter.

They were outdoors, all three of them. The sky was a vivid blue. The lawn was a plush, well-tended carpet of green. There was a wood and wrought iron bench in front of a pond with water lilies floating in no particular pattern on the surface. *How pretty*, thought Isla. The sun was warm but not directly above them. Late afternoon in the summer, Isla surmised. She felt a pleasant breeze caress her cheek and detected the sweet smell of flowers and freshly cut grass. Off to the side was a grayish-white stone mansion with a very long driveway.

The little boy with the clear blue eyes was quite animated. He held out his other hand to try catching a leaf that rode the breeze down from a very old tree.

Suddenly, everything stood still and everything around her went to black and white—everything except for the woman. She looked down at the child, smiling warmly. Then she looked right at Isla as if she recognized her. She smiled the same loving smile and beckoned for Isla to come join them.

It was only then that Isla realized that this woman's hair was a shiny dark copper color, like her own. A gold ring glittered on the hand she beckoned with. It looked just like her ring.

Isla woke, none too gently. She sprang up into a sitting position in bed even before her eyelids opened. When they did open, and her eyes adapted to the dark room, the first place she looked was her right hand. The Claddagh ring was there on her ring finger. Isla pulled it off in a panic without trying to rationalize her action. She heard a clinking sound on the night table where she dropped it unceremoniously.

Isla went into the bathroom with the intention of splashing cold water on her face. Morning light was starting to creep in, and she would have to be up soon anyway, so she might as well get straight into the shower, she decided.

After styling her hair, applying makeup and spraying on her favorite *eau de parfum,* Isla dressed for her meeting later that morning with her publicist. She chose the appropriate accessories but not the Claddagh ring. It clashed with what she was wearing, she told herself.

Isla always looked professional and polished for work, but she had some leeway when it came to her wardrobe. She was not restricted to the kind of business attire that she might have chosen if she were a lawyer or accountant. She was in a creative profession and people expected her to look like one of her stylish characters anyway: current and on the glamorous side. Isla did not disappoint.

She considered eating the first meal of the day at her place, then impulsively called up Ela to see if she was available for breakfast. She was.

Before leaving the apartment, something prompted Isla to go into the French antique secretary desk that had come from her parents' home. She had done her homework on it as a child and it had always held various family mementos. That was still its purpose, but it also served as a decorative piece of furniture and foil to the modern decor of her two-bedroom apartment.

In a frame that was appropriate for the time, there was a photo of her aunt and a little blond boy. Isla had seen this photo a thousand times and never thought to ask who the boy was.

The photo … Isla stared at it for a long time with the dream fresh in her mind. She had kept the photo in the desk since moving into her new place well over a year ago, about the time she was putting final touches on the book. She did not recall going into the drawer at all in that time but surely she must have.

Or perhaps the photo was ingrained in her memory, lingering somewhere in her subconscious mind and shaken loose by all her recent thoughts of her aunt and wearing her ring. Yes, Isla decided, with an imagination like hers, things like this were bound to happen. In fact, it was surprising that they had not already happened at least a half a dozen times. If she told Ela about her dream, Isla knew exactly what Ela would say. She decided she would tell her anyway.

Just before putting the photo back in the desk, Isla compared the composition to what she'd experienced in the dream. Something was nagging at her. The photo was in black and white, of course, but the woman's dress was right, as was the hairstyle, the boy's clothes and expression. The cloudless sky and the expansive lawn were the same in the photo as in her dream. What was very odd though, was that in her dream, she saw the mansion in its entirety and a long gravel driveway. In this photo, she could only make out the side and corner of the building and the angle did not show a driveway. The pond and bench in the dream were not visible in the photo.

There had to be an explanation. In her mind, she could perfectly see the elements that were missing in the photo. Was her writer's brain simply filling in some blanks … embellishing? She did that every day while working. Isla decided to jot down some notes of description, a technique to jolt her memory, should the images fade. Perhaps she could research this house. Isla hated loose ends. She researched things exhaustively for her books. She was driven like that. That was why her work was taken seriously.

When Isla arrived at the Sofitel Hotel, Ela was already seated in the restaurant, reading emails on her smartphone and sipping her first cappuccino of the morning. They had agreed to meet at Renoir because Isla's publicist's office was just across the street. It had made no difference to Ela. She would be spending the day on emails when she got back to her place. And, she liked the *œufs cocotte* at the Renoir.

After the usual two-cheeks kiss greeting, they got down to ordering the two poached eggs with mild goat cheese, prosciutto, tomato coulis and balsamic caramel.

When the server left with their order, Ela turned to Isla. "Okay, what's up? You generally don't get up this early and though you look perfectly composed—to someone who does *not* know you very well—I know something is bothering you."

Isla recounted her dream and how it matched the photo—but not quite.

"You had a visitation. Your aunt was communicating with you. What was she trying to tell you, I wonder?"

"You know, there has to be an explanation other than the paranormal one you are suggesting."

"Isla my dear friend, as a writer, should you not try to keep an open mind? In your books, all things are possible."

"Those stories are fiction. This is real life … my life."

"If you are so convinced this is implausible, why are you not wearing the Claddagh ring? Are you perhaps thinking that if you put it back on, something else will happen that you can't explain away? Why not keep wearing it and find out—one way or another."

When Isla left for her holiday in Positano on the Amalfi coast the following day, the Claddagh ring had not been on her finger. Nor was it among her luggage. It had been left behind … on purpose.

DIANA SOBOLEWSKI

CHAPTER 26

A couple of days later, Ela was off to Greece. Her flight to Athens was uneventful. She had even nodded off for about three hours because her seat, when pulled out, was nearly as comfortable as a bed.

The Champagne and reasonably tasty meal in business class made her rather sleepy. She had been up late the night before packing, and the night before that, doing last minute work on a couple of different projects with Robert.

No matter how many times her director of sales reassured her that he would handle everything, she went to that obsessive-compulsive place when preparing for a trip. It was nerves, anxiety, partly about her work but more about this trip and the presentation … and the fear of flying. At least she was in good shape with the presentation. Ela could do that part effortlessly, though she always stressed about it. She liked being up in front of people talking about what she knew and loved best, her work.

After over five years of working closely together, Robert knew her habits. He knew that she would relax only when the plane was in the air, and only as long as there was no turbulence. If she had forgotten to pack something, there was nothing she could do and she would resign herself to taking care of it at the other end. That was how her mind worked. Prior to cruising altitude, Ela was a bundle of nerves.

Ela Zalewski was an unusual woman, Robert often said to himself. She had these obsessive-compulsive tendencies, but her office was a total mess. On the other hand she knew where to find what she was looking for at any moment. She just could not be bothered to put things away.

"You never know when you are going to need something," she would tell him in a tone of authority and superior insight, daring him to contradict her. The rest of her dwelling was meticulous and she was very methodical when she worked. Ela's mind was uncharted territory. He sometimes thought she might have a split personality.

"Are you sure that you don't want me to take you to the airport?"

"No, that's alright. I booked a cab in advance."

Robert had not heard from Jonas since their face-to-face, and he wondered if Jonas had anything to do with this trip. He suspected so but was glad he didn't have any specifics. Robert hoped that all would go as planned.

Mr. Reimann had sent a car to meet Ela Zalewski's plane. The poor driver almost put out his back when he tried to lift the larger of Ela's bags into the trunk. She had paid extra when she had checked that one in. Ela noticed his strain and vowed to tip him big.

When they arrived at their destination, a porter was on hand to open her door and take her bags out of the trunk. The weight did not seem to bother him. The driver looked relieved. Ela tried to tip the man but he lifted a hand in protest. "It has been taken care of, miss."

Miss? He deserved a tip.

But in fact, the porter was not a porter at all. The letters in script on the front left side of his white polo spelled out the name of the yacht, which identified him as a member of the crew. The athletic young man led Ela into a functional looking building and explained that she would be asked to show her passport and that Mr. Reimann would have some papers for her to sign when he arrived momentarily. In the meantime, he would take her bags on board. The next time she would see them would be in her stateroom. He hoped that she found this satisfactory.

"Well, yes. Of course. Thank you."

A moment later, literally, a tanned man with a muscular build, strong masculine features and a full head of closely cropped, wheat colored hair that had started to turn silver at the temples made his way to her. There was a warm smile on his face, and his blue eyes sparkled merrily. Ela gauged his age to be approximately forty-five. It's not how she pictured Karsten Reimann. She thought she'd be meeting someone more average looking. He grasped her hand in both of his hands.

"Ms. Zalewski, Karsten Reimann. Welcome. I am so happy that you were able to join our little group."

His English was perfect, but there was a faint trace of a Germanic accent. It was familiar to her ear—it reminded her of Torsten.

"I am very happy to be here, Mr. Reimann. Thank you for the invitation."

"Call me Karsten ... please."

"Only if you call me Ela."

"Delighted, Ela. If you would kindly give me your passport, I will present it to the authorities for you. By the way, I must ask you to sign some forms for me and initial the paragraphs as I have already done because I'm responsible for you, as it were. You can take the time to read them if you like. It's just something we have to do for insurance purposes for anyone that comes on board ... you understand?"

Ela was tired and a little bleary eyed. There were three separate documents attached to a clipboard, each one several pages long.

"I don't need to read all of this, Mr. Reimann ... Karsten. I am sure everything is in order."

Mr. Reimann flipped the pages quickly muttering something about bureaucracy being so tedious. Ela had neither the time nor the desire to read any of the legalities. She never noticed that Karsten was breathing a sigh of relief.

Karsten had one of those illegible signatures. He had not written his name in all capital letters on the line below as requested on the forms.

"Oh don't worry about the block letters. I'll give the pages a once-over anyways and add our names at the counter when you're done."

All pages signed and paragraphs initialed, she handed the clipboard over to Karsten. He walked to the counter where a sufficiently bureaucratic-looking man waited. He verified that all of the signatures and initials were there and Karsten added their names in block letters in all of the appropriate places before turning the clipboard over to the official. Ela never noticed that the official took out three loose pages, placed them on top of the three sets of forms and stapled. This made them the first pages of the documents—with the details about the signatories.

When Karsten was done, he steered Ela towards the door at the back of the building which led out to an area where several luxury yachts were moored. Out further, in the middle of the body of water, was the yacht they would be boarding, Karsten told Ela. It dwarfed the others.

Ela put on her new black Chanel sunglasses. The brightness outside was painful to her sleep-deprived eyes. Having taken it all in, she looked a little stunned. Against the backdrop of a cloudless blue sky and deep blue water their yacht dominated the view. It seemed to be the size of an ocean liner.

"Is everything alright, Ela?"

"It's immense."

"She is an impressive vessel, all three hundred feet of her." It was actually three hundred and twenty-eight feet, but he wanted to make sure that he gave her different dimensions in case she remembered the size of Torsten's yacht. The whole crew had been briefed on this point. "I've asked the captain to give you a mini tour before lunch since you'll be the first on board and there will be a little time. There is nothing that he enjoys more. He is very proud of her. There will be a proper tour tomorrow morning after breakfast for the whole group."

"Who does she belong to?"

"A man who values his privacy. The company that rents her out on his behalf for events such as this, respects his wishes and keeps the information confidential. That's all I know, I'm afraid. Although I could put you in touch with the rental company if you're interested."

A landing boat brought them right up to the yacht and a member of the crew sporting the same polo and black pants as the young man she had mistaken for a porter helped her navigate the landing. Another dressed in formal whites helped her on board. Karsten took up the position directly behind her in case she were to lose her balance. Plus the position offered up a nice view of her rather lovely little ass.

"Ela, I would like you to meet the captain."

Ela removed her sunglasses. The captain was an impressive looking man in his late forties, dressed in a white shirt and pants. He was imposing in stature and demeanor with a weather-beaten face and sun-bleached blond hair under the white cap that he removed and tucked under his arm in one crisp motion. He reminder Ela of a Viking, albeit a clean, elegant one. The captain commanded respect to be sure. Ela was acutely aware that he was the law on board.

"Welcome aboard, Ms. Zalewski. I'm Captain Elis Linquist," he said in accented English, while putting out his hand. Ela's small hand disappeared in the firm grip of his massive hand. Scandinavian obviously.

"Thank you, Captain. I am very pleased to meet you." She squinted from the glare of the sun as she looked up, way up into his face. She used her other hand to shield her eyes, not wanting to appear rude by putting her sunglasses back on just yet.

"This is my first mate, Mr. Xavier Martinez." The captain introduced the man to his immediate left, who had also removed his white cap respectfully and tucked it under his arm with the same flare as the captain.

Another weather-beaten face, though younger and framed by black hair. Mr. Martinez appeared to be in his early forties.

He shook her hand next. First Mate Martinez was of average height and weight with hands to match, but his grip was just as firm as the captain's. His accent belied his Spanish heritage.

"Pleased to have you on board, Ms. Zalewski," he said smiling warmly.

"Thank you, Mr. Martinez."

The world of yachts was an international affair, thought Ela. Both men had an air of self-assurance about them that could only come from years of experience. Well that's what you wanted, she supposed. There was a reason that the owner had entrusted such a spectacular yacht to these two men. They certainly seemed capable.

Introductions over with, Ela was glad to put her sunglasses back on. The sun was strong. Thank goodness she had packed her sunscreen.

"I hope that after you have had a chance to freshen up, you will allow me the privilege of showing you around," the captain offered. "The *Second Chance* is an exceptional vessel. There are very few like her. She is what is known as a mega yacht."

"What flag are you flying? I don't recognize it."

"The flag of the Cayman Islands. The *Second Chance* is registered there. Many yachts are registered in the Cayman Islands. The crew will see to your every comfort while you are on board, Ms. Zalewski. You have but to ask. Mr. Logan Fraser, our head steward, will see you to your suite. I hope you will find it to your liking." The captain gestured in the direction of a man who was making his way towards them, in his late thirties, average build, flaming red hair, in his whites but no cap.

"Thank you, Captain. *Second Chance* is an unusual name. Any idea as to the significance?"

"I'm afraid not, Ms. Zalewski. Only the owner would know. He has not chosen to share that particular piece of information."

"I understand from Karsten … from Mr. Reimann that the owner is a very private man. I would assume that you know his identity since he spends a significant time on board? Or at least, I assume that it is a significant time …?"

"You are correct on both accounts, Ms. Zalewski, and I hope you won't be offended, but I am not at liberty to say more."

Ela almost asked the captain to call her Ela, but realized that it would put him in an awkward position and refrained. He would not have considered it appropriate. There were some formalities that simply had to be observed.

Ela took an immediate liking to the head steward. On the way to her suite, she learned that Mr. Fraser hailed from Aberdeen, Scotland; so ships were in his blood, several generations' worth, apparently. She loved the accent and kept him talking—which wasn't very hard.

Mr. Fraser loved his work but missed his home and his parents and five younger brothers. He was not married, but hoped to have a family one day. His brothers were all married, but no nieces or nephews yet. He preferred this climate over the rough frigid waters of the North Sea, she learned.

"Easier on the bones. Not likely to get arthritis sailing these waters," Mr. Fraser told her with an emphatic nod.

"The crew is a tight group," he explained, "because we are all in the same boat … if you know what I mean, ma'am?" Thinking he might have overstepped, he was relieved when Ms. Zalewski responded positively to his sense of humor.

Ela was laughing. Mr. Fraser was unexpected and had a relaxing effect on her. He cleared his throat and continued, "We all have loved ones somewhere and sometimes it can be difficult to be away from them. So we have become a kind of family. We rely on each other and I think we bring out the best in each other. Don't get me wrong, ma'am. We all love our jobs. It's one of those things. When we are working, we think about going home. When we are home, we can't wait to get that call and be together again and out on the open sea. It's a good life, though."

"Is the yacht in use many weeks out of the year?"

"The owner uses her for about six weeks a year."

"Does his family join him on board?"

"The gentleman does not have any family, ma'am."

Suddenly Mr. Fraser cast his eyes to the floor. He was starting to feel uncomfortable. Ela did not want to appear insensitive or overly intrusive and changed the subject, at least for the time being.

Ela's suite was larger and better appointed than some of the suites in five-star hotels that she had stayed in. She asked if this was the owner's suite.

"Oh no, ma'am. This suite is one of the two VIP suites," Mr. Fraser answered with a smile. "The owner's master suite is quite a bit larger and located on the top deck."

"How much larger?" She was incredulous.

"Well let's see … There is the living and dining area that opens up onto a private deck, the prep kitchen and bar, two adjoining bedrooms with his and hers dressing rooms, and his and hers bathrooms and also the owner's office. The master suite has a private lift as well as a private staircase with direct access to the area where we launch our small craft and the helipad. The expansive design includes a panoramic view to the exterior, and it is truly something. Actually the master suite takes up the whole top deck."

"It sounds like a penthouse apartment. The owner could live on this yacht for any period of time, I imagine."

"Are the other agents, producers and Mr. Reimann all staying on this deck?"

"Yes, you and Mr. Reimann have the VIP suites and everyone else will be staying in the double suites."

"Shall I collect you at noon for your tour, Ms. Zalewski? There will be a leisurely lunch at one o'clock on the main deck and then you can retire to your suite for a good rest before this evening's activities."

"That sounds fine. Thank you, Mr. Fraser."

Ela unpacked in the spacious bedroom. She hung her clothes in the oversized wardrobe, arranged her shoes and put away her delicates in the lingerie drawer, then she went to work on organizing her toiletries and cosmetics on the vanity in the bathroom.

Next order of business, back to the bedroom to put her money, jewelry, passport, plane ticket and laptop with tablet function into the safe that was discreetly built into the wardrobe. She hardly thought that someone would rip her off on a private yacht. It was just something she did. It quieted her mind.

Then she went on to familiarize herself with the rest of the VIP suite. In the sitting room, she located a piece of furniture that housed a wet bar, mini fridge and refreshments, including low carb, low cal, high fiber protein bars. Ela was starved. This would keep her going until lunch. She would wash it down with one of several bottles of water and re-hydrate.

Unpacking had been a daunting task in her jet-lagged state, but she was disciplined or, as Robert would say, exhibiting classic obsessive-compulsive behavior.

Ela, who was no stranger to luxury, still found her current situation a bit overwhelming. All of it was for her use. She couldn't even conceive of people living like this.

The large desk of light colored wood with its clean lines did not face a wall and have a chair tucked under it to save space. It faced out into the center of the sitting room. There was an executive leather chair and more cabinetry. There was even a sofa to fit three people, and a big comfortable chair with ottoman flanked by a couple of decorative tables, all in gentle beiges and neutrals, save for the occasional black accent piece that anchored the area ... *Anchored?* A nautical reference. Mr. Fraser was rubbing off on her, Ela mused, though she probably wouldn't be able to carry it off as well as he could.

The few black accents drew the eye and gave the suite a look of richness and depth was what she meant. In interior design, it was a thing to do. Everyone knew that.

The artwork on the walls and the stone sculptures were contemporary but Ela could not identify the movement or artists. It was not her area of expertise. Still the whole effect was pleasing. On a low glass coffee table, calla lilies, their long thick stems crisscrossed in a low round clear crystal vase only half filled with water, pulled it all together for a look of sublime sophistication. Ela liked the effect; she would be quite comfortable here.

The colors and textures carried over to the bedroom. The bed looked bigger than any king she could ever remember seeing, including her own. The linens, though simple in style, were freshly pressed and obviously of a very high thread count. The polished wood tables, tufted neutral leather headboard and glass lamps with streamlined shades gave the bedroom that contemporary comfortable look. Nothing stark or cold about this room either.

Though the VIP suite was huge, it was welcoming. The wide planked teak floor transmitted a feeling of warmth as did the luxurious silk and wool area rugs.

Only when she had completed her moving-in ritual, did Ela step into the dramatic marble shower with double showerheads and built-in seat for when a guest would like to unwind with *a steam.*

There was also a double soaking tub, double sink vanity and a separate toilet and bidet. The fixtures were modern and there was an unrestrained use of marble in this bathroom. Two people sharing this suite would not be bumping into each other, one could positively get lost in it.

It struck Ela as a little unusual that everything in the VIP suite seemed new, like it had never been used before. It even smelled new.

CHAPTER 27

Refreshed, dressed in a pair of skinny white jeans, Ela pulled on a very fine knit, off the shoulder silver metallic sweater with three quarter sleeves. The air-conditioning was quite effective on this yacht.

Donning a pair of silver leather, soft rubber soled wedge sandals, she reached for a white cross-body bag. It would not be cumbersome but could still hold her smartphone, card key, sunglasses and lipstick.

Ela had left her hair loose but brought along a clip in case part of the tour would take them outside. She had applied light makeup, and the freshly scrubbed look suited her. She looked rested, healthy and youthful.

Mr. Fraser met her in the hallway and together they re-traced their steps from earlier but only about halfway, until they were in front of a glass lift.

"The captain is on the bridge. He thought you would enjoy the view from there.

Lift or the stairs, ma'am?"

"The stairs, please. I'd like to stretch my legs."

"You may want to reconsider when moving about with the captain. He takes them two at a time."

"Noted. Thanks, Mr. Fraser."

A couple of chambermaids passed them as they headed for the staircase. Two young South American women, about twenty years of age, hair neatly tied back in ponytails. They looked alike. They also giggled when addressing Ela with a "Good afternoon, ma'am."

"Good afternoon," Ela replied.

"Sisters, Mr. Fraser?"

"Twins … Argentinian. They have been with us for about a year. It's like the United Nations around here. We get to learn about each other's cultures."

The captain looked a little pre-occupied when they arrived. He was poring over maps on a large interactive screen with Mr. Reimann and they were speaking in hushed tones. Two other members of the bridge crew were busy with what appeared to be navigational equipment. Mr. Fraser cleared his throat to announce them.

"Oh, Ms. Zalewski, I'm sorry. I was just going over some final details with Mr. Reimann."

"If this is a bad time, Captain …"

"Nonsense, my dear," Karsten answered instead. "Everything is coming together as planned. I've already taken up enough of the captain's time. I will leave you to your little tour of the *Second Chance* and look forward to seeing you this evening. Let us say, six thirty on deck. Everyone should be on board by three thirty. We'll be casting off at four thirty and expect to arrive at our evening's destination at six."

"That would be great, Karsten. I'm looking forward to meeting everyone."

"Now, Ms. Zalewski." Captain Linquist took charge. "Let me show you what it is we do here on the bridge."

The captain and Ela visited the galley, or kitchen, and met the chefs that ran it with military precision. They were a husband and wife team confusingly named Chef Vasseur and Chef Vasseur. So, everyone referred to them as Chef Celeste and Chef Pol. They obviously ran a *tight ship* ... Oh God, Ela could not help herself. She blamed Mr. Fraser again. At least she had not said it out loud.

The couple was from Beaune in Burgundy where they had run a successful, well-known restaurant for a few years and eventually turned it over to other family members. Then they had lived in Australia and the U.S. for several years prior to signing on with the crew of the *Second Chance*. Ela switched to French and told them that she was very familiar with the Burgundy region, much to their delight. Ela found out that with a staff of two, they prepared meals for not only the guests on board, but the whole crew as well.

The couple also purchased all of their ingredients personally whenever the yacht came into port. Suppliers who specialized in delivering the freshest ingredients to yachts like the *Second Chance* had learned the hard way not to deliver anything that was not absolutely the freshest. The captain had filled Ela in as they were approaching the galley.

This husband and wife team had exacting standards, he had gone on to say, and did not hesitate to turn away a delivery that disappointed. A tirade in English mixed with French would follow to demonstrate their displeasure. To know their wrath was one thing, but they had even blacklisted some repeat offenders. Those with whom they continued to do business, and were willing to pay top dollar to, held their breath as they inspected every ingredient that came on board. A nod was good. They would settle their account right away. Waving *all* of the boxes away was not.

The Chefs Vasseur in turn, introduced her to the sommelier, François who hailed from Tour. Ela was no expert on the Loire Valley, but she had stopped there for a mini three-day vacation one year. Their guest expressed an interest in seeing the wine cellar and François was happy to oblige. The captain followed behind, having been forewarned this was something that Ms. Zalewski would request.

The trio walked down a short, very dimly lit hallway towards total darkness as the sommelier took the lead. François passed his hand over a mechanism and a glass room became visible. He punched in a code on a key pad, and a glass door slid open in front of them. As they walked through the door, sensors picked up their movement and lit up one section at a time. The area they stood in was gently lit, while the area they had passed dimmed. The sommelier needlessly explained that the cellar was state-of-the-art. It was temperature and humidity controlled. It could accommodate five thousand bottles with additional space for larger formats and a section for cases. A computer program kept track of the inventory.

All very impressive but it was the inventory that made Ela swoon. Wines from Bordeaux, Burgundy, Champagne and other regions of France were well represented as were the most famous wines of Italy, Spain, Australia and the United States. Ela recognized the labels of Lafite, Latour, Raveneau, La Tâche, Krug, Gaija, Vega Sicilia, Pingus, Penfolds La Grange, Kistler … But, it was the Merlot based right bank Bordeaux wines that held her attention the longest: Petrus, Ausone, Angélus, Pavie, Figeac … Torsten would have been happy here. She dismissed the thought quickly.

On the same level, there was a formal dining room that could sit twenty-four at one long table or three round tables depending on the occasion. They had been known to host a lot more than that in different configurations when necessary. They could open up everything through to the deck, and built-in heaters would make guests forget all about the cool night breezes. The maximum number of guests that they had welcomed on board at one time had been forty-eight, the captain had explained, and it had been quite manageable. They even had room for live music, a dance floor and bar. Though limited as to the number of overnight guests that they could accommodate comfortably, they could host a larger group for an evening.

Breakfast and lunch would be taken outside on the adjoining deck, Ela was told.

Adjacent to the formal dining room was a sumptuously furnished living area with floor to ceiling windows and a fireplace. There were armchairs, ottomans, sofas and side tables throughout. This was where Ela could partake of conversation and enjoy an after dinner drink.

Ela was commenting on the extraordinary view, when the captain's eyes darted to one of the side tables. Under the lamp shade, in a heavy silver frame, was a photo of Mr. Furst and Mr. Koertig on the yacht in her previous incarnation as the *Lara*.

There had been photos of Mr. and Mrs. Furst at one time, but those had been removed when they divorced. This was the only photo that was still displayed.

It was one of those things. The crew was so used to seeing it there for so long, they just didn't notice it anymore. No one had remembered to hide it while Ms. Zalewski was on board.

The captain directed Ela out onto the deck. She never noticed that he was trying to catch the eye of a deckhand that happened to be walking by. He made himself understood with a scowl and a tilt of the head in the direction of that particular end table. The deckhand acknowledged with a barely discernable nod, silently crossed the room, picked up the frame and slipped away just as silently. Ela was none the wiser. The captain continued with the tour.

Ela got to see the full gym and meet the trainer on duty. There was also the spa and wellness center, which included massage facilities, a hair salon, an area for manicures and pedicures and professional makeup application. There were two multi-talented people assigned to these services.

Next on the list, a movie theater that could easily be transformed for live performances and an intimate night club with small stage of its own and equipment for a DJ. It would work for a small live band equally well. That was the trick whenever possible, the captain had explained, "To be able to convert a space from one purpose to another." For the purpose of this trip, the theater would serve as a meeting room for their presentations during the day.

Tomorrow, Ela was informed, the tour would include the crew's quarters; where they slept, ate, exercised and relaxed … without invading anyone's privacy the captain assured her. They would spend some time in the enormous engine room and meet the chief engineer. This was his domain, she had been told, so he would be the one giving the tour at that point. It gave him great pleasure to relay the impressive technical specifications, at least according to the captain.

"You will also be shown the garage. This is where the two small crafts that ferry guests and crew between the yacht and shore will be tucked away when everyone is on board the *Second Chance*."

The group would also see the helicopter stored under the helipad and get a demonstration of how they get it topside. She was told that when the *Second Chance* was on open water or when the weather was inclement, the helicopter was protected from the elements there. This also left the space topside free for a visiting helicopter. Two pilots were on board full-time. They were on call in shifts. They also did the maintenance and made sure the helicopter was flight ready at all times. They would be on hand for any questions. First Mate Martinez was a licensed helicopter pilot too, she was told. Also on the list would be the infirmary and the doctor and nurse on call, who were another husband and wife team, and would show them the latest in medical equipment on board. Ela wondered what they did with their time when they had no patients, but was comforted by the knowledge that they were on board.

After, the tour ... lunch. Ela ate her lightly seasoned grilled shrimp and mixed vegetables brushed with olive oil alone. Everyone was busy it seemed, and the others would be arriving about the time she had planned to nap. In the meantime, she was grateful for lunch. She needed some high quality protein about now.

They had prepared the shrimp with a squirt of lemon and forgone the garlic, as Ela had requested. The chilled dry Greek white wine from indigenous grapes was so delicious she had three glasses. Ela correctly identified the wine as one hundred percent Assyrtiko from Santorini.

It was a pale yellow because it was young. The nose was fruity and slightly vegetal, so it worked with all of the ingredients. On the palette there was sufficient acidity to give the wine freshness but it was rounder than she had expected. The fact that it was a medium bodied wine worked well with the richness of the shrimp. It had a nice long finish ... and it was ready to drink. It was also quite an easy wine to drink she was discovering.

They just kept filling her glass. A server would appear from nowhere and voilà, another glass. On very little sleep it went to her head quickly.

Karsten had stopped by and apologized for not being able to join her. There was still much to do, he had said. The producers were counting on him and everyone seemed to be slightly behind schedule. He needed for this to work to get his agency off to a strong start. Having been there herself, he said, he was sure she would understand. She did.

Karsten went on to say that he came looking for her because it had completely slipped his mind to tell her that the evening ahead had a white theme. Did she have anything suitable to wear?

"Well yes, but it is a very fitted dress. Very restrictive hemline. Not good for climbing in and out of a boat. The sandals are not exactly ideal for a beach either ... I was thinking to wear it on our last evening on the yacht."

"Nonsense, my dear. The pilot is more than capable of helping you in and out of the boat. You can wear the cotton slip-ons we have on the yacht until you reach the other side. There is a boardwalk that connects the dock to a large deck. You'll be walking on an even surface. The whole thing is covered with a decorative material that is in fact very sturdy. Even with stilettos, you'll be fine. If it is too much of an imposition, I will understand, of course."

"No, it's okay. Thank you for letting me know."

"Thank you for getting into the spirit, Ela. You're a great sport."

What Ela did not know was that while the captain was showing her around, Karsten, using his master key card, had let himself into her suite. Without disturbing anything, he'd looked through her belongings. What had she brought on board that would make her look even more irresistible to Torsten? It didn't take too long before he located the ideal dress. It would show off her assets to perfection. He knew just how he was going to get her to wear it.

Between the effect of the wine, the fresh air and the jet lag, a nap was definitely in order. She wouldn't have much time to rest, Ela calculated, but she would make the most of it.

This was her first time on a yacht, but certainly not in this type of situation. She had it down to a fine art. She would set the alarm on her television in the bedroom and her backup alarm that she had packed. She always did that.

Ela would lay out the dress and accessories ahead of time. She would take another quick shower, put some hot rollers in her hair for volume and devote the rest of the time to makeup. She would need an evening look to go with the dress that Karsten had talked her into wearing.

Well it was worth doing it right. Knowing she looked her very best would allow her to tackle whatever lay ahead that evening.

She slept hard … mostly. She also dreamed a little. Ela fought waking when the alarms went off, one after the other. She pulled the covers up to her chin and remained in bed. She was between dream state and consciousness. Ela was disoriented for a moment. She thought that she and Torsten were together in bed in Rome …

Something went off in her brain. Ela realized she had to get out of bed now or risk being late.

With heavy eyelids and a body to match, she dragged herself out of bed. Sheer willpower got her into the shower. Oh crap, she had gotten her hair wet. She had forgotten to put the shower cap on. Ela resigned herself to the fact that she would have to wash it all over again now. That meant more time in the shower than she had wanted to spend. She would need to style it all over again too and the other guests were probably already on board.

CHAPTER 28

In the shower fighting for control of her body and mind, Ela was not to know that a helicopter had landed on the yacht's helipad. It was different from the dark blue one that was secured in the garage below the helipad.

This helicopter, equally large and just as powerful, was also built to cover great distances quickly. It was a different model though and the paint color was battleship gray. Like the yacht's in-house pilots, this pilot was specifically trained to land on yachts even in windy conditions, though today was not especially windy. This helicopter belonged to a company that serviced yachts all around the area.

The man who got out on the front passenger side was dressed in casual clothes. He wore them in an easy way, white cotton pants, dark blue windbreaker, dark blue polo and dark blue slip-on shoes with rubber soles, no socks. Expensive looking silver rimmed aviator glasses and a platinum Rolex with bracelet completed his attire. The black leather Berluti briefcase was the only thing that looked out of place, but Torsten Lucas Furst was rarely seen without it.

Captain Linquist, First Mate Martinez, and Head Steward Fraser were on deck to greet him as was their custom. They were joined by Mr. Karsten Reimann, aka Jonas Koertig. Everyone waited until the helicopter departed before any kind of verbal exchange.

Flying in was the best part for Torsten. He could really enjoy the view of the *Second Chance* from the air and she was looking better than ever. Something struck him as strange though. Torsten had expected to see three or four half-naked women on the main deck, with Jonas right in the middle.

Yacht business attended to, the captain, first mate and head steward returned to their posts, and Torsten turned to Jonas. "It's rather quiet on board. Who are you and what have you done with Jonas Koertig?"

Smiling innocently, as if he did not know what Torsten was talking about, Jonas responded only with, "Everyone that needs to be on board is."

Torsten frowned at Jonas's evasive reply. That wasn't much in the way of an explanation. He wondered if perhaps he was conserving his energy for tonight. Perhaps his guests were as well.

"Why don't you go to your suite, check in with your office, read your emails, freshen up and meet me at six down below." Jonas pointed to the deck they would launch the small craft from. "You must have seen the activity as you flew over the island. That's where we are having the party you are throwing me. I need you to act as host on the island, while I get everyone out there. The caterers will be done by the time you get there. The crew will take care of the guests later on."

"Why a tiny, uninhabited island in the middle of nowhere, may I ask, Jonas? Why not on the yacht?"

"Anyone can have a party on a yacht."

"Anyone? Oh, really? Sometimes, Jonas …" Torsten was at a loss.

When they had flown towards the island that Jonas was referring to, on the way to the *Second Chance*, Torsten had been able to tell that it was quite small. At first it had appeared to be totally deserted. All he was able to make out was some sparse vegetation, which included a limited number of trees. The rest of the island was made up of some rocky hilly terrain and a sandy beach. It was rather pretty though.

As the helicopter had gotten closer, a canvas tent had come into view. Several smaller canvas structures had been erected just beside it. People had been scurrying around, their arms full. They were likely the caterers. The whole thing sat on some sort of deck and the deck was connected to the dock by a boardwalk.

Since it did not look like there were any permanent structures on this tiny island, everything must have been constructed for Jonas and his guests. This was going to be expensive.

Torsten focused once more on Jonas's odd behavior. With Jonas, there was odd, and then there was *odd*. This was the latter and it was on a whole different level. It was as if Jonas were deliberately trying to get him out of the way. Suggesting that he go work rather than join him for a glass of Champagne that would have eventually become the whole bottle was definitely not his friend's style. Torsten frowned thoughtfully. He did have to make a few calls in any case, and avoiding Jonas's guests for a while longer suited him fine.

CHAPTER 29

While Ela was still in the shower, they were underway. She only realized that the *Second Chance* had taken to open water when she noticed that the view had changed. No dock now, only water.

Satisfied with her appearance in the full length mirror, Ela looked for her smartphone. She did not recollect where she had left it in her fatigued state. A second of panic overtook her, but then she spied it on the desk.

Ela knew that though she was completely dependent on this device for her business, as were most people, it was more than that. There were photos, text messages and emails that she had saved. She had never quite been able to make herself delete anything that was part of her short love affair with Torsten. Though Ela found it too painful to look at the photos or read the texts and emails these days, she felt an attachment to them. It's like she carried the best part of their relationship with her.

For a split second, she wondered where Torsten was at this moment. What part of the world? Was he nearby? What was he doing? Did he ever think of her?

Ela knew she had to stop these kinds of thoughts immediately. To distract herself, she decided to check her emails. No signal. That distressed her. She would ask Karsten about it later.

Smiling at herself in the mirror hands on hips was a technique she used to help put her in a different state of mind. It worked and Ela made it out the door looking like she hadn't a care in the world.

Having had a brief tour of the *Second Chance*, Ela was able to find her bearings quickly and proceeded with vigor to the deck where she was to meet the group. She had replaced silver metallic leather sandals with the white cotton deck slippers that she found at the bottom of the wardrobe in her bedroom. She carried the sandals she would wear later by their ankle straps in addition to the matching leather clutch.

The only one she found on deck though was Mr. Fraser. It looked like he had been waiting for her.

Casting an admiring glance in her direction, but careful to remain professional, Mr. Fraser greeted her politely.

"I hope you had a good rest, Ms. Zalewski."

"Yes, thank you, Mr. Fraser. Where is everyone?" She looked puzzled.

"Mr. Reimann is already on the island. It was a last minute thing. The others will be along shortly. Mr. Reimann left instructions that I should advise him when the first of your group arrived on deck. That would be you, ma'am."

With that he brought a high-tech black walkie-talkie with thick antenna up to his mouth. She did not know what it was made of, but the casing looked pretty indestructible. Ela had seen several members of the crew using these while others used a hands-free version with a headset. Well with three hundred feet to cover, reliable communications equipment was a necessity.

"Ms. Zalewski is the first, sir." Karsten asked Mr. Fraser to pass the device over to Ela and Mr. Fraser had responded with, "Yes, sir."

After showing her very quickly how to hold and operate it, he handed the walkie-talkie to Ela.

"I'm here, Karsten."

"I'm sure Mr. Fraser told you that I am already on the island. I had to check on a couple of things before everyone got here. Would you mind joining me … to taste the wine and to see if it is at the right temperature? It's not really my forte. I'll send the boat back for you. We're down to one boat … Something about a problem with the engine of the second boat. They don't expect to have it running until much later. We'll have to make multiple trips with the one. Thank goodness it did not fail at the same time."

"Certainly, Karsten." With that Ela handed the walkie-talkie back to its rightful owner.

The pilot helped Ela into the boat slowly and carefully. She felt overdressed and her movements were hampered. She had not planned to wear a garment that fit so close to the body to this dinner. She had brought along a wispy sheath with asymmetrical hem and a pair of wedge sandals for the island. She had not considered that it might be chilly at night and neglected to bring anything to wear over her shoulders.

The sun would start setting in a couple of hours out here. It would be a breathtaking sunset. For now Ela kept her black Chanel sunglasses on for protection against the wind as much as the reflection of the fading sun on the water. She had tied a silk Hermès scarf 1950s style over her head and around to the back of her neck. This way she did not have to hold her hair as she had done getting to the yacht this morning. She hoped that it would stay in place.

Torsten was fiddling with the controls of one of the refrigeration units in one of the smaller tents. It appeared to be dead but he was unsure why that was his problem. He didn't know what he was doing. Jonas had asked him to check a few things, and all but shoved him in the boat and pushed it off.

The caterers had also departed. The galley crew was delayed by an emergency of their own making. The boat pilot had gone back almost immediately to stand by for other passengers. Torsten was the only one on-site. He was their only resource, Jonas had told him.

Torsten was relaying the readings on the unit to Jonas and Jonas, in turn, was consulting one of the galley crew for instructions on how to get it to function before they had a disaster on their hands. Torsten suggested they simply stay on the yacht but Jonas did not even dignify that with a response.

As the boat came closer to shore, the pilot cut the engine and allowed it to come in with the tide. After securing the boat to the dock, the pilot helped Ela out and offered his arm so she could steady herself while she slipped into her sandals. He hopped back into the boat with great haste, explaining that he had to go back immediately as they had the use of only this boat. The other was out of commission.

"Yes, I know. That's fine."

Torsten heard the engine of the departing boat. He had not heard it come in but then he'd been on the walkie-talkie with Jonas. Finally, they had sent someone.

He made his way from the other side of the deck because the view of the beach was blocked by the tent and the other structures.

Some of his vision was still obstructed by a couple of trees, but it was quickly apparent that there was a woman walking up the boardwalk.

Torsten took in the woman coming his way. She seemed classier than Jonas's usual party guests, wearing a head scarf and dark glasses Jackie O style. The silhouette was very familiar. White bandage dress with straps and a modest neckline hugging the gentle curves of her slender body. Great legs, nice ankles, stiletto sandals. But why had Jonas sent over a guest? And, why was there no one with the sense on his yacht to stop him and send over a crew member instead?

The woman stopped and tucked her clutch under her arm. Head down, she reached behind her head to loosen the knot of her scarf. She pulled it off in one motion and fluffed her hair. Bringing her head up, off came her sunglasses.

Ela. Who else could pull off a Hervé Léger dress on a deserted island? In white she looked fresh, summery, feminine and sophisticated. The French Riviera came to Torsten's mind. It was the way the bandage dress fit her like a second skin and the way she moved in it that would get anyone's attention. That's exactly why she wore Hervé Léger.

Ela was wrong about one thing though. She swore that when she put on a Hervé Léger dress, it gave her an instant dose of confidence ... transformed her. Torsten knew she did not give herself enough credit. These dresses just helped her to express who she already was.

When Ela turned to see how far the small boat had gotten, the dress with the modest neckline now gave off a whole different aura. The back plunged all the way to her shapely ass. There was no way she was wearing anything under it. This one would be his favorite, Torsten decided.

Ela was advancing again. She had not seen him yet, but Torsten knew she was here for him. She had to be, he thought. Jonas must have convinced her to give him another chance. How? When? No matter. Jonas had his ways. This was all part of a plan then. He was meant to be out here alone. There would be no guests. Torsten's mind was reeling. He stepped out of the shadows smiling, his heart gladdened that she had agreed to come. Judging by what she chose to wear, Ela was in a receptive frame of mind.

The blond man only a few yards ahead in beige cotton pants, single button checkered beige and blue silk and linen sports jacket with contrasting orange pocket square, blue cotton shirt and brown slip-ons was not Karsten, yet his stance was very familiar to Ela.

Ela no longer advanced, nor did she retreat. If she tried to take a step, her knees would buckle. Her mind tried to assimilate what her eyes were telling her. Torsten was smiling at her. He was expecting her.

"You look incredible, Ela. I am so glad you came," Torsten said while advancing towards her.

"You finally pulled it off, Torsten. A scheme so nefarious that the previous two, though well thought out, pale by comparison."

"Ela, you think that I lured you out here?"

"You've done it before, Torsten. It seems there is no shortage of people willing to be deceitful on your behalf. What did you offer Karsten Reimann? Or did you just buy his company?"

"I really don't know anything about this. I was just thinking you came of your own accord, to surprise me. I don't know any Karsten Reimann ... Wait, is he by any chance about my age and my height and build with closely cropped blond hair that is starting to turn silver at the temples?"

"So you do know him?"

Jonas's new toy covered the distance between the yacht and island in no time. Ela's and Torsten's attention was diverted to the beach by a whooshing sound. Air displacement.

A black object the size of a microwave oven was hovering about twelve feet above the boardwalk, roughly ten feet away from them. It was suspended in midair by four equally balanced oversized propellers. At its center were two lenses, each a different size and underneath, a metallic grill. It looked like a giant crab ... something from a sci-fi film where machines take over the world. One of the lenses moved. It seemed to be studying them.

"What the hell …?" The words came out of Torsten's mouth.

"The latest in drone technology … interactive," the giant crab replied. It talked. The words came across clearly—surprising considering the sound from the propellers.

"There's your Karsten. Only his name is not Karsten."

"Who is he? Is he with some government spy agency?"

"Worse. A bored billionaire and my best friend, Jonas Koertig."

"You keep strange company."

"He grows on you. It's just that he has an obscene amount of money and a lot of time on his hands. By the way, no spy agency would ever have him."

"I wouldn't be so sure." The giant crab sounded offended.

"You wouldn't be able to follow orders."

"I have a brilliant mind."

"He's quoting what they said about him in a business magazine. He has a very high IQ, you see."

"So your friend is one of those demented geniuses, then?"

"You could look at it that way. But, he does use his powers for good occasionally. Where did you get the drone, Jonas?"

"Thank you, Torsten. I borrowed it, but I'm thinking of keeping it. You look ravishing this evening, my dear," the drone addressed Ela. "So now you know that you were brought on the yacht and out to the island under false pretenses. Before you start hurling accusations at Torsten, let me assure you that he knew nothing about this. For my plan to work, you both had to be kept in the dark."

"But the crew was in on it?"

"Every single one of them. I could not have done it without their help."

"That performance on the yacht … worthy of *Masterpiece Theatre*. You went to a lot of trouble, Mr. Koertig."

"Nice of you to say. I dabbled in university. Shakespeare. Please call me Jonas."

"I wasn't trying to be nice. *Midsummer Night's Dream?* You played the part of Puck?"

"Why yes, Ela. How did you guess?"

"Same personality type: meddling. Call me Ms. Zalewski."

The drone ignored that last bit. "I had to intervene because the two of you were making a mess of things."

"This is none of your business, Jonas." This time it was Torsten who argued with the drone.

"You, Torsten, were losing the only woman who could truly make you happy. As for you, Ela … Has life really been so wonderful for you without Torsten in it? Pride, stubbornness, I do not know what it is with the two of you. Each of you is obviously miserable without the other. This is your chance. Talk it out over Champagne. A lovely meal is awaiting you—in the refrigeration unit that we did not sabotage. The one with the working generator. The tent will provide you with accommodations for the night and you can freshen up in the adjoining structures."

"You expect us to spend the night here?"

"You have everything you need. A boat will come to get you tomorrow morning but not too early."

"I demand that you send a boat right now," Ela sternly told the machine.

"No can do. I have given most of the crew the night off. The captain and I are going to play that game of chess we've always talked about while we drink Torsten's Hardy Perfection Grand Champagne Cognac and smoke his Cohibas … with a small wager to make things interesting. Some of the crew were talking about a poker game and there will be a showing of *The Scarlet Pimpernel* in the theater. The remake. I understand it's one of your favorite films, Ela. Witty repartee, a compelling love story …"

How did he know about The Scarlet Pimpernel? She was just about to ask, when Torsten interrupted, "You gave the crew on my yacht the night off? My crew?"

"That's right. So don't bother trying to get them on the walkie-talkie with any orders. Just so you know, there won't be any vessels coming within range of your walkie-talkie until tomorrow morning. Don't waste your time when you have better things to do. With that I must bid you good evening."

The drone climbed another five feet before retreating at a deliberately slow pace into the sunset.

Jonas looked at his watch and then at the captain, first mate and head steward. "Pay attention, gentlemen." They fixed their eyes on the large screen. The drone was still broadcasting.

Soft non-intrusive mood music could be heard coming from the island, due to the drone's superior sound detection capabilities, just as the manufacturer had promised. The warm glow of a dozen lanterns lit by invisible hands filled the screen. The conspirators all smiled at one another.

"Timers," shared Jonas. "And now for the pièce de résistance." A fire pit came alive with gold and red flickering flames. "There is something primal about fire," and with that last statement, Jonas brought the drone back.

The captain was quick to point out something no one in the room had taken notice of. "Mr. Furst knows as well as any of us that he could use the walkie-talkie to get someone from another vessel or island out there if he really wanted to. He has decided to play along."

Ela looked around. It could have been staging for a photo shoot for one of those luxury travel websites or glossy lifestyle magazines. "Your friend deserves a good thrashing." Her tone was not as convincing as she had intended. It was hard to be outraged when their environment was so appealing.

"I'd throw him in the brig, but I didn't have one put in when the yacht was being re-fitted. An oversight. I have not eaten since breakfast. I'm famished. Shall we have a bite? It would be a shame to waste the Champagne. Come, you can tell me all about you and Karsten Reimann. I'm sure it will be interesting."

"And you can tell me how the *Lara* came to be the *Second Chance* and how a seemingly intelligent man fell for whatever it is that Jonas told you to get you here." She took a halfhearted shot.

"So, Ms. Zalewski, if you were stranded on a deserted island and could only have one wine for the duration, what would that be?"

He had remembered. Now in turn, he was asking her ... Now that they were stranded on an *actual* deserted island. She could appreciate his timely sense of humor.

"Champagne de Venoge Cordon Bleu Extra Brut."

"Let's see what's for dinner," and with that pulled out an impressive platter of shucked oysters. "I think we are supposed to have our appetizers over there on the sofa under the awning in front of the fire pit. That's where they put out the ice bucket and the empty bowl for discarded shells."

Torsten placed the platter of oysters on the low rustic wooden table in front of the comfy shabby chic sofa with its overstuffed cushions. Not bad for outdoor furniture.

"We're going to have to rough it and serve ourselves this evening." He got a smile out of her.

Torsten was already popping the cork of the Champagne bottle that he pulled from its ice water bath before Ela noticed that they were going to be drinking Champagne de Venoge Cordon Bleu Extra Brut with the oysters. Too stunned to say anything, Ela just accepted the glass that Torsten had poured.

The Champagne was fresh and with a hint of white fruit and lemon on the nose and palette, just as she remembered. Superb pairing.

Ela waited for Torsten to fill his own glass. She knew those glasses. They were directly from Maison de Venoge. They were the shape of their Louis XV flacons, only upside down. While flutes were elegant looking and allowed one to admire the fine persistent bubbles of good Champagne, a glass that was less restrictive and closer to a wineglass was the best way to appreciate Champagne. This made perfect sense when one remembered that Champagne was, after all, wine.

Torsten raised his glass to make a toast. Ela hoped it wasn't going to be something that would make her uncomfortable.

Torsten kept it light. "To the woman I most want to be stranded on a deserted island with."

Ela was relieved and held up her glass in response, but did not make a toast of her own. Instead she took her first sip. "As good as I remember. I like the style of this particular Extra Brut. It's not quite bone dry. It's just a touch richer, but that makes all of the difference."

Torsten took a sip next and nodded in approval. "What's the *assemblage?*"

"Fifty percent Pinot Noir, twenty-five percent Pinot Meunier and twenty-five percent Chardonnay."

Torsten urged Ela to try an oyster.

"I don't think I have ever had these. I don't recognize them. They are huge. It will be impossible to eat them delicately."

"I believe they are the famous wild flat Cancale oysters. Very hard to get. I've only had them in France. Jonas must have had to pull some strings to get these here. The logistics would be mind-boggling."

"I know about these natural oysters from Brittany with their nutty flavor. I have always wanted to try them … with the Cordon Bleu Extra Brut. Oh, and they really are as good as advertised." Ela found that she had to take bites. They were just too big to handle any other way. "Are you sure Jonas is not with some sort of spy agency? This can't be a coincidence."

"Not to my knowledge … though he seems to have these connections that I have always wondered about."

The Champagne and oysters went down easily over the details of how Jonas got each of them to cooperate with him. When Ela got to the part about the white theme … it dawned on her that he had orchestrated what she would be wearing this evening. He had gone through her wardrobe. The man had no shame.

"I can't fault him there, Ela. You look amazing." He meant sexy as hell, but held back.

"Thank you, Torsten." She smiled shyly, a little self-conscious but pleased. "You look very handsome. Did Jonas pick out your clothes as well?"

"Jonas did not go quite that far with me. So, shall we have a look and see what they prepared for us in the way of a main course? I'm still hungry."

They had been making small talk in between bites and glasses of the Extra Brut. Mostly about what Ela had seen on her tour with the captain.

This time, Torsten returned with two plates. The main course, chunks of lobster, had already been plated for them. Ela adored lobster salad in the summer.

"Okay if we have the rest of our dinner here? We only need a fork. I saw some forks and some napkins too. I'll be right back."

It was fine with Ela. She didn't feel like moving over to the long table that was set up for the nonexistent agents and wine producers. Or, from Torsten's account of events, Jonas's supposed birthday party guests.

Ela followed to see if she could find them some wine. There was a second ice bucket covered with a white linen napkin and a set of glasses in the prep area. She knew the neck of that bottle: Champagne de Venoge Louis XV Brut 1996, a magnificent Champagne and one of the best vintages in recent history. So it was going to be a Champagne evening … gutsy pairing. Lobster sure, but in a salad … she wasn't so sure.

Ela poured a little to taste realizing they had forgotten to do that with the Extra Brut. There had been nothing wrong with it, but it was always wise to check, with any wine. There was absolutely nothing wrong with the Louis XV Brut 1996 either. It was perfection: A voluptuous Champagne on a carpet of fine bubbles. It had evolved nicely, but one could easily lay it down for many more years. Ela filled the second glass. She was interested in what Torsten would think of it.

Ela thought that it would be polite to make a toast this time. She was feeling more relaxed … more like herself. "To the man who is pretty good company on a deserted island."

Torsten took a sip and nodded his approval for the second time that evening. "I imagine you can tell me about this one as well?"

"Fifty percent Pinot Noir, fifty percent Chardonnay. Grand Cru vineyards. Aged ten years. The flacon pays homage to King Louis XV who allowed Champagne to be transported for the first time in history. Some say he was highly motivated, something about supplying his mistress. The 1996 vintage has been called the vintage of the century in the appellation. I really love this one. I just don't know if it's going to work with the salad part of the lobster salad. Well, only one way to find out."

Her reservations dissipated with the first forkful. It would work fine. The delicate flavor of vanilla bean in the dish put everything into perspective.

They went on to talk about Jonas and some of his escapades over the years. Ela had to admit that they were amusing stories. She could see that though the two men had different priorities, they had a real bond. It was true friendship. It made her soften her opinion of Jonas.

They came to the topic of how the *Lara* came to be the *Second Chance*. This was a little more difficult for Torsten to talk about. He did not want to bring up his ex-wife. They were having such a pleasant time. He just said that the name the *Second Chance* represented a new beginning.

"Time for desert, I think."

"I can't eat another bite, Torsten. I couldn't finish the lobster salad. It was delicious, but so rich."

"You'll change your mind once you see what it is. And you can have just one."

He was off before she could protest. When he returned there was a plate in one hand and he was carrying an ice bucket with the other. For expediency, he had placed the Champagne glasses in the ice bucket stem down, so as not to get any water inside the unique glasses. She had not seen a third ice bucket.

"More Champagne?"

"I don't know what you'll think about this one, but I know you'll approve of the house."

It turned out to be Champagne de Venoge Vin du Paradis. Before Torsten could ask, Ela volunteered, "Sixty percent Pinot Noir, twenty percent Pinot Meunier, twenty percent Chardonnay. A little floral with a hint of berries and honey, a Champagne that is ideal for a great many different kind of desserts."

"I see you are familiar with this label as well. This evening, it will be paired with strawberries stuffed with ricotta and tiny dark chocolate chips, Ms. Zalewski. I suggest you have at least one of these with a glass of the Vin du Paradis ... purely for research purposes, of course."

"Very well, Mr. Furst, if you insist, but before I do, I really have to find the ... All of that Champagne ..."

Ela went to investigate. There were the two small adjoining tents ... One housed a pretty big shower—an actual working shower on an island without plumbing. There was a tank that fed the hose that was attached to a showerhead. There was a pile of nicely folded fluffy cream colored towels on a brown leather and wood stool in the corner and under the stool a basket overflowing with toiletries. In the second tent, she found a dry toilet, a tiny sink, a suspended mirror and a couple of baskets with toilet paper, soap, hand towels, tissues, and hand lotion. Unbelievable. There was even a travel size blow dryer plugged into some kind of generator, combs in different sizes, a couple of hairbrushes, shower caps, dry shampoo ... What no curling iron? No hot rollers? She'd have to speak to the management.

When Ela returned, and Torsten excused himself.

"You won't believe what we have been supplied with in there."

Torsten was amazed at the attention to detail.

Dessert was decadent. The Vin du Paradis brought out the full flavor of the strawberries and the dark chocolate tamed the residual sugar in the dessert Champagne. Ela miraculously found room in her stomach for three giant overstuffed strawberries and a full glass of Vin du Paradis.

"My favorite foods all in one Champagne-themed dinner has been on my to-do list for a long time. I never thought of having it on a deserted island, mind you. Then there is Champagne de Venoge: One of my all-time favorite Champagne houses. Would it be paranoid of me to suggest a conspiracy? Someone did their homework. By someone, I mean Jonas."

"Jonas likes to think that nothing is beyond his abilities. The more of a challenge it is, the better he likes it."

The breeze coming off the water brought the temperature down. The island's only inhabitants were grateful for the fire pit. While it created a great ambiance, it was the heat that came off it, that they valued.

Ela shivered, put down the glass of chilled Champagne and moved closer to the fire. Her dress provided no protection. She rubbed the goose bumps on her arms and that helped a little, but nothing could be done about the hardened nipples.

Torsten had a dilemma. Should he do the gallant thing and offer Ela his jacket or wait a little while longer so he could enjoy the contour of her breasts through the material? It had been so long.

The gentleman in Torsten won out. He took off his sports jacket and placed it around Ela's shoulders. She did not flinch from his touch, but snuggled into the fabric that was warm from his body. Her wine agent's sensitive nose picked up his cologne. The scent was clean and masculine. She had always thought that it suited him well.

The compartment of her mind where she had locked up all of those memories and feelings was compromised. One by one they spilled out.

She was fighting her emotions, but to Torsten it looked like Ela might have taken ill. He was suddenly right against her, his arm went around her shoulders protectively and he pulled her into his chest so he could wrap both arms around her. She wasn't just shivering now. She was shaking and she was breathing strangely. Was she feverish?

"Ela, you don't look well." He sounded very concerned. When he put his hand to her forehead, it was cool, not hot as he had expected.

Oh God, Ela thought, he was making it worse. There was no chance that she would be able to regain her composure now. She thought she might be having an anxiety attack, not that she had ever had one before.

Torsten was trying to take care of her. He had been the source of her nerves, but suddenly she was feeling safe and secure. She slumped against him, as the trembling subsided and her breathing was returning to normal.

Torsten was relieved. She had really worried him. He didn't want her to relapse, so as a precaution, he held her closer and tighter, warming her with his body and waiting for her to relax in his arms. Having her this physically close seemed like the most natural thing in the world. As if they had not spent any time apart. She was where she belonged. He did not want this feeling to end.

Ela didn't fight him. She couldn't. She wanted this. It felt right. Hurt and anger receded. She was tired of holding on to these negative emotions. They had weighed her down for far too long. Happy memories and joy came to the foreground. She was euphoric at the physical contact.

While Torsten did not know what was going on with Ela, something had changed. She was different in his arms now. She was receptive to his light, comforting caresses and seemed to be gaining strength from them. He had not even realized that he had been trying to soothe her in that way.

Torsten had been concerned about her well-being before all else, but now realized that holding her in his arms—well familiar feelings were beginning to stir within him.

She was feeling something too. Ela looked up into his eyes with an unspoken need to know that he wanted her ... this moment ... always.

They didn't talk, though. In fact, it would have spoiled the moment and possibly where this was going. They both had so many pent-up feelings ... but mostly it was about an emptiness that only the other could fill.

Ela's pretty mouth was so inviting. Torsten cautiously bent his head to brush her lips lightly with his own. Ela parted her lips ever so slightly and he pressed his lips to hers for a real kiss this time. Their kiss was deep and long.

In this kiss, Ela felt lost and Ela felt found. So many emotions were welling up inside her. It was as if in that one kiss Torsten was able to communicate everything that was in his heart. He was sorry. He needed her. She had turned his life upside down and he was glad. He missed her. He loved her.

When Torsten broke away from Ela, reluctantly, it was to stand. He reached out to help her to her feet. Ela took his hand and let him take the lead. Hand in hand they walked over to the tent they were intended to spend the night in. Torsten picked up a lantern on the way. He pulled back the flap for Ela and she stepped through. The soft glow of the lantern exposed a comfortable looking bed on a wood platform; pillows, sheets, a duvet and a cashmere blanket in cream and brown tones; a side table, a small utilitarian chair. Close quarter living.

Torsten turned Ela away from him. The zipper at the back of the dress started at her lower back. With a steady hand he negotiated it the few inches down and turned her to face him again. Ela did the rest.

Ela reached up and brought one strap down and then the other under his gaze while her heart was beating wildly in her chest. She pushed the fabric down to her waist to reveal little firm breasts and hard pink nipples. Then, all the way down past her girlish waist, slim hips and perfect behind, until she was stepping out of the dress that she had worn for the first time.

Torsten picked it up and placed it on the chair, taking his time so that he could look at her. She was something to look at, nude like that. He liked the way the light from the lantern created a golden halo around her body. Her skin looked sun kissed. Her eye color was a deeper, liquid blue-green in this light. Her lips seemed fuller or maybe they were a little swollen from his last kiss.

Ela's breasts were begging for his fingers. She wanted to feel his hands on her again. Torsten could sense it. He was about to oblige when Ela stepped towards him and started undoing the buttons of his shirt. Why had he not worn a polo? Torsten berated himself, impatient with all of the buttons. Finally she was done and pushing his shirt away to place her palms on his chest.

It was Ela who sought out Torsten's lips this time and he gladly conceded. She tasted of strawberries and chocolate.

"Make love to me." Ela said the words that Torsten had thought he would never hear. He wanted nothing more than to claim her as she had claimed him those many months ago. He wanted to make her his for the rest of time.

"Do we need to use condoms? There are some in the little bowl on the nightstand along with individually wrapped moist wipes. I can see both from here. It seems that they thought of everything."

"I haven't been intimate with anyone since the last time we were together, Torsten."

"There is no need from my end either."

Though Torsten undressed with urgency, he decided that this night their pace would be slow. He lay Ela down on the bed gently and took the time to re-acquaint himself with her pleasure points.

Torsten traced her jawline with his fingertips and tilted her head away so he could kiss her neck. He caressed her sensitive breasts and sucked on the taut nipples. Ela arched her back in response. Ela was still ticklish around the stomach, Torsten was pleased to note. When he kissed her there she giggled, but did not ask him to stop. He kissed his way down her belly, to the juncture of her hip and thigh. Pausing, teasing.

When he buried himself between her legs, gently teasing her clit with his light, fast licks, she was literally quivering and making unintelligible sounds. Wave after wave of pleasure from deep within her came to the surface and spread throughout her whole body. Her fingers tangled in his hair as her body convulsed. It was one of the longest and most complete orgasms of her life.

Torsten wanted to continue, but she stopped him with her hands because she could not yet locate her voice. When she was able to speak again, she told him unabashedly what she wanted.

"I want to feel you inside me."

Ela saw that Torsten did not need any further encouragement. When she reached for him, he was rock hard. She squeezed his cock and ran her thumb over the tip in anticipation. Torsten was already fully aroused and ready to enter her. Ela was ready too and so very wet. She positioned him at the opening of her pussy and pushed forward with her hips, teasing them both.

Torsten started to glide in, then stopped himself. He had forgotten how tight she was. He did not want to hurt her, but damn it, she wasn't making it easy. She was wiggling her hips now, one hand guiding him in deeper while the other reached down to play with his balls.

Torsten was trying to restrain himself and Ela was fighting him on it. Torsten had no choice but to give in; he drove his whole length into her in one mighty thrust. He no longer held back. He wanted all of her. Again and again he withdrew his rock hard member, only to slam himself home over and over, with Ela arching up to meet him.

Each time Torsten moved inside her, she gave him more of herself, until her body was more his than hers. She surrendered to the powerful orgasm that came up from her toes to the core of her body—the walls squeezing and releasing Torsten's cock until he exploded with a level of passion that was beyond what seemed humanly possible.

Their lovemaking had knocked down barriers, erased the time they had spent apart, and removed the loneliness that had gripped them both for all of the months that they had denied themselves.

Two people who never felt the need to hold or be held in bed lay with limbs intertwined. Ela's head rested on Torsten's chest and she fell asleep listening to his strong heartbeat as his fingers lightly smoothed her hair.

Just before first light, Ela woke and watched Torsten in peaceful slumber for the next couple of minutes. She knew he would forgive her for what she was about to do.

Her hand reached for his sleeping cock. It fit well in her small hand, but not for long. A cock with a mind of its own … it twitched in her fingers. It was waking.

Torsten was fighting to stay in a wonderful dream. Ela was teasing him wantonly, daring him to take her on their balcony overlooking Rome, under the stars. She promised that she would be very quiet, so as not to disturb their neighbors. He was getting so turned on.

Torsten struggled to stay there, but something was pulling him out of his delightful dream. That something was Ela Zalewski who was working his cock with her lips and tongue. He tried to engage her, but she wouldn't have it. She did, however, ask for him to sit up in their bed.

When Torsten's cock was standing at attention, Ela straddled him and lowered herself onto the shaft. She was kneeling on her left knee and put her right leg into a forty-five angle with foot flat on the mattress. She had her palms resting on his shoulders.

In this position she had more mobility. She could raise herself easily to the tip of his cock and glide back down all the way. For better stimulation of the whole, she rotated her hips at the same time. And he had a good view of her pussy riding his willing cock. Torsten remembered when she had made love to him that way in Rome. He had complimented her on her technique. She had told him that she had just invented it right there and then blamed him for her lewd behavior.

In Rome, even though she was the one to initiate, and the position was for Torsten's enjoyment, Torsten's hands where everywhere and she had gotten so aroused that she came a couple of times before Torsten climaxed. Watching Ela come as she propelled herself up and down the shaft of his cock, just made it that much better, as far as Torsten was concerned.

This time, though, something more primitive appealed to Torsten. After her second orgasm, he flipped Ela onto her back. He pinned her arms over her head and he entered her in one unified motion. She sighed in pleasure. She liked to feel the weight of his body on hers. She liked how he took control. As Ela's body trembled with the onset of an orgasm, Torsten saw to his own pleasure with a few more deep thrusts.

Torsten turned onto his back taking Ela with him and wrapping her up in his arms. She snuggled in, content and smiling when she looked up and into her lover's eyes.

Torsten grinned. "Well I'm glad that wasn't just a dream. Can I buy you breakfast?"

Ela was very hungry and Torsten had quite the appetite himself. They decided to take a shower together—in the interest of saving water.

The shower accommodated them quite well and by design. Jonas had specified that the bed should be no larger than double width, while the shower should be big enough for two. It was obvious now. They were catching on. There was nothing that Jonas had not thought of.

Torsten got coffee going while Ela blow-dried her hair. He brought her a cup.

"Americano." It was what he had ordered for her in Rome. There was a hot plate, he explained, and he had warmed up the milk.

It was odd: In Montreal she started her day with cappuccino or café au lait and in Italy and France, she would ask for coffee American style, except with hot milk.

When she came out, Ela saw that Torsten had been quite industrious. He had set the low wood table they had eaten on the night before. They feasted on raspberries and Greek yogurt, French country style ham and French cheese, and washed it all down with a second cup of coffee.

As they were finishing the last of their coffee, Ela had to ask, "Where do we go from here Torsten? This has all been quite wonderful, but now what?"

Torsten had already decided that this time nothing was going to go wrong or stand between them. He would follow Ela to the ends of the earth if he had to, but decided it would be best to find out what was on her mind, so that he would not say or do the wrong thing.

"Ela, my darling, I never want to be parted from you again. Tell me what I must do to make that happen."

"You know, Torsten, when we are in bed, there is this perfect harmony. It is absolute bliss."

"I would have to agree, but does this somehow present a problem?"

"Not per se, but it's like we skipped a few steps. We automatically head to bed because we fit so well, but apart from the short interludes in Bordeaux, Rome and Montreal, we never took the time to get to know each other … who we are, what we want, what we want from this relationship. There are still things to resolve that we haven't talked about. I don't want to spoil the mood and I am feeling deliriously happy, but I think we have to take a few steps back and get to know each other on a different level. It will make the physical part even more meaningful, I think."

"Ela, I am crazy in love with you. Real love. The kind of love that few people on this planet have ever been fortunate enough to know—myself included until you. There is nothing I won't do for you. I want to spend the rest of my days making it up to you for the pain that I have caused you. I cannot imagine life without you, Ela. Tell me what it is that you need from me, so that we can figure how to make all of this work."

"I'm in love with you too, Torsten, and I know that it will be hard, but we have a few days ahead of us on the yacht and I was thinking that we should abstain from sex. It is an easy fix … a comfortable place to end up. We can use the rest of the week to talk, so we can figure out what the obstacles are and see how we can overcome them. I think we should agree right away, that we do this honestly, but without recrimination and with an eye on moving forward with our relationship."

It was not what Torsten had expected. Making love to Ela was an important expression of his true feelings for her, but maybe she had a point. If that was what she needed from him, how could he deny her? Hopefully, they would resolve everything in the next few days. He knew that he wanted to spend the rest of his life with this woman. He hoped that by the time the *Second Chance* docked in her home port, he would have his *Second Chance* with Ela Zalewski.

"Agreed."

The craft that had deposited first Torsten and then Ela on the island the day before was there to retrieve them. The pilot smiled as he helped them on board. With no need for subterfuge now, the pilot seemed more at ease with his passengers.

Another craft was right behind, caterers, who would remove their equipment, the dishes the glasses and so forth, and the team from the luxury safari company that would dismantle the tents and everything within, so that they could be loaded onto a barge later, the pilot had explained.

It was quite the operation that Jonas had masterminded. It had taken a small army to execute.

Just before Torsten and Ela made it onto the *Second Chance*, the yacht's helicopter took flight.

"Ela, would you mind waiting for me on deck? I need to have a word with my crew."

"I hope you're not going to be too severe with them, Torsten. It was Jonas's doing and their hearts were in the right place."

It was what he'd hoped to hear. Ela was kind and considerate by nature and she was feeling protective of *his* crew. How unlike Lara she was. Torsten hoped there would be many vacations on board in the years to come. His crew would come to adore her very quickly. His crew would be her crew.

First things first, though. Talk to the crew. Make it look like he was reprimanding them, then figure out how to keep Ela in his life permanently.

"That was Mr. Koertig making his get-away in my helicopter, I presume."

"He thought you and Ms. Zalewski should have your space. He'll send the helicopter back. Mr. Koertig was still a little drunk this morning. He asked me to tell you that he'd Skype you at the end of the afternoon. He was rather strange last night, sir. He seemed to be pre-occupied with this woman."

"That doesn't seem strange. That seems like Jonas."

"I think this time it might be different. Just an observation sir, but he seems to be really interested in this one."

"What makes you say that, Captain?"

"Because, sir, she wasn't interested in him."

"Really? A woman who was able to resist his obvious charms?"

"He did a little talking last night after his fourth snifter of cognac. He only met her once a few weeks ago and only for a few minutes. It seems she's a petite redhead and in her mid-thirties. On top of everything else, it seems like she might work for a living. He thinks she's some sort of businesswoman. Not his usual taste from what I remember. Wouldn't you agree, sir?"

"Nanny issues."

The captain was trying to figure out if Mr. Furst meant to be humorous. "Excuse me, sir?"

From Mr. Furst's serious expression, evidentially not.

"When our Mr. Koertig was a small boy, he always wanted to get his own way. No need to point out the obvious, Captain. Anyhow … he was a very clever child. And he was a good looking little boy, positively angelic I was told. He could wrap pretty much everyone around his little finger. If that didn't work, he knew quite well that a good tantrum would. His parents doted on their only child and were not very keen on disciplining him. They found it easier to just give in. His nannies, grown women trained in child rearing, were equally defenseless. When his second to last nanny left her charge to get married and start her own family, his parents hired this petite no-nonsense red haired woman by the name of Margaret Ferguson to look after their precious boy. Mrs. Ferguson had lost her husband only a few months earlier. He had worked for the railway and there was a derailment. He was one of the first on the scene. He managed to pull a woman and her infant son out of the wreckage. Unfortunately part of the passenger car fell in on him and crushed him. He died instantly. He died a hero of course, but the loss was almost unbearable for the woman who would become young Jonas's nanny. Her husband had been the great love of her life. She never remarried."

Torsten paused for a moment, finding it hard to imagine Jonas that age. He only knew him from their days at university.

"When Mrs. Ferguson first arrived, young Jonas did as he always did to get his own way. This time it did not work. Mrs. Ferguson spoke perfect German, but her approach to life, including Jonas's care, was rooted in her own Scottish upbringing. In other words, she would not allow him to wear her down. He could not get his own way regardless of what he tried. She just wouldn't have any of it. It was only when he did what she asked that he saw a look of approval on her face or was rewarded with a small gesture of affection. She seemed stern, but he had found her neither indifferent nor heartless. Quite the opposite. She cared enough to want him to grow up to be a well-adjusted and happy person. Soon, he was doing all that he could to please her. When he behaved well, Mrs. Ferguson would lavish affection on him. She was very devoted to him. She practically raised him. They became very close."

"What happened to her, sir?"

"Jonas … Mr. Koertig took care of her till the day she died. When she was advanced in years and somewhat frail, he found her the best nursing home that money could buy. He would visit her at least three times per week when he was in town and he tried not to be away for more than a week at a time, so she would not be too lonely for too long. He read to her, as she had read to him and they would talk for hours. Even though he was a grown man by then, she had worried about his future. She had hoped that he would meet a woman who would see through all of his nonsense, call him on it and go about loving him for himself, the good man she knew him to be. It had been like that with her and her husband. Though he had been taken from her far too soon, their marriage would have stood the test of time if he was still living. They loved each other passionately, but more importantly; they liked each other. She wanted that for Jonas."

"How did he handle it … her passing?"

"Not well. He was with her when she died. He had been expecting it, but he was pretty traumatized nevertheless. Sometimes it seemed that he was mad at her for leaving him."

"Mrs. Ferguson, being a practical woman, had put her affairs in order when she entered the nursing home. She had even made arrangements for her own funeral and the burial. She wanted to be buried next to her husband. Mr. Koertig said it was because she always had to have the last word, but I think that she knew that it would have been too painful for him to take care of those final details and wanted to spare him."

"I hope that I am not making you uncomfortable with all of this, Captain. I know that this is a very private matter and Mr. Koertig would be furious with me, if he knew about our conversation. I think I just wanted you to know that there is more to Mr. Koertig than what he puts out there for people to see."

"You're not making me uncomfortable, sir … and no one will ever hear of this. You have my word."

"Thank you, Captain. A lot of this, I learned from Mr. Koertig's parents. They are still alive and still living in the family home. They considered Mrs. Ferguson a member of the family and felt they owed her a debt of gratitude. They would visit her when they weren't traveling. Mr. Koertig's mother and father, by the way, are in robust health at the age of seventy-two and seventy-six respectively and very active. They had decided to spend their golden years traveling the world, but when Mrs. Ferguson passed, they took some time off to console Mr. Koertig. Unfortunately, Mr. Koertig was inconsolable. He has a deep affection and respect for his parents, but he and Mrs. Ferguson had a very special relationship. His parents understood that."

Torsten took a deep breath and continued with his own experience, "Mr. Koertig spent a lot of time visiting Mrs. Ferguson's grave. I did not see him for weeks at a time. From then on something changed. He was fighting some kind of battle inside. He went to great lengths to avoid any woman that his nanny would have approved of—any woman that might come to love him—

any woman that he could ever be in danger of falling for. It is as if he could not bear the idea of the loss of love again in his life. Beyond his parents and myself, Mr. Koertig does not invite meaningful relationships."

"And, you think that this might be behind his infatuation with this woman? He does seem to be drawn to her and trying to fight it at the same time. Why now, though—he doesn't even know her name?"

"This woman may be more than just someone that his nanny would have approved of. It sounds to me that she may be a lot like his nanny …"

"At the risk of sounding like an amateur psychologist, permission to go one better, sir."

"Of course, Captain."

"Perhaps that is why he is interfering in your personal life, sir … I think Mrs. Ferguson instilled something in him about the love of a good woman. He has the right idea, but absolutely no knowledge of how to apply the reasoning to his own life."

"Your hypothesis is a good one, Captain."

Mr. Fraser was coming their way, so Torsten changed the subject.

"No doubt she's looking." He tilted his head in Ela's direction. "Act like I'm reprimanding you. I'll gesture. You look at the floor. So, how was your chess game, Captain?"

"Mr. Koertig won."

"He usually does. How much did you lose?"

"I'd rather not say sir."

"How about you, Mr. Fraser, how was the poker game?"

"I fared better than the captain, sir," he was beaming with pride.

"Stop smiling, man. I'm supposed to be reprimanding you, remember?"

"Yes, sir."

"Mr. Fraser, would you please move Ms. Zalewski's things to the suite adjoining mine."

"Already done sir."

"It seems that I don't get to make any decisions on my own yacht."

CHAPTER 30

Lunch was served on the deck off the master suite. All of Ela's belongings had been transferred to the suite adjoining Torsten's. A suite within a suite ... It was quite a bit bigger than the VIP suite she had occupied for a few short hours, and she had thought that the VIP suite was massive.

Her new accommodations were also tastefully decorated in neutral tones, but it seemed like more ... well just more. If there was a word that beat *extravagant,* that would be the word.

Ela's belongings had been placed exactly as if she had laid them out herself. Whoever moved everything took note of how she liked things folded, hung up, grouped together, organized ... There was nothing for her to do. She knew where to find everything just based on how she had unpacked in her previous suite. Mind-boggling. This was a level of service that went beyond anything she had ever heard of.

It was another beautiful sunny day. The yacht was still anchored, so there was no wind to contend with. They would surely have some protection from the sun while dinning outdoors. She could wear the black chiffon shift with the white underskirt and the pair of black wedge sandals she had planned to wear on the island.

Lunch was quite the production. Someone had discreetly set a small table for two and left an iPad right in the center. Torsten was able to bring up the menu from which they could make their selections and the wine list, which was the whole up-to-the-minute inventory of the cellar that Ela had visited the day before.

There were local specialties on the menu, as always, but knowing Ms. Zalewski's eating habits and preference for French cuisine, courtesy of Mr. Koertig, Chef Celeste and Chef Pol had added some lighter bistro fare with a modern interpretation for lunch and more elegant dishes for dinner. Mr. Furst who had spent a lot of time in Italy and had a preference for Italian food, found a variety of his favorite modern trattoria style dishes on the menu and knew that he would likely find more elaborate preparations with Italian ingredients on the dinner menu.

Ela opted for chilled asparagus soup and cold poached salmon filets with dill and low fat Greek yogurt. She decided to skip the side dishes. Torsten thought that her choice would suit him as well.

Now for the important part: the wine selection. He passed the electronic version of the yacht's wine list to Ela, so that she could order her heart's desire.

Ela scrolled without hesitation to the White Bordeaux section. There they were; the glorious wines of the Pessac-Léognan appellation in Graves. She knew exactly what she was looking for. Judging by the selection she had seen yesterday, it would be there. Sixty seconds later, she was handing the iPad back to Torsten.

"Château Malartic-Lagravière White 2010. You're going to love this wine, Torsten. Grapefruit, tropical fruit... the oak is subdued. There is good minerality and it is backed by good acidity, but there *is* volume. That's the beauty of it. It is a complex wine with an astonishingly long finish. It is pleasing on the nose and pleasing on the palate—well you'll see for yourself. It is a particular favorite of mine, but I haven't had much opportunity to taste it. Anyone that has even a little bit of knowledge jumped on it."

Torsten rang down to the galley and Chef Celeste took the order personally. Torsten then called François' office on the yacht to order Ela's white to accompany their meal.

"An inspired choice, sir."

"I can't take the credit, François. Ms. Zalewski made the selection. François, Ms. Zalewski has informed me that this wine is a particular favorite of hers and I see that we only have three bottles in inventory. I know it is not going to be easy, from what Ms. Zalewski has told me, but you had better see about getting a case—for the next time that we are on board."

Ela liked what he had just communicated to the sommelier. It had a sense of permanency about it.

The meaning behind Mr. Furst's request was not lost on François.

"Of course, Mr. Furst."

"Excellent. Thank you. Would you please send up two bottles? I have ordered lunch and I know it won't be long before it is brought up, but we have a few minutes, so we might as well open a bottle right away—or at least, when it is at the correct temperature."

"I will bring them up myself, sir."

Seven minutes later, François was at the door with a young man in a white jacket pushing a cart with ice buckets filled with ice and water, fine crystal Riedel glasses, a handcrafted ebony wood Château Laguiole corkscrew—François was old school; Ela liked that—and the two bottles of the wine that she was so looking forward to.

François proceeded to taste the wine himself and once satisfied had Ela taste. It was everything she remembered. She was as excited as a child at Christmas.

"If you would like me to come back to do the wine service for the second bottle, you will find me in my office, sir."

"I believe we can take it from here, François, thank you."

"I think Ms. Zalewski would agree that you will find it to be at the ideal temperature in about five minutes, sir."

Ela nodded. It wouldn't do to serve it too cold. Serving a white ice cold was what one did to mask defects, but if this wine should be tasted when it was too cold, they would miss the fine nuances of its personality. This was not a wine with defects.

Wine and sex, thought Ela. Was that what their relationship was based on? No. That was a simplistic, maybe even imbecilic, conclusion. She didn't really believe that. She truly loved Torsten and she wanted to be with him forever. They just needed a road map. Hopefully the next few days would provide that and they would be on their way. Days close to Torsten, but not intimate with Torsten … how would she find the willpower? Suddenly, she was starting to have second thoughts about abstaining. And, it had only been a few hours.

Torsten was having reservations of his own. Before Ela had been installed in the adjoining suite, he never contemplated that they wouldn't be spending their nights together. She would be so close and yet unattainable.

Torsten looked at the lovely woman sitting across from him, lost in her thoughts. It would all be worth it … if he managed to hold up his end of the bargain.

He wanted to love, protect and cherish her for the rest of his life. He knew that in turn, he could rely on her strength and her fierce protective nature. Ela had a great capacity for love and would nurture their relationship in a way that would respect and celebrate their differences. She would not allow herself to be dominated. She would never lose her basic identity. She would, however, give of herself freely. *That* would be her greatest gift.

Something Mr. Fraser had said popped into Ela's head out of nowhere.

"Torsten, when I was asking about the owner of the yacht Mr. Fraser was being elusive and I had to drag things out of him. At one point when he had described the *his* and *hers* dressing rooms and bathrooms in the owner's master suite, I asked if there was a *her*. I caught him off guard, I think, and he told me that there used to be."

"He was telling you the truth. I divorced Lara. I was able to fast-track the divorce because she agreed not to contest it. I made her an offer she couldn't refuse, we might say."

"You're a free man."

"And all yours."

Torsten and Ela talked through lunch and well into the afternoon over the second bottle. They covered the unpleasant subject of his marriage to Lara and Torsten told her more about his childhood and his upbringing, his school days, his friendship with Jonas, his business successes and failures, and his current responsibilities. A lot of people counted on him and he took that to heart. Torsten did have an epiphany just then. Perhaps he could pull back some and not micromanage. He never had a reason before, but now things would be different. He had very capable men and women at the head of all of his companies. They had proven themselves over the years. Jonas was just as successful, and he had refused to be a slave to his businesses from the very beginning.

Ela was elated. Eager to get the hard stuff out of the way, she told Torsten about David. She was completely truthful about what their relationship was and what it wasn't. She also told Torsten about her history, personal and professional, and that evidently she was capable of growth at her age because she finally had a female friend and a best friend, for the first time in her adult life—like what Jonas was for Torsten, though the friendship was quite new.

Ela and Torsten shared what their expectations had been about life and relationships and they talked about disappointments without dwelling on the negative details. There was no reason to look back. All they needed to do was visit the past very briefly and then move forward.

Ela and Torsten's conversation ended with a better understanding of what had gone wrong between them and they both admitted they should have handled some things differently. They were in a good place.

Torsten felt that it would be best for them to be kept busy over the next few days otherwise he would never survive. All he could think of was the magical night they had spent together and the way he was awakened this morning. He would go see the captain about an itinerary; they could visit some islands. Usually these things were organized well in advance, but it might be possible.

Torsten wondered if Jonas had seen to this part as well. If so, Torsten wouldn't mind, he just needed to know the schedule and what they would be doing. Ela would always need a little advance notice, as he remembered.

Before Torsten had a chance to call the captain to ask if he could have a few minutes of his time, the captain called Torsten. "Mr. Koertig would like to speak to you, sir. You can take his video call in the communications room, Mr. Furst."

Torsten told Ela that he would be back in fifteen minutes and poured her another glass. She was content to just sit there, sipping a wine worthy of the majestic view—or should that be, taking in a majestic view worthy of the wine. Either way, she was happy in her solitude because she had never felt as connected to Torsten as she did this moment.

In the communications room, Jonas and Torsten were face-to-face, in a manner of speaking. Jonas had a big grin on his face.

"I hope I didn't pull you out of anything?" Jonas grinned with delight at his childish innuendo. "Judging by how relaxed you look, things went well."

Torsten couldn't help but smile. He couldn't possibly be angry with Jonas when he had been instrumental in reuniting him with Ela.

"I have to give it to you, Jonas. This was so well planned, that if you put it in your head to take over a small country, they would never see you coming."

"Is that what you would like to give Ela as a wedding present … a small country? I may be able to arrange that."

"Wedding present? That's a bit premature, don't you think?"

"Don't tell me that I did all of this, and you're not going to marry the woman?"

"What has gotten into you, Jonas? You have never been pro-marriage."

"Don't change the subject. Are you or are you not going to make Ela your wife?"

"That is my intention … yes."

"Do you think she will say no?"

"I'm quite sure she will say yes, if you must know."

"Then why don't you propose to her this evening after a romantic dinner, and let's move this thing along."

"Well for one thing, I don't have a ring and it wouldn't be fair to ask Chef Celeste and Chef Pol to come up with a special menu last minute. They may not have the ingredients and they have to prepare dinner for the whole crew. There would have to be flowers and candles to do it right. I have dinner jackets and the rest on board, but Ela loves to dress for an occasion."

"You underestimate me, Torsten. François had placed a very special order before Ela and you came on board. It does not show up in your inventory. Chef Celeste and Chef Pol have been planning a very romantic dinner for the two of you. There are some people coming on board soon to decorate the dining area of your suite. There will be an abundance of rare cream orchids—as rare as Ela; I was very clear and candles in appropriate candle holders. I know that the yacht has stabilizers and the captain told me that the sprinkler system has just been inspected, but we don't want to take any chances. Anyways, I have been promised understated and elegant. I thought of blindfolding some musicians, but you'll have to make do with the sound system that you spent a small fortune on. The people decorating will have soft romantic music playing before they leave. Ela will find a couple of dresses in her suite that she can choose from, with accessories, everything in her size. By the way, she has an appointment for a massage, hair, makeup … As for the ring … Don't ask me to explain, but you will find the ring that was in your safe in your home office is now in the safe in the office in your suite. The rest is up to you, my friend."

"I don't know what to say, Jonas ... This might actually be the best idea you ever had. Thank you. The breaking into my safe thing though ... I'm having a little trouble with that. By the way, Jonas, you look a little rough. Is it the four snifters of Cognac or the redhead?"

"So the captain talked."

"Did you swear him to secrecy?"

"An omission on my part."

"Well, there you have it. We are going to talk about this very soon. But first, have you by any chance arranged our itinerary for the rest of the week as well?"

"As a matter of fact I have, but I'll get to that tomorrow morning. In the meantime get engaged. Don't screw it up."

CHAPTER 31

"Ela, my darling. I have been informed that Chefs Celeste and Pol have a very special dinner planned for us and François has something special for us as well. You have an appointment for a massage, hair and makeup. You had better get a move on."

"Torsten, I don't have anything to wear."

"Apparently, you do."

"Jonas?"

"Jonas."

"Well then, I had better be on my way. See you this evening. What time should I be ready for?"

"Nine, my darling."

Ela rose and planted a soft kiss on Torsten's lips.

Torsten poured himself another glass and planned to remain there a while longer. The old Torsten would have gone off to his office to work. The new Torsten was only thinking of proposing to Ela, their wedding, their marriage and all of the adventures they would have together. He was turning over a new leaf and it felt good.

Ela had not had this kind of pampering since Bordeaux and Rome. It was so relaxing. She had forgotten to ask about not being able to get a signal on her cell phone. She had not thought about the office until now, and that lasted a mere twenty seconds.

While strong hands massaged her, Ela's mind re-played last night, this morning, the leisurely lunch with Torsten and all of the things they covered and sorted out.

How would she get through this night? All she could think about was making love with Torsten. Maybe he was thinking the same. Maybe he would relent. She wouldn't hold him to their agreement to abstain from sex … especially on a night like this.

Here she was on a yacht where every one of her needs was anticipated and attended to. Here was this man who could have pretty much any woman he set his sights on, but he chose her.

Torsten retired to his suite for a nap, but it wasn't going to happen. He was wide awake. The adrenaline was pumping, but not in a fight-or-flight sort of way. He just wanted everything to be perfect this evening. He wanted to show Ela what the rest of their lives would be like if she said yes. He wanted to make her believe that she would always be the center of his universe and that she would always be her own woman ... even as Mrs. Furst.

The bright, lively, fiercely independent, spirited, passionate, sexy, sensual Ela Zalewski loved him. He was a lucky man. He hoped that he would not give in to a moment of weakness and carry her off to bed. He had given his word. There was a lot riding on his ability to control himself. Mr. Fraser had laid out his evening clothes, there was nothing to do but to get the ring from the safe, take a cool shower, bordering on cold, and think about the words that would make his darling Ela say yes.

Ela followed the massage with a long cool shower. She made use of the toiletries in her private changing cabin and was ready to proceed to hair and makeup.

Ela had taken a look at what was hanging in the walk-in closet in her suite within the master suite ... two incredibly beautiful feminine wispy dresses. She would feel like a goddess in either one. How would she ever decide?

Hair washed and blow-dried for maximum volume, the stylist used a curling iron to give her long hanging waves. He then swept the waves to one side over her shoulder, pinned them into position invisibly and gave them a light misting with hairspray to keep the fullness for the whole night.

The hair stylist was also the one to apply her makeup. Ela had great skin, so she only needed light coverage and a hint of color to make her face glow. He wasn't going to mess with her signature red lips, so if the lips were going to be the focus, he would give her a softer eye. He achieved that with a light neutral color all over the lids and brown shade in the creases. He curled her lashes, applied black mascara only to the top lashes and shaped her brows with a medium brown pencil. He finished their makeup session with a lip pencil and lipstick, which he applied with a brush. Her upper lip had that perfect bow shape and her lips were naturally full, so he merely followed the contours ... no need to trace outside the actual lip to create an illusion of full lips. The lipstick would not smudge easily, but he used a sealant in any case.

She thanked the hair stylist–makeup artist for making her look so good as well as the masseuse for the wonderful restorative massage, and decided to return to her suite wearing the white robe that they had provided for her so that she would not mess up her hair or makeup.

All she had to do now was try on the two dresses and choose one for this evening. It sounded easy enough, but Ela knew that she was going to eat up the hour ahead by trying both on two and three times before making her final decision. Luckily she only had to walk out of her suite into the dining area of the master suite.

Whoever supplied these glamorous dresses, had also supplied a couple of strappy evening sandals.

Ela's thought that one dress might fit better on her body than the other and the choice would be made for her—not so. Both size 0 dresses fit her as if they had been sewn on her body.

The first one was a halter with daring cleavage. Silver crystals covered the bodice and continued down to just above the knee. From there it was sheer with an appliqué of crystals several inches apart, as if a mist was floating around her legs and ankles. She felt like she was not of this world. Ela selected the silver crisscrossed sandals for this dress, but she wouldn't have gone wrong with either.

The second dress was a transparent nude with a spray of non-traditional ivory lace in the shape of flower petals and crystal beading. Who would think that lace could be used in such a design? It covered her breasts, midriff, and upper thighs in the front, and in the back the lace and crystal embellishment was strategically limited to the lower back and upper thigh. A slim belt made entirely of crystals added a touch of luxury. Next she donned the silver sandals with the delicate ankle strap.

Ela paraded past the full length mirror in the dressing room of her suite in one dress and then the other. She looked at herself in the mirrors in the bathroom … the light was different. She repeated the exercise until she got the feeling that she was looking for, for the second time. Each dress was exquisite, but one dress spoke to her for this occasion … for this night.

Earrings and her newly purchased fragrance Cologne Indéléble by Dominique Robin at the nape of her neck and on her wrists and she was ready.

When Ela entered the dining area of Torsten's suite, she found him already there. He had been pacing nervously until she made her entrance.

Oh my God, he's handsome, she thought. He was wearing an ivory dinner jacket, formal white shirt, black trousers, black bow tie and black evening shoes. He was wearing the clothes like they were part of his everyday life.

While Torsten was thinking that Ela looked like some ethereal creature in the short dress that covered very little of her slender figure. And the part that was covered with the ivory lace flower petal motif drew the eye anyway because of the crystal beading that was also part of the design. It sparkled in the candlelight. She was resplendent in that cocktail dress. He couldn't take his eyes off Ela and felt like an adolescent just standing there and gaping. Not very suave …

"Good evening, Torsten. You look very handsome. You put James Bond to shame. Look at these incredible cream colored orchids, and there are so many of them. I love all of the candles, and this table is so dramatic. The music definitely sets the mood. Jonas's elves have been hard at work."

"Good evening, Ela, darling. Forgive me for staring, but you're a vision. You take my breath away." Torsten walked over to Ela, picked up her right hand and brought it to his lips. He did not recognize the luxurious seductive scent she was wearing.

"New scent?"

"Yes, you have a good nose."

"I like it. It smells like the Mediterranean. It suits you well. By the way, François has brought up something he hopes that you will approve of. It is going to take us right into the first course. He has already tasted it. May I pour you a glass?"

"Yes, please. I'm intrigued.

"The flacon and the color are a dead giveaway. This one is available in Quebec and I have had the pleasure of tasting it, but I long to get re-acquainted."

"So you're pleased?"

"More than I can say."

"Champagne de Venoge Louis XV Extra Brut Rosé 2002. Pink Champagne with a lower degree of sugar than a brut. So why not start an evening this way?" It was grandiose … it was glamorous.

"I wonder what they are going to serve with it?"

"It's a surprise, even to me. But, we are going to find out in about fifteen minutes. Chef Pol is going to come up to tell us about the first course.

Torsten raised his glass in the direction of his beloved. "First, though, I just want to say that I love you, Ela my darling, and I am the happiest that I have ever been because you love me too." At that moment Torsten said a silent, *Thank you, Jonas, wherever you are, but if you bugged the room, I'm going to kill you.*

"Torsten, I never knew that love could be like this. That it could feel so good. So perfect. I am looking forward to a wonderful future together. In her head, Ela thought, *If it wasn't for you Jonas, we wouldn't be here. Thank you. If you bugged the room, however, I swear I will hunt you down and kill you.*

"Pinot Noir and Chardonnay from the best vintages, aged six years, with fine persistent bubbles, the mark of great Champagne."

"I guess we'll be stocking this one?"

"Well, that's up to you, my love," Ela said coyly.

Chef Pol rang up. "May we serve the first course, Mr. Furst?"

"Ready when you are, Chef."

While they waited, Ela regaled Torsten with some history about the house de Venoge.

"The family hails from a region in Switzerland crossed by the Venoge River. The name dates back to 1411. The business was set up in 1837 and the founder Henri-Marc de Venoge was the first one in Champagne to illustrate labels. This is just one of the reasons that this Champagne house is of historic importance. Not much later, they were exporting to a number of cities in various countries in Europe. This should interest you, Torsten: One of those cities was Munich. They branched out to other countries in the world, including the United States. They went on to create brands within the house de Venoge and in 1876 Champagne de Venoge won the Grand Prix at the World Fair in Philadelphia. Isn't that fascinating? Yvonne de Venoge, the last in the line, married Marquis Adrien de Mun, and his name raised the profile of the Champagne house among Paris's high society. In the years to come, the Champagne would become a favorite of the rich and influential in other countries as well. Champagne de Venoge recently moved from a very respectable property to a beautiful historical mansion; befitting the producer of such a wide range of high-quality Champagnes."

"Would you like to visit Champagne de Venoge together?"

"I would love that. It would be like a pilgrimage for me."

"No doubt."

A few minutes later, there was a knock on the door. Torsten opened the door and one of the young men that Ela had seen in the galley wheeled in a cart. The first course was plated but the presentation concealed.

Torsten held the seat out for Ela and when she was seated, he took the chair opposite her at the table covered with a white linen table cloth. The young man placed linen napkins in their laps starting with Ela. The table was set as it would be in a Michelin Star restaurant, with its fine porcelain tableware, heavy silverware and delicate crystal. The decoration was limited to a single candle in a heavy crystal candleholder. Nothing to interfere with the two people about to dine.

"Good evening, Ms. Zalewski, Mr. Furst. While Simon pours you another glass of this excellent Champagne, it will give me great pleasure to tell you what Chef Celeste and I prepared for you this evening. We know that Ms. Zalewski favors the Champagnes of Maison de Venoge. For our first offering, we took the recipe from their website, reduced it to appetizer portion and decided to serve it as your first course. "It is: *Homard Bleu à la nage de son consommé en gelée*," announced Chef Pol as he uncovered their plates simultaneously.

"*Bon appétit, Madame et Monsieur.*"

"Blue lobster swimming in its jellied consommé; that was very clever of them."

They ate slowly, relishing every morsel and sipping on the Champagne. They continued getting to know each other. Each gaining a respect for the other when they talked about accomplishing things against all odds. Each feeling compassion for the other when they talked about losing their parents. Each understanding that it is possible to be lonely in a room full of people seeking your attention, while it is possible to feel the opposite with only one other person present, like this evening.

Chef Pol knocked on the door again … having timed his appearance perfectly. It had been understood that he did not need to send anyone up to refill the Champagne glasses in between courses. Torsten would handle that.

"I hope everything was satisfactory, *Madame et Monsieur?*"

Ela voiced her pleasure and gratitude before Torsten had a chance to say anything. "Chef, your first course does Maison de Venoge proud and it was one of the best dishes I have ever tasted. Thank you so much. Please extend our thanks to Chef Celeste."

"I think Ms. Zalewski said it all."

"Thank you, *Madame et Monsieur.* That is very kind. My wife will be very happy also. Now for your second course, to accompany the wine that Simon is about to pour for you, you will be dining on scallops with a blood orange and shallot sauce. They are being served on a bed of wilted greens."

"That sounds delicious, Chef. Thank you," came from Torsten.

Just then, Simon who had managed to conceal what he was opening even if the popping sound was a partial clue, turned to face them with another flacon. This time it was a magnum. He held out this unique vessel that looked more like a decanter than a bottle, so that they could see the label. It was Champagne de Venoge Grand Vin des Princes Brut 1993. He poured a little for Chef Pol to taste. Once the chef nodded his approval, Simon poured the golden elixir into Ela's glass and then Torsten's.

"One hundred percent Chardonnay aged for fourteen years prior to disgorgement and release, though *Madame* may already know that. If so, forgive my forwardness."

"I know of the existence of this Champagne, but nothing about it, so thank you, Chef … I simply cannot restrain myself. I must taste it." Ela took a second to admire the rich golden color and fine continuous stream of bubbles and then took a sip. She did not speak for thirty seconds. Then there was a smile while she closed her eyes.

"Toasty, nutty brioche, orange peel … It has a floral side too, but it is also spicy and there is a hint of baked apple. The mousse is so creamy. I'm in heaven. It's a magnum, though. It would kill me if this rare Champagne would go to waste; Torsten and I cannot possibly finish it."

"Not to worry, *Madame*. Champagne of this caliber would never go to waste on this yacht. Celeste, François and I would find that as distressing as you do, Ms. Zalewski. We'll enjoy a glass in the galley and toast to your health and Mr. Furst's."

"That's a relief."

Ela and Torsten thanked Chef Pol and his talented wife, and were alone once more.

Torsten raised his glass again. "To the woman who has captured my heart, and is teaching me to appreciate things that I either took for granted or never took the time for."

"As for you Torsten Lucas Furst … I would have no other," toasted in return.

It was Torsten's turn to take a sip, "Now *this* we are definitely stocking, though I imagine that it will be a challenge to obtain. Never mind, François does like a challenge."

Ela and Torsten decided the Chefs Vasseur were geniuses. The blood orange and shallot sauce found the orange zest and spices in the Champagne. The creamy mousse complemented the texture of the scallops.

Their conversation flowed once again, until there was that well timed knock on the door.

This time a smiling Chef Celeste walked through the door with Simon pushing the familiar cart.

"Good evening, *Madame et Monsieur*. My husband has conveyed your kind words. I am very happy that you enjoyed your first course. How was the second course?"

"It was absolute awe-inspiring, Chef." Torsten's praise made Chef Celeste blush, something she was not usually prone to.

"It will be etched in our memory, Chef. Please tell Chef Pol," Ela added.

"Gladly. *Merci, Madame et Monsieur.*"

The next delicacy was not hidden. Ela and Torsten found a rectangle of dark chocolate in their dessert plates. The center was either stamped or etched with the shape of the *Second Chance*. Gold foil had been painstakingly laid over the edges. It had been placed on a miniature easel. It looked like a painting on display.

"I know that *Madame* does not eat traditional desserts, so I have created this to finish with. It is seventy percent dark chocolate. The gold foil is edible. We are serving it with Mas Amiel Maury 1969 from Languedoc-Roussillon. If this *vin doux naturel* would have been young, I might have infused the chocolate with wild cherry. Since it is an older vintage, my husband, François and I agreed that this pairing would be ideal. The 1969 is ninety percent Grenache. We opened the bottle downstairs to taste it and to make sure that it was in perfect condition. It is.

You will still find sweet ripe fruit, but you will also find spices, tobacco and a hint of cacao powder. I have heard that you do not take coffee this late *Madame* and I know that *Monsieur* does not either, so there is no coffee. If you should change your mind, please let us know. Otherwise just call to let us know when to clear. Simon will come up promptly. Good evening, *Madame et Monsieur.*"

"Your creation is too beautiful to eat, Chef."

"You may just have outdone yourself with this presentation Chef. Our thanks to Chef Pol and François for their contribution."

"Your words give me great pleasure, *Madame et Monsieur,* but it will give me greater pleasure if you enjoy how it tastes. It was my intention to please the eye and in so doing, to create curiosity and anticipation for the taste buds. The taste buds must confirm … Only then, will this creation be a success. *Bonsoir, Madame et Monsieur.*"

"This is a rare woman, as much artist as chef."

"Chef Celeste studied as a pastry chef in addition to her other culinary accomplishments. She was probably crushed to learn that you did not eat dessert and this is her solution."

"It's very imaginative. I dare not leave anything after such an effort. Oh my, that is good and with the 1969 Maury, it is a luxury dessert … And I don't feel guilty. That is the best part. Well actually, the best part is sharing it with you here in this magnificent suite on this magnificent yacht. I feel very spoiled."

"Well, Ms. Zalewski, you had better get used to it because I am going to continue spoiling you every day for the rest of our lives. You may feel this is too soon, Ela, but we have missed out on a lot already. I know that I bear the blame because I was not willing to make the commitment you deserved. I will not make that mistake a second time."

Ela saw Torsten reach into the side pocket of his dinner jacket and take out a ring … but not just a ring. The size of it was astonishing. It was simply the most beautiful ring she had ever laid eyes on. Ela's heart skipped a beat and she started to tremble. The ring sparkled in the candlelight. It was a flawless, pear shaped white diamond. Three sets of double claws attached it to the platinum setting. Micro-pavé white diamonds made up the slim band.

"Torsten." Her lips formed his name silently. Ela could not take her eyes off the ring.

"If you marry me, Ela, I will spend the rest of my days making you happy." Torsten took Ela's left hand and placed the ring on her fourth finger. Ela did not recoil. "Ela Zalewski, I want you as my friend, confidante and partner in life. Would you please do me the honor of becoming my wife?"

"Torsten, my love, nothing could make me happier. Yes, I will marry you and the sooner the better. I can't wait to be able to call you my husband. There could never be a more beautiful ring or a more meaningful marriage proposal. I can't believe the ring fits. How did you know the size? I don't even know my size."

"Dumb luck. I thought I would have to have it re-sized."

"Or maybe it was the universe telling us that we were meant for each other."

"Darling, it's a cliché, but you've make me feel like the luckiest man in the world. We will have so much to plan over the next few days. I am looking forward to all of it. It's going to be an exciting journey. First though, I should ask if you can see yourself living in Bavaria—at least some of the time. I have a very large estate outside of Munich and it's my favorite place to be. I know it's a long way from your home, your friends and your business but it's not so far from your producers; perhaps we can make it work?"

"*You* are my family now, Torsten. I want to be where you want to be. It will be exciting. A new life in a new country."

"That's great, darling. If there is something about the estate that doesn't please you, we'll change it."

"I'm sure that I will love your home and the grounds just as they are."

"*Our* home."

Torsten grimaced briefly and continued. "There is, however, one thing you might object to. Jonas's property and our property border Jonas's parents' property. It was all theirs at one point, but they wanted to have us nearby. I will, however, make it clear to him his drone is unwelcome on the estate so you needn't worry."

"My opinion of Jonas has quite softened these past few hours." Ela grinned mischievously. "Not that it matters, but did you live there with Lara at any time?"

"No. Jonas and I built from the ground up. When Lara and I got together, the work wasn't finished, so we lived in a mansion on a big lot closer to town; she picked it out. It was never much to my tastes. I had intended to sell it and move to the new house in the country when it was ready. What I didn't know at the time was that she had never any intention of moving there with me. That house was part of her divorce settlement, and I am happy to be rid of it. The new house is part of my new life with you. I have offices in Munich, but most of the time I plan to work from home. On the second floor, there are two large offices, with a meeting room between them. We can set you up in the one that stands empty. I know it will be a challenge but I believe you can still run your business from Munich. You will, however, have to turn more of the day-to-day operations over to Robert. I am planning to step back as well, so I'm not asking you to do anything I'm not willing to myself. I want us to be focused on each other first and foremost but also to support each other in our endeavors."

"That would be fantastic. There's just one thing that's bothering me, my love. How is it that you just happened to have the ring on board when you didn't know about Jonas's plan? I'm not saying that you were in on it. I know you weren't. I'm just curious."

"The evening at Laurence's château, I was going to tell you about my divorce and ask you to marry me. I had the ring in my pocket. When you had excused yourself for the second time, I was thinking of the right words. I decided that the straightforward approach would be best: I would tell you how much I loved you and needed you; then I would just ask you to marry me. Except you never came back.

"I didn't go after you again because I was convinced that you did not want me in your life and that you had moved on."

"Oh, Torsten, I had no idea. I was still so hurt. I just wanted to hurt you back. In the process I hurt myself. Now knowing this, I feel like such a fool. I'm so sorry."

"I should have told you as soon as I walked through the door that the divorce had been finalized. I should have asked you to be my wife, right there and then. Since then the ring has been in my safe at home … And, then suddenly it was in the safe in my office here."

"Jonas?"

"Yes."

"He has the combination of both safes? Or is that a foolish question?"

"He does *not* have the combinations … The enigma that is Jonas Koertig."

"He's a little bit scary … But, I suppose we should be glad that he is on our side. He would make a formidable enemy.

"Darling, now I shall see you to your suite and return to mine. I made you a promise to abstain and I want you to believe that whatever you ask of me, I will move heaven and earth to do. So, on that note, let me walk you to your suite and kiss you good night before I go back on my word. It's just that there is only so much temptation that a man can take. You're so damn appealing right now, and I have visions of last night and this morning dancing around in my head, which does not help matters. But I want to show you that I can be the man you want me to be."

No, no, no, Ela's brain was screaming. What had she done?"

Ela let Torsten walk her to her suite, not knowing how to reverse her edict.

Torsten picked up her left hand and brought it to his lips. "The ring is where it should be. I despaired that I would never see you wear it."

"I'm surprised that you hadn't returned it."

"It was chosen for you from the heart. I could not stand the idea of it being on some other woman's finger. It was a bittersweet reminder of what we had and what we could have had. Even if you'd never worn it, it would have been giving away something of yours and I couldn't do that."

"Oh, Torsten. What an idiot I was not to have seen beyond our difficulties to recognize that I was giving up on a man who was capable of such abiding love. I blamed you for not fighting for us, but I didn't fight for us either. I crawled into my shell where I thought it was safe. Instead I was miserable and aching for you, while you were missing me. We did make a mess of things. Jonas was right to intervene. I swear that nothing like that will ever happen again."

With that pronouncement, Torsten took her in his arms and kissed her deeply with passion and love, giving wholly of his heart and his soul as a man, and as her future husband. Then summoning every ounce of self-control that he possessed, he turned away from her and walked back to the dining area.

DIANA SOBOLEWSKI

CHAPTER 32

Ela had fallen asleep eventually ... early in the morning. She woke up groggy. Did she dream that Torsten proposed and she had said yes? The hand under her pillow told her otherwise. There was the ring. She had not wanted to take it off. She would never want to take it off. It was nine o'clock. She would not be able to fall asleep again, and besides she was impatient to see her fiancé.

Ela stuffed her hair into a shower cap. The style had held and not having to wash and dry it, she would be ready to meet her intended sooner.

When Ela left her suite dressed in a white silk robe to her ankles and a pair of white silk slippers, she walked through the many arrangements of cream colored orchids and remembered the evening they shared. She found Torsten in a white terry bathrobe out on their private terrace. He was reading on his tablet. She'd have to check her cell and see if there was a signal ... later. It seemed less important now.

Ela thought he looked like he had not slept too well himself. He caught sight of her from the corner of his eye, turned his head in her direction, smiled and greeted her warmly but with only a chaste kiss on the cheek.

"You're glowing, darling. Did you sleep well?"

"No, terribly."

"Is there something wrong with the bed?"

Yes, you weren't in it, Ela wanted to say, but settled on, "Just the excitement of last night. How about you, my love?"

"Not very well either. I'm not made of stone, and you were so close by. You have a certain effect on me." Torsten needed to change the subject. "I see you're wearing your ring."

"I had it on all night ... just to assure myself that it wasn't all just a dream. I am already very attached to it."

"Good, darling. That makes me very happy. Shall we order some breakfast?"

"Yes, I'm rather hungry."

"What would you like? I'll ring down."

"We can just order like that? We don't need to consult a menu?"

"Not for breakfast."

"May I please have two scrambled eggs then, and some fruit, and I desperately need a pot of American coffee with hot milk?"

Torsten made it for two.

When breakfast was served with the same courteous manner as their dinner had been, Simon indicated to her engagement ring and respectfully offered his congratulations to the future Mrs. Furst and to his employer.

Ela blushed with pleasure and thanked him.

The meal was not just the straightforward breakfast they had ordered. There was freshly squeezed orange juice, which turned out to be a mimosa, the fruit was on the exotic side and the scrambled eggs came with shavings, not a sprinkling, of truffle. Those were some expensive eggs. The mimosa was probably made with Champagne rather than a sparkling wine. Ela sighed with delight. This was going to be her life from here on. Paradise on earth with the man of her dreams. A real-life fairy tale. But Ela wasn't the type to spend all her days in idle self-indulgence.

"Torsten, once we are married, I don't think that I want continue in my present type of work. I want to spend as much time together as possible. I want to be unencumbered to accompany you when you travel on business, so that we can always take a couple of extra days to enjoy the surroundings. On the other hand, wine and especially prestige wine has been such a big part of my personal and professional life for a long time and I love what I do. I do not want to completely give up something that I am so passionate about. I would like to incorporate it into our lives beyond the pleasure of drinking it… do something meaningful around it."

"I love your thinking, darling. There are a number of annual charity events that invite the producers of fine Bordeaux wines, Burgundy wines and Champagne to sponsor the gala dinners. I am aware of the power of the Furst family name, and if it can be used to bring about something good, I'm all for it. I'll introduce you to Jonas's mother, if you like; she knows a lot of people involved with a lot of organizations. It can be something of a minefield trying to sort the genuinely concerned people from those only interested in the press coverage."

"That would be wonderful, I'd appreciate a little inside information. I would prefer a low key approach, using the Furst name to benefit a worthy cause and not aggrandize myself."

"Jonas and I set up an organization many years ago, when we were young men. It did not escape us that we had certain advantages that only a minuscule percentage of the world's population could ever lay claim to. We knew full well that we were living extraordinary lives. They were not perfect lives, but we were very privileged. Sure there are thousands of people that are making a living because of the companies we own and manage and that contributes to the health of the economy, but here you and I are on a three hundred and twenty-eight foot yacht … All of this for the pleasure of two people, eggs with white truffles, the wine cellar below, private planes, luxury residences. Jonas's drone probably cost more than the average middle-class home. Talk about conspicuous consumption, and the carbon footprint is deplorable."

"So why do you have these toys?"

"We're imperfect humans. Our toys don't define us, but we do enjoy them. Thus we made a pact. We set up a philanthropic umbrella organization jointly. Wherever we have an office or a branch, our people go into the community there and determine what some of the more urgent issues are: Kids needing breakfast to start their school days, food banks, women's shelters, computers for schools, homelessness, there's always a need, believe me. Our organization creates a program to offer assistance as quickly as possible, as the first step. The second step is to raise funds among our suppliers and others that benefit from our presence, as well as approaching philanthropic organizations that want to put their money somewhere where there is proper accountability. Apart from that, we have departments that contribute and raise funds for causes to do with the environment and even the prevention of the extinction of endangered species. We work to bring attention to these issues and put up our money to set an example. We use the best minds in marketing communications to get the message out. With the emphasis on being good corporate citizens, Jonas and I knew we had to start on the inside with our companies and work outwards. We wanted our people to be treated fairly. All of our companies respect a strict code concerning the environment, human dignity and equal pay for the sexes and discrimination. We also agreed that it was important to create a work environment that people can excel in. We encourage new ideas and reward initiative. We work to earn the loyalty of our employees. That's not to say that we have never encountered situations that required a firm hand within our respective businesses, with suppliers and to fight off competitors. Neither Jonas nor I are fools or pushovers, and we do not like our good names to be sullied or to be taken advantage of by unscrupulous individuals or corporations. We are in business to succeed and make a profit. But everything is tempered with in-depth analysis and logic."

"It makes me feel guilty about my engagement ring."

"I can understand that, but don't worry, my love. I would only buy diamonds that were ethically mined; I'm very careful about such things and I'll show you some of the tricks I picked up so you can be too. You know, Ela, Jonas and I have been known to press our toys into service, if we know that we can raise money that way. This yacht has hosted special fund-raising weekends, for example. It's been very effective. Perhaps you can do something similar with prestige wines, since you have the relationships. You are an unstoppable force all on your own, my darling, but remember you will have the use of the Furst name and my people will be at your service."

"Torsten, you and Jonas amaze me. I had no idea ... I probably could have imagined that you would get behind something like that, but not Jonas."

"It's only that you don't really know very much about Jonas yet. You will see that he is actually a very decent person."

"Yes, you're right. It seems that your organization is doing an exemplary job, my love—on so many levels and for so many worthwhile causes. I believe that you and Jonas and your people are making a huge difference and I want to do that too, in my own way. I have a cause that is particularly close to my heart. Perhaps I can start there."

"You can do whatever you wish, my darling. I will put whatever resources you need at your disposal and you and I will be able to offer our own financial support as well."

"Thank you, Torsten. That would be the perfect wedding gift."

"Well, I can do a little better than that, but if you would like to look at it that way, that's fine. So what is this cause that is close to your heart?"

"Animal rescue groups and animal shelters; sometimes they are one and the same. I could start small; maybe do something for those organizations in and around Montreal and branch out. I realize that we will be living in Germany, but I have lived in Montreal my whole life without doing anything significant except for making some donations. I would like to begin my charity there. Perhaps I can set something up with Robert that will benefit these groups on a regular basis. We will be able to help support them financially as well, due to your generosity. These groups save the lives of all kinds of animals, but if we just take cats and dogs, the difference they make is really to be admired. They give so much of themselves to cats and dogs that have been abandoned, neglected and abused. They show them affection and teach them to trust, so that they can become part of a family. They also work very hard to find them the right family. These groups rely on donations, and people to volunteer their time and often to foster animals in their homes, but sometimes it takes a while to get an animal to where it's adoptable or to find the right forever home. Some of these cats and dogs are old or very ill when they come in. Some have lost their will to live, their spirits broken. It takes awareness and it takes money. I just had a thought. It could be called the Second Chance Fund. I would so much like for these animals to get their second chance just like we have. That would be my pet project. What do you think?"

"I think that's a wonderful idea and it will keep you connected to Montreal, and Robert and his wife and your new friend. Tell me, darling, would you like for us to have pets?"

"I would adore a house full of pets, but I don't want to scare you."

"I grew up in a house full of pets. We were tripping over them. You're not scaring me. I love animals and on the estate we have enough space for a zoo. My parents always believed that animals could teach people a lot about love and life and I agree. I miss having pets, dogs especially. Funnily enough, my housekeeper and my chauffeur have been after me to get a couple of German Shepherd dogs from a breeder they both admire, so they would be very pleased and more than willing to dog sit. Raina grew up on a farm and her family always had two GSDs. Tavin's family had an obedience training school and he loves the breed as well. He also offered to help train them."

"I think German Shepherds are great dogs. So why didn't you get a couple?"

"I was always so busy, so focused on work, that I couldn't imagine finding the time to properly care for pets. But now I see my future differently. I see us at home and our big dogs sleeping by the fire as we sip fine wines."

"I'm falling in love with you all over again. You're spoiling me already, Torsten."

"I plan to keep on spoiling you, my darling, but you must also be aware that this lifestyle requires certain precautions. It is important you have a security person nearby at all times. They have an office on the estate and someone is available twenty-four/seven. They also maintain the estate's state-of-art security system."

"So this is what it will be like to be married to Torsten Lucas Furst …"

"I hope this is not too off-putting, my darling. When you have wealth, you have to employ a certain amount of vigilance. Jonas and I are used to living this way, but for someone who moves around freely, it can be a hindrance."

"I only have one question."

"Go ahead."

"Are the cameras limited to the outside of the house?"

"Yes. There is no one looking in."

"Good."

"Is there always security when you travel, like we had in Rome?"

"Yes."

"What about on the yacht?"

"Among the crew and also Chef Celeste."

"What is her specialty?"

"Knives."

Ela doubled over with laughter, clutching her stomach.

"Well there are certain suppliers that are quite fearful of her. You should know that we have a very advanced security system on board and we are linked up to all kinds of agencies. Oh yes, and then there is the secret escape submarine."

"The captain never mentioned it."

"That's because it's a *secret* escape submarine."

"I know that you take security seriously, but in this case, I think you're pulling my leg."

"I am. Jonas, on the other hand, would have had one installed. Or he would forgo the yacht altogether in favor of a luxury submarine."

"Now *that* I would have no trouble believing."

Torsten loved to see his Ela laugh. She was so full of joy. He looked forward to making all of her dreams come true. Ela thought about others and truly cared for people. She deserved everything he could give her and make happen for her.

Torsten noticed that there was a video call from Jonas on his iPad.

"A call from Jonas. I neglected to tell you, but yesterday he told me that he would be in touch today and that he has made some arrangements for us for the rest of our time on board. Apparently he's not done yet. Should I take it?"

"You know better than I that there's no avoiding Jonas. Whatever his plan is, it's already in motion, so why fight it?"

"Good morning, Torsten. Is Ela with you?"

"Good morning, Jonas. I see you are back home. She's right beside me."

Ela got up and Torsten pulled her chair beside his so they both had a good view of Jonas.

"Good morning, Jonas. I must say that I prefer this method of communication over the flying toaster oven."

"Spirited as ever. You're going to have your hands full, Torsten, but then that's exactly what you need. Do the two of you have anything to tell me?"

"Ela has agreed to become my wife. It's official."

Ela held out her hand to show that she was wearing her engagement ring.

"Being engaged suits the two of you. You both look happy."

"We are, Jonas. Thank you for your ... *assistance*."

"You're quite welcome, my dear. That brings me to the reason for my call. While Operation Reconciliation is a success thus far, there is one thing that would make it a complete and indisputable success."

"Operation Reconciliation? Jonas, isn't that a bit melodramatic?"

"It's my plan, Torsten, I get to name it. Anyway, I've just sent you both a schedule but it would be best if I explained. The yacht will be returning to port. An English gentleman by the name of Cyril Bishop is going to come on board. He is a wedding planner from London who works with partner agencies in Rome, Paris and Berlin. He will be accompanied by a fitter and a seamstress. They will be bringing some things on board with them. Mr. Bishop is going to go over wedding details with the both of you while the crew transforms the dining room into a mini bridal salon and fitting room with screens and mirrors and lighting that Mr. Bishop is sending over. The ladies are going to unpack about a dozen different dresses: half wedding dresses and half reception dresses. There will be some accessories for you to try on as well, Ela. Torsten, at this stage, you will be required to stay up in the master suite. You have to be out of the way and I am sure Ela would like her wedding dress to be a surprise. Tomorrow *Monsieur* Gilbert Destan will come on board with his own security so that the two of you can pick out your wedding bands and whatever else you might need for the grand affair."

"And when and where is the grand affair going to take place?"

"In one month's time, Ela, give or take a day or so. I'll let Mr. Bishop tell you the rest. He has photos to show you. He and his team have been working nonstop since you agreed to my invitation to come on the yacht, Ela. I had a feeling about the outcome, so I hired him back then."

"There is not enough time to get all of the documents."

"I assure you, Torsten, that everything is in the works. About a week before you were to join me on the yacht, your lawyer stopped by your office to have you sign some insurance papers for the *Second Chance* ... new regulations."

"Yes, I remember."

"Well you were signing authorization for the law firm to act on your behalf to take care of all of that. Ela, when you signed those documents that I handed you prior to boarding, you were doing the same. There are people on it. Nothing to worry about."

"This is kind of fast. We just got engaged. I have arrangements to make, Jonas."

"A law firm in Montreal will handle things for you and your agency ... you'll just have to meet with them a couple of times when you decide what you wish to do about your agency and if you wish to sell or keep your apartment. A moving company will move your furnishings if you decide not to leave them in the apartment. They will also pack up all of your personal belongings and forward them to Torsten's house in Bavaria. The wedding and all of these arrangements are my wedding gift to the two of you, so don't think about refusing. It would be rude. Oh, and there is one more thing. My parents will be hosting the reception at our family's ancestral home. Your wedding planner has been working with my mother on it, since you agreed to my invitation—or rather, Karsten's invitation. My parents think of Torsten like a son, Ela, so I hope you won't mind."

"That's very generous of you and them, Jonas."

"It really is very generous, my friend. Please convey our thanks to your parents."

"The guests have also already been invited on your side, old friend. They think my parents are throwing a party in honor of you, Torsten. We all felt it would be best to protect Ela's privacy while she is in Montreal. An official statement and wedding photo can be released after the reception. Ela, if you can email my assistant a list of names, I'll handle your guests as well. I estimated two hundred people from your side but obviously we can adjust that."

"That's very generous, Jonas, but I only have a few people I'd like to include and so prefer to extend their invitations face-to-face."

"As you wish, I'll have my assistant email you the details then. By the way, the honeymoon is up to the groom, but I should think that it might be nice to get back on board and continue where you will leave off. Back to the wedding. It's all going to happen quickly, but it should be relatively stress free for you between now and the wedding. Mr. Bishop, on the other hand, might have a nervous breakdown. He's doing Klarissa's wedding at the same time, so he has a lot on his plate."

"Klarissa is getting married?" Torsten asked about Jonas's last on-again-off-again girlfriend. Like all of the others, she was half his age, tall, leggy, ample breasts.

"Yes Torsten, she shared the happy news with me over lunch a few weeks ago. Poor girl didn't expect the reaction she got. I think she wanted me to stop the marriage. She seemed rather disappointed when I didn't drop to one knee, but wished her well instead. The meeting proved fruitful though. It's how I found out about Mr. Bishop."

"So you're coming solo to the wedding?"

"I'm afraid that my parents don't really approve of any of my lady friends."

"Well then, I had better give you something to do. Will you stand up with me, Jonas?"

"I would be honored, Torsten. Ela, you're not saying much. Are you alright?"

"It's a lot to take in."

"Yes, of course, that's why I'm trying to shoulder some of the organizational burden."

"Are you always going to be interfering in our lives?"

"Just for the first year or so; I want to make sure that the marriage takes."

"Hmm ... Well, I do want to marry Torsten and the sooner the better. I can't argue with your reasoning. So, thank you. Torsten, could you step inside for a few minutes, I'd like to speak to Jonas privately. Bride business."

"Certainly, my darling. I'll go get dressed."

When Ela was certain that Torsten was out of earshot, she turned her attention to the iPad. "Jonas, you're already doing a lot for us, and I am very grateful, but I need your help with something."

"For the only woman who could ever make my best friend happy ...

anything."

"Do you know if Torsten has a painting of the *Second Chance*, now that she is the *Second Chance*?"

"No, he does not. Why?"

"I'd like to commission a painting ... a fairly good size painting by a reputable artist, and give it to Torsten as a wedding present. Though I do not have wedding expenses, thanks to your kindness, my budget is about twenty-five thousand dollars Canadian. Can you find someone and get it done before the wedding?"

"That is the perfect wedding gift for Torsten from his bride. He will love it and I know just the painter, but you don't have to worry about money, my dear. You're marrying one of the wealthiest men in Europe. By next week, knowing Torsten, he will have an account set up that you can draw on. He'll expect you to spend ... otherwise it could trigger a world-wide economic crisis. Everyone will think Torsten has lost his fortune."

"Very funny. I know that things will be different once we are married, but this is something that I would like to do on my own financially. I just hope that the artist will be able to capture her splendor and dignity ... and in a way, her heart and soul if I can explain it that way. She really reflects who Torsten is and I want that to come across."

That impressed the hell out of Jonas. No wonder Torsten was in love with Ela Zalewski. He wondered what it would be like to be adored like that, something he had never known. Klarissa had never expressed a sentiment like that, and she had been the closest thing to a girlfriend that he had ever had. Jonas remembered how he had thought that Torsten had taken leave of his senses by wanting to give up his independence. But in reality, Torsten was giving up nothing. He was gaining everything.

"It would be my privilege and pleasure. As soon as you are on your way to Montreal, I will take care of it, and have the invoice sent to you. I will also take possession of the finished painting until you decide where you'd like it hung. By the way, on Friday when you are due to go back, you'll be flying first class. I had planned to send you back on my jetliner, but there was a delay with the interior design work I am having done."

"I had a perfectly good return ticket for business class, Jonas. You didn't have to do that."

"You might as well get used to the lifestyle, my dear."

"Well, having spent some time on the *Second Chance*, I am beginning to acclimate. Thank you, Jonas. Thank you for everything you've done; I really don't think we'd have managed it without you. We'll speak soon?"

"I am happy to do it, my dear. Yes, we'll speak soon."

Torsten returned, looking every inch the owner of a yacht as spectacular as the *Second Chance*.

"Did the two of you have a nice chat or did you scold him the whole time?"

"Honestly, Torsten …. As a matter of fact, we had a very nice chat. He's growing on me."

"I assume I'm not allowed to ask what about?"

"Nope, a bride has her secrets. Love you, but I have to get dressed too. By the way, you look smashing in that white linen shirt, white slacks and dark sunglasses … Like a tycoon on a yacht off Greece … Oh wait, you are a tycoon on a yacht off Greece." With a laugh, Ela was gone.

CHAPTER 33

After breakfast, Ela and Torsten strolled the lower deck hand in hand. Torsten gave her the rest of the tour in place of the captain. Every time a member of the crew passed them, they offered their congratulations to the happy couple. Torsten and his bride-to-be made the rounds to thank the captain, the first mate and the head steward for ... well everything. How else could one phrase the extraordinary chain of events? Though they announced their engagement each time, it was obvious that the whole crew was already buzzing with the news.

Jonas's chief co-conspirators were very happy for their employer and his lovely fiancée. They were aware that their time on board would be very short, but hoped that the couple would return quickly for a proper cruise.

"Well it appears that you gentlemen"—Torsten told his staff—"and the crew have some shore leave coming but not for too long. You'll be returning to your loved ones for a short while before I am going to ask you to get the *Second Chance* ready for a longer voyage. If my future bride has no objections, I would like for us to have our honeymoon on board; with some day trips."

"That is very good news, sir. Ms. Zalewski, it will be good to welcome you on board ... this time without the ..." The captain tapered off, trying to find the right words.

"That's alright, Captain. Mr. Furst and I are actually very thankful for your ... err ... efforts on our behalf. Yes, I would love to come back here for our honeymoon, my love," Ela said turning to Torsten.

When Ela and Torsten stopped by the galley, the Chefs Vasseur and Sommelier François were ecstatic at their announcement, though already aware of the engagement like everyone else on board. The way they looked at each other, Ela was convinced that they were taking some of the credit ... because those dishes and wine pairings had gotten *Madame et Monsieur* in the right frame of mind. *Well it hadn't hurt,* thought Ela.

"Torsten, may I please have a moment to speak to the chefs and your very knowledgeable sommelier in private."

"I'll be on the main deck."

Perplexed, but not wanting to be too inquisitive about all of this secrecy of late ... Torsten left them alone.

"What can we do for *Madame?*" Chef Celeste was the first to ask.

"Chef, do you by any chance have veal shanks in the fridge?"

"For osso bucco?"

"Yes. I know that it's Torsten favorite Italian dish, and it just so happens to be the *only* dish that I know how to make."

"I am expecting a delivery the day after tomorrow. I was going to put it on the menu for dinner on your last evening with us. I think it is better in autumn and winter, but Mr. Furst eats it during the warmer months as well."

"I know that there are a hundred ways to prepare osso bucco. My version requires these ingredients." Ela pulled out a list from her little bag. "I would like to make it for Torsten. Would you mind?"

"Certainly not, *Madame*." It was thoughtful of Ms. Zalewski to ask, thought the chef. She didn't have to.

"That would be great."

"What about a side dish of sautéed broccoli rabe, with just a little olive oil and garlic? If you both eat it, it will be alright." Chef Celeste laughed.

"That is very considerate of you, Chef, and I will make sure that we both eat it."

"Something to start with ... or maybe dessert? I will also be taking delivery of some fresh figs."

"Please forgive me, Chef, and I cannot speak for my fiancé, but I find osso bucco to be a rich and filling dish. I usually can't eat much of anything else. But I do like fresh figs and your cuisine is hard to resist. Besides, I do not wish to deprive Torsten. He won't eat a course if I'm not eating it, so maybe we can have either an appetizer or a dessert."

"I could cut a couple of fresh figs in half, drizzle aged balsamic vinegar on them and crumble some goat cheese on top. I would roast them until warm and if François agrees, serve this starter with a Gewurztraminer from Alsace to get those layered notes of honey, spices and apricots."

"Yes, from Domaine Weinback."

"Or I can prepare a simple but elegant dessert ... chocolate covered figs. There are only three ingredients: Fresh ripe figs, chocolate with seventy percent cocoa and a tiny bit of high quality coconut oil. All you do is melt the chocolate with the coconut oil in a double boiler, dip and place the dipped figs on a tray lined with parchment paper. Then it's into the freezer for twenty minutes and afterwards into the fridge until you are ready to serve. The first time that I made this for my husband, he proposed marriage. No ring ... it was not planned ... just like that. Figs are a sexy fruit, some would say a sexual stimulant, and we know that chocolate is thought to be an aphrodisiac. You put the two together and well ... you know how the evening will end."

Chef Pol was shaking his head in disbelief at his wife's forthright manner but Celeste continued, undeterred.

"If *Madame* does not reserve the dessert now, it is possible that my husband will devour it, and then we may not be in the kitchen in time to prepare breakfast Friday morning."

"Since this dessert comes so highly recommended, I think we should have a taste. I suggest you make enough for your husband as well. We'll order our breakfast a little later the next morning."

"*Formidable.* François, what do you suggest?"

"A fortified wine from Roussillon, Abbé Rous, Cuvée Christian Reynal, Banyuls 2000. This Grand Cru is one hundred percent Grenache Noir. The baked fruit, prunes and warm spices in this semi-sweet wine would marry well with the sweet earthiness of ripe figs and dark chocolate."

"Well then, it is decided. And once the osso bucco is in the oven, would you be so kind, Chef, as to take it out for me two hours later. Apart from the prep time, I would like to spend as much time as possible with Torsten. We will not be seeing each other for a whole month."

"My husband and I have never spent more than a couple of days apart since we were married. We would find the separation very difficult, so I understand completely. Are there any other ingredients I should put out?"

"Just a half a bottle of a dry white wine … something from the North of Italy maybe, that has some spicy notes."

"I think a bottle would be better. It is always nice to have a glass while cooking no?"

"Excellent initiative, Chef. Thank you for allowing me in your kitchen; I know it's an imposition."

"It will be our pleasure to have you in our kitchen, Ms. Zalewski. Mr. Furst has come down to cook with us quite a few times," Chef Celeste said in her matter-of-fact way, then added, "He finds it relaxing."

"Really? He cooks?" Ela was intrigued by this new information about her fiancé.

"I can honestly tell you that Mr. Furst can cook. One evening, he insisted on helping with the food preparation for the whole crew … and then he insisted on helping to serve the meal at both dinner sittings. He joined the first group for the first course and the second group for the main course. You should have seen the look on their faces. They are still talking about it. And Mr. Furst too, he had a wonderful time."

Ela had to laugh, picturing the expressions of the crew.

"François, I was thinking Barolo for the osso bucco."

"I have just the wine: Barale Fratelli Barolo Cannubi Riserva 2006. Mr. Furst is very fond of the Nebbiolo grape from Piedmont, especially when the wine is Barolo from the great cru vineyard site of Cannubi. I have also ordered three wines by this producer for the yacht and Mr. Furst's wine cellar in his home, but they are for laying down. These wines were recommended to me by some Italian sommelier friends and also they were very highly rated by *The Wine Advocate*. The Barolo Bussia 2010 scored 97 points, the Barolo Castellero 2010 scored 95+ points and the Barbaresco Serraboella 2011 scored 93 points.

"That is very interesting, François. I wonder if Barale Fratelli is represented in Quebec. Sorry … old habits die hard."

"Even if they are not, I imagine it would be hard to get an allocation. The demand is quite high."

"I will have my colleague, Robert, look into it. It would be nice for the agency's portfolio. I am happy to go with your suggestion and look forward to tasting the Barolo Cannubi Riserva 2006 from this producer."

"It would be nice to ease into the Barolo … with something. May I suggest a sparkling wine from Italy? It seems appropriate."

"Franciacorta, from the Lombardi region?"

"Yes. Bellavista Vittorio Moretti 2004; fifty-two percent Chardonnay and forty-eight percent Pinot Noir; smoke, brioche, dried fruit and good minerality. The Italian answer to high-end Champagne."

"Perfect … who needs an appetizer? It's like a first course all by itself."

"You are so right, Ms. Zalewski. We'll bring it up an hour before the osso bucco."

"I imagine that you will want to decant the Barolo to smooth out the edges?"

"I plan to decant it an hour before we serve it. That should be sufficient to tame the tannins."

"One of these days, François, I will have to take a serious interest in the wines of Germany since that is to be my new home. Perhaps in the future, we can do some tastings together and you can educate me."

"There are some excellent wines being produced in Germany, including really outstanding dessert wines. I think you will be most impressed with the wines of Herman Dönnhoff for example, but there are others that are quite the revelation as well. In turn you must introduce me to Canadian wines from Quebec and Ontario and British Columbia. I understand that there are some interesting wines being produced in Nova Scotia and Prince Edward Island as well."

"I hang my head in shame. I know a little, but not nearly enough about these wines. Not my area of expertise, I'm afraid. There are big gaps in my education, these included. Perhaps we can discover them together. As a matter of fact, maybe down the road we can even tackle other wine producing countries in the same way."

"That would be ideal, Ms. Zalewski. When you are on board for your honeymoon, we can always arrange visits to the wineries on our route."

"I love that idea. Meeting the producer, and learning about his or her philosophy while standing on the soil that gives a wine certain characteristics ... well, nothing compares."

"I could not express it better." François would hold Ms. Zalewski in the highest esteem from that moment on. She would bring things to life on the yacht and make his job even more rewarding. Mr. Furst's good fortune was also his good fortune, and the good fortune of everyone else on the *Second Chance*.

DIANA SOBOLEWSKI

CHAPTER 34

When the immaculate Cyril Bishop came on board with two ladies and a lot of stuff, whatever it was, he looked a little flustered. The wind had played havoc with what would have been perfectly styled hair at the outset of his boat ride. He kept trying to pat it into place obsessively, *Never mind,* thought Ela. After Jonas how eccentric could he be.

Ela and Torsten greeted him on the main deck and thanked him for coming so far. They invited him into the living space next to the large dining room, where the transformation had begun, and offered refreshments. He gladly accepted a bottle of water, saying he was absolutely parched.

Cyril Bishop had come armed with a very well organized file for the Furst wedding. Wasting no time, he briefed them on what he swore would be the most memorable day of their lives. There was no interrupting him, so they didn't try.

"You will be getting married in a civil ceremony in Rome … since Mr. Furst is divorced. By law, you must be married in a government building by a government official. For expediency's sake, I have selected the venue, though several are available for this purpose. You will be married in a late afternoon ceremony at the Campidoglio. It's located in the heart of Rome where you find antiquities like the Roman Forum, the Coliseum and Piazza di Venezia. It was once the epicenter of the Roman Empire, where the city's first temples stood, including the temple of Jupiter. It has been the seat of the civic administration of Rome for centuries. The interior is very regal, befitting such a marriage. The style is of the Renaissance period, red and gold with period furniture and large tapestries. We will have it decorated with large arrangements of white roses to personalize it for your wedding. It is best to keep it simple. It is not like working with a blank canvas. The building is ornate and a historical treasure. To try to compete with the architecture, art and antiques, would just confuse the eye, but neither is it a good idea to play to the venue for the attire. The effect would be costume-like." Mr. Bishop pulled out a couple of photos to show that he was not prone to exaggeration.

"There will be a harpist. There is a sense of history about the sound and harps are always appropriate for weddings. One instrument will be enough. The sound carries. There will be a photographer to capture every moment. Though it is not a religious ceremony, you may exchange vows. The officiant will do everything in Italian, but there will be an interpreter on hand to translate for those who may not understand. You will arrive separately. We are in the process of reserving the cars and drivers, matching Mercedes sedans, black, late models. Excuse me, may I have another water, I find that I am still very dehydrated."

Ela was pleased to have a moment to assimilate all of the information.

Having soothed his throat somewhat, Mr. Bishop continued, "You and your wedding party will be staying at the Rome Cavalieri Hotel. I am told that you are both familiar with this five-star luxury property that is part of the Waldorf Astoria Resorts, as are Mr. Koertig and his parents. You can let me know individually about your wishes regarding a bachelor and bachelorette evening. We have to respect some traditions. Since we are mentioning traditions, you will also be sleeping in separate suites until the wedding night. No hanky-panky before the ring is on the finger."

"Mr. Furst, you and your witness—I received a call from Mr. Koertig to say that you had asked him—will be fitted for your tuxedos while Ms. Zalewski is back in Montreal. Ms. Zalewski, you will be required to make your decision from the samples here today. Please remember that these are only samples. While they are all suitable for the venue and are in your size, measurements will have to be taken and you will have to be pinned. Some of them have beading all of the way down. It's not just a matter of cutting and hemming."

"I understand, Mr. Bishop. My height does present certain challenges. I am sure that I will find something that I like and my future husband will approve of."

"Thank you, Ms. Zalewski. I'm afraid that I will have to ask Mr. Furst to stay away while you are trying on the dresses. We don't want to invite bad luck, now do we?"

"I look forward to seeing my bride in her dress for the first time on our wedding day, Mr. Bishop."

"Ms. Zalewski, when will your witness be available to fly to London to try on dresses? Depending on what you select, we will pull dresses to correspond to your look."

"Mr. Bishop, Torsten and I just got engaged, I have not had the time to tell my friend about our engagement or the marriage. I don't even know if she will be free to be my maid of honor. I will take care of that when I return to Montreal in a couple of days. We should take some photos of the dresses that I select and I will show them to her. I can assure you that she is a woman with a heightened sense of style and an innate understanding of how to put herself together for any occasion. We do have some shops in Montreal and in Toronto that can handle a wide variety of styles … vintage romantic, traditional, contemporary …"

Cyril Bishop took a moment to center himself as his guru had taught him.

He was not pleased with this development, but the situation was manageable. He would just ask to see photos of the bridesmaid's dress for final approval. There were ways around these things. If Ms. Zalewski was right, then everything would fall into place. If not, he would find a solution. That was what he did and what he was paid to do. It would just be another line on the invoice. "Of course, Ms. Zalewski. To put you into my vision for your glorious day, I will now reveal the theme of your wedding. It will be an all-white wedding and the theme is"—Cyril paused and arched one eyebrow melodramatically—"Diamonds and Pearls."

"That sounds fine, Mr. Bishop, but my best man and I will *not* be wearing white tuxedos."

"Oh. But, Mr. Furst, perhaps you could reconsider. We would never do anything low-brow. This will be very tasteful."

"White dinner jackets and black trousers would suit us better."

"With all due respect, Mr. Furst …"

"White dinner jackets with black trousers, Mr. Bishop."

"White dinner jackets with black trousers it shall be. Ms. Zalewski, any objection to having your witness in white?"

"None. She looks good in white."

"That's a relief. By the way how many guests should we be expecting for the wedding and wedding dinner?"

"Just Mr. Koertig and his parents from my side."

"Ms. Zalewski, what about from your side?"

"My maid of honor, my colleague and his wife, so that's three as well."

"This could work nicely. We won't need a reception room. I see a table for eight on the private roof terrace of the penthouse suite, which is where you will be spending your last night as a bachelor, Mr. Furst. There is a gazebo that we could do up with billowy sheers. We'll have weights sewn into the hems so that they won't blow around, and we'll tie them back with strands of cut crystals and pearls … A heavy white table cloth, white lanterns with ropes of pearls, flower arrangements with white roses and white hydrangeas, dripping with cut crystals … and a triple-tiered butter cream cake decorated with tiny edible pearls and a ribbon tied into a bow and secured with a crystal broach."

"I don't eat cake, Mr. Bishop."

"But it is your wedding cake, Ms. Zalewski. Just a morsel? Your guests might want to have a piece … and for the photos …" Cyril Bishop looked at Torsten for help, and was offered none.

"Alright, Mr. Bishop. We'll go with the wedding cake."

"Thank you, Ms. Zalewski. You scared me there for a second."

"Sorry."

"Now for the schedule." Cyril launched into a minute by minute accounting of how everyone would assemble for the ceremony in Rome and the reception in Munich. As Ela listened, she came to appreciate the value of a wedding planner and felt relieved she wouldn't have to worry about transportation or anything but enjoying her day.

"Ms. Zalewski, would it be too much to ask that your colleague's wife wear white? The photos will be spectacular … Mrs. Koertig has already agreed."

"I am sure she will go along with the theme as well, Mr. Bishop."

"And … does your colleague have a white dinner jacket by any chance?"

"He'll rent one."

"Rent? Really?"

"That's what normal people do, Mr. Bishop. Even with all of the events we attend, I doubt he will have much use for a white dinner jacket."

Now it was Torsten's turn to toy with their wedding planner. "Perhaps Jonas and I should rent as well."

Cyril Bishop was probably seconds away from an anxiety attack.

"Don't tease Mr. Bishop, darling. My fiancé and the best man will not be renting, Mr. Bishop. They will stick to the plan. There's nothing to worry about."

"I didn't mean to make anyone uncomfortable, Ms. Zalewski."

"You didn't, Mr. Bishop."

"By the way, Ms. Zalewski, if you would be so kind as to provide me with your email address and the email addresses of your party. I will contact everyone to find out about food allergies or other dietary considerations. The menu for your wedding supper will be a surprise. Rest assured, Ms. Zalewski, Mr. Furst, neither you nor your guests will be disappointed … quite the contrary."

When Mr. Bishop broke to make a call regarding some of the details they had discussed, as time was of the essence, Ela asked Torsten, "So what are the parents of Jonas Koertig like?"

"Elsbeth and Richart are warm, caring, generous people. They are very adventurous and enjoy traveling. They've certainly earned it. They both worked very hard to build the companies that Jonas took over. They have a wonderful sense of humor, they love their son and they have treated me like a son since Jonas and I became best friends. They have been married for fifty-three years and you should see how they look at one another. They are always holding hands. They even sneak away sometimes when they're attending a big function to steal a kiss. They're like teenagers. They are the happiest married couple I know."

"So, why then does Jonas come off like the perpetual playboy? You would think that he would emulate his parents."

"Nanny issues ..."

Torsten proceeded to tell Ela about Jonas's nanny and his theory ... the abridged version as Mr. Bishop would eventually end his phone call and expect their full attention.

"The good news is that Jonas seems to be interested in someone who is not his usual type."

"Then why is he coming solo to the wedding and reception?"

"I'm not clear on the details, but I think he just met this woman and she does not yet share his feelings."

Cyril Bishop escorted Ela to the makeshift bridal salon after lunch, resolutely shooing Torsten away from the area where the dresses were on display.

Full length mirrors and augmented lighting allowed Ela to take in all of the details of each dress; the screens made for a makeshift changing room that was more than adequate. There was a rack where they could hang the dresses, a shelving unit for all of the accessories, enough room for Ela and the two ladies to move around in, plus a mirror and a platform where she could be pinned.

Each dress was more beautiful than the last. Ela tried on a super sexy lingerie inspired silk dress that was almost indecent because of how low it was cut in the back and how the ruching emphasized her behind. It was held together by two of the thinnest straps that Ela had ever seen. She liked the fluidity of the dress and the small train as well as the lace on the bodice and the crystal appliqué.

Then there was the lace dress with sheer bodice and three quarter sleeves over a white camisole top. It had a slit in front that went up just over the knee and it flared out at the bottom. Ela was not one for lace because she always thought of traditional dresses when she thought of lace. The use of lace with this design achieved a contemporary romantic look she had never seen before. She was looking forward to finding out how she would look in it.

The next three dresses were more modern. One was an unembellished halter column dress with a very short train. Another had thick crisscrossing straps, low back and very small train. It too was an understated column design. The second to last one had a low back and the straps, though on the thicker side, went straight over her shoulders and down. This one was a fit and flare without a train, but it did have significant bling all over.

When Ms. Zalewski came out in the sixth and final dress that did not in any way resemble any of the other dresses, Mr. Bishop jumped to his feet.

"That's it. That's the one." His tone brooked no argument.

"It seems we agree, Mr. Bishop."

The reception dresses were next. There was a halter dress, a one-shoulder dress with a slit in the front, an off the shoulder dress with a slit on the side and a dress with a low back. Two had embellishments. Ela had a pretty good idea, which one would be the one so she saved it for last, but she shouldn't have bothered with the other five.

"*This* is my reception dress, Mr. Bishop."

The dress that Ela had selected as her reception dress was completely different in style from the wedding dress.

"You're very decisive, Ms. Zalewski."

"When you know, you know, Mr. Bishop."

CHAPTER 35

Ela and Torsten said goodbye to Mr. Bishop, and since *Monsieur* Gilbert Destan, the jeweler was not due until the following morning, they could relax for a bit until dinner.

"I would like to discuss something with you, Ela."

"That's your serious tone. What is it?"

"I have been on the phone with my lawyer. I am having him draw up a prenuptial agreement and I am revising my last will and testament."

"The pre-nup is a good idea, Torsten. You have to protect yourself."

"I truly believe that you and I will stay married forever, but a prenuptial agreement will also protect you."

"So, I could take you for a lot of money, then?"

"Don't joke, Ela. This is a serious matter. After one year plus one day of marriage and living together for that time, if we divorce, you will receive three hundred fifty million euros. One year is all that I will ask, so that we can have that time to work through any bumps in the road. If you are the one who wants out before then, you will receive one hundred million euros. If I am the one who wants out before then, you will still receive three hundred fifty million euros. My lawyer tried to convince me to add clauses and conditions, loopholes for me. I have not agreed to this."

"Torsten, I wouldn't stay with you for one year to get three hundred fifty million euros, stupid as it sounds. Nor would I leave you if you lost all of your money and didn't have a dime. *I* would work to support *us* and put food on the table, if it came to that. You can give me nothing in the pre-nup and I'll sign it." Torsten was still learning about what an incredible woman Ela was. He felt incredibly lucky he'd managed to find someone who loved him for himself. Still he ignored her objections.

"When you get back to Montreal, you will need to find a law firm that can advise you. You will have to pay them out of your own money, so that they work in your best interest. My lawyer will send them the prenuptial agreement and also my will which names you as the main beneficiary although about fifty percent of my total wealth will go to various charities."

"I will do whatever you need me to do and when I get back to Montreal, I am going to make the same kind of changes in my own will. There won't be much of an inheritance, I'm afraid but it will be yours—well, maybe a bit for the rescue fund."

"What? You mean I am not marrying a fabulously wealthy woman? I might have to rethink all of this."

"There is still time to get out of the wedding."

"I feel that it would devastate Jonas. He is so invested. The crew would be very disappointed. Mr. Bishop would probably never recover."

"Oh, so you're going to marry me for Jonas, the crew and now Mr. Bishop? Well, perhaps I should rethink this marriage."

Torsten took her in his arms. "I'm going to marry you for only one reason: I am desperately in love with you."

"That's more like it. What do you think if we invite Captain Linquist, First Mate Martinez, Mr. Fraser, the Chefs Vasseur and François to dinner *en famille* this evening, to thank them properly."

"I think you are going to bewitch these people with your warm heart, as you have bewitched me."

CHAPTER 36

Dinner really was *en famille*. Chef Celeste, Chef Pol and François put their heads together and came up with ideas for a Greek feast of fresh fish and seafood.

The cozy little group would start with an appetizer dish of boiled shrimp that were peeled, deveined and refrigerated before being served with latholemono sauce, which as Chef Pol explained was extra virgin Greek olive oil and lemon whipped to creamy consistency. Simple and tasty.

François had served Boutari Santorini Kallisti Reserve 2010, which was a complex vibrant white with green apple and melon coming through at the beginning, then creamy lemon and a hint of ginger, tarragon and good minerality.

As soon as all of the glasses were filled, Torsten raised his. "I would like to thank Chef Celeste, Chef Pol and François for making this evening possible. I would like to thank my brilliant and enchanting fiancée for having suggested it. I think that we should make a point of spending one evening like this every time we are on board. I would like to thank all of you for everything you have done to reunite us."

"Mr. Koertig deserves the credit, sir," Logan Fraser offered. "Operation Reconciliation was one ingenious plan."

"I agree that he deserves a great deal of credit, but without the execution, it would only have been a plan. I think this is the first time that anyone has ever gotten anything over on me … that I know of. It's the kind of deception that I would never reproach anyone for. I believe my fiancée agrees, otherwise she would not have asked that you share this evening with us. We thank you."

The group responded with applause and then it was time to eat.

The main dish turned out to be six. All of the main dishes were placed in the middle and everyone was expected to pass them around family style. There was octopus with eggplant, a fish dish called gavros with peppers, spetsiotiko fish made with sea bream, a dish made with sea bass that was stuffed with garlic and herbs, topped with slices of tomato and baked, stuffed squid in a spicy tomato sauce and prawn sagancki in a tomato sauce made with ouzo and feta. Chef Celeste and Chef Pol thought they should have made some vegetable based side dishes, but everyone protested that they would have a hard time eating all of the dishes set out before them as it was. Besides they could get their fill of vegetables from these dishes.

François had a challenge on his hands. Yes, it was fish and seafood, but the ingredients were not exactly for the timid. He served Mitravelas Agiorgitko Nemea 2011, a vibrant red with red fruit and violets backed by distinct citrus and spice flavors with a mineral finish.

Dessert was uncomplicated but delicious: Greek yogurt drizzled with honey. The dessert wine François had selected was Argos Santorini Vin Santo 1987. It coated the palate with an abundance of flavors like ripe apricots, vanilla, spice, cream, honey and candied ginger. It was a great match for the creamy sweetness of the final dish of the meal.

No one overstepped with their employer and his fiancée, but the conversation had been animated and lively. Torsten smiled at Ela. What a marvel she was. She engaged absolutely everyone at the table, and they were all thoroughly enjoying themselves. She had taken over his yacht and the key people on his crew. This was the kind of mutiny Torsten couldn't have been happier about.

The evening came to an end when the members of the crew at the table realized that it was midnight. Mr. Furst and Ms. Zalewski were generous with their time, but they wouldn't have many more hours together before they would be saying goodbye for a whole month.

Torsten walked Ela to the door of her suite.

"Thank you for this evening ... from me and from the crew."

"I had more fun than all of you, so don't thank me. I should be thanking you ... where do I start? For having listened to the suggestion, for making me an important part of your extraordinary life and quite simply, for making me feel incredibly loved."

"I had no idea that in a matter of days— hours really, my life could change like this, from not having love in my life to having a lifetime of love and happiness to look forward to. It's surreal."

"Tell me about it."

"Well I had better go. Mr. Bishop probably has spies on board ... or something. He did say no hanky panky."

"Are you kidding? There are at least six among the crew that looked as if they would have liked to make him walk the plank or just plain throw him overboard for making them lug all of the stuff he had brought with him and then having the nerve to tell them to put their backs into it ... but alright."

Ela smiled a sweet smile of compliance, craned her neck to give Torsten a chaste kiss on the lips and walked into her suite, leaving Torsten more than a bit disappointed that she hadn't tried to talk him out of returning to his suite.

Enough was enough, Ela told herself resolutely. Self-imposed torture ... How ridiculous. They had only hours together before they would be spending a month apart. She had gotten herself into this, it was up to her to get herself out of it.

Regretting that she hadn't brought something really sexy in the way of nightwear on board, she decided that she would just have to make herself alluring in other ways.

After showering and moisturizing her skin with a rich body lotion, she sprayed Signorina Eleganza by Salvatore Ferragamo on strategic parts of her body, neck, between her breasts, wrists and behind her knees. A flimsy ankle length white silk robe would be all the attire she would need. She planned to walk over to Torsten's suite dressed only in her fragrance, silk robe, engagement ring and signature earrings. Since she was vain and a little self-conscious about her height, she wore her silver heels from the island.

The door to Torsten's suite was closed but not locked. Unfortunately it was pitch black in there. Ela bumped into a piece of furniture in the sitting room. The configuration was the reverse of her suite. She felt her way around and eventually found the door of his bedroom. It was wide open. She bumped into some other kind of furniture. If she didn't locate the bed soon, she would be bruised all over her body by the morning.

"Shit," Torsten heard and smiled to himself, giving no indication that was awake. He decided to pretend that he was snoring, to help her find her way to his bed.

Ela didn't remember Torsten ever snoring, but this was good. At least she could move in the right general direction.

Her toes and then her shins told her she had collided with the frame of the bed. She wondered how he could he sleep through the noise she was making.

Ela felt the bed and found the cover. Torsten was not sleeping on that side. She undid her robe and dropped it on the floor since she had no idea if there was a chair nearby. She stepped out of her sandals and slipped under the covers. The snoring stopped as abruptly as it had started.

Ela contemplated her next move then snaked her way across the bed in the direction of Torsten's even breathing. She was still navigating by sound ... like some sort of bat.

Her body made contact with the full length of his body, but still he did not stir. On her side, supporting her head with hand, she caressed his chest and stomach. Then it was only a short journey to his nether region. She was delighted to find he was already becoming erect.

"You're not asleep. You're getting a hard-on."

"Maybe I was dreaming of you."

"Aha. I knew it. You were just punishing me because abstaining was the worst idea I ever had."

"I was just enjoying all of this. Marrying me a month from now was clearly the best idea you ever had, so that evens things out, don't you think?"

"Technically, it was Jonas's idea, but I think we should keep him out of our bed tonight."

"Agreed. Our bed … I like the sound of that. Now where were we?"

"I'm so aroused, I could climb out of my skin: I need you inside me right now or something terrible might happen."

That was all that Torsten needed to hear. He rolled on top of her, shucking his pajama bottoms along the way. Her lips met his as he moved between Ela's shapely legs. He found her so wet and ready that his erect cock slid inside her in one effortless motion. She moaned and bent her legs to receive all of him, pushing her hips up. Their denial had them both on the edge of ecstacy from the moment they were joined. They were lost in passion and lust, Torsten moving his rock-hard cock in and out of her slick folds as Ela met his thrusts, urging him to go deeper, give her more. Her frenzy was infectious and he drove his member home as he kissed her passionately, both of them succumbing to passion until they climaxed together in mere minutes. Ela wrapped her legs around Torsten to bring him as deeply as possible, grinding against as she waggled her hips, wanting to wring every last drop of pleasure from this, the first time she made love to her fiancé.

"Torsten …"

"Yes, my love?"

"Don't tell Mr. Bishop."

An hour later … "Torsten are you asleep?"

"Yes. Are you?"

"Yes."

"Torsten …"

"Yes, my love?"

"I'm ready for some foreplay."

CHAPTER 37

Monsieur Destan, was a quiet, dignified man. He offered his congratulations to Ela and Torsten as he entered the main living area of the yacht with his own security detail the next morning. Two of the four men that accompanied him took up position on either side of him. They never let the case he carried out of their sight. The other two positioned themselves with their backs to *Monsieur* Destan, looking outward in each direction like the Hapsburg eagle. No one except Mr. Furst and Ms. Zalewski was allowed in the living area.

Monsieur Destan had brought wedding bands for the bride and groom in sizes that would be larger than the actual rings. These demonstrator wedding rings allowed the client to see them on the hand. He would size the bride and groom before leaving and the rings would be made for them in their sizes. *Monsieur* Destan also brought along a few pieces for the groom to choose from for his wedding gift to the bride. Those he would keep hidden from Ela. All of the items would look good with the shape and style of the engagement ring.

Monsieur Destin opened the case and Ela saw five beautiful wedding bands displayed in a row of little slots of black velvet. It would depend on what she wanted to do, *Monsieur* Destan explained. She could wear a wedding band and the engagement ring on the same finger, in which case, the wedding band would have to be slim, as her hand was small. Or, she could switch her engagement ring, which he could not resist commenting on, "Truly extraordinary, the photo did not do it justice," to her other hand and wear a thicker band.

By thinner band, *Monsieur* Destan meant a band of white micro pavé diamonds set in platinum or a band the same thickness, without the micro pavé diamonds. In both cases, the bands were designed to be worn flush with the engagement ring. By thicker, he really did mean thicker. He provided three options that would do just as well if one was to be shopping for diamond and platinum eternity bands. There was a circle of brilliant cut diamonds. There was a band of smaller double tiered diamonds and a band of the same width with micro pavé diamonds in a lace-like pattern.

Having tried them all on, Ela made her decision. It would be the thin micro pavé band that matched the micro pavé band of her engagement ring. As much as she admired some of the others, she liked having both rings together. Torsten selected a thin platinum band for himself.

"Now, Ms. Zalewski, I have something that I need to discuss with Mr. Furst.

Would you be so kind as to leave us? Forgive my rudeness but time is a factor."

"Not at all, *Monsieur* Destan. I'm going to check in with Chef Celeste … I have a secret of my own."

When one of the security guards let Ms. Zalewski out and closed the door behind her, *Monsieur* Destan removed the top tier of the case, put it aside, and then placed the second and third tiers in front of Mr. Furst.

"Since it is customary to give the bride a wedding gift, I took the liberty of bringing some pieces. While he was on the yacht, Mr. Bishop took photos of the dresses that Ms. Zalewski selected and emailed them to me along with the photos of the engagement ring. I am sworn to secrecy about the style of the dresses, but I can tell you which pieces would enhance the dresses your fiancée has chosen. There are also pieces that you may want to order at a later date for a birthday, an anniversary or as a Christmas gift, Mr. Furst."

Torsten looked the whole collection over. There were pendants, necklaces, and bracelets in addition to the eternity rings. He made a mental note of pieces Ela might like for some upcoming occasions, but not anything right for their one-year anniversary … plus a day. No need to mention that last part to the jeweler. "For our one-year anniversary, I am going to surprise my wife with a renewal of our vows, *Monsieur* Destan. I'm going to have to see more rings, when we are closer to the date."

"Very good, Mr. Furst."

"Now what about earrings for her wedding and reception dresses?"

"Well the dresses are quite different, so the earrings would have to be as well. The pearl and diamond ones would work well with the wedding dress and the diamond ones would be ideal for the reception dress."

"You are obviously a man of taste, *Monsieur* Destan. You have seen my fiancée and you know what the dresses look like, which would be your first pick for each dress?"

"Thank you for your confidence Mr. Furst," and with that, the jeweler placed two sets of earrings in front of his new client.

"We will go with your selection for the pearl and diamond earrings, *Monsieur* Destan, but I just had a thought for the reception dress. Did you by any chance notice the earrings that my fiancée was wearing?"

"Yes. One does not see that design every day … with pear shaped diamonds."

"That is where I got the idea for her engagement ring. Ela worked with a jeweler and had those earrings custom designed for her. She wears them all of the time, it's her signature jewelry. If you were to re-create them with larger, higher quality stones in a platinum setting, would they be suitable for the reception dress?"

"Indeed they would, Mr. Furst."

"Good, then please go ahead, *Monsieur* Destan."

"How large, were you thinking?"

"I would like for my fiancée to be able to wear them at any time of the day or evening, with casual wear as well as an elaborate evening gown. They should not weigh her down too much. She won't wear them very often if they are uncomfortable. They should, however, make a statement."

"Certainly. Is there anything else I can do for you, Mr. Furst?"

"I will need a gift for my best man, *Monsieur* Destan. He is the one responsible for re-uniting Ms. Zalewski and I. I believe he retained your services as well. In light of Mr. Koertig's contributions the gift has to be something special. Can you please locate a specific watch for me to give to my best man?"

"I'm sure that I can, Mr. Furst. What timepiece did you have in mind?"

"The Franck Muller Aeternitas Mega 4, if the collector that has the first one is willing to part with it for a substantial increase in price, of course, or the second one made if it is still available."

"I believe the wristwatch you have in mind was valued at over two million euros at the time, Mr. Furst. It's supposed to be the most complicated watch in the world, meaning that it has the most complications in watch-speak."

"It's perfect then … The most complicated watch in the world for the most complicated man in the world."

DIANA SOBOLEWSKI

CHAPTER 38

Ela joined Torsten on the main deck to see *Monsieur* Destan and his stoic security guards off. The jeweler offered his congratulations again and he and his team of security people stepped off the yacht into the waiting motor boats that would take them to shore.

"So did you have a nice *tête-à-tête* with Chef Celeste?"

"Yes, as a matter of fact. I am going to have to return this afternoon for about forty-five minutes, but then I am all yours."

"What mischief are the two of you up to?"

"You'll just have to wait and see."

"What would you like to do between lunch and then?"

"Have you ever seen *The Scarlet Pimpernel* … the re-make?"

"I can't say that I have."

"Well, Jonas did mention that some of the crew were going to watch it, so presumably we should be able to access it."

"You wish to take in a movie in the theater on our last day together?"

"I was thinking … more like in bed."

"Well then, I'll see to it right away."

After an afternoon's torrid lovemaking, Torsten took a fortifying nap while Ela snuck off to the kitchen. When Ela had returned to their suite, her fiancé had only one thing on his mind. Ela, who seemed to have boundless energy, was in the same frame of mind. They would have an hour and a quarter to kill before their apéro, she informed Torsten. Then their early dinner would be served an hour after that.

"Not kill, darling … use productively, is what you meant to say."

"Long foreplay … is that what you meant?"

"So long you are going to beg me to take you."

Torsten had been right *again*.

This time they both fell asleep and woke only minutes before the Franciacorta would be served. Ela hurried into the shower, and Torsten came in after her. Ela's helpful groom-to-be started to soap up her back, then when she turned, he repeatedly passed the sudsy sponge over her breasts and hardening nipples. That's not all that was hardening and the sponge was soon forgotten as Torsten's hands began to do the caressing instead. Suddenly there was a loud knock on the door that was heard in the shower, even with the water running, because the bathroom door was wide open. Ela looked at Torsten in panic. Their Italian sparkling wine was at the door.

"Torsten, my instructions were that Simon should let himself in at the designated time. I left the door to the suite unlocked. I don't know what I was thinking."

There was no time for Torsten to dry himself. He put on his robe and sprinted to intercept Simon, closing the bathroom door behind him as Ela stifled a giggle. They were like horny teenagers.

With Simon gone, Torsten came to tell Ela that the coast was clear.

"Torsten, they are all going to realize how we've been spending our time."

"I should hope so. They would have something to worry about if they found us fully dressed and playing chess. I am sure that someone would place a call to Jonas …"

"When you put it that way … Still I think we should get dressed for when Simon comes back."

While they sipped the Franciacorta, Ela told Torsten that François and she collaborated, but gave him the credit for the idea and the information that she was going to share with Torsten about the sparkling wine that would set the tone for their dinner.

"He is very intuitive, Torsten. He understood right away."

Dinner was served exactly sixty minutes later. Osso bucco with a side dish of garlic scented sautéed broccoli rabe.

"Ms. Zalewski requested that there not be an appetizer, sir. François tasted the wine downstairs, but Ms. Zalewski will tell you about it."

"Thank you, Simon. Would you give us an hour before you serve dessert, then?

"As *Madame* wishes."

"Once again a collaboration with François. Once again, the perfect wine for the dish. This is why François suggested it …"

"I didn't even realize we had it on board. I'll have to keep up with the inventory. The Barale Fratelli Barolo Cannubi Riserva 2006 is going to be amazing with osso bucco."

"So you know this wine, Torsten."

"I know the wine and the producer. Barale Fratelli is one of the oldest estates in Langhe. It was founded in 1870. I think you will like the minerality and the herbal notes. It's a robust wine. The 2006 is velvety and harmonious when decanted. It's a great match for tomato based savory meat dishes.

"Jonas's parents served the Barbera d'Alba Superiore La Preda 2010 not long ago. I remember the ruby red color and that the nose was intensely fragrant ... all kinds of red fruit, but mostly cherries. All in all, a well-balanced, full-bodied wine with a long finish. We ended up opening a second bottle ... due to popular demand. The osso bucco smells great, by the way."

Torsten placed a little of the veal that was falling off the bone, onto the back of his fork with the aid of his knife, as Europeans do, and brought it up to his mouth.

After allowing for the flavors to come through, he spoke. "This is very delicious, but not Chef Celeste's usual recipe."

"That is because I made it ... using my recipe. I didn't want to tell you right away in case you felt you *had* to say it was good. I really wanted to make it for you, my love. Surprise."

"Well, you are going to have to teach it to Alphonse, our chef in Munich. It's *that* good."

"You're not just saying that?"

"I'm really not."

Ela jumped out of her chair spontaneously and hugged the startled Torsten.

"Darling, I'm enjoying all of the affection, but you need not be so shocked. Your osso bucco is utterly and indisputably a pleaser. Chef Celeste and Chef Pol and their team should make it for the whole crew."

"They did."

"Well then, you are going to be even more popular around here, my love."

Torsten ate every bit of Ela's osso bucco and most of the broccoli rabe, but understood why she had not wanted a starter. The veal was very filling ... especially a double serving.

"I'm so glad that someone thought about the bone marrow spoons. I like to scoop out every bit. It's the best part."

"I agree, but I think you should have mine as well, Ela, since you love it so much ... For all of your hard work. The things I do for love."

"Can we put that in the pre-nup?"

"If you make it up to me later."

Dessert was timed as per Ela's request.

"What is this, darling?"

"Fresh figs dipped in dark chocolate. This particular dessert was Chef Celeste's idea. There's a story that goes with it. Apparently, one evening Chef Celeste made these for Chef Pol while they were dating. He took one bite and proposed marriage. He didn't have a ring. It was not planned. It was an instinctive reaction, but a good one, obviously. Look how happy they are to be husband and wife. So I couldn't resist. I suggested that she make a whole batch for her husband for this evening and assured her that we would not call down for breakfast too early tomorrow morning. I am dying to have a bite … and look at the 2000 Banyuls that François selected for us to enjoy with our dessert. Oh wow. The combination is so good, it's insane."

"This is going down as another of our most memorable meals ever … for taste and for the memories. I love that you planned this all out for us."

"I just love you, Torsten … now and forever. I don't know how I am going to be able to leave for Montreal tomorrow. I don't even want to think about it."

"Then don't. Though thirty days will seem like an eternity for us both, after that, we will not have to spend a day apart, if we don't want to. This is a promise that I am making to you right now. Please believe me."

"You're right, my love. I am just being silly. I'm a woman in love."

They decided to have a second glass of Banyuls out on their private terrace under the stars after changing into their robes separately. The built-in heaters would keep things comfortable, but there would be no lights, so that they could really appreciate the night sky. The breeze off the water brought a briny scent to their nostrils.

Ela and Torsten half sat, half lay beside each other on a double lounger. They started kissing softly. Torsten put his glass and Ela's down on the table beside him.

With his hands free, he placed one at the back of her neck and drew her to him. He pressed his lips to hers and the pressure caused her lips to part. His tongue found hers and the kiss was long and deep. She shivered from the strong physical reaction it created in her and not from the sea air. Ela wasn't cold. She was burning up.

Torsten kissed her neck passionately inhaling her scent. When he reached into her robe, her nipples were hard and she arched her back to press her breasts into his hand; longing for a rougher caress.

The belt of Ela's robe came undone on its own and she was freed from the restrictive material. Torsten never tired of looking at her body and never failed to get aroused by it.

Ela slid down into a kneeling position on both sides of Torsten's legs. She then sat down between his legs, elongated her right while she kept the left one bent. She moved her weight onto her left cheek and supported herself in a semi-reclining position with her left hand. She untied his robe to expose his well-exercised body. He was as hard as she was wet.

Ela took hold of Torsten's shaft, stroking it up and down and making him harder still. When the head was nicely lubricated, she worked the head of his cock over her clit and the opening of her pussy; the sigh she heard was affirmation that her lover was not going to object. She was using his cock like a dildo and masturbating with it. The orgasm was thigh-melting. If she was not seated, she would have collapsed. Yet, Ela was greedy for more; she thrust her hips forward, to feel more of his cock pass over her wet clit and pussy. Waves of pleasure overcame her. The second orgasm didn't even take a minute to arrive and was almost as earth shattering and as long as the first.

Torsten remembered how he had asked her to show him how she would make herself come in one of his texts. And, she had in Rome. Now she was taking it to a whole new level, making herself come while teasing and taunting his cock by stopping at the opening of her pussy and then running it over her slick clit.

Torsten had been trying not to come so that she could take her pleasure, but there was only so much that a man could endure. The sensation was completely new; the way she had used his cock was completely new. Not only was he stimulated physically, but the visual magnified all of the sensations. If only Ela would stop teasing him; he longed to take control but was rendered powerless by pleasure.

She dared him, with her actions and her eyes, to do something about it. And finally Torsten did. He moved Ela off him and onto her back. He reached for the lever that flattened the top part of the lounger. He got between her legs, taking her hard while kissing her full on the mouth; his tongue engaging hers. The muscles of his ass flexed as he drove deep into Ela's welcoming pussy. She moaned with delight. Some people thought the missionary position was unimaginative. Ela thought they obviously hadn't had a lover who applied himself the way Torsten did.

On Ela's fourth orgasm, she had company. Torsten felt his orgasm start in his abdomen and balls, travel through the shaft of his cock to the tip. The two of them exploded together, panting and grasping at each other as Torsten strove to bury his cock deep inside her and Ela did everything she could think of to help him. When they both stopped spasming, Torsten managed to speak.

"What was that? Where did you get the idea …?"

"I don't know … probably a side effect of Chef Celeste's chocolate dipped figs. She did say that figs are a very sexy fruit and we have all heard that chocolate is an aphrodisiac."

"I'm going to give that woman a raise."

"Well, one thing's for sure, my darling. I don't think we're going to be a boring old married couple any time soon."

True to her word, Ela did not call for their breakfast too early the next morning. Instead they took a little extra time to enjoy each other in bed. Their lovemaking was sweet and tender. It was like their minds and bodies were trying to absorb everything they were feeling and sharing, so they would have these recollections to sustain them during their separation.

Their last physical embrace in bed came to an end too quickly, and they had to rise, eat breakfast and make ready for their departure from the yacht.

"I don't know how I'm going to be able to sleep without you, Torsten."

"I was thinking the same thing, my darling."

Both Ela and Torsten had been used to sleeping alone, though Ela never slept all that well. Now they could not imagine sleeping without each other. They both slept more soundly when some part of their bodies were in contact.

Ela finally had what she had been searching for, even though she had pretended that she hadn't been searching for this kind of fulfillment ... even though she had rebelled against it.

Ela and Torsten both ordered Greek yogurt with berries, two scrambled eggs and coffee Americano for their last meal together.

What they received was Greek yogurt with fresh blueberries, two scrambled eggs with crabmeat, mimosas and coffee Americano.

"I do not know which chef made our breakfast, but whoever it was had to be in a good mood ... And if one is, the other is too."

"I'm telling you, Torsten ... there is *something* to those chocolate dipped figs."

CHAPTER 39

Saying goodbye to Torsten was hard, but Ela knew that she would be very busy in the month leading up to their wedding, so time would go by fast. She had better make a list.

First on the list was Robert, who had kindly offered to pick her up at the airport. Ela had telephoned ahead to ask him if they could have dinner that night. She had to talk to him right away about something important.

Robert's wife, Diane, would be working at the hospital, so the timing was perfect. Robert said he'd cook at his place, and then send her home in a taxi because he was going to open some wine.

"No wonder the good doctor agreed to marry you after only a short courtship. The meal was out of this world. Simple but delicious. This was some of the best smoked salmon I have ever eaten. The Domaine Feuillat-Juillot Montagny 1er Cru Les Platières 2013 worked really well with the silky texture of the smoked salmon. The steak was so tender and flavorful; I can't believe I ate the whole thing. I love a good steak on a charcoal barbeque, medium rare. The Château Fleur de Boüard 2009 has a little spice to it, and brought out the spices you used on the steaks. So many people have told me that the producer is *la référence* when it comes to Lalande de Pomerol. What drew you to these particular wines? I presume you have tasted them before deciding to serve them this evening."

"Diane and I tasted them just last week. As you know the Montagny 1er Cru Les Platières 2013 from Domaine Feuillat-Juillot being a white Burgundy is one hundred percent Chardonnay, so it would normally be a good choice for a variety of fish dishes and shellfish anyway. It's young, so it has that pale yellow color you would expect. I like how brilliant it is in the glass. It has good minerality and some white fruit, but what attracted me to this particular wine is that it also has these appealing floral notes. Another thing I like is that it is a little racy and therefore fresh on the finish. That's what cuts through the richness of the smoked salmon, so your palate is not fatigued.

"That last time that I was in Burgundy for *Les grands jour de Bourgogne*, Ela, I tasted two other *premier crus* from this producer. Les Jardins was very expressive on the nose … lots of yellow fruit. On the palate, the wine was supple and round with intense notes of yellow fruit. It would be amazing with one of your favorite dishes, salmon tartare. Les Coères was really something. It was this brilliant light gold color with rich aromas of white fruit, a hint of vanilla and pastry cream. The wine had good volume on the palate and a long generous finish. Personally I would serve it with a lobster or scallops. The owner of Domaine Feuillat-Juillot produces other *premier crus,* but she was swarmed by importers. Her wines must be very popular. If I hadn't been the height that I am with long arm range, I would probably not have had the opportunity to taste even the Les Jardins and Les Coères. I kept coming back, but there were just too many buyers tightly crammed in around her … tasting and asking about the wines and the prices. I'll just have to wait until some of her other wines get to Quebec."

"I'm sure that they will do very well here."

"As for Château Fleur de Boüard 2009 … it's a very worthwhile discovery, I think we would both agree. The 2009 is eighty-five percent Merlot, twelve percent Cabernet Franc and three percent Cabernet Sauvignon. It spent twenty months in oak. In some ways, it's still young. I'm sure you've noticed that the color is very dark with purple highlights. You get dark fruit and red fruit, mingled with vanilla and mocha, so there is a lot going on. I find that though it is structured and powerful, the tannins are velvety, so it feels ample in the mouth, and it has that long finish that keeps you thinking about the enjoyment of having tasted this wine, way after you have taken your last sip. It is not overwhelmed by the flavors of the steak, nor does it overwhelm the flavors of the steak."

"Well put."

"You know, I never thanked you for talking Diane and I into finding a house in N.D.G., your old stomping ground. The Newton Group, you recommended way back then really came through for us and we've loved every minute in this house—something else I never thanked you for properly by the way. I guess it's just dawned on me because we're having dinner here."

"It's us, Robert. Forget it."

"Well, if it wasn't for you we would not have looked into N.D.G. at all. We love being in the Monkland village. We're discovering the neighborhood from the culinary side as well … like Monkland Taverne. It's upscale and down to earth at the same time. The wine list is to our liking. We can even walk to it."

"It sounds like you've had many a date night there."

"Yes, but since Diane likes my cooking, we eat in quite a bit too. The shops on Monkland Street are great whether you just want to pick up something quick and easy or put on a big spread. The smoked salmon and steaks came from Maître Boucher. They only deal with top quality suppliers. Even their fruits and vegetables are something very special. The cheeses are friggin' unbelievable.

They carry the best cheeses produced in Quebec and the best cheeses produced in France, and are very knowledgeable when it comes to pairing cheeses with wines. You and I know, that's not always an easy thing to do."

"I remember well."

"By the way, you were right about Tranzo on Somerled … Nice cuts of meat, really good cheeses, many of them Italian, and they carry all kinds of other Italian delicacies. If you go there hungry, you'll be taking two big shopping bags home. The Italian style roast chicken is addictive. Diane and I get it for lunch on the Saturdays when she's not working. And the guys are very nice and helpful. You can always count on them for cooking tips when you want to try a new recipe."

"It's like visiting family when you go in there."

"The location is great. Diane is very happy to be so close to the new hospital. It takes her no time at all to get to work now. We both love everything about N.D.G. It's such a vibrant community. I can see why houses don't stay on the market long and why landlords don't have any problem getting top dollar. I'm actually kind of surprised that you didn't move back."

"I had different needs, but I will always have a soft spot for N.D.G. I have been going for manicures and pedicures at Lyly Nails on Monkland for twelve years. They are absolutely the best. So, you see, I haven't totally abandoned the neighborhood. I like what you and Diane have done with the house, incidentally. This deck is fantastic."

"The house is not quite fully furnished yet, as you saw. We have a lot of space to fill, especially with a finished basement. Well, almost finished. We have the family room, guest bedroom, home gym, laundry room, full bath and a good size storage room. There is one more space, that we don't know how we are going to use yet, so we've left it for now … maybe a cold room. At least all of the other renovations are done."

"I might be able to help you fill it up a little more. It seems that there is some commonality in our decor. Shall we start by addressing the elephant in the room? I haven't exactly been trying to hide the rock on my left hand, and you never asked."

"I knew you'd get around to it sooner or later. You're the one who wanted to talk."

"I'm engaged to be married."

"I see."

"I see? That's all you're going to say? I recall the trepidations when I was flying off to Rome on short notice. That was you, wasn't it?"

"Well, you returned unharmed."

"What would you say if I told you that I am going to be marrying Torsten

Lucas Furst?"

"I would first have to acknowledge that he's a brave man. Then, I would say congratulations. Is that not the appropriate response?"

"Are you on medication?"

"I may have had my doubts in the past, but I think it's the right thing for you."

"Even if it's in a month from how?"

"That soon? But why not? You're not getting any younger."

"I'm going to overlook the age remark because of the excellent wines and superb meal. Anyhow, I'm going to be living in Bavaria after the wedding."

"That makes sense. Marriages usually fare better when both parties are on the same continent, don't you think?"

"You're not curious about what's going to happen with the agency?"

"I'm sure you're going to tell me any minute now."

"I want you to have it. I don't mean buy it. I want to turn it over to you. I am going to be discussing how to do this with some lawyers this week. Our producers couldn't be in better hands and you will have a viable agency. You will be able to take it to the next level. You've always wanted us to hire outside sales representatives, an inside salesperson and a marketing coordinator. You will even be able to develop the private importation side now. I will advise the producers, who all know and adore you, so it will be a very smooth transition. Keep the name, or change it if you like, Robert."

"There's a lot of equity built into the name Les Vins EZ Inc., Ela, and I'm kind of attached to it. I would prefer to keep it."

"You're not getting all sentimental on me, by any chance, are you?"

"Perish the thought." Robert frowned as if she had said something utterly preposterous.

"What was I thinking? I'm glad you'd like to keep the name." It was Ela that was getting emotional. "Robert, I'm very proud of all that we've achieved with the agency, but there's something that I have left undone."

"You've never said anything before."

"Well, it wasn't really pertinent to our sales."

"What is it?"

"You know how at the events in Bordeaux, they serve Champagne at the cocktail hour? Well I've always wanted to get some of the châteaux we work with to serve the Champagnes of our producer at their grand *soirées*. It was just a personal goal I had, that I never got around to. Could you maybe work on that?"

"Of course."

"Thanks. I'm sending some personal items ahead to Munich, but I would like you and Diane to have anything you want from my apartment, all of the furniture, the sound system, the paintings, the massive beveled mirror with the heavy frame that you always admired, the dishes, the flatware, the glassware, the area rug, the lighting and my wine cellar with contents, if there are any bottles left by then, and whatever else there is. Also I'm only taking my laptop, the rest of my computer equipment is yours. You'll need it to run the agency. If you want these things, that is."

"We could use all of that. Thank you."

"It will be like I'm living with you."

"That's a scary thought."

"Once again … I going to pretend that I didn't hear that. Where was I? Oh, yes. Everything will be packed up and delivered to you after the wedding and once that is done, my lawyers will arrange for the sale of the apartment."

"That gives me an idea: Diane and I bought this duplex with the intention of renting out the top floor to help pay the mortgage. In view of the fact that there are all of these changes coming, and I will need a proper office, it might make more sense for me to set up an office on the second floor instead of leasing somewhere else. There is a separate entrance and we soundproofed both floors in every way possible. I will have to discuss it with Diane, but I think she would like it if I were to be one floor up in the same building. It would save on commuting time and when we have kids, it would be very convenient."

"I can see that working. Now, I am going to ask you for a big personal favor. I want to establish a permanent charity with fund-raising events for animal rescue groups and animal shelters in and around Montreal. The city has been my home my whole life, and I know the organizations that operate in this geographical area. My project has to do with wine sponsorships, and, while I plan to do most of the heavy lifting from Munich, I want you to administer it locally. Torsten and I will compensate you for your time. We're also going to put quite a bit of money behind this initiative. If you agree, we'll still be working together in a way. I'd like that."

"That is incredibly generous, Ela. You can count on me. Diane and I are planning to adopt a little rescue to make our house a home. As you know, N.D.G. is a very dog-friendly community."

"When is this going to happen?"

"Soon. We started looking on websites. We've also asked around about the vets in our area, and of course, we needed to get the yard fenced first. My wife, the doctor, has been doing research on food. We've even strolled into a couple of pet stores to see about doggie beds and safe toys. Diane has been eyeing the rain coats, winter coats and booties. This girl or boy is not only going to be dry and warm, but fashionable as well, if my wife has anything to say about it."

"I can see that Diane and you are going to be very responsible doggie parents."

"If the addition to our family is a *she*, we'll name her Ela."

"Well then, Ela might just get a trust fund."

"Ela it is ... Even if she ends up being a *he*."

"I will need to Skype with my namesake ... regularly."

"Naturally."

"Do you have plans for obedience training?"

"With a name like Ela, what do you think?"

"I should have seen that coming. Now, I have one more request: Would you and Diane come to the wedding and wedding dinner in Rome and then the reception in Bavaria?" At his enthusiastic nod, Ela proceeded to give Robert the details. At this point, he found it necessary to pull out a pad and pen, so he could take notes and tell Diane. Ela assured him that Mr. Bishop, the wedding planner, would be getting in touch with him and Diane in a couple of days with all of the details, so he shouldn't worry about writing it all down now. She did prepare Robert for Mr. Bishop's personality, though.

"Just think of him as one the more *unusual* producers we've represented."

Robert, I think you, Diane, Isla and I should have dinner once Mr. Bishop sends us everything, so we can go over it together."

"I'll cook."

"I was hoping you'd offer. I'll bring the wine."

CHAPTER 40

Second on the list was Isla Duncan. Ela asked Isla if they could have lunch at L'Express on St-Denis. L'Express was a Montreal institution. This was French bistro style food at its best. Dishes didn't always have to be over thought. These were prepared with fresh wholesome ingredients and they were delicious. That was only part of the reason that the well-heeled and the artists sought out this establishment, though. The same for people in the wine industry. The wine list was excellent. Plus L'Express had that Paris bistro vibe. It was always filled to capacity when Ela and Isla got together there. Management and staff were super knowledgeable about wine and very friendly. Ela had even taken some of her producers to L'Express for lunch and dinner. When she needed to have a business meeting early in the morning, she'd have it there over breakfast.

Ela knew that Isla made it a point to be punctual, so Ela arrived a few minutes in advance and was seated when Isla arrived. Ela rose to exchange the two-cheek kiss, as was the custom not only in France, but in Quebec. She was careful to conceal her ring. She had twisted the ten-carat pear shaped diamond around and closed her palm over it.

"How did it go on the mega yacht? I'm sure it was a very glamorous experience, but was it productive as well?"

"More like life-changing. As in my life is going to be changing … in a novel-by-Isla-Duncan kind of way."

"I am intrigued."

"First, some wine?"

"When have I ever turned down wine when we're out together? We'll start with a Chablis? I think something special is in order since you obviously have good news. You're positively beaming."

"It's very good news. That's why I decided on Domaine Raveneau. I already ordered. We're in for a real treat. This is one of the most celebrated properties of Chablis. The wines are so rare that some of my French producers have a hard time getting them in France. So, I take them here and surprise them."

"You're very good to your producers."

"That's what they've told me."

After taking the time to show proper reverence for the sublime white

Burgundy made with one hundred percent Chardonnay grapes, the two friends put down their glasses.

"Don't keep me in suspense."

"Are you doing anything three and a half weeks from now?"

"Neither my agent nor my publicist have anything scheduled until the Frankfurt Book Fair in October. I was just planning to write and go out with you to taste rare wines like this. Why?"

Ela held up her hand, smiling from ear to ear.

"You could poke someone's eye out with that thing. It's the most beautiful ring I have ever seen— not that I have ever seen a diamond even close to this size before. Was David worried that with all of the men around you when you travel on business, eventually one of them would steal you away, and proposed upon your return from Greece?"

"No, it's not David. He doesn't know yet. I'm dreading having to tell him."

"He's not going to take it well. From everything you've told me about him and the two of you, I'm pretty sure he's in love with you, you know."

"I've sensed it for some time."

"So ... a Greek wine producer that is very, very rich by the size of your sparkler, I presume."

"It's not a Greek wine producer. It's the owner of the yacht."

"Are you sure you want to marry someone you just met? You didn't bump your head on the yacht or anything like that?"

"I didn't just meet him, Isla. Remember when I mentioned that there was a man I was going to tell you about one of these days?"

"I was going to ask you about him a couple of times, but thought that it would be better to let you get around to it, when you were ready."

"His name is Torsten Lucas Furst. He is a double digit billionaire. He is German and lives in Barvaria, but he has lived all over Europe and even in the United States for a period of time.

We met in Bordeaux during Vinexpo."

Isla raised an eyebrow, interested in hearing more.

"Two days in a row I rode the hotel elevator down with this really handsome man: He was tall, muscular ... masculine and refined at the same time. On both occasions he was wearing a well tailored suit. I remember thinking that I had never seen a man wear a suit as well as he did. I liked the way his sandy blond hair was cut into that retro style too—you know parted on the side. He had this presence about him, and expressive blue eyes and engaging smile that drew me to him. I was so attracted to him and couldn't believe it when he asked me to join him for breakfast the second day, after some small talk. Well we ended up having Champagne at the hotel that night and sitting together the following evening at this gala banquet that he got himself invited to because I would be there."

Ela paused and took a sip of the extraordinary Chablis.

"Anyhow, he came to Montreal on business the following week and we had this amazing dinner. I was peeved because he seemed to be very attracted to me, but sent me home after dinner, rather than inviting me to his suite. I couldn't figure him out. He was going to be occupied with business for the three weeks that followed, but made out like we'd see each other again. I wasn't entirely sure he'd carry through. During this time he never missed an opportunity to send me a text. Eventually we started sexting, which led to an invitation to join him in Rome. Just thinking about it makes me weak in the knees. Torsten was the best lover I have ever had. But we connected emotionally too and that made the lovemaking even more fulfilling. I was falling for a man that I barely knew. I was surprised that he felt that way too. We made plans to see each other in Montreal to discuss being together. I couldn't have been happier."

"So what went wrong, Ela?"

"There was this hitch. He was married. It was in name only and they maintained separate residences, which they kept from her high-society friends. He didn't want to divorce her because he wanted to protect her reputation. But he also wanted me."

"So he wanted you to be his mistress?"

"I was really mad that he cared more about her feelings than mine and we had this big fight. He walked out on me and I fell apart. He tried to get me back by buying a company in Vienna and having the president offer me a contract without me knowing that he was behind it. I found out. Then he had one of my producers invite me to an event at her château in Bordeaux and he was the only one there. He didn't say any of the things I longed to hear, so I told him about David and let him jump to his own conclusions. Then I pretended to go to the bathroom, left a hurtful note, snuck out the back door and got into a waiting car. He didn't come after me. I didn't hear from him after that. That night Torsten was going to tell me that he was divorced, that he was in love with me and ask me to marry him. He was nervous and looking for the right words. He had the ring in his pocket. When he read the note, he thought that I didn't want anything to do with him and that I had moved on. The truth was that I had never fallen out of love with him. I really screwed it up. That one was on me."

"So, Torsten finally came up with a better plan?"

"He didn't have anything to do with it. It was his best friend that devised the plan and the crew helped him to execute it."

"So, this Karsten Reimann is Torsten's best friend and the one behind the plan?"

"Yes, only his name is not Karsten Reimann. It's Jonas Koertig. At first I was furious. I didn't appreciate being manipulated like that. But it seems that I was rather hasty in judging him because he just wanted Torsten and I to be happy. Torsten revealed that people think all of the wrong things about Jonas and that's just how he likes it. He wants people to believe that he would rather play than work, for example. He's so good at creating this illusion, that sometimes even Torsten forgets that it's just an illusion. Apparently, Jonas plays it that way, so that business rivals never see him coming. Torsten told me that Jonas knows exactly what's going on with every single company he owns and he owns a great many of them. Like Torsten, he started off with family money and family businesses, but he expanded their holdings and increased their fortune way beyond what anyone could have predicted. He's just *that* brilliant. I am becoming quite fond of Torsten's best friend, myself."

"Fascinating, but I need details about what took place."

"Let's order and I think we better have another bottle of something on standby. This is going to take a while."

"Wow, Ela," Isla exclaimed after taking another sip of wine, "it sounds like your trip was a lot more exciting than mine. Congratulations, and I really mean that. I love to see you this happy. I truly believe that you and Torsten belong together from everything you have just told me. I couldn't have written a better story. But … I'm not crazy about the idea of losing my closest friend. It took me all of these years to find this kind of friendship."

"I'm still going to be your technical advisor on wine, so we'll be working together and we'll probably have to meet up eventually to taste the wines together. Robert and I will be working together on a charity, so I'll be coming to Montreal at least twice a year. You're in Europe a couple of times per year for one thing or another, so you can come out to visit Torsten and me in Munich. Come for some R & R after the Frankfurt Book Fair, for example. If it's anything like Vinexpo, you'll need it."

"That doesn't sound too bad."

"We would always be locked in, if you would be my maid of honor. Mr. Bishop keeps referring to you as my witness because it's going to be a civil ceremony, but I don't like that title. It's impersonal, like you're an onlooker. I don't much care for maid of honor either though. 'Maid' makes me think of a giggly maiden or a servant. Jonas is going to stand up with Torsten and Torsten refers to him as his best man. What if we call you my best woman? Yes, I like that better. Isla Duncan, will you be my best woman?"

"I would be honored … but, you're going to give Mr. Bishop apoplexy."

"I suspect so."

"So, what is going to happen? Do I need to be recording this?"

"No. Mr. Bishop will email you everything that you will need to know about our wedding, down to the minute. Besides the ceremony is going to be an intimate affair. Torsten and I, you and Jonas, Jonas's parents and Robert and Diane. Jonas is giving us the wedding and wedding dinner in Rome, plus Mr. Bishop's services, as a wedding present. His parents, who are like second parents to Torsten, are giving us the reception in Bavaria, at their ancestral home ... or should I say, mansion. It's their wedding present to us. There will be quite a few guests that evening.

"Anyhow, Mr. Bishop has a theme for each venue ... Let me show you on my phone what I have selected for my wedding dress and the reception dress. We're having an all-white wedding with crystals and pearls. For the reception, Mr. Bishop went with white and silver. I have to admit that I like what Mr. Bishop is doing. He had great anxiety about allowing you to select your own dresses, by the way. The man wants to control everything. I assured him that you were quite capable in that department."

"Thank you. Would you like to go shopping with me, so that you can have the final say?"

"If I didn't have so much to do, I would—but not for approval, just to see how great you look. Have one of the salespeople take a photo with your phone of the dresses you've selected, and send them to me."

"Absolutely."

"Oh! Can you do me a favor when you are trying on dresses?"

"Sure ... what?"

"Can you find the most hideous ill-fitting dresses in white and some other color and have someone photograph you in those and send them to me?"

"I have never shopped in stores that sell hideous ill-fitting dresses and I don't plan to start now."

"Well then, have some shots taken in a couple of dresses that are at least two sizes too big or something like that."

"That I can do, but why am I doing this? Are you planning to blackmail me?"

"I'm going to send the photos to Mr. Bishop and tell him that there is no time to have them altered. Then, I'll let him know that I was only kidding and I'll send him the real photos."

"I swear you're trying to kill that man."

"Mr. Bishop needs some fun in his life."

"Can you please send the photos of your wedding dress and reception dress to my phone, so I can refer to them when I'm shopping?"

Ela pressed *send*. "And ... they're gone."

"These are gorgeous. I like that you chose modern vintage for the wedding.

It's romantic and so right for Rome. I also like that you went sophisticated sexy for the reception dress. Now I'm really excited to go shopping."

"That's what I want to hear."

"This will be the right occasion to pull out some family heirlooms. My mother inherited a diamond and white gold Art Deco bracelet and a pair of pearl and diamond earrings set in white gold in the same style, from a favorite aunt who was fairly well off. We never had much money but my father insisted my mother keep the jewelry no matter what and she wore it for special occasions. I associate the jewelry with very happy family memories. Now, I have a reason to wear the earrings and bracelet."

"I love that. Speaking of jewelry, I don't see the Claddagh ring on your hand."

"It clashes with my other jewelry."

"You haven't been wearing it, have you? You were spooked by the dream, weren't you?"

"Nonsense. It's just that it's not my style …"

"I'm going to ask you to wear it in Rome, where I can keep an eye on you. As my best woman, I don't think you can refuse me. I believe there is some sort of code …"

"It' not going to work with either dress or the Art Deco jewelry."

"No, it's not, but you can wear it before and after. Who knows, if your aunt was right, you might meet your soulmate in Rome. Wouldn't that be fabulous?"

"Why are you so stuck on this?"

"You are an incredible woman, and I am newly in love and I want you to be with an incredible man … that's all. Besides Rome is such a romantic city. Maybe you'll bump into a handsome Italian while out shopping—if Mr. Bishop allows us any free time, that is."

"Well, since there's a code … Is it okay if I wait until we are on our way to Rome to put the ring back on?"

"Yes. I am capable of compromise, now and then … well in this matter, anyway."

"So how are you and Torsten coping with being apart?"

"We Skype every day and text each other a couple of times a day … very suggestive texts. I'm not sure if that makes the separation easier or more difficult … It depends on the day."

"Anything you want to share?"

"Nope. Anyhow, Torsten is busy too. He is reorganizing his corporations so that we can have more time together as a couple, even after the honeymoon."

"The man is completely devoted to you … that's obvious. I'm so happy for you, my friend."

CHAPTER 41

Third on the list was David Vaughn. Ela couldn't sleep the night before she was going to be meeting David for a glass of wine. She was about to break the man's heart. He deserved better. She felt like such a horrible person.

Ela contemplated breaking the news to David by video call, but that was the cowardly way out. She owed it to him to tell him in person.

David had been surprised that she said "glass of wine" rather than suggesting one of their favorite restaurants, where they would normally go through a couple of bottles of fine wine. He had a feeling something was up and it was not good. She had been acting distant since she got back from Greece.

"Hi, beautiful. What's up?"

"What do you mean?"

"You didn't sound like yourself when you called about meeting for a glass of wine … not even dinner when we haven't seen each other in two weeks. It can only mean that you want to make a quick getaway."

"You've always been able to read me, David."

"Get it over with, Ela, before you lose any more sleep. Those dark circles under your eyes tell me something is bothering you."

Ela pulled out her left hand from under the bar where it had rested on her knee.

"Who's the lucky man? Or, do I have to ask?"

"It's the man I was with in Rome, the man I broke up with before you. Torsten."

"This happened while you were away in Greece?"

"Yes, it's a long story but I want you to know I had no idea he would be there; his best friend re-united us."

"How soon?"

"Three weeks."

"That soon?"

"Yes, it's all arranged. It will take place in Rome. I will be living in Bavaria."

"You're sure?"

"I'm sure. I'm sorry, David. I feel really bad … about us."

"Don't feel bad, Ela. You never led me on. You were always very honest about where I stood with you. It's just that I had hopes … What I realize now is that you can't make someone love you … especially when *the someone* is still in love with another person. So, I guess this is goodbye, Ela. I just want you to know, that I will never regret the time we spent together. I relished every moment. I have to be truthful though, this does hurt. Like, I said … not your fault, but it's going to take a little time to come to terms with how things turned out, and to get over you … I think that I had better go now."

"I'm so sorry, David."

"Just be happy." David stood up and kissed her on the forehead. "If you ever need anything, you know where to find me," and with that, he placed cash on the bar and exited without looking back.

"Goodbye, David," Ela said to herself, because David was out of the building and out of her life. Ela would not be sleeping well that night. She couldn't help it … she felt a profound sense of loss. She could relate to how David was feeling. She had felt like that, when Torsten had walked out on her.

CHAPTER 42

Cyril Bishop opened the email from Ela Zalewski on his phone. She had sent along a couple photos of her best woman in the dresses for the wedding and the reception. She warned him that unfortunately, there was no time to have either dress altered.

Best woman? He'd never had a client like Ms. Zalewski. She had a peculiar way about her.

That was not the worst of it. When Cyril Bishop opened the attachments, there was a lovely woman with delicate features staring out at him from a couple of oversized dresses. They hung of her small frame like potato sacks.

Oh no, no, no. This would not do. Cyril's panic rose. The photographs would be spoiled. If anyone saw them, his reputation would be ruined. Why had he allowed Ms. Zalewski her own way? She had showed such good judgment … up until now. How was going to undo this colossal mistake?

A second email came up; it was from Ms. Zalewski as well. There were attachments—Cyril took a calming breath and sat down; bracing himself before opening up the email. He read:

Mr. Bishop,

Please disregard the previous email and attachments. I was playing a prank on you. I hope you'll forgive me. The dresses that my best woman is wearing in these photos are the dresses that she will be wearing for the wedding and for the reception. They require very little in the way of alterations, except for hemming and the boutique assured her that she would be able to come by in a week, to check the fit.

Ela Zalewski

Cyril Bishop opened the first attachment and breathed a sigh of relief. This time Ms. Zalewski's best woman was dressed in an exquisite white dress that matched the bride's dress perfectly and fit her proportions exactly. The earrings and bracelet were just the right touch. She looked to the manor born.

He was hopeful about the second dress now. Oh, thank goodness. The black dress for the reception was spot on. Ms. Zalewski had been right. This woman knew how to put herself together. He could almost forgive Ms. Zalewski for taking ten years off his life.

DIANA SOBOLEWSKI

CHAPTER 43

Ela's last day in her apartment made her feel very nostalgic. Many of her things were already boxed or packed, waiting for the moving company to take them away. This would be the last time she would be sleeping in her bed. Tomorrow evening, the limousine would come for her. Isla and her luggage would already be in the car. They would be picking up Robert and Diane on the way to the airport. Ela would hand her keys over to the doorman, who would get them to her lawyers. She always gave him a Christmas gift. Tomorrow she would give him an envelope with a few bills to thank him for his years of keeping the building secure, opening doors for her, accepting wine samples for her and a wide array of other services. She had done the same with her cleaning lady two days ago. The car had been taken care of the previous week. Tomorrow, Ela would be leaving behind her home, her city and her old life.

She had contemplated holding on to the place and using it when she'd be back to meet with Robert or get together with Isla, but that would not be very practical. She would be Mrs. Furst and Mrs. Furst would need to get around with security and would have to stay in a more secure location, like the Montreal Ritz. Tonight she was still Ela Zalewski and Ela Zalewski reflected back on what a gratifying life she had had.

Isla had offered to come over and sleep on the Murphy bed if Ela didn't want to be alone. She didn't want her best friend to be sad. Isla wanted to keep her focused on the happy and exciting life that lay ahead.

Ela declined. She wanted be alone with her thoughts, memories and emotions. She talked with Torsten via Skype at the beginning of the day, but let him know that she needed some time to herself, until the following morning. He knew why without Ela having to tell him.

Ela Zalewski wanted to remember every inch of her apartment and walked the small space over and over. She sat on the sectional. She sat at the dining table which doubled as a work table. She sat at her desk. It was the first time in a long time, she could see her desk. Gone were the piles of files. She remembered Robert saying that she had more files on her desk than in the filing cabinet. It had been true.

Not to have to rely totally on memory in the years to come, Ela re-traced her movements and took photos of every corner of her apartment.

Ela would take photos of her balcony and from her balcony, so she could relive the view at dawn, during the day, at dusk, during the evening and at night. She'd save all of the photos on her phone and send them to her computer as well.

Ela had her breakfast of berries and yogurt and morning coffee out on the balcony. She ordered lunch in from a bistro in Old Montreal that prepared a kick-ass meal-size salmon tartare, and ate it out on the balcony with a bottle of Langhe Chardonnay 2013 from Fratelli Barale, the producer of the Barolo Cannubi Riserva 2006 that she and Torsten had enjoyed with the osso bucco on the *Second Chance*. This Chardonnay, with its pale straw yellow color, was known for its exotic fruit, floral notes, and freshness on the lingering finish. Ela just thought of it as liquid sunshine.

When evening rolled around, Ela ordered the same thing for dinner. The people at the bistro probably thought she was nuts, but she couldn't get enough of this dish. She wouldn't be able to taste it again for a long time, so why not. This would be her last meal of the day and her last dinner in what had been her refuge and the nerve center of her small but dynamic agency. The occasion called for something special to drink. The something special had been chilling to the correct serving temperature and was waiting for her to release it. Ela eased the cork out of the flacon and poured herself a glass of Champagne de Venoge Louis XV Brut 1996. It would be the symbolic bridge between her old life and her new life. She had first tasted it in this very space as a wine agent and the last time she had tasted it was with Torsten … that night on the island. The next time she would taste it would be as Torsten's wife. It was a fitting choice for this evening. She would enjoy it into the night and when the clock struck midnight it would be the first day of the rest of her life and she would take her last sip and retire to the bedroom. Ela hoped whoever would buy her apartment would be as happy here as she had been.

CHAPTER 44

Ela had hours to get ready before the limousine would be out in front of the building. She had done most of her packing a couple of days earlier, and only needed to do some light laundry and throw a few items into the suitcase last minute.

Though Ela assured Robert that she had plenty of food on hand to nibble on throughout the day, he insisted on coming over with the ingredients to make her a crustless cheese and tomato quiche.

Robert told Ela that he would be having lunch with her, to make sure that she had a good helping of the high protein dish.

"If it's as tasty as that veggie and cheese pizza with the no-carb cheesy cauliflower crust that you made me, then there may not be much left for you."

"I'll take my chances. I'll start cooking, and you can open the wine. It's going to work well as our aperitif and with the quiche. It's a rosé from Languedoc, so it's more full-bodied in style."

"You brought wine and you're going to drive home?"

"I came by taxi."

"Okay … just asking."

Ela reached into one of the large re-usable bags and pulled out the bottle that was sitting in a wine chiller.

"Already chilled. You thought of everything."

Before reading the attractive modern label, she reacted to the stopper. "What is this and how do I open it?"

"It's a cork with a twist … literally."

"It looks a little like a Champagne cork, only flatter on top."

"It's the Helix twist cork for still wine. There is an interface thread finish inside the bottle. You twist it open and you can reinsert the cork the same way. It's the latest technological innovation that does the job of a traditional cork, has the elegance of a cork for that premium look and is sustainable. At the same time, it's user-friendly with the practicality of a screw top. No corkscrew required."

"You know a lot about this, I see."

"I'm a wine agent. I did the research."

"So how is the Helix cork made?"

"From cork fragments pressed into a mold. I read that this cork and bottle system only requires a minor adjustment to existing filling lines."

"This is pretty cool ... but some people will miss that pop sound you get with a traditional cork."

"You still get that experience with the Helix cork. Go ahead. See for yourself."

So Ela did, and Robert was right. She had gotten so carried away, she hadn't yet looked at the label.

"How do you know this and how did you get your hands on this bottle?"

"Look at the label."

"Domaine Guizard Folie d'Oc Languedoc 2014. This is the producer that your friend Sylvain was raving about."

"Sylvain and his wife went back to where they honeymooned for their vacation. This time they brought back four bottles of this rosé. They gave me one as a thank-you for driving them to the airport and picking them up. They purchased it at a big wine store called Megavins only days after it was launched there ... First time ever in France. So, today I was looking through my wine cellar for something that would go with the tomatoes and other ingredients and there it was. It's sixty percent Grenache, twenty percent Syrah, and twenty percent Mouvèdre. Whites wines would have been too aromatic and red wines too heavy."

"I do know that a worthwhile rosé is difficult to make. People should not think of it as a lesser wine because it is meant to be consumed young or for any other reason. They should think of the wonderful versatility of rosé wines. I'm partial to the dry ones personally, where the sugar is less than 4 g/L."

"My preference as well. So, we should like the Folie d'Oc."

"You'll be tasting it for the first time, with me."

"That's right."

"We haven't done that for a while."

"So let's get to it. Would you please pour? I'll taste it as soon as I wash my hands."

"I like the pale color with a touch of coral. The nose is intense. Red fruit and a hint of vanilla. Love that. Citrus fruit on the palate. It's mellow ... the type of rosé you just keep on drinking ... and it has a nice long finish. I would build a whole picnic or brunch around just this wine—many bottles of it—if I could cook, that is. It's the perfect summer day in a glass. I'd want to drink it from spring into fall, in anticipation of summer and so that summer would linger when fall approaches ... and there's Indian summer."

"Shall we drink to good choices, then?"

"Oh yeah."

CHAPTER 45

Isla thought Ela looked radiant, like a bride should. She jumped out of the limousine before the driver had a chance to open the door for her. Isla hugged her friend, sharing in Ela's obvious happiness. Both women were wearing slim fit pants, fitted top and cropped jacket. Not the exact same pieces, but close enough. Ela and Isla both burst out laughing.

"Why didn't I just send you to shop for me, Isla?"

As the skyline of Montreal receded behind them and they took the exit for N.D.G., Ela and Isla were chatty and smiling. Moments later, the limousine pulled up in front of Robert and Diane's house and they found the couple outside with their suitcases. This time the ladies waited for the driver to come around and open their door. Kisses were exchanged, while the neighbors looked on with curiosity. Robert's wife was giddy with excitement: Diane had never been to Rome. Robert appeared more reserved, but Ela had worked with him long enough to know he was already having a good time … and, the adventure was only just unfolding.

So this is how the indecently rich live, Robert thought as he looked around the private aircraft. It wasn't out of envy. It was awe. The colors were subdued. The luxury came from the richness of the materials used. The custom-made carpet had a sheen to it … probably silk. They had used the very best wood and treated it in a way that made it thin and light while it appeared solid and heavy to the eye.

The foursome had been greeted by the pilot and co-pilot as well as two flight attendants when they came on board, all offered their congratulations to the bride before they took turns introducing themselves to Mr. Koertig's esteemed guests. Ritter Luft was their pilot. The self-assured man in his late forties had been with Mr. Koertig for five years. The cheerful, younger co-pilot, Lother Sommer, had been in Mr. Koertig's employment for the last three years. Liesel Engel, with the attributes of a lingerie model, was looking forward to making them comfortable on their flight, as was her equally gorgeous colleague, Margit Lang. Both had been working for Mr. Koertig as flight attendants for the last three years.

Mr. Koertig's jetliner, explained the captain, was sometimes referred to an airliner because it was in fact, a commercial airliner. Mr. Koertig had the interior designed to his specifications and overseen the refitting personally.

The pilot announced that he and the co-pilot would be returning to the cockpit to prepare for the flight. They would be taking off in thirty-five minutes.

Margit excused herself and disappeared into the galley, stating that she needed to check on their refreshments and meals.

Liesel was their tour guide on the aircraft. At the front of the wide-bodied plane was the galley and an area where the flight attendants strapped themselves on takeoff, landing and turbulence and where they took their breaks in comfort plus the crew lavatory. In the next part of the plane, there was seating for twelve.

The seats were like those you would find in first class when you flew on a commercial airliner and equipped the same way. They converted to full size beds, had their own screens for movie viewing, reading lamps and storage compartments. There were four doubles; so that a couple could sleep side by side, if they wished, and four singles. A lavatory for the comfort of the passengers was located in this section as well.

Further down, there was a space with two double seats that faced two double seats with a large table between them on both sides. Eight people could dine there or work there. The part after was what Liesel called the lounge. There were two sofas for four across the aisle from each other. A well-equipped bar and entertainment center dominiated that area. Another spacious lavatory was only steps away. The part of the plane that they walked through next was dedicated to a conference table that doubled as a dining table for eight.

At the back of the plane was Mr. Koertig's private suite. The first area entered was his private office and sitting room with entertainment unit. That led to a bedroom with king-size bed and side tables, storage compartments, entertainment unit, and an en suite with shower, vanity and sink, and dressing area.

This Jonas knows how to live, thought Robert before the flight attendant led them back to the front of the plane to prepare for takeoff and instructed them on safety on board and what would happen in the event of an emergency.

Ela who was usually white-knuckled on takeoff and landing, didn't grab hold of her armrest when the plane taxied into position and the engines started up.

Robert, who was well aware of how Ela felt about flying, looked over with a concerned expression on his face.

"Are you going to be okay? This is a well-maintained plane. There is nothing to worry about," he reassured her.

"I'm fine ... see." She held up her hands.

Maybe it was that the decor fooled her mind into believing she was in a luxury apartment and not on an airplane. Maybe she felt invincible because she couldn't have come this far only to die on the way to her wedding. Maybe it was that Isla had worn her aunt's Claddagh ring.

The vintage Gaelic wedding ring, reminded Ela that Isla's aunt had something planned for Isla and it was going to be epic. Though Isla didn't believe or had tried to talk herself out of believing, Ela knew her aunt had given her a message from beyond the grave and she believed it strongly enough for the two of them. If the aunt was anything like the niece, she wouldn't give up that easily either. There would be more. Since Isla's aunt was on the other side, Ela reasoned, she would have had the inside track and would not have been reaching out to impact Isla's future, if they were destined to meet their demise on this flight. No, they would arrive safely at their destination. Ela vowed to be Aunt Isla's accomplice on *this* side although she didn't mention it to Isla.

After the plane had leveled off, Liesel and Margit asked them if they would like to take their refreshments in the lounge.

"We're serving Champagne de Venoge Extra Brut this evening, in honor of Ms. Zalewski. Of course, we have a well-stocked bar and a good selection of wines on board, should that be your preference, ladies and sir."

They all selected the Champagne, which now held a special meaning for Ela and by association, the other three passengers. Their flight attendants came out with a variety of *amuse-bouches* to munch on with their Champagne.

Since, they were only four people, dinner would be served to them at the table between each set of double seats. It would be more intimate and ideal for conversation. Everyone had pre-selected their choice of appetizer, main dish and dessert from a menu that Mr. Bishop had emailed to them a few days earlier and Liesel rolled out a serving trolley that also held the ice bucket with their Champagne.

"Ms. Zalewski, your shrimp and avocado. Ms. Duncan, I believe you ordered the smoked salmon and cucumber rolls. Dr. Beauchamp, the chilled summer vegetable terrine for you. Mr. Leclerc, here is your shrimp and avocado. More of the extra brut Champagne?" All four of the guests replied in the affirmative.

When Liesel returned to remove their empty plates, Ela made it a point to tell her that they all agreed that the appetizers were perfect … fresh, light and tasty.

Liesel's colleague came out next with their main dishes on the serving trolley.

"Ladies and sir, you have all chosen the same dish for your main course; the chicken in a light morel sauce and julienne vegetables. We will be serving Champagne de Venoge Le Blanc de Noirs with your meal. The chef has looked into the Champagnes from De Venoge and found this one quite to his liking with savory dishes made with ingredients like mushrooms, for example. Obviously that is due to the fact that the Blanc de Noirs is produced from Pinot Noir and Pinot Meunier grapes." Ela and Robert nodded their agreement as Margit began to serve.

Dessert was a fruit salad in pink Champagne with a dollop of whipped cream and a spring of mint, there was no reason to have a dessert wine. Liesel explained that they had just prepared it with Champagne de Venoge Brut Rosé. Ela thought that the Champagne, made from the two red grapes and one white grape of the region, would be delicious over berries too. The foursome drank Italian non-sparkling water with their extravagant final course.

After the meal, Ela asked everyone not to return to their seats at the front of the plane yet and excused herself.

"I have to get something out of my carry-on bag. I'll be right back."

Ela returned with a box several inches long, not very wide and somewhat flat in one hand and an envelope in the other.

"I believe it is customary for the bride to give her bridal party gifts to thank them for their participation."

"Ela, we're being flown on a private luxury airliner, and nobody asked us to chip in for fuel. We're being put up in a suite at a five-star hotel and treated to the cuisine of one of the world's most famous restaurants. If that wasn't enough, we are then being flown to Munich via private jet, which I am sure will be as luxurious as this plane, where we will attend a reception on an estate owned by the parents of one of the richest men around. Gifts are not necessary."

Diane and Isla agreed.

"Listen, all of you. It's tradition … This is for you, Diane and Robert. Please open the envelope."

Robert opened the envelope and a business card fell out. He was puzzled as was his wife.

"These people are going to give you a call when you return to Montreal. They are going to make an appointment to come to your house, take measurements, show you photos and samples of materials. They are going to convert that space you and Diane don't know what to do with into a temperature and humidity controlled, walk-in wine cellar. They have been instructed by *me* to only show you the very best and not to discuss the cost with you. They will be sending the invoice directly to me. I know it's not a conventional gift, but it will have to do."

"We'd worry if you suddenly went conventional. Thank you for your thoughtfulness," Robert answered. He and Diane got out of their seats to hug Ela.

"This is so sweet of you, Ela. We'll stock it with your favorite Champagne and wines for when you come to visit," added Diane.

"Your turn, Isla."

Isla was all smiles as she unwrapped her gift. Ela was almost as excited as her best woman.

"Oh, wow. This is the Montblanc Meisterstuck Solitaire Tribute Rollerball. I love the white lacquer and platinum plating. It's white for the wedding. How appropriate. Thank you."

"Not only because of the wedding. You wear white so well. Every great writer should have a special pen for book signings, but you should have a writing instrument that is really Isla Duncan. On the practical side, you won't have trouble finding refills, though these should last you for a while." Ela handed Isla another slimmer package.

"I will always treasure it, and not only because it is what it is, but because it was a gift from you and it marks a very special occasion that I am thrilled to be part of." It was Isla's turn to hug the bride.

Having exhausted every topic of conversation over dinner, everyone craved a little alone time.

They returned to their seats up front and strapped in.

Diane went back to reading *The Claddagh Ring* and Robert listened to music.

Ela picked up another fashion magazine. Isla pressed play for *Casino Royale* with Daniel Craig and Eva Green. There were more recent films to choose from, but Ela couldn't believe she had never seen it, so maybe it was time. Ela had told her to look for a bottle of Château Angélus in the train scene … very apropos for James Bond and his love interest. The conversation they are having over the Saint-Émilion wine, which is now a Grand Cru Classé A, incidentally, she said, is like foreplay. *You* should like that, Ela had added.

DIANA SOBOLEWSKI

CHAPTER 46

Ela, Isla, Diane and Robert awoke one by one to the morning sun. Liesel and Margit had been walking around and raising the shades. Their passengers were all a little groggy but the sunlight and smell of coffee slowly roused everyone. Liesel informed them that they could take a few minutes to freshen up before breakfast.

Breakfast was copious and satisfying … something for everyone. They ate in the lounge as they had at dinner. Every member of the group was ravenous and soon they returned to their chairs. Not long after, the plane began its descent and Ela barely even noticed.

The ride to the Rome Cavalieri Hotel went well. Their driver, of course, was none other than Sebastiano Byron Bassetti. He offered his congratulations to Ms. Zalewski and introduced himself to her party. Sebastiano knew who everyone was, and he addressed them by name and even called Diane, Dr. Beauchamp. Ela had to admit that Mr. Bishop was good, there was no denying it.

The group was ceremoniously escorted to their suites.

Ela and Isla took a few minutes to get acquainted with their accommodation and decide who would sleep in which of the two queen size beds.

"Ela, this suite is incredible. Look at all of the eighteenth century antiques and the artwork. It's like living in a palace in a bygone era except with modern conveniences."

"It's the largest of the suites in this hotel. With the massive sitting area and formal dining for eight, we won't need to go out for the bachelorette party."

"You're actually marrying a billionaire … like in one of my books."

"We got here in a flying five-star hotel. Now you're noticing?"

The two friends unpacked and put their traveling clothes in a bag to be picked up for cleaning. Isla also put her dress for the wedding out, so that it could be pressed, and called down to ask that someone pick up these items. Ela only took out what she would need until her things would be moved to Torsten's suite tomorrow. Mr. Bishop's coordinator would be bringing Ela's wedding dress, already pressed, along with the accessories.

Isla jumped into the shower, put on some fresh clothes, and asked, "Are you sure you don't want to join us for lunch? Or want me to stay?"

"Go. I'm going to take a shower and lie down for a while before Mr. Bishop attacks. Don't forget your key card."

"Okay. I have my cell phone in my bag, so if you change your mind, call. I'll be back in a couple hours in any case."

"You're wearing your Claddagh ring?"

"Yes ... look." Isla held up her hand.

"Just checking."

When the door closed behind Isla, Ela had a silent chat with Aunt Isla. "I did my part, now it's your turn."

Isla stepped into the glaring sun. She reached for the Chanel sunglasses she had purchased for the trip. Any excuse to get the latest pair of Chanel shades, but this had actually been a good one.

They weren't in her bag. That's right ... she had removed them and placed them on the table when they were done with lunch. Isla had stepped inside to check her emails. The others had gotten up to go for a walk so she never returned to the table. Isla walked over to where she, Diane and Robert had been sitting. The table had already been cleared.

She spotted the waiter who'd taken such good care of them.

"Excuse me ... Hi again. I think I left my sunglasses on the table."

"*Si, signora.* I brought them to reception. I told them that I knew who they belonged to. They were going to call up to your suite. I will get them for you."

"I can go."

"It's no trouble, really. I will be right back."

Isla didn't mind having an opportunity to look around again, so she waited. She was going to go exploring for a bit anyway. Maybe she'd bump into Diane and Robert, if they weren't being amorous in their suite.

As Isla looked back in the direction of the reception counter, her jaw dropped open. There he was. She only caught the side profile, but there was no mistake. This was the same man from the malfunctioning elevator. Oh, God, she couldn't let him see her. The server came back with her glasses before the man turned around. She grabbed the oversized shades and thrust them on for a disguise. The safest thing would be to get back up to the suite. Could she make it to the elevators before he looked her way? She'd have to risk it.

Ela was surprised to see her friend return to their suite so quickly.

"So soon? Why do you look so panicked?"

"The man I told you about from the hotel elevator ... the one I was trapped with … he's here in the lobby of the hotel."

"No! What are the odds? Did he see you?"

"I hope not; I didn't want him to. I managed to make it to the elevator … probably just in time."

"Maybe he's a writer for a luxury travel magazine."

"Do you think so?"

"No. Maybe it's just a very weird coincidence. Or, he's stalking you. Actually, there could be one other explanation."

Ela was looking down at Isla's right hand.

"You were wearing your aunt's Claddagh ring trapped in the elevator with this man and you're wearing it now."

"That's ridiculous," Isla said as she frantically tried to tug the ring off.

While his parents and Torsten were already in their suites, Jonas had stayed behind in the lobby of the Rome Cavalieri Hotel to check on some arrangements.

Riding the elevator up, Jonas thought he detected a familiar fragrance. It was faint and he couldn't put his finger on it right away. Then, it came to him. The last time he smelled this scent was also in a hotel elevator—in Montreal. It was the perfume that bewitching redhead had worn when they met. Jonas shook his head, wondering if the scent was Italian.

DIANA SOBOLEWSKI

CHAPTER 47

Isla opened the door of the suite she was sharing with Ela to a trolley laden with refreshments. A few minutes later, she opened the door again, this time to a smartly dressed woman about five foot eight inches in height and very slim. She looked like she was in her early sixties. The visitor at their door was wearing a modern pale blue pantsuit in a thin fluid material with a boxy jacket and wide ankle length pants with side pockets. Her light golden blond hair had been cut into a long bob and Isla noticed that she had robin's-egg blue eyes and great skin. The woman wore a white silk tank top that was longer than the jacket outside the pants. Her flats were the same hue as her jacket and pants. Though Isla could not have guessed what label the woman was wearing, the bag over her shoulder was definitely Hermès, the reversible Double Sens tote in sky blue and Maltese blue. She wore her hair behind her ears and Isla admired the diamond that hung from each earlobe. Those diamonds had to be three-carats each. On her wrist was an oval white gold and diamond watch with diamond pavé dial and diamond studded bezel. The only other jewelry she wore was a brilliant cut solitaire about six-carats in a very simple platinum setting and thin band, along with a matching wedding band. She had a French manicure and her nails were short. Two shades of gray eye shadow and black mascara on the top lashes brought attention to her eyes, but did not overpower her features. Her lips were glossed in light pink and the apples of her cheeks were a lighter shade of pink. She was a beautiful and beautifully put-together woman.

"Good afternoon, Ms. Duncan. I'm Elsbeth Koertig; I am very happy to meet you. You look just like your photograph on the back of *The Claddagh Ring*." Elsbeth held out her hand and Isla shook it.

"Please call me Isla. So, you know my work, Mrs. Koertig. Anything I should be apologizing for?" Isla asked in fun.

"On the contrary, my dear. You have given voice to female sexuality in a way that was long overdue. I'm a big fan. So is my husband … but then he is an enlightened man." Elsbeth winked.

Isla found herself liking this woman right away.

"It's a pleasure to make your acquaintance Mrs. Koertig. Please let me introduce our bride, Ela Zalewski."

"I'm very happy to finally meet you, Mrs. Koertig. Thank you in advance for the reception. It's a very generous thing that you and your husband are doing for Torsten and me."

"We are thrilled to be doing it. Torsten is like our own son, only better behaved. Please call me Elsbeth. Jonas doesn't look like he is going to take a bride anytime soon, so this may be our only chance to have this kind of enjoyment."

"How is Torsten, Elsbeth?"

"Very much in love and deliriously happy. I'm somewhat of an authority … I have known Torsten for many years. I just want to say that my husband and I are ecstatic that he has found someone as wonderful as you to share his life with. Jonas filled me in. He has expressed a great deal of admiration for you, my dear."

Ela blushed.

"I love Torsten very much, and all I want is to make him happy."

Diane joined the ladies just before the wedding coordinator was due to arrive. She looked a little flushed. Ela had a pretty good idea why, but decided to tease her before she introduced her to Jonas's mother.

"You have a little color. Where you and Robert out taking a brisk walk in the sunshine to stretch your legs and get the blood circulating?"

"No. We, eh …"

"You laid down to … rest … and realized the time and ran over here?"

"Uh, yes …"

Jonas's mother chuckled along. Moments later, Elsbeth and Diane, on first name basis too, where chatting like they had known each other for years.

Just before the wedding coordinator arrived, Elsbeth spoke up. "I have something for you from Torsten. He would have liked to give this to you in person, but since the two of you are not supposed to see each other, I volunteered to be the go-between. He is sending you this, with all of his love, to wear tomorrow."

Elsbeth located the small leather box in her bag and handed it to Ela. Ela opened it and saw a pair of earrings that were designed to look vintage. There were three sets of delicate diamonds clustered to resemble tiny four-leaf clovers. Dangling from the bottom was a perfect cultured pearl. The setting was white gold. The note in Torsten's handwriting read, "Darling, For you to wear on the most important day of our lives. With my undying love, Your soon to be husband."

"These are exactly perfect for my dress, Elsbeth." Ela could not hide her excitement and pleasure. "Please tell Torsten, when you see him, that I absolutely love them. It was what I was missing, though I didn't realize until just now. I love my diamond earrings, but these will make the dress."

"You will make the dress, my dear, but I know what you mean. Mr. Bishop showed me what your dress looks like. He did this for another reason. Your dress and the earrings take care of your something new, but you still need something borrowed. So, I brought along something that might do."

Elsbeth was back into her bag of tricks. This time she pulled out a leather case, slightly larger and not as new looking. She let Ela open it for herself.

Ela was smiling like a kid on Christmas morning. Elsbeth knew that she had chosen correctly from her collection.

"My mother gave it to me to wear on my wedding day. Her parents had it made for her wedding day.

Ela stared at the antique comb in white gold with three pear shaped diamonds about a half carat each, with some small cultured pearls, a spray of delicate brilliant cut diamonds and swirls of pavé diamonds. Ela had the desire to hug this woman, so she did. Words were not needed.

Now it was Isla's turn to step forward.

"There is one more thing … to get you married properly."

Isla pulled a package from a lingerie brand that Ela recognized out of her carry-on luggage. "This is from Diane and me." When Ela was unwrapping the layers of white tissue paper, she almost missed the contents. Then, the prize fell out on to Ela's bed. It was a blue silk garter trimmed in delicate white lace. Isla and Diane had had it customized. It was monogrammed … in seed pearls with the initials *E.F.* Ela burst out laughing and wrapped her arms around Isla and then Diane.

"Now you just need the groom," Isla pointed out.

DIANA SOBOLEWSKI

CHAPTER 48

The wedding coordinator, a very competent woman in her late forties, came with the seamstress from the yacht. They had Ela's dress, undergarments and silk pumps with them. The first order of business would be for Ela to try everything on in case something needed a last minute alteration. The seamstress had a sewing machine in her room.

Isla helped Ela into her dress very carefully in the washroom to avoid wrinkling the fabric, then opened the box with Ela's white silk pumps. Ela would have done something fun like silver sandals for her wedding as brides tended to do nowadays, but that would have worked only if her dress was modern in style. So, she had gone traditional.

Isla smiled mischievously and flipped the pumps around. Embedded into the back of the heel of the left shoe in seed pearls, was the initial E and the back of the heel of the right shoe, the initial F. Since the seed pearls were embedded, the fabric of Ela's dress wouldn't get caught on them, Isla explained.

"I talked Mr. Bishop into it. I hope you don't mind."

Ela didn't mind at all. Seed pearls had been used in vintage jewelry in Britain and some other countries for at least two hundred years, so that was nothing new, but the way they were used on her footwear was pretty innovative. It took someone like Isla to come up with an idea like this.

"I am now officially crazy about my shoes for tomorrow."

The wedding coordinator and seamstress were satisfied that Ela's wedding dress skimmed Ela's body in all of the right places. Ela concurred that no adjustments were needed. Isla was on standby to help Ela out of it, and once done, the wedding coordinator passed out copies of the itinerary for the next day, to review with the ladies. No one had any questions. It was all very clear and would go smoothly. Before departing, the wedding coordinator gave them each a business card. They could call at any time if they needed to be in touch, otherwise she would see them all the next day.

Elsbeth was the first to get up to leave.

"I'll see you back here when the men will be leaving for Torsten's bachelor party at Imàgo, then we'll get your bachelorette party started."

"You don't mind that it's in the suite, Elsbeth? I didn't want to be a party pooper, but with the jet lag and everything …"

"You don't have to explain, my dear. It's your bachelorette evening and you can do whatever you wish. This suite is perfect for entertaining."

When Ela and Isla were alone, Isla commented on Elsbeth's vitality and youthful looks.

"She must have been a child bride … didn't you tell me that Jonas is the same age as Torsten?"

"Though Jonas doesn't look it, he just turned fifty-one. She and Jonas's father have been married fifty-three years … very happily too. She's actually seventy-two and her husband is seventy-six."

"I would have given her sixty-two."

"Apparently, Richart doesn't look his age either."

"So, Torsten's best friend comes from good stock."

"He has the same eyes as Elsbeth, by the way, and Torsten tells me that he looks like his father. Jonas's father must be very handsome because Jonas is a pretty damn good looking man … in case you're interested."

Isla held up her hand by way of response; the Claddagh ring was back in place.

Richart was already in their suite when Elsbeth got there.

"So how did it go?" he asked his wife.

"Very well. Ela is every bit as lovely as Torsten described and she is very much in love with our Torsten. She has a very endearing personality. I feel like our family is expanding. Christmas will be even more fun this year."

"And Ms. Duncan?"

"I knew you'd want to know about her," Elsbeth teased her husband. "She's exceptionally bright, witty, spirited, brimming with self-confidence, with personality plus, very fashionable … oh yes, and she's stunning. Why can't Jonas get together with a woman of substance like that? I would absolutely adore someone like Isla for our daughter-in-law."

"It's probably that a woman like Isla wouldn't put up with our son's nonsense."

"A mother can dream."

"What is your impression of Dr. Beauchamp? Her husband is a good guy, by the way, self-appointed big brother to Ela, did you know that?"

"Diane told me. We had a few minutes to talk. She is very smart, compassionate, quite easy to like, by the way, and a real looker. She and Robert both think of Ela as family. She doesn't have any, so …"

"Robert told me. Well, she has them, and all of us now. By the way, do you know that Robert comes from a large family and that both of his parents are university professors?"

"We didn't get that far. How many in his family?"

"His parents raised four happy, well-adjusted boys, and Robert is the oldest. Being the oldest, he looked out for his brothers. Now that they are on their own and living all over Canada, I think it's Ela that brings out that protective nature in him. She's the sister he never had, but always wanted."

"How did things go with your wedding coordinator?"

"Just fine. I think Torsten wants to ask you about Ela's reaction to the earrings. It's an excuse. He's hungry for details about his bride to be. Why don't you ring his suite … or his mobile?"

"I understand. She was the same."

DIANA SOBOLEWSKI

CHAPTER 49

The bachelorette party was a resounding success. Ela, Isla and Diane got to know the fantastic woman that was Elsbeth Koertig and Elsbeth got to know three fascinating women herself.

Generational lines blurred as they delved into serious topics and hilarity. Nothing was off-limits. The wines were refined, the dishes delectable and the ladies had donned their finery for this evening.

They talked about how Ela became a wine agent and she answered some questions about Elsbeth's favorite wines. They talked about how Isla had become the author of erotic romance novels that women Elsbeth's age could also enjoy. Isla shared some anecdotes, including the most recent development: A travel agency in the U.S. wanted to offer tours based on *The Claddagh Ring*.

Ela repeated the anecdote Isla had told her about the man in the elevator that Isla was trapped with and added, "Isla spotted him in the lobby of our hotel today, but he didn't see her."

Elsbeth laughed at the part where Isla had told him that she would rather stick a fork in her eye than have dinner with him. "Quite right, my dear. He was asking for it. How rude. It seems like a big coincidence that he's here, but in truth, it's a small world. Richart and I are always bumping into somebody we know when we're traveling. You know what they say: all roads lead to Rome."

Elsbeth wanted to know all about Diane too. "What led you to a career in medicine, Diane?"

"My parents are doctors. They met in med school, as a matter of fact. They're still practicing. My father went into neurology and my mother went into pediatrics. I just knew, even as a child, that I wanted to go into medicine. My parents were working a lot and sometimes my sister and I found it tough, but there was something so noble in what they were doing. They used to discuss cases at the dinner table without going into some of the more graphic aspects in front of us kids. When our parents were working, we were well looked after by our grandparents. And my sister and I never resented that they were so involved with their patients. We just thought of them as great humanitarians, doing important work, and we looked up to them. We both wanted to help people like they did; when we grew up."

"Are you a family doctor ... general practitioner or did you specialize?"

"I practice general orthopedic surgery."

"And your sister?"

"Julie went into nursing. She works in the ER of the same hospital as I do."

"You are to be commended, Diane. Your sister as well."

"Thank you. Our parents deserve a lot of the credit. Ela told us that according to Torsten, you've had quite an illustrious career."

"That is very kind, my dear. It's certainly been interesting. In my day, it was unusual for a woman to have career aspirations and even more so, for a husband to indulge them. A couple of years before Jonas started school, this wonderful woman came into our lives. She wasn't the first nanny that we hired, but she was the last. She was the only one that our little man could not manipulate. She wouldn't allow him his way. At first he resorted to temper tantrums and holding his breath. She would just wait it out patiently and when he was done, she calmly went about taking charge. He came to love her very much. I never begrudged their special bond, and neither did his father. She became a member of our family. She was a good influence on our son. He doesn't allow many people in, but those who know him well, know how good-hearted he is. I give her credit for that.

"Having this woman in our home looking after Jonas, freed me to pursue a career. I wasn't trained for anything useful, but I ended up working alongside my husband. Some businesspeople that Richart was involved with, partners, didn't approve, so he bought them out. He trusted my business instincts … we trusted each other. Neither Richart nor I came from poor families. There was a certain infusion of money to get us started, but we basically built our companies ourselves, together. Of course, our brilliant son has taken them way beyond what anyone ever foresaw and he just kept on going. I don't think he's done yet. The funny thing is that there are people who don't know how he does it. They are aware that he has above average intelligence, but believe that having brought in the right people made him and our family very wealthy. He did bring in the right people. He always hires the brightest and the best, but just because Jonas rewards initiative and does not micromanage, does not mean that he is not at the helm."

"So, you and Richart just allowed Jonas to take over one day?" Ela posed the question.

"Not exactly. His father and I always believed that Jonas was exceptionally bright and could achieve anything he put his mind to, but we were more practical than that. We devised a plan with Torsten's parents, God rest their souls, to prepare both young men for their leadership roles. Richart and I met the Fursts when our sons became friends in their first year of university, and we found we had similar hopes and concerns.

"When classes ended for the summer after their freshman year, we put the boys to work in our businesses, in entry level positions and under assumed names. Only Human Resources knew who they really were, so that there would be no special treatment for the heirs apparent. Each summer, they did a paid internship in a different company and a different department. They had to pull their own weight. Torsten's parents and Richart and I would receive a report at the end of the exercise. You've seen the American television show *Undercover Boss?*" The ladies nodded. "Well Jonas and Torsten were undercover trainees each summer, during the years that they were pursuing their undergraduate studies right up until they finished graduate school."

"And, they didn't mind not having summers off?"

"They didn't have a choice. But they were given two weeks off before classes resumed, to do whatever they wanted."

"How did they do as trainees?" Ela wanted to know.

"They excelled in school and they excelled as interns. They surprised us in another way as well. The Fursts and Richart and I paid for our sons' education. They both had a decent new car, but nothing extravagant. They were given a reasonable allowance and they had to manage their living expenses with that money when they were living away from home. We wanted them to understand the value of money and what it was like to work for it, so that's the reason for the *paid* internships. We did not dictate how they spent the money they earned, but we were very pleased to find out that the two of them were investing the money from their summer jobs.

"When they were finished with school, we gave them a year off to travel, so that they would experience things that you can't learn about from textbooks, and a modest sum of money to do it with. They tried to fight us on this. They wanted to get right to work, but we insisted.

"That year of travelling did them a lot of good. They saw how people lived in other parts of the world. They were exposed to different cultures and traditions, many different economies, other political systems and a number of religions. They learned the need for tolerance and the need to stand up against injustice. They witnessed the kinds of hardships that people face, but they also learned where these people found inspiration.

"Jonas and Torsten's friendship was strengthened by these shared experiences and when they came home, they had a deep appreciation for how fortunate they were. So they made a pact, to make things better, when and where they could. There was a certain maturity about them … a sense of responsibility.

"Anyhow, when they came back, my husband mentored Torsten for one full year, while Torsten's father mentored Jonas for the same amount of time. That is why they know a lot about each other's core companies, and sit on each other's boards. After that, Jonas joined our organization … in middle management, and

Torsten went to work with his father. They still had to prove themselves and win the trust and respect of the employees, clients and business community, before we gave them full autonomy. Eventually they developed their own effective style and we knew that it was time to let them fly. We also knew that the companies we had built would be in good hands. Torsten's parents were overjoyed by the man he had become, while Jonas had surpassed all of our dreams for him.

"Sorry, ladies ... I'm just a little proud of my son."

"I have a feeling that your son is proud of his mother," volunteered Isla.

"Thank you, dear, I hope so. Your Claddagh ring ... I meant to ask about it earlier today. Your book is titled *The Claddagh Ring*." Elsbeth had noticed that Isla wore the ring the way a woman who is unattached would wear it. She didn't want to just come right out and ask if Isla was single, but she was curious.

"I inherited it from my namesake, Aunt Isla. I never actually met her. She passed before I could."

"I should tell you, Elsbeth ... I'm making Isla wear it."

"Why, dear?"

"Her aunt was convinced that it was a talisman, documented by family history I might add. According to Aunt Isla, this vintage Claddagh ring would act as a beacon to attract a woman's true love or soulmate ... something like that. Isla doesn't believe, but what if ...?"

"A worthwhile experiment, I would think."

"See, Isla. I have told Isla, Elsbeth, that maybe the man from the elevator is here because of the Claddagh ring. She was wearing it both times."

Everyone laughed, except Isla.

Elsbeth was still up when Richart got back from the bachelor party. By all accounts, it was a great evening. In turn, Elsbeth filled Richart in about all of the things she learned about the three ladies, including how Isla had a stalker, and Ela's theory about how the Claddagh ring was responsible.

"He's not really a stalker is he? That could be dangerous."

"From the way that Ela told the story, from what Isla had told her, he doesn't sound like the type that would be an actual stalker. You know how it is when you are traveling; sometimes you see the same people over and over, usually the ones you'd rather not."

CHAPTER 50

Ela and Torsten's wedding day had arrived. Everyone was in full preparation mode and there was excitement in the air. That's not to say, that Ela and Torsten weren't a little nervous. Ela kept looking at the time and Torsten had reminded Jonas three times not to forget the wedding bands.

Isla got ready first, so that she would be able to help Ela get into her wedding dress without messing up her hair or smudging her makeup.

"Isla, you look fabulous."

When Ela was dressed and looking the happiest that Isla had ever seen, she returned the compliment. "You, my dear friend, are going to take Torsten's breath away."

"Isla, I just had an idea. Could you call Diane and Robert's suite and ask Robert to come by our suite, please, while I put some items in my clutch."

Robert was at the door in less than five minutes. "Is anything wrong?" he asked anxiously when Isla let him in.

"Not a thing. Ela just wanted to ask you something."

Robert's expression went from worried to relieved. Then, Ela came into view.

"You are a beautiful bride, and it isn't just the dress or your hair and makeup. You have that inner glow."

"Thank you. You're pretty dashing yourself."

"Well, Diane and I didn't want to look like the poor relations, so we put a little effort into it."

"Relations? That's like family?"

"That's how we think of you, Ela."

"Damn if you didn't just get me misty eyed. I can't have that. Think of my makeup. I feel the same way about the two of you. That's why you're here. Would you walk me down the aisle?"

"You want me to give you away?"

"No. I want you to walk me down the aisle."

"There's a difference?"

"Of course there's a difference. Isla, tell him."

"There's a difference … we're talking about Ela, Robert."

"My mistake. I'd be honored, but from what you've told me about Mr. Bishop, he's not going to like a last minute change."

"It's not his wedding. He'll have to adapt."

"If you could please let him know, as soon as you get to the Campidoglio … so he can work it out with the photographer. If he gives you a hard time, just tell him that he can come see me about it. That should stop him dead in his tracks."

Robert looked at his watch. "It's almost time. By the way, Isla, you look great." He walked over to Ela and kissed her on the top of her forehead, so as not to ruin her professionally applied makeup. "Take care of our girl."

It was Ela and Isla's turn to get a knock on their door to announce that the cars with the other members of the wedding party had departed for the Campidoglio. All that was left for Ela and Isla to do was to pick up their bouquets and their clutches and climb in the waiting car. It was arranged that Diane would come get the little bags just before they started down the aisle, in case a touch up or tissue was required at the last minute.

Ela saw that Isla had left the Claddagh ring on a side table. *Not so fast, my friend,* Ela said in her head. When Isla's back was turned, she scooped it up and went over to Isla's bed to retrieve Isla's clutch. She opened it with nimble fingers, slipped Aunt Isla's ring inside and closed it. Then she handed the clutch to Isla, who was none the wiser.

Cyril Bishop and the wedding coordinator that hadn't stayed behind to supervise preparations for the wedding dinner were waiting for Ela and Isla's car in front of the ornate government building. Everyone else was inside getting acquainted, since many of the wedding party were meeting for the first time.

Through hand gestures, Mr. Bishop indicated that the driver should lower the back window facing him. He stuck his head in to inform the ladies that in five minutes he would escort them up the many steps and into the historical edifice. They might as well stay seated until then.

While Mr. Bishop was talking, Isla saw a head pop out from the doorway and look in their direction. It was *that* man again. The one from the hotel elevator in Montreal and the lobby of their hotel in Rome.

Mr. Bishop pulled his upper body away from the window and blocked Isla's line of vision. Isla strained to see past him to the top of the steps of the building they were going to be entering, but the man was gone.

"Ela, I just saw *that* man again," she said nervously, grateful that they had a security person with them.

"Are you talking about the man that is following you?"

"Yes. He's in the building."

"I think that this man is here because of your Claddagh ring."

"The ring is back at the hotel ... you know that."

"Look in your bag."

Jonas returned to stand beside Torsten who was impatient to see his bride walking towards him.

"The car is here."

"Did you see Ela?"

"No, Mr. Bishop was blocking my view."

Jonas looked at his new watch longer than necessary, because he was appreciating it all over again. It was a gift from Torsten for performing his best man duties so well and for so much more. It was nearly impossible to impress Jonas to this degree, but Torsten had pulled it off. To own something so carefully chosen for him meant more to Jonas than the price tag ... though he had an inkling of what this rare timepiece sold for.

"They should be coming in any minute now."

Jonas glanced over at his parents who were sharing a moment. Torsten had quite generously offered them the use of the yacht after the honeymoon and after the crew had a couple of weeks off to spend some time with their families. It was Torsten's way of thanking them for everything they were doing for Ela and him.

While Isla and Ela stood out of sight, the wedding planner signaled to Diane to come get Ela's and Isla's clutch bags and for Robert to take his place with Ela.

Diane sprinted out. She could easily have been an ER doctor, running to save a life. Robert was close behind.

"Ela, you are so beautiful."

"Ah, go on ... No, I mean it. Go on." Ela was making light, because she saw that the doctor was getting teary eyed, and once that started, they'd all be in big trouble.

It worked. Diane laughed and gave the bride a big hug.

"Isla, you look incredible ... like some sort of goddess."

"Good, I was going for goddess. You, Diane, are drop-dead gorgeous."

"I keep telling Robert that he is one lucky man, Isla."

"Don't I know it," Robert chimed in, smiling at his wife.

Diane was wearing a modern interpretation of a dress that was vintage Hollywood royalty in white silk chiffon. It was sleeveless and loose fitting on top with a cowl neckline. The waist was cinched in and it fell close to the body all the way down to the ground. She was in silver satin sandals visible when the filmy dress floated around her ankles as she walked. There was a small broach of crystals on the left shoulder. Diane's earrings were quite original. They were knots of diamonds dropping down to a single pearl. She had worn them only once before ... on the day she married Robert. They had been her wedding gift from the groom. She hoped that their daughters or daughters-in-law would want to wear them on their wedding days, if she and Robert were lucky enough to be blessed with children. They would start a family tradition. The stylist had swept her bangs to the side and pulled her honey blond shoulder length hair into a very glamorous chignon. The makeup artist went bolder than Diane thought she wanted, until she saw the results in the mirror. Her cornflower blue eyes popped.

Dark haired Robert with his warm brown eyes, took his place beside Ela and offered her his arm. He looked very *GQ* in the white dinner jacket, with shawl collar, black pants, white shirt with French cuffs that were just a little longer than the sleeves of his jacket, onyx and silver cufflinks, black silk bow tie, black silk pocket square, and black shoes with a polish. He wore his white gold wedding band, as always and the large steel watch with the black face, white Roman numerals and black leather strap that Diane had given him as a wedding present ... because he had always been late for their dates.

Diane went back in and placed Ela's clutch, covered in seed pearls, and Isla's clutch of tiny crystals on the gilded red chair that lined the bride's side of the room, leaving the seat to her left for Robert to occupy.

Mr. Bishop, whom she had heard a lot about in the preceding weeks, did a great job with the decorating. He didn't try to compete with the red and gold period decor. It would have swallowed up anything you could throw at it. So he went simple and classic ... Just large arrangements of white roses in white containers that were rushed in before the first of the bridal party got there and which would be donated to wherever the government officials would choose to send them, at the bride and groom's expense, or left in the room for the couples that would marry there the following day.

Rather than provide Elsbeth and Diane with traditional rose corsages, clever Mr. Bishop came up with a clip-on version that could be attached to their white satin clutch bags. The corsages were identical ... three white roses, sheer white ribbon and crystal embellishments. It was like carrying a mini-bouquet into the wedding venue.

Diane smiled at Elsbeth and Richart who were seated in the first two chairs against the opposite wall, on the groom's side. Richart was a good looking man about an inch shorter than his son, with a full head of closely cropped silver hair and aqua blue eyes that crinkled when he smiled, which was often. He wore a white gold wedding band that matched Elsbeth's and a recent model white gold watch with a round silver face and a shiny black alligator strap. He had the physique of one who was physically fit. These two would not be susceptible to osteoporosis, Diane observed, thinking like a doctor. The couple was holding hands. Diane smiled at how sweet they were.

Elsbeth was wearing a white fit and flare dress to the floor in a heavier silk with some structure. It had cap sleeves and a cowl neckline trimmed in crystals. Her freshly styled hair usually worn in a long bob, had been pulled back into a chignon for uniformity. The style showed off the earrings that she had bought for the occasion: a pear shaped diamond, below it a brilliant diamond and then the earrings forked out with two marquis diamonds from which was suspended a white cultured pearl. The heels of her white satin pumps were embellished with tiny crystals. Since she was so fair, the makeup artist didn't want her to be washed out in all of that white, so he gave her a more dramatic look like Diane's.

While all of the ladies wore dresses that were in the same theme, they varied in fabric and style. Dressing the gentlemen presented a challenge, however, for Mr. Bishop. They all wore pure white single breasted dinner jackets with relaxed shoulders, shawl collars, white shirts, black bow ties, black trousers and black shoes with a high polish. The boutonnieres presented a bit of difficulty as well.

How to differentiate the groom from the best man, the best man from the other two gentlemen? The differences were very subtle but there. Mr. Bishop had made sure that Torsten and his best man had a white silk pocket square and that the buttons of their shirts were also white, while the other gentlemen had black pocket squares and black buttons. Jonas's cufflinks were black onyx like the other men, but with diamonds and set in platinum. Torsten's cufflinks were diamond and platinum.

Mr. Bishop had had the florist add some fine green leaves to the white rose boutonnieres so that they wouldn't disappear against the cool white wool dinner jackets. Torsten's double roses were wrapped tightly with white ribbon, as was Jonas's single rose. The single roses in the boutonnieres of the other two gentlemen were wrapped in a dark green ribbon to emulate the stem. Everything was perfect, awaiting Ela's arrival.

Diane looked over at the man Ela was marrying. Torsten was very charming and engaging. In a conversation, he held your gaze and heard every word spoken to him. It's as if there was no one else in the room and nothing more important than what you had to say to him. He was very much the same body type as Jonas. Both men were six feet tall. Like Jonas, Torsten had significant muscle mass. Ela had told Diane about what Torsten called his limp, but Diane had seen almost no evidence of it. It was important that his spine had not been affected. There she went again, thinking like an orthopedic surgeon … but that's what she was. Torsten probably worked out extensively as another way to compensate for his leg. Diane marveled at how close she already felt to a man she had previously only read about. He had a way of making you feel that if you were his family or his friend, you would never need or want for anything. Ela must feel safe with this man who was larger than life. Diane had to admit, that Torsten was really good looking too. If she had to describe him to someone, she would say that he looked like the actor Aaron Eckhart. Ela had alluded to a very strong sex drive and their compatibility in bed. Yes, Diane was a doctor, but Ela was still a private person. That's all Diane got out of her, but she had a few ideas to fill in the blanks.

Diane did not have to speculate about what this colossus of the business world was attracted to in the complicated, quirky and totally loveable Ela Zalewski, who had sex appeal to spare, all kinds of time for the people she cared about and real depth of character.

Isla had been looking around since they had come into the historical building, but it wasn't the architecture or the period decor that she was taking in. Isla's eyes were scanning for the man that was obviously stalking her. She was anxious to be inside the room where the wedding would take place, because their security people would keep anyone who wasn't supposed to be there out.

Holding on to her bouquet of tightly wrapped white roses with both hands, Isla waited impatiently to hear the harp music. That would be her cue to precede Ela down the aisle, as the wedding coordinator had explained.

Ela was amused. Here was this strong, independent, poised woman who was normally ready to take on the world, and all she could think about now was how she could hide from some guy she barely knew. Which was an exercise in futility. If he was in the vicinity, he wouldn't be able to miss Isla. Everyone who passed them or who they passed had stared at both women with great admiration. One good looking Italian man in an expensive suit, had even been bold enough to smile at Isla and say *complimenti* in a very flirtatious way.

Isla did look really good in the white silk sheath that skimmed her body in all of the right places and danced around her ankles with fluidity. It had shoulder straps that were about two inches in width and the cowl neck was relatively modest, but the low cut *V* of the back was super sexy, and her white silk sandals were adorned with rhinestones and very feminine. The heirloom jewelry made her look like the modern version of an heiress from decades ago. The hairstylist had given her an old Hollywood movie star chignon and glamorous makeup.

Ela did a final check in the mirror in the hallway outside of the room where Torsten waited.

She hoped he would like what he saw.

The column dress she had selected to marry Torsten in had elements of the twenties and forties. It was an updated version of what a young woman from a prosperous family might wear if she were getting married during the time of *The Great Gatsby*. It was also reminiscent of the glamorous women of the forties. The layer of white sheer silk chiffon over a denser silk was embellished with seed pearls from the knees down to the scalloped hem. It went to the floor over her white silk and seed pearl encrusted pumps. The cowl-neck brought attention to Ela's delicate collarbones and the belt of seed pearls accentuated her small waist. Thin straps made entirely of seed pearls went over her shoulders and shoulder blades and formed a *V* halfway down the back. From the top of the dress to the waist in the back were four pearl buttons. The trim around the sides and back of the dress was also in seed pearls. Her hair had been styled into a voluminous chignon with bangs to the side in a period inspired wave. The hairstylist embedded the vintage comb with diamonds and pearls in the up-do. She wore the diamond and pearl earrings from Torsten, and of course her engagement ring. Although Ela had switched her engagement ring to the opposite hand for the day, so she could wear the band on its own to better enjoy everything it represented. The makeup artist had also taken a dramatic approach with Ela's makeup, because it suited her personality, the style of the wedding and it would balance with the makeup of the other ladies for the photos. The look included red lips. Like Isla, Ela carried a tightly wrapped bouquet of white roses, only her bouquet was larger in circumference.

After what seemed like an eternity, they could hear the harp music and with a quick look back at Ela and Robert that communicated *here we go,* and one last glance over to Ela's shoulder to make sure that her stalker was not lurking back there, Isla started towards the doorway.

When she stepped over the threshold, Ela and Robert would move into her spot then commence their walk into the room.

Isla was at the doorway and about to take the step inside, when she was suddenly propelled backwards and to the side as if hitting an invisible wall. She almost smacked into Ela and Robert.

"He's is in there."

Robert didn't understand, but Ela seemed to.

"Robert, who's inside?" Ela asked calmly.

"Our wedding party, Mr. Bishop, the wedding coordinator, the woman playing the harp, the officiant, the interpreter and the photographer."

"I know the photographer is a woman from Mr. Bishop, but the officiant and the interpreter, are they men?"

"Yes."

"What do they look like? The officiant is about sixty, with salt and pepper hair. He is dressed in a black suit, red tie and white shirt." Ela and Isla both shook their heads so Robert moved on. "The interpreter is standing beside him. He is wearing a black suit, white shirt, no tie. He's probably thirty and has a full head of dark hair."

"No. This man is blond and dressed like you, Robert. He's standing in front of the desk, and his boutonniere is a single rose," Isla said nervously.

Robert looked at Ela. "Jonas."

It was Ela's turn to stumble back in shock, her mind processing quickly.

So, Jonas had been to Montreal. That's how he knew about Champagne de Venoge Extra Brut and the Cancale oysters. And why Robert didn't seem that surprised about her engagement. "Is there something you want to tell me, Robert?"

"Jonas and I had lunch. He told me about this idea he had about getting you and Torsten back together. He asked for my help."

"Was Diane in on this?"

"I didn't want to involve my wife, but I have a hard time keeping things from her. On a scale of one to ten, how mad are you?"

Ela looked abnormally calm. *The quiet before the storm,* thought Robert.

"Thank you, Robert, for caring so much about my happiness." Standing on tippy toes, she kissed his cheek.

"Do you still want me to walk you down the aisle?"

"Yes … as soon as we get Isla sorted out. I'll explain later."

Ela turned to her best friend and spoke sharply but not unkindly. "Isla, you have got to pull yourself together. You can't not walk in there."

Inside, Diane, Elsbeth and Richart looked at each other, wondering what was going on with Isla. They saw her about to step into the room and suddenly duck out. The officiant and interpreter talked rapidly in Italian and shrugged their shoulders. Mr. Bishop and the wedding coordinator looked concerned; the harpist just kept playing. She had seen a couple of runaway brides over the years, though never a runaway witness.

Torsten, who was confused about what just happened, was even more confused when he saw the odd look on Jonas's face.

"That's Ela's best friend?"

"Yes, of course. What's the matter?"

"She's the woman from Montreal I told you about."

Mr. Bishop leaned out of the doorway.

"Is everything under control here?"

"Perfectly. We'll be right along. Perhaps the musician can take it from the top."

Mr. Bishop seemed satisfied and went in to cue the harpist to start again.

"Isla, take a deep breath."

"I'm okay. I can do this. He just caught me off guard is all."

The music started up again, and Isla did not falter this time. She walked down the red carpet completely composed.

Everyone was smiling at her and she made eye contact with the assembled guests—all except for one. When she got to the four red and gold chairs in front of the desk, two smaller ones each on one side of the two large chairs meant for the bride and groom, she veered to the left, leaving room for Ela to pass, just as the wedding coordinator had instructed.

Jonas was in position on the groom's side. Isla had felt his eyes on her during the walk. She was used to men looking at her, but this was in a different context. She refused to look in his direction.

It was still sinking in for Jonas that the woman he'd encountered by chance in a Montreal elevator was in their wedding party. Actually, she was his counterpart in the wedding. He noticed that she wouldn't meet his gaze. Obviously from her rapid withdrawal a few minutes earlier, she also realized that they had met.

That day in the elevator, Jonas had thought that woman was very attractive, but today she was exquisitely beautiful. She embraced her femininity while her body language conveyed fortitude. Jonas forced himself to concentrate on the ceremony; the redhead could wait a bit longer.

Ela and Robert, who was beaming with pride, started their walk to where Torsten waited. Ela's heart was beating fast out of excitement and happiness. If not anchored by Robert, she would probably have run down the aisle to Torsten.

There was something to be said for having a couple of minutes to enjoy the whole experience, though. When Ela looked at Torsten, her heart skipped a beat. He looked even more handsome than when she had last seen him in Greece a month ago. Video-conferencing didn't count. It wasn't just the fine Italian fabric of the dinner jacket and trousers, or the way they had been expertly fitted to his masculine form. It was about the way he was looking at her. There was such love in his expression.

Ela took a moment to look around the room where she would become Torsten's wife and he her husband. She smiled her thanks to Elsbeth and Richart, for being part of this happy occasion and for everything they were doing for her and Torsten. She met Jonas's eyes and whispered, "Thank you." She winked at Diane as if to say, *Thanks for loaning me your husband. I'll get him back to you in a second.* Ela didn't dare look at Isla; that was too much for her brain to process. As she and Robert approached Torsten, she looked into her fiancé's eyes, her expression serious and emotional. The woman who had shown him his heart and offered hers without reservation, was saying, *you are my love ... you are my life,* with her eyes.

Torsten saw the most breathtakingly beautiful bride he had ever seen. It was almost painful to look at her. He thought his heart would explode in his chest. He whispered, "I love you," and she smiled at him.

Standing in front of Torsten, Ela disengaged from Robert. "Thank you." He kissed her on both cheeks, shook Torsten's hand and went to sit with his wife. Torsten lifted the hand on which he would place a circle of pavé diamonds only a few minutes from now, to his lips. They broke free to walk around the chairs and stand in front of the massive, carved desk. Ela handed her bouquet to Isla as she passed her and joined Torsten.

The officiant invited them to sit for a moment, in Italian; gesturing with his hand toward the chairs. Ela and Torsten sat side by side, holding hands while he welcomed them and explained what would happen next. The interpreter spoke the words in English.

Mr. Bishop and the wedding coordinator were standing on the sidelines. Like any good wedding planner and wedding coordinator, they were equipped with a sewing kit, stain remover, extra tissues, wipes, hairspray, hair pins and makeup for touch-ups, among other things.

Mr. Bishop nodded to the officiant, who via the interpreter announced that the bride and groom would exchange vows they had written and rings.

The photographer was ready to capture every movement, every look and every emotion.

The bride and groom rose to their feet. Ela looked at Torsten and then at the ground before speaking up. "We didn't exactly write vows. We thought, we'd ad lib." She distinctly saw Mr. Bishop roll his eyes, which made her smile.

Ela and Torsten faced each other.

Torsten took both of Ela's hands in his. "Darling, tell me you're mine, because I'm yours till the end of time."

"I always was, and I always will be." The good news, Ela thought, was that apparently you *can* re-write history.

"Well then, I take you, Ela Zalewski, as my lawfully wedded wife to have and to hold from this day forward."

"And I take you, Torsten Lucas Furst, as my lawfully wedded husband to have and to hold from this day forward."

Mr. Bishop was at a loss. Their strange exchange had some sort of meaning that only the couple was privy to. Moving along, he nodded to Jonas, who took the wedding bands out of his pocket.

Mr. Bishop had provided the bride and groom with the appropriate words ahead of time, "With this ring, I thee wed …" They could read from the cue cards that he was about to hand them, in case they forgot due to nerves.

The bride and groom waved the cards away. Mr. Bishop tensed.

Jonas handed Ela's band to Torsten.

"With this ring, I make you the most important person in my life. Your happiness is all that I want. Your love and faith in us surpasses anything I could have ever dreamed of. Take this ring, and know that there will never be another for me."

Jonas handed Torsten's band to Ela.

"With this ring, I make you the most important person in my life. I promise to love you more tomorrow than I do today. I don't know how that is possible, but it's how it will be. I will always be considerate of your needs, and listen to what you say and also to what you don't. Take this ring, and know that there will never be another for me."

Those seated jumped to their feet and applauded. Jonas clapped, as did Isla. Mr. Bishop pulled out a hanky. It wasn't what was scripted, but it would more than do. The wedding coordinator was visibly moved. The harpist started to play again with renewed vigor. The officiant, having received a reverse translation from the interpreter in his ear, slapped the interpreter on the back. "Ah, love … that's what Rome is all about," he said in Italian.

After pledges of the heart, came the formalities and paperwork. So, Ela, Torsten, Isla and Jonas put pen to paper and made it official.

There was one last custom to observe. The officiant announced that if the couple wished, they could kiss to seal the deal.

"Finally," Torsten spoke up. Ela giggled.

Holding both of Ela's hands in his again, Torsten kissed his wife lovingly, but not the way he would have liked. For that, he'd have to wait a few more hours.

The officiant, through the interpreter, introduced Mr. and Mrs. Furst and offered his congratulations. The two men headed to the office to file the papers and deal with the legalities.

Jonas hugged Torsten and kissed Ela on both cheeks. Isla hugged and kissed both Ela and Torsten. Then Torsten and Ela again embraced while Isla and Jonas regarded each other cautiously. Mr. Bishop and the wedding coordinator offered their congratulations to the couple, as did the photographer and the harpist.

As the harpist played, Mr. Bishop and the wedding coordinator led the wedding party out to begin Ela and Torsten's life together as husband and wife. The photographer was snapping the shots that would record the first moments of the married lives of Mr. and Mrs. Furst and the special people who had shared in the glorious event that united them.

The harpist was a superstitious woman. When so much love was released in a building, that building could withstand anything for hundreds of years. They deserved her best send-off. They were helping to preserve a major monument of Rome.

Ela's arm was locked through Torsten's. Jonas offered his arm to Isla who took it, but still refused to look him in the eye. She looked ahead instead, so she missed the smile. Diane and Robert were behind Isla and Jonas, arms intertwined, with Elsbeth and Richart bringing up the rear energetically with their arms also intertwined.

"We haven't been properly introduced. Jonas Koertig at your service."

"Isla Duncan."

"Now don't be coy, Ms. Duncan, you gave yourself away with that false start. I'm not the only one who remembers our time in the elevator."

The photographer posed the group for photos, while Mr. Bishop and the wedding coordinator looked for anything that might need straightening, like a shoulder strap, pocket square or bow tie. Ela was a bit fidgety, but told herself that if she could be patient a little while longer, she and Torsten would have wonderful photos to pull out on their anniversaries and re-live the happiest of days.

During the car ride back to the hotel, Ela and Torsten snuck a kiss, but dialed back the intensity in the presence of their driver and security person.

"Torsten, do you know that Isla and Jonas have met and that Jonas and Robert have also met?"

"I put two and two together. I saw Isla take one look at Jonas, recognition registered on her face and she ducked out. Jonas recognized her as the woman from Montreal. After Jonas confessed the extent of his machinations to me; he admitted he'd been to Montreal and told me about this woman he'd met. But they had never introduced themselves. He didn't go into any of the details. He's been somewhat preoccupied with her since, and planned to have some people find out her identity. The only thing he had to go on was that she was well acquainted with the hotel they met in. But, you know Jonas loves a challenge.

Ela had filled Torsten in on Isla's elevator experience, when she had told him about her new friend on the yacht.

"It should make for an interesting wedding dinner."

Diane and Robert were reminiscing about their own wedding on the drive back, when Diane asked, "What was going on with Isla? She looked like she had seen a ghost."

"Remember how you told me about the bachelorette party and you got to the part about Isla's mystery man?"

"Yes. You were cracking up."

"It's Jonas."

"What?"

"When he came to Montreal to meet with me, it looks like he ran into Isla."

"He was acting weird when he first saw her."

"I can't wait to see how the evening is going to turn out."

Elsbeth and Richart were cuddling in the backseat of their car.

"Wasn't that romantic?"

"What if we renewed our vows, Mrs. Koertig? If you would have me again."

"Well, Mr. Koertig, I think there's a pretty good chance. We already have an in with Mr. Bishop. He's doing Klarissa's wedding, you know. So, once that's out of the way…"

"So Klarissa is really getting married? I wonder how long that will last."

"Our son does not seem to be too bothered by her upcoming nuptials."

"No, he does not."

"By the way, wasn't it strange how Isla bolted out of the room?"

"About as strange as Jonas's expression when he looked at her *before* she fled."

"I think this is going to be an interesting evening. Call it a mother's premonition."

In the car transporting Isla and Jonas … silence. Fifteen minutes into the drive, Jonas tried making small talk, but Isla wasn't very receptive. She either nodded or gave him a one word response. Jonas wondered if he was going to be able to make any headway over the course of the evening.

Isla wondered how quickly she could make her excuses and retire to her suite, without seeming impolite to the rest of the group.

DIANA SOBOLEWSKI

CHAPTER 51

The penthouse suite was the epitome of luxury and superlative taste. Torsten gave everyone the tour. The furnishings were in palatial style. Modern and antique art coexisted in elegance. The staircase led to a glass ceiling that opened to the panoramic private roof terrace where they would enjoy cocktails and the wedding feast, as there was no other way to describe the menu and selection of wines … all handled by the hotel, with Ela's approval of course.

Posing for photos ate into the time allotted for cocktails, but no one complained. Mr. Bishop and his team had outdone themselves on the decor and the view did the rest.

Before dinner would be served, there was sufficient time for wedding presents. They could have left that to the end, but it was fun to change things up and Ela loved presents.

Torsten reached into a drawer and pulled out a small jewel case wrapped in the theme of the evening. He presented it to his wife. Ela opened it eagerly. Earrings … her earrings … only more spectacular. Her husband really had a sense of who she was. He had paid attention. Ela kissed him with a promise of what was to come, then blushed remembering that they were not alone.

"I understand that they might suit your dress for the reception."

"And everything else." Ela laughed. "I haven't even thanked you for the ones I am wearing yet. I love both sets."

"I'm very glad."

"I have something for you too, my love." Ela went over to a large white easel draped in white satin. She painstakingly undid the rope of pearls and crystals that secured the fabric. Stepping aside, she pulled off the covering, revealing a painting of impressive dimensions with a heavy contemporary frame. It was the *Second Chance* on canvas. The details were there, but it was as if she was a living entity, rather than something mechanical, driven by technology.

Torsten knew at that moment, that he had married the woman who understood him better than anyone ever could. She had someone create the visual of how he felt about the vessel.

"You know my mind and my heart. Thank you."

Then Diane and Robert presented their gift to the bride and groom. They had pledged $5,000 to the Second Chance Fund in Ela and Torsten's names, as soon as it was up and running. Isla was up next. Her gift to Ela and Torsten was also a donation to the Second Chance Fund: one percent of the net profit of *The Claddagh Ring* until now, in their names.

Everyone expected the wedding gifts to have come to an end, when Jonas spoke up.

"There is something I want the two of you to have."

"Jonas, you are giving us all of this. Please …"

"Torsten, I must."

So, Torsten accepted the envelope with Ela looking on. He opened it, read, laughed and passed it to Ela, who read it and laughed.

"Torsten, you tell them …"

"You have all heard of Operation Reconciliation; well, Jonas is giving us the island where we were marooned and he had the name changed—officially—to Torstenela Island. I'm not making this up." He held up the deed.

Everyone roared with laughter, Isla included.

"I'm throwing in the luxury safari structures and components. Everything is warehoused in Greece and can be transported to Torstenela Island and set up in no time. You can always re-visit the island on the anniversary of your reconciliation and stoke the embers of romance …"

Leave it to Jonas to upstage everyone in entertainment value. It earned him a round of applause from the group … Isla included.

"Torsten and I will invite all of you to join us at some point, since there is a table and seating for a group. We can also host people for business and charity purposes on Torstenela Island, so thank you, Jonas."

Soon enough, it was time to sit for dinner. The members of the wedding party realized how privileged they were to be in this place, for this auspicious occasion. The bride and groom realized how lucky they were to be amongst people who cared about them so much and took a moment to tell them so.

Jonas rose to propose the official best man toast. "It was a tough job to get the two of you married, but worth the effort. No two people are more right for each other. You are both so strong that there is no way that either of you will lose that which makes you who you are. You have each gained a partner that will make you stronger and impervious to any influence not in your best interest. May your love grow in the years to come, as it has for my parents." He looked at Elsbeth and Richart with a loving smile and admiration in his eyes. He was rewarded with a look of immense pride and love from them. "I think I can speak for everyone here, when I say that we are all in your corner and always will be. You can count on us. To the bride and groom."

"To the bride and groom," the others repeated while raising their glasses and taking a sip of the excellent Franciacorta.

Isla was the next to propose her official best woman toast. "Ela and Torsten,

I could not have written a love story as profound as yours. This will always be the bar for me now. I feel that my main characters will have a lot to live up to. Yours is a love that is inspirational and lasting. Be happy forever. To the bride and groom."

Once again, everyone repeated. "To the bride and groom."

So Isla Duncan was some sort of writer, Jonas noted.

Ela and Torsten thanked Jonas and Isla for the toasts and for having performed their duties as best man and best woman so well. Everyone thanked Jonas for flying them in and doing so in luxury. They also thanked him for putting them up in suites fit for royalty.

Torsten saw a mischievous look in Ela's eye as Jonas was basking in the accolades.

"Jonas, if you're ever looking for a good book to read, I can recommend one. Love found, love lost and redemption through love by the author of celebrated romance novels sitting next to you. Unless you think that such a book is nothing but fluff."

Jonas lifted an eyebrow to the almost word-for-word remark that he remembered uttering.

Then Ela turned her attention to Isla supressing laughter. "So Isla, *here you are;* having dinner with Jonas afterall, rather than doing something drastic with a fork. Phew … What a relief."

Robert was shaking his head, thinking marriage had not changed Ela.

Elsbeth and Richart looked from Jonas to Isla, then at Ela. Elsbeth had to know if the crazy thought that she had was right. "You mean our son is the stalker from the elevator?"

"Uh-huh. He was in Montreal to meet with Robert."

"Jonas, you said those things?" His mother was using her scolding voice. His father's eyebrows were raised in disapproval.

Jonas was in shock. It seemed that everyone at the table knew what had gone on in that elevator. He tried to redeem himself. "Ms. Duncan and I seem to have gotten off on the wrong foot. Please accept my apology, Ms. Duncan, for my boorish behavior."

Isla almost felt sorry for Jonas. He did sound sincere, and he was probably not used to being put in this situation. It wouldn't be very gracious of her not to accept his apology.

"Apology accepted, Mr. Koertig."

"Thank you. Would you then agree to call me Jonas? And, may I call you Isla?"

"That sounds reasonable."

Dinner was imaginative and supremely enjoyable, as were the expertly selected wines. Conversation was animated and easy among the eight people. They shared their plans for the following day. They had made their arrangements that morning. Ela and Torsten would stay in to enjoy their suite. Ela had booked an in-room couple's massage. Elsbeth and Richart were going to do some shopping. Diane and Robert were going to head out early to visit the Vatican since it was their first time in Rome. On Ela's recommendation, they were going to have a late lunch in Trastevere. Isla was looking forward to her four-hands massage and thought she would enjoy sitting out by the main outdoor pool afterwards. She would be having lunch at the hotel. Isla had been to Rome several times and had already done the sightseeing thing. Jonas was noncommittal, other than to say that he was going to get some time in at the gym early the following morning.

The group decided to take their after dinner drinks inside.

Jonas pulled Ela aside. He wanted to speak to her about what life ahead would be like.

"So a simple low key life is going to be out of the question?"

"I'm afraid so. Besides, that's not really your style, my dear, is it? Good thing too, because your husband is high profile. You're going to be quite an asset to Torsten. The two of you will be entertaining some very important people as a couple. There will be those who will underestimate you at first, because they feel superior to pretty much everyone. That's to be expected in Torsten's world. When they realize how much Torsten values your opinion, they will try to court you. They will send emissaries to lobby you. Always talk to Torsten. Always present a united front. When they realize that they can't manipulate you, they will come to respect you. There will be a learning curve, but it's nothing you can't handle. You're too smart to be used by anyone. Turn the tables on them so the outcome is in your favor and in Torsten's favor. You and Torsten are a team now. There will be times when you will see a very different side of Torsten, when it comes to business. He's fair and wants everyone to get something out of a business deal, but he will not acquiesce if he is not the one with the greatest advantage and he will never, ever capitulate. He is a very tough negotiator. He has to be. He would have never gotten to where he is, by softening his position in a crucial negotiation. It's something you'll have to get used to, Ela. Then there is a side to him that I hope you will never see. If someone comes after his loved ones, they will regret it very quickly. In the event that this should ever happen, Torsten would act instantly, and he would be quite ruthless. You will be very safe with him … always."

"I knew you are loyal to Torsten, Jonas, but I didn't give you enough credit for your insight and wisdom. For that I am sorry."

"Torsten is my dear friend, Ela … and now, so are you."

CHAPTER 52

The evening had come to its logical conclusion. It was time for the feted couple to enjoy the first part of their honeymoon, and they didn't need an audience.

Elsbeth and Richart were the first to depart. Elsbeth had been making eyes at her husband from across the room, and he knew what that look meant.

Diane and Robert pleaded fatigue, but they didn't look particularly tired. They looked like two people who couldn't wait to be alone. Weddings did that to people. Rome did that to people.

Isla was looking forward to a soak in the hydro-massage bath in her suite.

For Jonas, it was still early and he was wide awake. He decided to go downstairs to the lounge for a drink before they closed up. Jonas wanted to ask Isla if she would care to join him, but thought better of it. Tomorrow was another day.

"Alone at last, Mrs. Furst. Do you need help getting out of your lovely wedding dress?"

"If you would be so kind as to undo the buttons at the back, I can take it from there, Mr. Furst. Before you do, I think you should see what Isla and Diane gave me for my something blue." Ela raised the dress to reveal the blue silk garter trimmed in lace and monogrammed with her initials.

"Isn't there some sort of tradition, where the groom removes the garter?"

"Something like that."

"Well then, if the bride would care to take a seat …"

"If the groom is going to take so long to get it off, we're never going to get anywhere."

"I thought we were getting somewhere. I for one, feel a distinct elevation in my heart rate, and you appear a little flushed my love," he teased.

Ela presented her back to her husband and his nimble fingers accomplished the task she had set for him. "I would like to take a shower and slip into something more revealing and sexy for your pleasure, my love."

While Torsten was in the triple shower, Ela located her belongings in the large dressing area. She had what she had been looking for in her arms, when Torsten came out in the bathrobe provided by the hotel. She could find him in the sitting room when she was ready ... and he hoped it would be soon.

It took Ela a little longer than she had planned. It wasn't the shower that took up so much time. After she removed Elsbeth's comb, she had a million hairpins to deal with that had secured her chignon. It could have withstood a hurricane. Finally, she was able to run her fingers through her hair and it felt good.

She'd remove the makeup later. It still looked fresh after all of this time. She put on the promised revealing and sexy item, purchased specifically for their wedding night. It wasn't the traditional white. It was better.

Ela accessorized with satin slip-ons in the same hue, her engagement ring, her brand-new wedding band and her husband's wedding gift. This would be an appropriate occasion to wear her new earrings, she decided. Ela was relieved that they didn't pull on her earlobes, even though they were considerably larger than the ones they were modeled after. Properly attired, Ela went to find her husband.

The sitting room was dimly lit when Ela entered it. Legs crossed, Torsten was sitting comfortably on the oversized divan. Ela stood for a moment letting her eyes adjust to the semi-darkness. Here, Torsten had the advantage. He got to look at the sexy silhouette of his wife, backlit by the bathroom light. A film ... a translucent fabric the color of skin from neckline to ankles. Swirls in the design covered her in strategic places, but only there.

How Torsten resisted the temptation to scoop her up in his arms and carry her off to bed, he wasn't sure. They hadn't made love in a month. He was starved. He was aching.

When Ela was before him, he took her hand, the one with the wedding band and kissed the palm. She stroked his cheek with the other. *When you are so in love,* Ela thought, *such a small gesture can be more meaningful than a thousand professions of love.*

Torsten guided her onto his lap and cradled her petite frame in his arms. He placed his hand behind the back of her head and brought her lips in line with his. Then he kissed the soft, parted lips of the most important person in his life. His kiss was tender ... an oath of his everlasting love. Ela kissed him back the same way, her hand on his cheek once more.

Anything could have happened anywhere in the suite, since they were two people with a healthy sex drive, but Ela decided to take it into the bedroom. She got off Torsten's lap with the intention of pulling him along. Torsten stood up, but didn't move forward. Ela holding his hand, was propelled backwards. This time, Torsten gave into the impulse to pick her up and carry her to bed. She felt like a feather in his arms.

Torsten lay Ela on the bed that had been turned down by someone from housekeeping. He took a moment to look at his bride. It seemed to her that he was caressing her with his eyes. It was loving. It was sexual. It aroused her. He broke away to dim the lights slightly ... only slightly because he wanted to see her ... her body and the way she would look into his eyes. He wanted to see her expression of pleasure. Ela's eyes followed him, and when he returned, she welcomed him with outstretched arms.

Torsten lay beside her. His kiss was more passion driven this time. He kissed her neck and breasts through the thin barrier of the sexy nightgown. He even sucked on the nipples. His fingers found the outline of the lips of her pussy. She was already wet.

Ela sat up, about to remove her illusion of a garment. Torsten sat up behind her. He pushed the straps down her shoulders and arm. He moved her hair and kissed the side of her neck from behind. His fingers traced her spine. She quivered and swallowed hard.

Ela lay down on her back again, and Torsten slid the sexiest nightgown there ever was over her flat stomach and her narrow hips, down her thighs and past her ankles. Her slip-ons had fallen off in the process and lay askew on the extra large king bed. Torsten loved having her in front of him totally nude. It was the most arousing of all.

Ela tugged at the belt of his robe from her position, so Torsten got off the bed and removed it. Ela was as visual as her husband. His body was pleasing to the eye, and that body gave her so much physical pleasure.

Torsten took his place beside Ela on the bed. He propped himself with one hand, while the other roamed the familiar places of her body. His mouth followed in lazy exploration. Her neck, the line of her collarbone, one breast, then the other, sucking the nipple into his mouth and giving it all his attention. She tasted good and he went lower, kissing his way down the side of her waist, kissing her belly button as he positioned himself between her legs. Slowly, slowly making his way to the junction of her thighs. His tongue kissed and licked her bare folds as his fingers traced along her pussy. His tongue craved more and he thrust it inside his wife, ready to claim her as his.

Ela was oblivious to where she was. She was in a non-drug induced state of euphoria. Each flick of tongue on her clit and each penetration of tongue in her pussy was taking her outside of herself. She had no control over her body. It belonged to someone else. At the mercy of Torsten's intimate knowledge of his wife's body, Ela was climbing a steep hill of sensations, teetering on the brink of an orgasm that threatened to shatter her. She would eventually reach the peak and then descend, but he would be there to raise her up again. So, Ela decided to just let go, and put her trust in her husband. The way that Ela was responding to him, gave Torsten a full-blown erection.

Torsten was feeling a connection to his wife that went beyond what they had known before. When finally he put his mouth to hers and he entered her, he understood why. It was the melding of hearts, minds, bodies and souls. It created the symbiosis for the best and most intense expression of emotional and physical love possible.

Ela felt it too. The way he was making love to her, expressed all of his feelings of love and desire. When she came, she became a part of him … and then he took her there a second time. Ela felt truly his. When Torsten came with a few more thrusts, he became part of her.

Ela lay in his arms looking up at the fiber optics star-lit ceiling, smiling her contentment. There was no need to speak. Their bodies had said everything for them.

Twenty-minutes later, Ela was in a playful mood. Her fingers caressed her husband's torso with a teasing touch, then with more conviction. She got him semi-hard with just a few strokes to his shaft. He was not objecting. Then she sat up and bent over his cock. She closed her mouth around him and rolled her tongue over the head. She felt him grow. Ela took him in deep and out again at a deliberately slow pace to prolong the pleasure. She knew what this did to him. She also knew when to stop so that she might go on to please him with her body.

Ela wanted to make her husband feel as good as he had made her feel. She straddled Torsten and he reached for her breasts. They were responsive to his touch. The nipples were hard against his palms. The caresses and stimulation that her clit was getting from Torsten's cock were talking Ela into the third orgasm of the night. Torsten felt it from inside and he pushed her hips down onto his cock for deeper penetration and she came. Her heart was beating hard from the exertion. He could feel it when he caressed her breasts.

Ela intended to continue, but she was worn out. Torsten moved her onto her back and she didn't protest. He moved a pillow under her behind and knelt between her legs. Holding Ela by the ankles, Torsten entered her. As arousing as this position was for him, he would not allow himself to come until he could give her another orgasm so he let go of his wife's ankles and leaned in, Ela's feet were now over his shoulders.

This was not a position that they had explored before. The newness of it all and the deep thrusts that were arousing in a very primal way, built a need in Ela as well as in Torsten. Hands on Torsten's chest, eyes closed, Ela was coming again. Not a second later, so was Torsten. This was the wedding night that Ela had once thought happened in fairy tales … adult fairy tales.

CHAPTER 53

Ela woke and as she stirred, Torsten woke. They both checked their ring fingers and grinned ... lovestruck and acting like they had invented sex.

"That was some wedding night, Mr. Furst."

"I'm glad it lived up to your expectations, Mrs. Furst."

"It surpassed my expectations, and I love being Mrs. Furst."

"I'm glad we're spending the day in, darling. I think we might want to re-visit some of your techniques."

"Or try out new ones ..."

"We have all day ... except for the couple's massage. We can pace ourselves."

"We'll order in, as planned."

They showered together to save time. It was very tempting to take it further, but they limited themselves to some overzealous soaping as they were both very hungry.

"Torsten, would you please order my favorite breakfast, if you remember ..."

"Of course, I remember."

"In Italian, like last time. I love to hear you speak Italian."

"Anything to please my bride."

Breakfast was delicious of course. Once Ela had some scrambled eggs in her and a few sips of her coffee Americano with hot milk, she became very talkative.

"Darling, after dinner tonight, maybe we can enjoy some bubbly in our roof-top Jacuzzi?"

"We certainly can. Who knows where that will lead? I'm willing to *test* the waters."

"Do you think we can come back here on our anniversary every year? I adore this hotel. It has good karma."

"I was thinking that we should do exactly that."

Ela finally told Torsten what Jonas had said, and how impressed she was.

It made Torsten very happy that Jonas and Ela were becoming close.

"It's too bad that Jonas is interested in someone, because I think that he and Isla would be good together, though she would need convincing."

"Ela, Isla is the woman Jonas is interested in."

"After five minutes in an elevator?"

"I take offense to that. Do you remember where we met, and how something passed between us?"

"That's true, but Isla told him off and then she rejected him. Even now, after hearing the accolades from me and his mother, she doesn't exactly hang on his every word or swoon in his presence. It seems that she could care less that he's charming or a billionaire many times over. Jonas seems to be the kind of man that gets what he wants. Do you think he is interested in Isla just because she hasn't reacted like other women?"

"There is some truth to what you are saying, and it's exactly what I thought at first. Jonas is likely to pursue something that is out of reach, just because it's out of reach. He may lose interest when he has it in his grasp. I don't think so in this case because I have seen small changes in him that make me think that there may be more. They're subtle, and most people wouldn't notice, but when you know Jonas, the implications are monumental. Are you going to tell Isla?"

"Maybe not. She might think what you and I thought. Maybe we should see how this plays out."

"You're close with Isla. Do you think that Jonas stands a chance?"

"She told me that she did find him good looking. He fits the description of one of her alpha males: overtly masculine, attractive, sexually appealing, fashionably dressed, well groomed, self-confident with superior intelligence. The problem is that she also said that he was full of himself."

"So the billionaire has to trade on his looks … and do it with some humility."

"The brain is the most important sex organ as far as Isla is concerned. Jonas would have to seduce her mind first. I'm sure there are quite a few women that have thrown themselves at Jonas, but Isla is different. She's also the author of erotic romance novels … She's explored all kinds of scenarios to do with seduction."

"He's going to have an uphill battle. Should I tell him?"

"Like I said, maybe we should just let it play out. The funny thing is that they have a lot in common … including a resistance to love. Mind you, I was of the same opinion until I met you. My hypothesis is that neither one has met the right person."

"Maybe we'll be a good influence on them."

"Can you imagine if something came of this, though? Two people who we care a lot about would have what we have. Elsbeth and Richart would be overjoyed."

"You just want everyone to be happy. I love that about you."

"As happy as we are … now that we've overcome certain obstacles and challenges."

"Jonas helped in that department."

"Loads. Maybe one day, we'll repay the favor, if they don't work things out for themselves."

"We might have to. In the meantime, let me make you happy now, dear wife."

CHAPTER 54

Isla's fifty-minute massage was for ten and she had planned to sit by the main outdoor pool directly afterwards. Allotting time for showering and getting into her swimsuit, she would probably be out at eleven fifteen by Jonas's calculations. Relaxed, she would hopefully be in a receptive state of mind.

At eleven eighteen, Isla got her white towel from a poolside attendant who was just about to help her find an unoccupied sun lounger. Hair in a high ponytail and wearing a white bandage Hervé Léger bikini with halter top and a partially sheer white cover up from the same fashion house, Isla looked very fashionable and sophisticated. She wore sandals in neutral leather with wide straps and her customary four inch heels. They were easy to slip on and off and made the leg look good. She carried a beach bag in the same shade as her sandals, into which she had stuffed her essentials: sporty Chanel sunglasses, a white floppy beach hat with soft wide brim, lip balm, red lipstick that would hopefully not melt, a mirror, a comb, hair elastics, non-greasy sunscreen for the face and body with a 60 SPF, tissues, wipes, toothbrush, toothpaste, dental floss, cell phone, key card, some money, a bottle of water, a fashion magazine as well as a notebook and pen—because you never knew when you'd get a good idea for a character or storyline.

"Good morning, Isla. It's such a beautiful day. Mind if I join you?"

Isla turned around and found Jonas standing behind her, dressed in loose fitting royal blue mid-thigh swimming trunks, white polo, royal blue swimming shoes with a white stripe and a pair of silver rimmed aviator shades. In his left hand was a white baseball style cap and a small blue sports bag.

She couldn't very well say no, but she could read the magazine in her beach bag or feign sleep if she didn't feel like talking.

The attendant had already provided Jonas with his own towel, so Isla responded politely with, "By all means." As if she had a choice.

As they walked up to a couple of available white sun loungers right in front of the pool, Jonas saw several men look over their glasses or remove them altogether. Their eyes followed the redhead. They were being bold because their wives or girlfriends were either in the pool or resting on their stomachs. One was reclined in her lounger, but saw what her partner was up to and removed her own sunglasses to give him a look of warning. Caught in the act of ogling, he smiled apologetically, pushed his sunglasses up the bridge of his nose and bent his head as if he was reading the newspaper, but Jonas was sure that he was still staring at Isla. Isla's admirers gawked while she laid her towel out, removed her cover-up, folded it neatly and placed it at end of the lounger. Jonas stared too.

Isla worked out quite a bit. That was obvious. Her body was super toned. She probably weighed no more than a hundred pounds, but there was a nice swell to her breasts. Her collarbones, spine, and hip bones were discernable because she was slender, but they just added to her femininity. She also had a tapered waist, flat stomach, and narrow hips, but not in a boyish way. There was a definite womanly curve to those hips. Her thigh and calf muscles were well defined and she had a firm girlish ass.

Isla proceeded to apply sunscreen over her face, neck, and chest, then shoulders, arms, midriff, legs, and feet. The men kept staring.

Jonas removed his polo and attracted the attention of a few of the women by the pool. Their husbands and boyfriends were oblivious. Some unaccompanied ladies were admiring his athletic form quite openly *and* trying to catch his eye. Jonas didn't notice, but Isla did. She had to admit that he did have a really good body: There was that square jaw to start with that many women found attractive, and yes, she was one of them. Then there were the broad shoulders, well developed biceps and triceps, the narrow waist, the eight-pack, powerful thighs and calves and the tight muscular ass. A quick glimpse at the front nether region had Isla thinking that he had to have a good size package.

"Would you like me to do your back, Isla?"

She could decline and contort herself to get at those hard to reach parts, but that would have been plain silly.

With a "thank you," Isla passed her sunscreen over to Jonas and turned so that he could apply it.

Jonas spread the sunscreen on Isla's soft fair skin, careful to give her a good layer of coverage. The touch from his strong hands was gentle. He may have kept his right hand in contact with her back a little longer than was necessary, while his left hand rested on the shoulder he had already done. When Jonas was finished, he pulled out his own 30 SPF sunscreen for the body. He had applied the one for his face, in his suite.

When he had the desired coverage on the parts of the body that he could reach, he held out the bottle to Isla.

"Would you mind?"

How could she refuse? So Isla returned the favor. The muscles beneath her fingers felt as hard as they looked. That took years of working out with heavy weights.

Jonas had thought the pool, where everyone kept to themselves, would be a nice, quiet place to ambush her. He was wrong.

Two women in their early fifties walked out of the hotel onto the terrace and eventually installed themselves across the pool from Isla and Jonas. It wasn't even five minutes later, when they jumped up and walked over.

"Excuse me," said one of the ladies. "Are you Isla Duncan, the writer?"

"Yes. I am."

"Ms. Duncan, my sister and I are currently reading your latest, *The Claddagh Ring*. See. We both have a copy. We're really enjoying it, but then we've enjoyed all of your books."

"It's very kind of you to say. Thank you for your support. By the accent, you're English."

"We're from London."

One of the ladies was probably fifty-two years of age. The other closer to fifty-five.

"I'm Brianne Cox," said the slightly younger of the two. "And, I'm her sister sister, Cara Milburn," said the other. Both women were svelte, attractive and stylish. Right now, though, they looked a little starstruck, thought Jonas, who found himself being totally ignored.

"Are you ladies here on holiday?" asked Isla.

"Yes, we do two weeks away together every year in the summer. It gives our husbands a chance to miss us. Rome is one of our favorite destinations and we simply love this hotel. We take in the sights, but we also enjoy the restaurants and the shopping. Still it's good to take the time to relax in lovely surroundings … like today with your book. By the way, Ms. Duncan, you've added some spice to our marriages with your novels. Please keep them coming."

"I'm delighted to hear that."

"Are you on holiday in Rome?"

"Actually I'm here for the wedding of a very close friend. It took place yesterday."

"Would it be an imposition for you to sign our books?"

"Of course not." Isla found her new pen at the bottom of her bag and went to work on a personalized message for each of the ladies. She valued all of the fans of her books and when they were face-to-face, she had to accord them the time that it took to show her appreciation.

Cara had an idea there and then. "Sir," she addressed Isla's neighbor. "You may not know this, but this lady is a famous author. My sister and I are big fans. Would you be so kind as to take a photo of the three of us with our mobile phones … if Ms. Duncan doesn't mind?"

"It would be my pleasure, ladies," Jonas responded. He hoped that would make them leave.

Isla put on her sandals and applied her red lipstick. She undid the ponytail and suggested they stand away from the loungers. With Isla in heels and the ladies on either side of her in flats, the three were close in height, so it was easy for Jonas to get everyone in the frame. Brianne held her copy of *The Claddagh Ring* up, with the front cover facing the camera. Cara did the same with the back cover because there was a large photograph of the author. She couldn't wait to show their family and friends. They would be so envious.

When the ladies were satisfied with the photos, Jonas went back to his lounger. Just before returning to her lounger, Brianne quietly suggested to Isla and her sister nodded in agreement, "The gentleman who took our photos, reminds me of the main male character in the book. He seems to be someone who has done reasonably well for himself. He probably hasn't attained your level of success, Ms. Duncan, but if he's single, with those looks and that physique, he would do quite nicely as arm candy."

"I'll take that under advisement. Enjoy your day, ladies. You've made mine."

Isla returned to her lounger, laughing at a joke that she was not sharing with Jonas.

Every now and then, Brianne and Cara looked up from their book. Isla Duncan was interacting with the man on the lounger next to hers. The sisters looked at each other knowingly. His body language indicated that he was interested in their favorite author. They hadn't spent years reading Isla Duncan novels without learning something about picking up on the signs.

"Does this kind of think happen often?"

"Once in a while."

"And, do people always thank you for spicing up their sex lives?"

"Sometimes."

"So what did your biggest fan say that was so funny?"

"That you have real potential ... as arm candy." Isla was in stitches. This morning was not going so badly, after all.

Jonas raised an eyebrow and decided now would be a good time for a swim.

Isla watched him get up from the lounger and walk the few steps to the pool from behind her dark sunglasses. If Daniel Craig wasn't available for the next James Bond film, Jonas could fill in. She was an author of erotic romance novels ... It was her job to notice physical attributes, she reminded herself.

When Jonas returned refreshed, he found Isla had dozed off. He enjoyed the view ... especially since he was unobserved by the woman he was looking at. A few droplets of water landed on Isla and she woke up and stretched.

"Good swim?"

"I feel refreshed, but I have also built up an appetite. How about lunch?"

"I was going to order from in-room dining. The balcony is great in my suite. I should write about this hotel and the suites in my next book."

"You haven't seen mine."

"Is that some sort of indecent proposal?"

"I was just thinking of the research and we both have to eat. Why not together?"

"Sure. I'll just throw on ..."

"A suit of armor?"

"Sweatpants and I'm putting my hair up in rollers. I'll be at your door in forty-five minutes."

"If you have already consulted the in-room dining menu for lunch and know what you would like, I could order in advance."

"I'm pretty hungry, but I'm not in the mood for anything too filling. Dinner is going to be out of this world, I understand. I was thinking fish and vegetables."

"Then that is what you shall have."

Jonas probably thought she'd show up as covered up as possible ... so obviously, Isla decided to do the opposite.

When Jonas answered the door in a fitted shirt, straight leg fitted slacks just to the ankles and soft leather loafers, Isla was standing there in a short, close to the body white summer dress that showed off her toned arms. She had on the same neutral sandals she had worn to the pool and carried a neutral clutch. Isla who was rarely without some type of jewelry, chose a heavy gold ring with two large crystals and geometric matte gold earrings inset with little brilliant cut diamonds for her lunch with Jonas. She had washed and curled her hair and applied makeup—all in forty-five minutes. Her makeup had not been applied with a heavy hand, but it did emphasize her best facial features, and there was that scent. It was potent, so she had applied it judiciously, but it reached Jonas's nostrils from where she was standing.

"Please come in. This is much better than the sweatpants. I see that you took the rollers out."

"They didn't really work with the dress."

"May, I pour you a glass of Chardonnay from Umbria while we wait?"

"Already chilled to the ideal serving temperature?"

"What can I say? I believe it's rude to keep a lady waiting in matters of pleasure ... such as this fine wine."

Oh he's good, thought Isla. Years of experiences. But the sword play was entertaining.

"To happy coincidences." Jonas raised his glass in Isla's direction.

"Uh-mm, yes."

There was a knock at the door and the trolley was wheeled in with their lunch along with bottled water. Jonas pointed to the balcony a very short distance from where they were standing and requested in Italian that their meal be set up there.

"Why don't we eat first, and then I'll show you the suite. You may want to take some photos with your mobile, so that you can have the visuals on hand, should you wish to recall the decor and art at a later date, as well as our *stimulating* conversation and pleasant lunch."

And, there's the innuendo, Isla registered. It had to be automatic with this man. "I'll do that."

"Do try to relax, Isla. I'm not going to hold you hostage in my suite ... Not even if you pleaded with me. We're just getting acquainted and we may not even be each other's type."

"I'm not worried, Jonas. If *I* wanted to stay, your resolve would quickly melt away—trust me." More sword play, but no casualties.

"You're very sure of yourself, Isla."

"I'm just stating a fact."

"More wine?"

"Yes. Thank you."

Lunch was healthy, but delicious and fortifying: sea bass carpaccio with citrus fruit sauce, followed by steamed fillet of sole with seasonal vegetables. Isla and Jonas got a little better acquainted over their meal.

When they were done, Isla decided to move things along. "Thank you for lunch. Nice wine, by the way. I don't want to appear ungracious, but if you don't mind, I would really like to take the photos and return to my suite to rest up for this evening."

"Let's get started then." Jonas showed Isla around and she took in the rare antique Empire furnishings and original paintings. The carpet and wall coverings were unbelievable. This was going back in time to luxury in a different era. Then the inner sanctum, the bedroom with its king size floating bed.

"So, this is where one sleeps like an emperor and wakes up feeling like one can conquer the world."

The world would be a piece of cake, thought Jonas, *compared to Isla Duncan.*

The Imperial bathroom with all of that rare marble had to be one of the most impressive bathrooms in existence. Isla took pictures from several angles and thanked Jonas for his hospitality.

As she walked back to her own suite, Isla mused that she already had photos of her suite and the penthouse suite. This evening, she would ask Elsbeth and Richart as well as Diane and Robert, if she could take photos of their suites the following morning. She would also ask Ela to email her the photos of the suite she had stayed in with Torsten when they were here the last time. Before their flight out tomorrow, she'd walk around the hotel and grounds and take some photos to add to the collection. The location would be fantastic for a major romantic scene in her next book.

DIANA SOBOLEWSKI

CHAPTER 55

Elsbeth and Richart were the first to arrive at the Tiepolo Lounge. Elsbeth was dressed in a fuchsia sheath with cap sleeves, matching pumps and handbag. On someone else, it would have been too much of a good thing, but the color complemented Elsbeth so well, that going monochromatic had been a good call, Richart had told his wife. With soft, almost neutral makeup, her sleek bob and her usual jewelry, everything looked right.

Elsbeth thought that Richart looked dapper in his tailored summer gray suit with a small pattern in the shirt, striped tie in the same hues and white pocket square. The black lace-up shoes from their shopping excursion that day, were exactly what he had needed for that polished modern look.

The next time the elevator opened, Diane and Robert stepped out. The doctor was in a black backless halter jumpsuit with a deep V in the front. The pants were wide with side pockets. She wore black sandals and carried a metallic silver leather clutch. Diane had done a smoky eye and neutral lips this evening, the way the makeup artist at Sephora in Montreal had demonstrated, and her hair was styled straight. She wore a five-row silver chain necklace, diamond studs, her five-diamond engagement ring and thin white gold wedding band. Elsbeth thought Diane looked like a *femme fatale*.

As her husband and escort, Robert did her proud in a lightweight black tailored suit, open collar white shirt, and white pocket square, and black-lace up shoes.

Ela and Torsten walked out of the elevator next, hand in hand … looking ridiculously happy.

"I know that dress," said Diane to the other three.

"It has to be Hervé Léger. Even I know that, by now," inputted Robert.

Ela was keeping the white theme going with a body con sleeveless empire waist bandage dress. Her accessories were jewelry that should have been in a vault, a silver leather clutch, and strappy silver leather sandals. Makeup was classic Ela: a neutral eye, light foundation, bronzer and sexy red lips and her hair fell to her shoulders in those tousled waves that Alain had introduced her to.

Her husband looked devastatingly handsome in a tailored navy blue suit, with a fine checkered shirt, navy blue tie with minimal design, a white pocket square and dressy lace-up shoes.

The last to arrive were Isla and Jonas—*together*.

Everyone recognized by now that Ela had a mischievous streak, so when she was true to form, nobody batted an eye lash.

"Good evening, you two. It seems that you are destined to ride elevators together. Wow, that's some hot Hervé Léger number, Isla. You're attracting all kinds of attention. I swear I just saw a man turn his head so fast, I thought he was going to need medical attention."

Isla was in a short, sleeveless alabaster Hervé Léger dress with a round neckline and an open back. It almost looked like the sides were cutouts. She had on neutral gladiator sandals that heightened the leg, and her neutral clutch from earlier. Her jewelry was what Ela had seen her wearing the day they met, and what Jonas had seen her wearing at lunch. Makeup was typical Isla which happened to also be typical Ela. Loose sexy waves framing her face, red lips.

"Were the two of you separated at birth?" The question directed at Ela and Isla, came from Robert.

Then everyone looked from Jonas to Torsten. "Do the two of you have the same tailor?" This time the question came from Elsbeth.

Torsten and Jonas looked at each other. Their attire for the evening was very close. The same cut, two buttons, with only the top one done. The lapels were a medium width. The pant leg was a semi-retro straight style. The shirt was similar. The tie was not that different. The pocket square was there too, and the shoes were very much alike.

Torsten groaned. Jonas said that he was glad Torsten had finally picked up some pointers.

"Maybe he wasn't trying to emulate me on purpose. It could have happened on a subconscious level."

Richart, the voice of reason, asked, "So, what is everyone drinking?"

"Bubbly ..." suggested Ela, and everyone was nodding in agreement.

"Franciacorta or Champagne?"

Ela, being the bride, had the deciding vote, though Richart had not polled the others.

"When in Rome ..."

When they were comfortably seated on the outdoor wicker furniture with big wide striped cushions that fit in so well with the lush vegetation on the grounds; Elsbeth asked about everyone's day.

Since she looked at Ela and Torsten first, Torsten told their group that their day was the perfect combination of romance and relaxation in a suite designed for lovers overlooking a city to fall in love in and with. What could be better?

Torsten returned the query. "How did you and Richart enjoy your day of shopping?"

It was Richart who answered. "I purchased the shoes I'm wearing. My wife on the other hand, has singlehandedly brought up the economy of Rome. Some shopkeepers are going to name offspring after her and several thanked her for contributing so generously to their children's education fund."

"Mother, is that true?"

"Your father is prone to exaggeration." Elsbeth then deflected with, "Diane, Robert, was the Sistine Chapel everything you expected?"

Diane answered enthusiastically for herself and her spouse, "We were so enchanted that we are going to come back and do a whole two weeks just in Rome, as soon as Robert sets up the wine agency and I can get two weeks off in a row."

"Isla, the four-hand massage, was enjoyable?" Elsbeth wanted to know.

"When they finish, you feel like you're floating on a cloud."

"How did you spend the rest of the morning?"

"I lay by the pool and even entertained a couple of fans. Jonas helped."

Now that everyone was aware that the two had spent time together, they were all ears. It was Ela though, who took control of the interrogation. "How did Jonas help?"

"He took some photos of the ladies and myself."

"That was considerate of him."

"Yes, it was. Unfortunately something disturbing happened."

"How so?"

"He was objectified."

"No?" Ela was incredulous.

"I'm afraid so. They only saw him as a sex object. Is this what modern women have come to? It's shocking. It's too bad that they left before I had a chance to speak up for Jonas. I would have defended his honor and chided them for seeing him only as an instrument of sexual pleasure. He has a brain."

Elsbeth was thinking, *What a woman.*

Richart was thinking, *Son, you have met your match.*

Diane was thinking, *Shades of an Isla Duncan novel?*

Robert was thinking, *Shit, she's even worse than Ela.*

Torsten was thinking, *Here is the woman that you have been waiting for, but just didn't know it.*

Ela was thinking, *This dueling is foreplay. You're into him, my friend.*

No one was willing to say what they really thought. So, they went with: *No. Really? Strange. Not possible. Inconceivable. Outrageous.* No one was very convincing though, because no one ... not even one of them, was able to keep a straight face.

La Pergola was everything that Ela, Torsten, Jonas and his parents remembered. For Isla, Diane and Robert it was their first time. Each of them had read about the restaurant that had been awarded three stars and five forks by the Michelin Guide and viewed the photos, but it was quite another thing to be here in person to admire the Imperial furniture, rare Aubusson tapestry, antique bronze candelabra and seventeenth century Celadon vase that the hotel's master florist had filled with fresh flowers, and other *objets d'art* from several different periods.

The ambience played a big part in the dining experience in this famous restaurant as did the views of the Eternal City through the panoramic windows.

Isla, the writer, was mentally recording all of the details and the emotions that they evoked for future reference. Robert, the wine agent and foodie, devoured the menu and wine list with his eyes. His wife simply let all of the splendor come to her in due course and absorbed it gradually for fear of being overwhelmed.

The service was exceptional and every part of the meal was a revelation. They would surely be dreaming about the wines for months to come, yearning to return. The chef had kindly stopped by their table. Torsten, Jonas, Elsbeth and Richart complimented him and his team in German, then switched to English to express their thanks. Ela, Isla, Diane and Robert joined in, trying to find the words worthy of such an experience in fine dining.

During dinner, Torsten happened to mention that Jonas had quite the wine cellar in his home in Bavaria … well stocked with rare Bordeaux, Burgundies, vintage Champagnes; especially Krug, but not limited to these wines. He also collected the most prestigious wines from Germany, Italy and Spain predominately, but the United States and Australia were also represented in his collection.

Torsten also told Ela, Isla, Diane and Robert that though Elsbeth and Richart relied on their son for advice now and then in his areas of expertise, being widely travelled, they had discovered wines from Austria, Portugal, Switzerland, New Zealand, Hungary, Greece, Canada, Chile, Uruguay and Brazil. The flavor of the land, Richart called it.

"Our current favorites come from Argentina. Elsbeth and I visited this winery that is situated in the Uco Valley, to the south of the city of Mendoza, with some friends. The producers are big into wine tourism and they offer activities that appeal to wine lovers who are also nature lovers, so it was right up our alley. You should see this place. We were in awe of the architecture and the way it respects the environment. It was designed specifically not to compete with the beauty that surrounds these vineyards but to work with it."

"Jonas, you may be interested to know that the family behind this endeavor is very well known for their red and white Grand Cru Classé Pessac Léognan wines. You have recommended these wines to your mother and myself."

"Château Malartic-Lagravière?"

"That's right. Do you know that that they also own another property right beside Château Malartic-Lagravière that is worked by the same team in the same way?"

"I am aware. It's Château Gazin Rocquencourt. They produce a very high quality white and red."

Ela was just sitting back with a silly grin on her face, saying nothing for the moment. She loved being around people who were passionate about wine and had discovered something amazing, which they absolutely had to share.

"There's an interchange between the Bordeaux and Argentinian teams, which would explain why the wines are opulent and complex. I'm quoting, but it's a very accurate description."

"Why have you not mentioned this until now, Father?"

"I would have, if you spent a little more time with your parents."

"Point taken. I shall try to remedy that. So, what is the name of this property and what did you and Mother taste over there?"

"Bodega DiamAndes. The name is a combination of *diamante,* Spanish for diamond, and Andes because the property sits at the foot of the Andes Mountains. The reflection of the volcano nearby in a lake nearby inspired the name of the estate."

We were very impressed with the DiamAndes de Uco Gran Reserva, which is aged for a minimum of twenty months in French oak and released onto the market only after three years. The majority is Malbec, the grape that Argentina is famous for. This is where the wine gets its roundness and velvety tannins from. They blend it with some Cabernet Sauvignon for complexity and structure. The Gran Reserva is a serious age worthy wine that does not fatigue the palate. I suspect that it's the Bordeaux influence. You want to keep filling your glass. It's what I want to drink with a very thick grilled steak, rib in and medium rare … more rare than medium.

"We also tasted the Malbec … dark fruit, dark chocolate, spices and smokiness. The vineyard is planted at a high attitude so there is a pleasing freshness about the Malbec.

"The Viognier de Uco was luscious, as my wife put it, with a freshness to it, again a benefit of the altitude, as I understand. I distinctly remember that it was very aromatic—on the floral side and that there was good minerality, which I had not expected, and apricot notes.

"Then there was the Chardonnay de Uco. I recall notes of peach, pear and some exotic fruit, and good acidity … once again, due to the altitude."

"That was very informative, Father."

"I should say so," Ela joined in.

"We have all four of those wines in Quebec, and you have just motivated me to taste them," said Robert with admiration.

"Hello ... though not a wine agent ... wine lover," Diane reprimanded her husband. "Richart, you have motivated us to taste them. Thank you."

"You haven't said very much, Ela," Robert observed. "That's not like you."

"That's true. I enjoyed listening. Jonas, I completely understand about Château Malartic-Lagravière. I adore their wines, as Torsten knows. The red and white wines from the adjoining property are very good too, because they put in the same kind of effort. I tell people about Château Gazin-Rocquencourt all of the time. Isla, the wines of Bodega DiamAndes sound like something you would enjoy, since your introduction to wine was by way of the New World. You should get in on that tasting with Diane and Robert."

Jonas smiled at Ela. Now they had *that* in common.

Isla nodded eagerly at Ela's suggestion.

Jonas wondered if Isla might like the Pinot-Noir wines from the Beaux Frères estate in Oregon, and how and when, he might get her to taste them.

"Isla is going to be incorporating wine references into her novels," Ela announced. "We will be collaborating. I have contacted some of the French producers that Robert and I have been working with ... for starters. Her books have been translated into French, so they knew immediately who she was. They love the idea. Isla will be busy very soon with invitations to visit their properties."

"I'm looking forward to it. There is no substitute for that kind of firsthand knowledge when you are writing. Everything on the page is richer."

"The négociant in Bordeaux that Robert and I have been working with is going to offer a limited series of wines to correspond with the launch of each new book. He is going to have a special case designed with Isla's signature. The case will always be the same, but what will be different each time is the title of the book, and the message from Isla to her fans. Each time she puts a book out, he will select six Bordeaux wines that Isla has included in that book. Also, he just purchased a small vineyard that is producing well priced high quality wines, and would like to offer a Cuvée Isla. The only thing to work out for both the limited series and Cuvée Isla, is the financial compensation to Isla."

"It was Ela's idea. Edmond is very excited, as am I," proclaimed Robert.

"And I," came from Isla.

"Isla, I forgot to tell you that Edmond will fly you in for the next Vinexpo, at his expense, business class, if you will agree to spend one day in their booth so that they can announce your presence in advance to their clients. He would also like to have a large poster of you done for the booth and he plans to fill the space with samples of the Bordeaux wines in your book for clients to taste by appointment. He would like to give out your book in the languages of his best clients, and have you sign their copy when they meet you … as a little incentive. He would also like to have you at the party that they put on for their best clients during Vinexpo, and at their table at Fête de La Fleur. Robert will be at their table. He hasn't attended Vinexpo in the past because I did, but he'll be going next time, since he will be the official owner of Les Vins EZ, not I. In any case, he knows all of the same people as I do. So you'll have someone from home there who will introduce you to lots of interesting people. I understand that Edmond would be putting you up at the Grand Hôtel de Bordeaux … the spa is fabulous, by the way. If you prefer, you can stay at any one of the châteaux in your book. The owners would be only too happy to have you as their guest. They would probably want to throw a dinner in your honor or at the very least, have you as the guest of honor at a dinner they are holding. Edmond thinks that one day, you may be inducted into La Commanderie du Bontemps de Medoc, des Graves, de Sauterne et de Barsac. It's one of the oldest and largest wine brotherhoods in France."

Robert was floored. "It's considered a great honor."

Isla took a deep breath. "I am thrilled to have this opportunity. With Ela and Robert as my coaches, I think that I can rise to the occasion."

Jonas made an announcement of his own. "Well since we're on the subject of great opportunities related to wine, this would be a good time to tell you that Torsten and I have teamed up to look for a property in Bordeaux … to buy."

"Darling, you didn't think to mention this? Are you keeping secrets from your wife already?"

"It didn't come up. Actually Jonas and I had first talked about it two years ago. It can take time to find and acquire the right property. This is confidential, but Laurence is thinking of selling."

"Have you let her know that you and Jonas are interested in purchasing her property?"

"We've had some preliminary discussions. She and her team would stay on, of course. It's because of Laurence and her people that the brand is synonymous with high standards. What do you think, darling?"

"That would be quite a coup. It's not a terribly large property, but it's planted to Merlot, Cabernet Franc and Cabernet Sauvignon. The average age of the vines is thirty-five years, which is perfect; old enough to produce complex wines, and there is nothing to replant.

"Laurence is scrupulous when it comes to vineyard management, especially green harvesting. It's painful to see those unripe grape clusters on the ground after the pruning, but it's necessary to limit the *yield* to the clusters with the most potential. When the plant doesn't have to divide its energy, you get the desired ripeness and flavor in the clusters left on the vine. Plus, you eliminate crowding, so the sun and wind can get to the grapes and keep the plant healthy in the process. It ensures that the skins will not be damaged which would make the grapes susceptible to disease.

"It's not about volume. It's about obtaining the highest quality; vintage after vintage. Laurence has a reputation for achieving it too. Her wines are dense, with dark berry aromas and flavors, as well as espresso and dark chocolate. They are plush on the palate … with juicy ripe fruit on the long finish.

"The château is pretty, but with an influx of substantial cash, it can be made into a real showplace … as spectacular as those of her neighbors. Several have completely transformed their châteaux, while maintaining historical integrity."

"Jonas and I believe that Laurence's property would be a worthwhile investment … and then there is the *private reserve* wine."

"Yes, there's that too. You know, the property has been in Laurence's family since the mid-1800s. Did she give you any indication why she is considering selling?"

"Laurence has devoted most of her adult life to the property. In addition to vineyard management, there are the salons—and you know how many there are every year. Then there are all of the other promotional activities such as winemaker dinners. She's on a plane almost as many days as she is in the vineyards and the cellar. Plus she conducts visits on the property and hosts dinners for négociants and their clients. Then there is the administration. Laurence would like a change of pace. She doesn't have a personal life. She would like to have more time for herself, buy a home on Cap Ferrat like so many of the owners of neighboring châteaux have done, so she can truly relax by the water in the summer, and not just over the four week vacation period in August that everyone in France takes off, but on weekends in warm months. Plus, she would like to travel for pleasure at least two weeks out of the year. She would also like to move out of the château and rent a spacious apartment in Bordeaux for a while, to see if she likes living in the city. There is one other important factor. Laurence has no children or family that can take over the property, and to whom she can leave the château and vineyards. She would have to sell sometime anyway. Laurence has told Jonas and myself, that the property has been both a blessing and a curse. She hasn't had time for a personal life and if she'd had one, she might have married and had children. If the work was distributed between herself, her spouse and her children, it would be manageable and if just one child was interested in that life for the future, she would have a reason to keep the property."

"Why is she entertaining the idea of selling to you and not to one of the adjoining properties? Considering who her neighbors are, I would think there would be a bidding war."

"Astute as usual." It was Jonas who answered. "Laurence would want to stay on for the vineyard management part primarily. It's what she loves. Laurence has been her own woman for many years. With Torsten and myself, she knows that she will have the autonomy she desires. We will not impose any practices on her such as a château owner may have adopted for his or her property. Our vision would be congruent with her vision. We want that continuity. There would be a transition. She is prepared to take the time to work with a candidate that is less experienced, but more open. She has told us that to withdraw from that responsibility too quickly would be a shock to her system. It will take her a few years to transfer her skills anyway. So it seems that we are a good fit. We can meet her demands."

"Well then, Jonas and husband of mine, it sounds like the perfect scenario."

"Will you come do *vendange*, Ela?"

"No, Jonas, I most emphatically will not. I have visited plenty of properties during the fall harvest, and it's very hard work. I have all kinds of respect for people who do it for a living and even more so for those that do it for the experience. It's a hell of a commitment. People who volunteer get a lot out of it. They know that they had a *hand* in that particular vintage and will always be part of the history of that wine and by association, the history of that wine producing château. I'm afraid that I prefer to involve myself with the wines when they are ready to drink … and I have always enjoyed selling and promoting them. Robert has come for *vendange* … Laurence's property coincidentally. Laurence asked him and he accepted. I think she figured that there was no point in asking me. Do you and Torsten realize that if you buy Laurence's property, Robert will be your agent for Quebec and we'll be keeping it in the family? Laurence is very fond of Robert. Even more so, because of how he impressed her during *vendange*. She is very happy with his work. And that would be some of the continuity you were speaking of. Besides, if you tried to replace him, you'd have me to deal with."

"Wouldn't dream of it," Jonas assured everyone.

"That would work out very well," added Torsten.

"Isla my friend, Laurence is a fountain of knowledge. You could spend a few days with her, follow her around and ask questions, take notes and some photos … do field research … literally. I could join you. As a matter of fact, Torsten, Jonas and I could join you."

"That's a super idea, Ela. Do you think Laurence would mind?"

"We'd make sure that Laurence had the time, obviously, but I have known her for years and she enjoys talking about the property and her approach to winemaking. Laurence will recognize how favorable it will be for the property, if you write about the wines in the next book. It might even lead to some serious oentourism.

"It takes time to get permission for renovations in Bordeaux … history and all of that. Then renovations can take years. It's highly specialized work and it takes craftsmen who are much in demand. So, the château may be uninhabitable for some time. We would be very comfortable at either Hostellerie de Plaisance overlooking the medieval village of Saint-Émilion or the Hôtel Grand Barrail, a nineteenth century château set among the vines outside of the town. Both are luxury hotels known for their fine cuisine and wine cellars filled with prestigious wines.

"Isla, La Jurade de Saint-Émilion opens Vinexpo, so Laurence is going to want you for her table. I'll be going. I was inducted. Torsten and Jonas, as the new owners of Laurence's château by then, will be expected to go. Robert, as the new owner of EZ Wines, will be there too. That still leaves four places for important buyers at the table. Business relationships are solidified while everyone is immersed in the experience of amazing food that highlights the outstanding wines of the region. It's a *hedonistic* voyage to financial gain. That's how Saint-Émilion does it."

"I like the sound of that. So, Torsten, with your wife making all of these plans, we had better find a way to buy Laurence's property."

Ela could see even beyond the possibilities she had described. "It's important to have dreams and goals and more so, to realize them. It's one of those things that makes you feel revitalized … alive."

"There are other things?"

"Why yes, Jonas," was all that Ela would say for now, with a sly smile alluding to the kinds of things that their resident erotic romance novelist wrote about.

The couples were anxious to get back to their suites to say goodbye to Rome in their own way and make more memories of a personal and romantic nature to take with them.

Jonas asked Isla if she would care to join him in the Tieopolo Lounge for a nightcap. Having rested some that afternoon, Isla was not ready to call it a night. She looked forward to enjoying the live music, she said.

The others bid them a good night and kept silent until the elevator door closed, should they be overheard.

Ela instigated the discussion. "Is it me, or is something happening between those two?"

Torsten substantiated his wife's hypothesis. "I've never seen Jonas like this. Something is definitely going on with him. Isla and I just met, but she seems to be coming around … from where they started."

"You know, this is very much like an Isla Duncan novel … and it's unfolding before our eyes," was Diane's observation.

"It does seem that he wants her and she wants him. The problem is that with *those* two it's going to be complicated. Probably more complicated than with the two of you." Robert looked from Ela to Torsten. "No offense."

"None taken," Torsten replied, then thoughtfully suggested, "If they should veer off course, we're here to steer them back."

"Torsten darling, are you talking conspiracy?"

"It might come to that."

"I'm in." Ela was the first to voice support for a yet unformed plan of interference.

Elsbeth was only too happy for her husband and herself to play a part if necessary. "Count Richart and I in."

"Definitely," Richart added.

By the way his wife was smiling, Robert knew that she was eager for them to participate too.

"If there is anything that Diane and I can do …" Robert resigned himself not to swim against the tide. With this bunch, and Ela spearheading the campaign, it was pointless.

DIANA SOBOLEWSKI

CHAPTER 56

Jonas's large-cabin jet, though smaller than the jetliner, was nevertheless, just as luxurious. There was the cockpit, the full forward galley with crew rest area and crew lavoratory. There were four single berthable seats up front, then a four-place conference-dining configuration opposite a credenza, mid-cabin, plus lavoratory and two opposing four-place berthablable divans at the back.

The pilot and co-pilot were women. *Okay, so he's not a chauvinist,* thought Isla. Lamberta Hartwig, the pilot, and Landra Siferd, the co-pilot, had been flying Jonas's planes for over five years now. Lurline Enns, the older of the two shapely blond flight attendants, at about twenty-eight years of age, had been working for Jonas for nearly four years and Adette Halle for two and a half years.

When it was time for the group to take their seats, Elsbeth, Richart, Diane and Robert moved quickly to occupy the single seats up front, nearly trampling poor Isla in the process. Ela and Torsten sat themselves side by side strategically in the conference-dining seats. The only available seats were opposite Ela and Torsten, so Isla and Jonas sat down next to each other, never noticing Ela's sly smile and the look she exchanged with her husband.

Once they were in the air and the plane had leveled off, Jonas welcomed his guests with two chilled bottles of Champagne de Venoge Extra Brut La Cuvée 20 Ans 1988 that Lurline and Adette brought out.

"Just a little preview of this evening. Lurline and Adette are going to bring out a few bite-size delicacies for us to nibble on. That should keep everyone going until we have lunch at the house."

With the party started while they were still in Italian airspace, Jonas Koertig toasted his guests. "What do you think of the aperitif we are going to be enjoying at the cocktail this evening, Isla?"

"There is a freshness, due to the acidity I imagine, this being an extra brut. But the acidity seems rounded out by the long aging. Though I detect fruit through the delicate stream of bubbles, there are those beguiling aromas of nuts and honey that were years in the making. It's a very sophisticated style. One that I like very much. I look forward to tasting it again this evening."

Four luxury automobiles lined up to await the arrival of Jonas's private jet. They were different models, but all were black and recently waxed. Smartly dressed drivers and security people exited and took up position on either side of the vehicle.

Drivers greeted their passengers, then saw to the luggage. The security people acknowledged the presence of the people whose safety they were responsible for, but did not partake in conversation. They had done a dry run, and now their eyes scanned the perimeter for anything that might be out of place.

"Darling, this is Tavin. Tavin … my wife."

"Welcome home, Mr. and Mrs. Furst, and may I offer my congratulations on your marriage." Tavin addressed them formally, but there was warmth in his voice.

"Thank you, Tavin," responded his employer with equal warmth, and then added, "It's good to be home."

"Thank you, Tavin. I know you have been in my husband's service a long time and he values you immensely," were Ela's first words to the man who had been with her husband longer than she had known him, and was loyal to a fault.

Tavin smiled his gratitude at the gracious woman. She was very different from the first Mrs. Furst. He could tell that his employer was totally besotted with his bride and that she was very happy to be his wife. Ela Furst would bring life to the house. The staff would like and respect her, of that there was no doubt.

"How is Raina, Tavin?"

"Very well, sir … and, awaiting your arrival at the Koertig residence."

"Oh dear."

"I'm afraid so, sir."

Torsten seemed to know what Tavin meant, just as Tavin understood what Torsten implied. Both men appeared amused, rather than concerned, though. *Years of service,* Ela reminded herself.

"Is something wrong, Torsten?"

"Not really, darling. It just means that Raina and the Koertigs' housekeeper are ganging up on the caterers about now. Both women have exacting standards, imagine them teaming up."

The procession of black automobiles drove down a picturesque road and passed a long high stone wall. Ela was thinking that whoever lived beyond it, would have all of the privacy in the world.

"We are passing Jonas's estate. We'll be coming up on his parents' shortly."

The cars came to a stop in front of two stone pillars on either side of massive wrought iron gates. They opened to a very long paved driveway, which led to an imposing light colored stone building. *So, this is the Koertig family home,* Ela thought.

Looking through the windshield from the backseat of the car that she shared with Jonas, Isla strained to make out the architectural details of the building looming before them.

"Has your family home been featured in a British or U.S. magazine recently?"

"Mother mentioned something about a photo shoot. I guess people are interested in historical homes. My parents restored parts of the house that were in disrepair and took the opportunity to re-do the plumbing and electricity and bring everything up to code. So plumbers and electricians worked alongside craftsman who were knowledgeable about historical restoration. My parents worked with a couple of historians, an architect, an engineer, several antique dealers, and a museum curator in addition to a contractor that specialized in these kinds of projects, to get everything right. It was understood that my parents weren't prepared to sacrifice modern conveniences … It's just that they couldn't be obvious. So, it was a challenging and time-consuming project. The house was overrun by workmen day and night sometimes. They even had crews staying in these large trailers, right on the property, with their own trailer for rest periods and another for meal service. At times it wasn't possible to inhabit any part of the house. My parents, their staff and the dogs took refuge in my home, since we have adjoining properties, for weeks at a time … Correction, they took over my home for weeks at a time. This way they were close by to supervise. Of course the property that adjoins theirs on the other side belongs to Torsten, and they are always saying that he's like a son to them, but they didn't dream of inconveniencing *him*. My parents didn't travel for three years during this restoration. So, I traveled … to keep my sanity and I gave my staff a lot of time off and put them up in hotels so they wouldn't quit."

Isla had to suppress a giggle.

"I must have seen your family home in that magazine … at the hair salon most likely. They have all kinds of magazines piled on the tables in the reception area. Sometimes I flip through a couple while I wait for my appointment, without really registering what I'm looking at. Strange, though … I don't remember anything about the interior of the house. Maybe I hadn't gotten to that page. Well, I'm here now, so I can experience all of the wonderful work that your parents have done to preserve the historical accuracy and original beauty of the house in person."

"Oh, my mother *will* give you the tour."

Jonas was thinking to himself, that it felt right somehow to have Isla here. He hoped that she would like everything about the house. It held many happy memories for his parents … and for him. His Mother would say that a house was truly a home when loved ones gather in it, and when laughter could be heard in the common areas.

CHAPTER 57

The whole staff was gathered outside to greet the group, Downton Abbey style, Ela noted. Elsbeth was about to introduce the staff, when a huge, surprisingly graceful beast with a medium-long reddish brown coat, large powerful head, black muzzle and floppy years, came running out of nowhere and was building speed while it headed in their direction. It came to a full stop in front of Torsten bum wiggling and tail wagging. Then it leaned into him.

"Hello, girl." Torsten acknowledged the dog while scratching her behind the ear. "I've missed you too."

Then another came running in their direction and greeted Jonas with the same kind of affection. When Jonas bent down to kiss the top of its head, the massive creature covered his face with kisses. But, the moment he told the big dog to sit in English, it did so ... very eager to please.

"Meet the girls. The boys should be right behind them."

Just as Jonas said that, two more dogs came running. They were big-boned and muscular, like the first two, but even larger. Ela squealed with delight. Isla was laughing. They greeted the returning Elsbeth and Richart, Jonas and Torsten, but were reserved with the strangers.

So Elsbeth's introduction of the staff, was pre-empted by Jonas's introduction of the canine contingent.

"Now the whole family is here. The younger of the girls is Leyna." He pointed to the dog so happy to be getting attention from Torsten. "Her name means 'little angel.' She's anything but. She absolutely loves Torsten. She's probably going to try to sneak into your room later."

"She loves everyone, Jonas."

"Not true. She growled at your ex-wife, if you remember." The others didn't take to her either. They kept their distance ... but they never let her out of their sight."

"You have a point."

"They are good judges of character," Jonas smirked. "But, I digress. The one that just gave me a face wash is Uli. Her name means 'mistress of all' ... and that pretty much sums it up. The big brut next to Mother is Burgh. His name means 'protection.' He always has to know where everyone is. Finally we have Donner." Jonas pointed to the biggest of the dogs sitting beside Richart. "His name means 'thunder,' and he lives up to it. You can hear him coming, and hope he can put on the brakes in time."

"They are Leonbergers, a very old German breed ... and these four are just magnificent."

"You know your dogs, Isla. Do you have a dog?"

"No, but I would like to one day. We had a couple of cats who thought they were dogs when I was growing up, Dior and Hermès ... you had to know my mother. I know about your giant breed from attending the annual dog show in Montreal."

"Research for a book?"

"It started out that way, but I kept going back for the pleasure of learning about different breeds. Do you have any dogs of your own?"

"No."

"Leonbergers are great companions and watch dogs," Ela added.

"They are. This breed is also known to be smart, confident and dependable. Though they are calm, they do have a lively personality and are very energetic. These girls and boys love to go hiking with my parents, and with all of the trails between our three adjoining properties, they can be gone for hours. My parents pack a picnic, and water and treats for the dogs, as well as a very big blanket, and the dogs carry everything in backpacks. You can't keep them out of the pool either. They have webbed feet and are great swimmers. My parents had this massive natural pool constructed with beach entry and a waterfall more for the dogs than for them. You'll see it later. The problem is that if you are in the pool, they keep trying to rescue you."

"You said *sit* in English. Is it your tone of voice that they understand, or are they in fact bilingual?" Isla wanted to know.

"They pick up on your tone of voice and body language but they understand German and English, as well as hand signals."

Elsbeth joined in the conversation. "The Koertigs have had Leonbergers for generations.... Usually four at a time. We have the space, though they also have the run of the house. Don't worry, they are well behaved ... most of the time. We've had others before these. Jonas grew up with the breed. If that wasn't enough, his nanny had a Scottish deerhound by the name of Lacey. Lacey was gentle, loving, well-mannered and friendly. They are courageous dogs, but they are not watchdogs or guard dogs. They are good with children though and Lacey was devoted to Jonas. A stranger could have come into the house and walked out with priceless works of art, silverware and my good jewelry, and Lacey wouldn't have done a thing about it, but when someone that Lacey didn't know got near Jonas, she would rise to her feet and put herself between Jonas and that person, and she meant business. We called Lacey, Jonas's other nanny."

Ela was inspired. "Torsten, I would like to give our dogs German names ...

with meanings that fit with their personalities."

A tall, straight woman stepped forward. "Excuse me, sir … you're getting dogs?"

"Raina. I'm sorry. We got carried away."

"Ela, this is *the* Raina. Raina, I would like you to meet my wife."

"Mrs. Furst. Welcome. Congratulations to both of you. I look forward to welcoming you anew at your home tomorrow."

Ela took Raina's hand in both of hers. "I am so happy to finally meet you. Your husband mentioned that you would be here."

"Yes, we're getting dogs, Raina … when we return from our honeymoon. It seems that my wife likes German Shepherds. We'd like to get rescues though … a male and a female. Since you and Tavin know something about German Shepherds, do you think the two of you could look into that for us?"

"Oh, yes! Thank you, sir. Thank you, Mrs. Furst. Does Tavin know yet?" Raina had shed her housekeeper persona, and acted like young girl getting a pony for her birthday.

"No. You can have the pleasure of giving him the news."

"He is going to be as pleased as I am, Mr. and Mrs. Furst. Tavin's cousin Hans and his wife operate an animal hospital and they donate their services to several animal rescue groups. They foster and even house dogs, when there's no place for them. Tavin and I will speak to them."

Ela became self-conscious. The staff was still waiting patiently. "I'm so sorry, Elsbeth."

"Don't be, my dear. The staff is used to the dogs stealing the show. When Dietricha, our housekeeper, who you will meet in a minute, interviews someone for a position with us, the dogs sit in… and it was the same with their predecessors. They conduct part of the interview, their way. Dietricha has been with us a long time, through the life span of a few dogs. She has done this since the beginning. She gauges the dogs' reaction to the person she is considering hiring and pays careful attention to how the person reacts to them. Dietricha doesn't just spring it on them. They are told ahead of time. If they agree, that keeps them in the running. So, you see, Ela, every member of our staff is here because they passed the pup test. They have been approved. They are all very fond of the four-legged members of our family."

Ela, Isla, Diane and Robert, eyes wide at the eccentricity of this family, burst out in laughter.

Having exchanged pleasantries with the staff, the group entered the Koertig residence. Their luggage was being loaded onto an elevator concealed behind wood paneling.

"Very clever," Ela said in admiration.

"There's another like it at the back of the house," Jonas informed Ela, Isla, Diane and Robert. "I was telling Isla in the car that when my parents were doing the restoration work, they took the opportunity to add some modern conveniences. They did not want to detract from the original look of the house, so compromises had to be made. The elevators are very practical with all of these floors. My parents still take the stairs when Mother's not in heels, but the staff and guests make good use of these elevators.

"We'll take the other elevator and I'll show everyone to their rooms." Elsbeth took over. "Perhaps you will want to take a half an hour to unpack or freshen up. I'll see about lunch. We'll meet up on the patio. Just ask one of the staff where to go when you come down."

"Our suite is on the floor above, but everyone else will be staying on this floor," Elsbeth told their guests. "Ela and Torsten, the suite at the end of the hall that way is yours." Elsbeth pointed to the front of the house. "Diane and Robert, yours is here at the back of the house. Jonas, you're in your old room. Isla, you have the room next to Jonas. It was Jonas's nanny's room. I'm afraid that you'll have to share the bathroom between the two rooms. It's in the style of the house, but quite big and we've modernized it. It's just that we couldn't do anything about the configuration of this part of the house."

Elsbeth was telling the truth, but when Isla and Jonas had entered their rooms and Diane and Robert were about to head to their suite, Ela asked Elsbeth quietly, "Was that on purpose?"

"No. I didn't call ahead. Also, there are no other guest rooms. It couldn't have worked out better though, don't you think? By the way, there are no locks on the bathroom doors, and if one isn't careful, they could just swing open." Elsbeth shared with a sly smile.

The Koertigs and their guests met up on the patio as planned. It was a private area with fully functioning large outdoor kitchen with tons of counter space, a massive grill and wide vent to suck out the smoke, an outdoor living room with seating for twelve, an outdoor fireplace, audio system and large screen television. They were seated at a massive table of indoor-outdoor design.

Robert told Elsbeth and Richart that this was his fantasy space. "It's too bad you can't use it in the winter."

"Oh, but they can," Jonas interjected.

"Yes," his father confirmed. "Even the grill. We close this whole space off and it turns into a kind of solarium. The smoke from the grill is sucked out winter and summer."

Robert was in awe. The things he could do up on that grill … fish, seafood and poultry in the warmer months and meats of all kinds in the cooler months, he thought.

No one had felt the need to change their clothes. They had each used their thirty minutes to unpack.

Their late lunch was buffet style, and they agreed unanimously to stick to water, since there would be so many great wines that evening.

When they were done with lunch, the eight sat around for a while just talking. Then Elsbeth announced that it would be a good time to give their first-time guests a tour of the house.

Richart, Jonas and Torsten decided to sit this part out. They moved over to a gazebo by the swimming pool to wait for the others to join them. "It could be a while," Richart warned the other men.

When Elsbeth, Ela, Isla, Diane and Robert joined Richart, Jonas and Torsten by the bio pool after the tour of the mansion, the newcomers were all very impressed with its design. The extra-large pool looked like it had been created by nature. There was no evidence of anything mechanical. There was a very large regeneration zone with plants, which Richart explained not only kept the pool clean, but also acted like a passive solar collector and warmed the pool. The whole purpose of a bio pool was to eliminate the need for eye irritating, skin drying, fabric bleaching chemicals, he went on to say. This one was an irregular shape with non-slippery beach entry three quarters of the way around. So the dogs could get in and out easily, Richart told them.

"It slopes down, but even the deepest part isn't very deep. So if anything should happen to one of the dogs, though unlikely, we would be able to get him or her out right away. The dogs wear a light but strong waterproof harness that doesn't interfere with their enjoyment. It's something that we can grab on to and even attach a floating device to in the event of an emergency. The floatation devices are located behind the biggest of the rocks on three sides, along with alarms that will be heard everywhere on the property. Many of our staff have been trained in CPR—human and canine. By the way, it was one of Jonas's companies that designed and built this bio pool and everything to go with it. Our dogs know that they are not allowed in the pool without the harness, and only when supervised. The pool is deep enough, long enough and wide enough though, for man and beast to enjoy a good swim. There are sensors that alert the people in the security building and in the house when someone is in the pool. Actually, they can tell how many someones and if they are in distress with those sensors. We like our privacy, but there are cameras that can be turned on from either location for a visual confirmation. Before they do that, they check in with audio. If there is no response, then they go to visual.

"Of course if Elsbeth and I decide on a midnight swim"—Richart winked—"we make sure that it is understood that we want total privacy, until we say otherwise."

"Richart," Elsbeth tried to sound disapproving, but ended up giggling.

"As an additional safety measure, with respect to the dogs; there is a very tall fence that comes out of the ground a few meters from the pool. It's too high for the dogs to scale, even in the winter when snow can pile up and become compacted. That's what worried us the most. We almost never have it up until it's time to close the pool at the end of the season though. Then it stays up until it's time to open the pool. One part of it is a wide gate in case we have to have maintenance done. In the winter we have to remove the snow in front of it and de-ice the latch, but it opens outwards, so it's manageable. Before you ask, with the way it was constructed, there is no danger of electrocution."

Elsbeth joined in. "Since this pool was built, Jonas's company has had a lot of requests for custom designed bio pools that are dog friendly. It's now a very big part of their business."

"Maybe we should look into that, Torsten?"

"Way ahead of you, my love. I talked to Jonas about it while Elsbeth was giving you the tour. Obviously we'll need a pool house. Perhaps one that will double as our private retreat.

Ela had caught his meaning, of course, so she looked directly into her husband's eyes and smiled.

"Where are the dogs now?" Ela wanted to know.

Richart laughed. "Detricha is keeping them out of the way, and they're none too happy about that. They always want to be where the action is."

What Ela liked most about the bio pool, she told everyone, was that while it looked completely natural in every way, she could see the bottom. Ela mentioned that she thought she would find a murky pool in which you could not see your feet, and the idea kind of freaked her out. Richart told her that she was not alone. Elsbeth had felt the same way.

"What is that building over there?" Isla asked Elsbeth.

"That's our pool house. My husband felt that since we were putting in a pool, we had to have a pool house, so there it is. Anyway, it is practical. There's a sitting room with some enormous divans, a fireplace and large screen television, plus quite an audio system. It's also equipped with a mini kitchen, bar and built-in wine cellar, as well as two bathrooms with showers and changing rooms where you will find extra towels. There is a separate part that houses additional loungers, outdoor tables, umbrellas, cushions as well as reading material, including Isla Duncan novels in paperback … there's another set in hardcover in the library." Elsbeth was pleased tell everyone. "Anyway, it's nice and private. It's away from the house and it has a wonderful view of the pool which we light up at night. Sometimes when it's too cool to sit outside at night, we go there to enjoy a good bottle of wine."

Just then, something occurred to Elsbeth that had her concerned.

"Richart, the florist has not shown up yet. He and his people should have been here by now. I'm getting worried."

"There is nothing to worry about, sweetheart," Richart told his wife reasurringly. "There was a little mix-up with the flowers that will decorate the cocktail space, and they will be delivered a little later than planned, that's all. But, it looks like everything is being sorted out.

"They'll get all of those yellow and tangerine flowers here in plenty of time. It's just that they had mistakenly put them into pink pots, rather than the red ones."

"What? No, no, no …" Then, Elsbeth saw the mischievous glint in her husband's eye and the smile on his lips. Jonas and Torsten coughed discreetly to hide their own mirth.

"Richart Koertig, it's a good thing there are people around, or you'd be in big trouble. Has the car left for the airport to pick up Mr. Bishop and the wedding coordinator?"

"Were they supposed to be picked up?" Richart tried to keep a straight face, but couldn't.

"Father, you're taking your life in your hands." The rest were trying not to laugh, but failed miserably.

"It's just that even though there are a dozen people running around here with checklists, meticulously attending to every detail, if I know your mother she's going to be making the rounds to see that they haven't missed something … Your mother needs to relax. Elsbeth, as your husband and the man of the house, I'm telling you that we are going to change our clothes and take the dogs for a nice long walk. Everyone who is supposed to be working is. We're just in the way. She likes it when I'm forceful," Richart added and winked at the others.

Elsbeth rolled her eyes and shook her head.

"Good idea, and with the dogs out of the way, I'll actually be able to take a swim," Jonas told his parents. "We have to be downstairs at eight thirty, right?" Jonas directed the question at his mother. He looked serious, but Elsbeth was onto her son.

"Like father, like son. Unbelievable. Don't you dare be late."

Ela and Torsten decided on a nap, though maybe not right away. Diane and Robert thought that was the thing to do, to look and feel their best. Isla was a little tired herself. A nap would be good.

Jonas snuck into the pool house in search of reading material. He hadn't missed the fact that his mother had all of Isla's books in there. Jonas remembered that Isla's two English fans from Rome, had said that *The Claddagh Ring* was her latest novel. To get to know the author, he'd have to meet her characters. He wondered if she had written herself into the principal female character of her latest work.

With the book in hand, Jonas Koertig returned to the pool, ready to unlock the secrets of Isla Duncan.

CHAPTER 58

Already made up with hair styled and half dressed, Isla realized that she had forgotten to spray on some perfume. She looked around for the bottle, but it was not in her room. Then she remembered that she had left it on the vanity in the bathroom.

Isla opened the door hurriedly and walked all the way in before she realized that Jonas was hunched over the sink removing the last traces of shaving cream. He was totally naked. She started to withdraw while trying not to make a sound in her black high heel evening sandals, when he lifted his head and caught sight of her in the mirror.

"Sorry. I was just looking for my perfume." She hadn't heard the water running. Elsbeth and Richart had done an excellent job soundproofing the rooms.

Having dried his face with a towel, Jonas located the pink porcelain egg-shaped bottle, picked it up and brought it over to Isla, not at all self-conscious that he was giving her the full frontal view. Rather than handing the perfume over right away, he brought the bottle up to his nose.

"Very nice." He wasn't just referring to the seductive scent when Isla was standing in front of him in nothing but a nearly sheer black bra with some delicate lace and the tiniest of panties from the same collection. She was blushing profusely.

"Thank you," Isla replied acting as if he was complimenting her fragrance and nothing more. "I really have to finish getting ready, so if you don't mind?" Isla held out her hand.

"Of course." Jonas placed the bottle in her hand and watched as Isla turned and walked away. He didn't move from his spot until she had closed the door behind her.

Isla wasn't exactly composed as she tested the handle to make sure that the door stayed closed. She now felt as naked as Jonas had been.

She couldn't get the image of the naked Jonas out of her mind though. If only she could have seen what she saw without having been observed, voyeuristic as that would have been. The last thought she allowed herself before dressing was: *So his penis matches the size of his ego.*

After spraying on her signature fragrance, Isla got into her floor length black silk chiffon evening dress. It fit close to the body but opened up on one side with a slit from mid-thigh that was hidden by a wispy feminine frill from the waist all the way down to the floor. It gave the dress movement, and revealed leg when she walked. The shoulder straps were of medium width and the neckline was just low enough to show a little cleavage. The back was cut a little lower, but didn't dip as low as some of her other dresses. This dress was more romantic in style than what Isla usually wore, but she had been swept up in the occasion. The last thing that Isla had to do was attach her mother's earrings and fasten the clasp of her mother's bracelet. With a dress that only Isla would have considered low key, she would carry the clutch of Swarovski crystals for a little more sparkle, as she had at the wedding.

Isla reminded herself to hurry otherwise she might arrive at the elevator at the same time as Jonas. She preferred to avoid him.

The coast was clear. Then she realized that she had forgotten her clutch and went back for it. As she headed out the door for the second time, the elegantly dressed Jonas was coming out of his room.

There he was, working that tuxedo the way few men could, and she was still seeing him naked. Isla started to blush again.

"Stunning ... though I prefer what you were in earlier."

"As a gentleman, you didn't have to take such a good long look."

"May I remind you, that you walked in on me? Perhaps it was on purpose?"

"It was an accident."

"You can tell a lot about a woman from her lingerie ... and her perfume."

"I can see that you actually believe you're an expert on such things."

"Said the woman who's wearing Agent Provocateur on at least a few of her pulse points and under that dress."

Taken by surprise, Isla wondered how he knew that her bra and panties were from Agent Provocateur.

"In any case, whatever gave you the idea that I am a gentleman?"

CHAPTER 59

The three couples were in the ballroom with Mr. Bishop and the wedding coordinator when Isla and Jonas made their entrance. Mr. Bishop was expressing his approval for the photograph that the bride and groom had selected as their official wedding photo for the press release. It was flattering and they looked insanely in love.

"Ah, Ms. Duncan … Mr. Koertig, if you would like to look around the room, we have some great photographs from the wedding. There is one of the two of you that is just outstanding. You could have easily been bride and groom. Mrs. Furst has requested that you each receive that photograph … nicely framed, of course, as a special memento for doing such an excellent job as best woman and best man."

"Thank you, Mr. Bishop." Then Jonas turned to Ela. "That's very thoughtful, Ela."

"What a good looking group we are," said their hostess who was in a pink silk off the shoulder mermaid gown with black lace on the bodice.

"Mother, you look beautiful. Are those pink and white diamond earrings new?"

"Yes. Do you like them?"

"They're exquisite. You purchased them for the occasion?"

"Of course not. I just mentioned to your father that we had an anniversary coming up. You look handsome, son. Almost as handsome as your father. Isla dear, you wear black very well. I must tell you that you look absolutely gorgeous this evening."

"You're quite chic yourself. Richart had better not let you out of his sight this evening."

Robert was starting to get used to this whole tuxedo thing and liking it. He looked good in his black tux, his wife told him with admiration.

"Aren't you glad that you listened to me and had one tailor made … even if it was a little pricey?"

"My wife is usually right about things like that. By the way, have I told you how great you look in that pink dress?"

Robert didn't know that the column style dress was silk chiffon. He only knew that he liked the low back and thin crisscross straps. His wife had accessorized with the earrings he had given her as wedding gift; which pleased him, a pink evening bag with crystal clasp and dressy pink sandals.

There was no doubt who the bride and groom were this evening. Torsten in his fine black tuxedo had the look of love in his eyes every time Ela came into his line of vision.

Ela had decided that the gown for the reception would be dove-gray in keeping with Mr. Bishop's theme. It was gathered over one shoulder and as it went over onto the back, the gray silk turned a transparent flesh tone. A corset of appliqué from under the bust to over the hip and a silk cumberbund accentuated Ela's small waist. From knees to the floor, there were only layers of translucent silk chiffon in the same hue. When she walked, it looked like she was walking in mist. Ela wore delicate silver evening sandals with very fine cross straps across the top of her feet and around her ankles. Her evening clutch was a plain dove-gray satin and she wore her engagement ring, wedding band and the earrings that were her wedding gift from Torsten with great pride.

Mr. Bishop reminded the group that the two coaches with their guests would be arriving momentarily. Unlike in a situation where guests arrived separately and trickled into a reception, coming by coach meant that they would be arriving all at once. He assured them though, that the team was ready and would have a glass of Champagne in everyone's hands in minutes.

Mr. Bishop suggested that the Koertigs go out now to greet their guests. All three of them would be needed. Diane and Robert could go out too if they wished, so they followed Elsbeth and Richart out. When Torsten stepped away for a moment to have a last word with Jonas, Ela whispered to Isla, "You don't seem yourself. Did something happen? And did it involve Jonas? You came down together ... again."

"There was a little mishap in the bathroom. That's all I'm going to say."

"I see. Are you going to be alright this evening?"

"I'll be fine."

Ela couldn't wait to tell Elsbeth.

"Ladies and gentlemen, thank you for coming to our dinner to honor Torsten Lucas Furst. As all of you know, Torsten is my oldest and dearest friend, and like a son to my parents. My parents and I agreed that it was time we threw Torsten a proper party and invited people who are important to him, to help us celebrate his life and accomplishments.

"There has been a new development recently as well, and we thought that this was the appropriate way to share the news with you. Please put down your glass of Champagne for a second and help me welcome the man of the hour, my friend Torsten."

Torsten walked through the crowd to applause and took his place beside Jonas. No one noticed that Torsten was wearing a wedding band.

"Friends and my corporate family, I am overwhelmed. Thank you for coming. I know some of you probably thought that you had to show up. Not so, but I am grateful that you did. I have an announcement to make about something that occurred only recently, but is the most important thing that has ever happened to me."

The guests were on pins and needles.

"I'm afraid that you have been invited here, in part, under false pretenses, but I hope that you'll forgive the ruse once you know the whole story. I'd like to ask someone very special to join us. Some of you already know her." He looked at Edmond Mallet, the Bordeaux négociant that Ela had worked with for so many years. He was accompanied by his wife. Torsten also turned in the direction of a group of wine producers that Ela was close to and he was friendly with. Among them was Laurence Bonnet.

That was Ela's cue. The crowd parted to clear a path for the woman with sparkling eyes, red lips and the warmest of smiles. Her soft gray evening gown floated around her as did waves of dark lustrous hair. She had this aura about her that made it impossible for anyone to look elsewhere.

"Ladies and gentlemen, for those of you who don't know; this lovely lady used to go by the name of Ela Zalewski." Torsten reached for the hand on which Ela was wearing her wedding and engagement rings and raised it to his lips.

Their guests were captivated and desperate to know where this was going.

Torsten did not keep them in suspense much longer. "But, this evening it gives me great pleasure to introduce her to everyone as Mrs. Torsten Lucas Furst."

The announcement was greeted with wild applause. When the clapping finally died down, Torsten continued. "Ela and I were married in Rome two days ago. I know that many of you will have questions, but my wife and I are intensely private people, so please don't be offended if we do not go into great detail about our courtship or engagement. Just be assured that as my best friend, Jonas Koertig, pointed out, there are no other two people more right for each other. Those of you who know Jonas, know he's never wrong."

The crowd roared.

"Jonas by the way, was not only my best man, but he was responsible for taking care of everything to do with the wedding, which goes well beyond the duties of best man. Thank you, Jonas. I am more grateful than I can express. As talented as Jonas is, he did have excellent help from the most gifted of wedding planners, Mr. Cyril Bishop and his army. Thank you, Mr. Bishop."

Mr. Bishop acknowledged the compliment with a bow of his head.

"I would also like to thank our host and hostess, Mr. and Mrs. Koertig, who were part of the wedding party. I have known them forever, and they are family. Elsbeth and Richart worked with Mr. Bishop and his people to pull off this wonderful reception, as did the Koertigs' staff, especially Deitricha and my own Raina, who are back in the kitchen working at whatever level is above perfection."

Richart waved and Elsbeth blew Torsten a kiss.

"On behalf of my wife and myself, I would like to thank Ms. Isla Duncan over there in the black evening dress. Some of you may recognize the name. Isla is my wife's closest and dearest friend and stood up with Ela as her best woman. Yes, that's what I said, best woman. As you come to know my wife, it will all make sense. She's like no other. Now Isla means as much to me as she does to Ela."

"Finally, I would like to thank that beautiful lady and handsome gentleman next to Isla. That is Dr. Diane Beauchamp and her husband, *Monsieur* Robert Leclerc, who is a very knowledgeable wine agent. You are bound to enjoy talking to Robert, if you are a wine lover. They were also in our wedding. They are more family than friends to my wife, and now part of the family that includes Jonas, Elsbeth, Richart, Isla, Ela and myself.

"Isla, Diane and Robert are from Montreal like my wife, but we expect to have them visit us in Bavaria often.

"I would like to take a little time during the cocktail hour to have Ela meet all of you, but first will you kindly raise your glasses with me."

And the guests complied happily.

"To my darling wife and to family and friends." Torsten made a point of looking from his wife to Jonas, Elsbeth, Richart, Isla, Diane and Robert before looking out among the guests.

"Oh, one last thing."

"Expect to see a lot less of me around the office. I have the best, most capable people working for me and with me, and it's time that I adopted a different management style. I've decided that I am not going to micromanage anymore. I'm going to be spending more time on the pleasures of life … starting with a one month honeymoon. No need to applaud, though."

No applause, but he did get collective laughter.

One gentleman was about to snap a photo with his mobile, but a look from Jonas dissuaded him. "Ladies and gentleman, we ask there be no photos taken with your mobiles. You may have noticed that there is an official photographer here this evening. You will receive copies. Also, would you please treat this information as confidential until there is an official press release with photo, while the newlyweds are on their honeymoon … to protect their privacy."

The first to offer congratulations was Ima Kurtz.

"Darling, this is Ima Kurtz, the head of corporate legal for all of my companies."

"I am so happy to meet you, Ms. Kurtz, or is it Mrs. Kurtz?"

"It's Ms. Kurtz, Ela, but in three months it will be Mrs. Konig," announced Aldrick, Ela's high profile deal-making acquaintance from Bordeaux, who came to stand beside Ms. Kurtz.

"Aldrick, it's so good to see you. What wonderful news. Small world. Isn't it?" Ela teased and kissed him on both cheeks.

"Yes, it is. Congratulations, my dear. You too, Torsten. You're a very lucky man."

"I know that I am, Aldrick. Glad you could come, and congratulations to the both of you on your engagement. I didn't know."

"It's very recent, and thank you," Ima told her employer on their behalf.

"I heard that Jonas brokered *this* deal."

"Did you now?" Ela couldn't resist.

"I wish it had been I," Aldrick added mischievously.

"Spoken like the Aldrick that I know," Ela acknowledged.

"Aldrick, how do you know Mrs. Furst? Never mind. You know everyone," his financée stated matter-of-factly.

"Oh and, Torsten, a word of advice: Treat her well. I'm very fond of your wife. If you do not, I will have half a dozen billionaires lined up who will. And some of them are even richer than you are."

Ela laughed. Torsten was speechless.

When Ima and Aldrick were out of earshot, Ela turned to her husband and said, "Aldrick cracks me up ... that bit about the billionaires ... if you don't treat me right."

"The thing is, he means it."

Ela had a great time meeting the guests, and she and Torsten graciously accepted their congratulations and heartfelt wishes. These people had great respect for her husband and few called him by his first name, even when he used their first names. The same for her.

It was no wonder they respected him. Wherever they stopped, Torsten would pull out a story about the person's family or some amusing business anecdotes. He had a relationship with each and every one of these people.

Just before dinner, Jonas took to the microphone.

"Ladies and gentlemen, we will be sitting for dinner in a minute, with Mr. and Mrs. Furst leading the way, but my parents and I have been asked during the cocktail hour about wedding presents.

"The bride and groom would appreciate a donation to a charity of your choosing or if you prefer, one of the charities that they support. By next week, my office will email you a list. I see that Mr. Bishop is assembling us for our entrance, so I won't take up any more of your time."

Jonas joined Isla and offered his arm. Isla took it and instantly thought of Jonas naked. She didn't dare look at him, in case he realized. By *not* looking at him, Isla told Jonas what she was thinking, and he smiled to himself.

Ela and Torsten had enjoyed some Champagne during the cocktail part of the evening, but with so many people to see, they hadn't eaten a morsel of food. Both were relieved that they were going to be dining with their wedding party, so they could enjoy the fabulous feast ahead.

With the Les Crêtes Chardonnay Cuvée Bois 2010, Ela, Torsten, Isla and Jonas asked for the seared scallops and parsnips cream, while Elsbeth and Diane requested the chilled pea, avocado and mint soup, and Richart and Robert ordered the paper thin slices of smoked trout with lemon wedges.

The medallions of lobster in Champagne sauce served with Champagne de Venoge Millésimé 2002 were a big hit with the ladies. Torsten and Jonas had opted for the pomegranate glazed wild Alaska salmon with apple horseradish that was served with Domaine Armelle et Bernard Rion Vosne-Romanée "Les Chaumes" 2006 and found it utterly delicious. Richart and Robert went for the medium rare filet mignon of Black Angus in Merlot and wild mushroom sauce that was served with Château Beau-Séjour Bécot Saint-Émilion Grand Cru Classé 2005 and argued that they had made out the best.

Everyone had a little cheese with fig confit, and after a short break and much sparkling water, the passion fruit cream with wild berries was served.

Ela and Torsten posed with the cake and when their table was served, ate but a forkful just like the rest, to make it look good. They skipped the mignardise, but not the Champagne de Venoge Cordon Bleu Demi-Sec. Unlike their guests, they did not order coffee, tea or Armagnac, so the leader of the band that had been playing background music, signaled for the band to stop playing because he had an announcement.

"Ladies and gentlemen, the bride and groom specifically requested that there be no speeches and asked that on their behalf I express their thanks to the chef and his staff for these exquisite dishes served on this auspicious occasion, which our band was lucky enough to have had a sampling of before your dinner. Chef, would and your staff come out please."

The chef and his team came out to a round of applause.

"And now, ladies and gentlemen, the bride and groom will open the dancing."

Ela was panic-stricken. She tried to signal to the band leader that they would not be opening the dancing, but Torsten rose from his seat and held his hand out to Ela.

"May I have this dance, Mrs. Furst?"

"Torsten, you don't have to do this ... in front of all of these people."

"But I want to hold my wife in my arms."

"Are you sure?"

"I'm sure."

Ela was still nervous as Torsten moved with her in her arms. He wasn't awkward, as she had feared. He was graceful and sure of himself. If anything, she had to step up *her* game. So she relaxed in his arms and followed his movements. They looked so happy and so in love. No one had ever seen Torsten Lucas Furst like this. The room was visibly moved and gave them a standing ovation.

Elsbeth and Richart joined them on the dance floor and then they changed partners. Jonas invited Isla to dance and she accepted, but moved awkwardly, self-conscious from being so physically close. Robert led Diane onto the dance floor right behind them. They all changed partners during the next few numbers, until they found themselves with their original partners and it was time for the guests to join the dancing.

When Ela and Elsbeth excused themselves and were sure that they were alone in the ladies room, Elsbeth asked Ela, "Do you find Isla a bit strange this evening?"

"Apparently there was a mishap in the bathroom that she shares with Jonas, but she wouldn't tell me the nature of that mishap."

"I take it that it was more enjoyable for Jonas, because he hasn't stopped smiling."

"By the way that the unflappable Isla Duncan is avoiding making eye contact with Jonas, I'd say that she hasn't been able to stop thinking about what happened. She's fighting the attraction that she's feeling for your son."

While Ela and Elsbeth were forming their hypothesis, Jonas asked Isla if she would like to finish their dance on the terrace where it was cooler. Isla agreed because the cool night breeze would be welcome after all of the dancing.

Inside, Jonas had kept it respectable, but now he was holding her close as they moved to the slow sensual rhythm of the music. Isla was acutely aware of Jonas's hard body and his clean masculine scent with woody and spicy notes. She was heating up, not cooling off.

Suddenly the music stopped, and so did Jonas. He looked right into Isla's eyes, placed his hands on either side of her head, fingers disappearing in the waves of her thick hair and kissed her deeply and passionately. Isla's mouth responded to his kiss before she had a chance to process what was happening.

The kiss lasted a good long time; then Jonas broke away. He thanked Isla for the dance, and took her by the hand to lead her back inside, as if nothing had happened.

"Shall we go in and join the others? It's probably time to see the guests out."

CHAPTER 60

The reception had ended at midnight, but it was after one a.m. when the last guests boarded the coaches that would take them to their hotels. The core group should have been fatigued, but Elsbeth, Richart, Diane, Robert, Ela, Torsten, Isla and Jonas were overly stimulated. In Isla's case, it was for reasons as yet unknown to the others, with the exception of Jonas, who gave no indication.

The only way that anyone was going to get to any sleep was if they could wind down. Having foreseen this, Elsbeth had Mr. Bishop make some last minute arrangements to have the caterers put out refreshments in the Koertig family room, for when the guests departed. Having been fed earlier and let out for the last time, the dogs now joined them there.

It was a large space, paneled in dark wood true to the period, and dominated by a large fireplace, also original to the house. The furniture was massive, but did not look oversize in the context of the room. For some reason, the room, for all of its dark wood furnishings, didn't feel oppressive. The room felt cozy … comforting.

And, it was decorated with several ornate silver vases, each filled with a dozen lavender roses. The color looked good against the dark wood in this room. It seemed that while Elsbeth and Richart wanted to preserve their family history and the authentic character of their home, someone had a flair for beautification.

"Isla, look. Lavender roses."

"I know. They're beautiful. Lavender roses have a long history, but people don't realize. They think this is the next wonderful thing to come along, when really … they are rediscovering something that has always been. Something old is something new."

"Well then, one is ahead of the curve by going back in time."

"You could put it that way."

Oil portraits of family members that had occupied the house before Elsbeth and Rickart, hung on the walls. The present-day occupants continued the tradition with photographs.

There was a wedding photo of Elsbeth and Richart in a heavy silver frame, and another of them and their newborn son on one of two side tables. It was hard to imagine that Elsbeth and Richart had lived through decades of changes in fashion and technology, and bore witness to political upheaval and social change, when they looked so much part of the present.

Elsbeth pointed to the other table. "One of the group photos from the wedding will be going there, to mark another important event in our family history."

"That's very touching, Elsbeth." Ela smiled warmly at their hostess.

Jonas looked over the refreshments. "I see the Champagne de Venoge stemware, but where is the Champagne, Mother?"

"I saw the caterers filling two ice buckets with water and ice in the preparation area beside the kitchen before they left. I presume the Champagne has been chilling there the last twenty-five minutes. Unfortunately, they forgot to put it out."

"I'll take care of it, Mother."

"Thank you, sweetheart." To everyone else she said, "Shall we sit?"

There was only one more photo in the room. Isla had not seen it until just now. It was displayed on the mantel above the fireplace, a place of honor. It must represent something very special to the family, assessed Isla the observer. While the others sat, Isla went in for a closer look to satisfy her writer's inquisitive mind.

The group heard an intake of breath before seeing Isla's fair complexion take on a ghastly pallor.

"Isla dear. What's wrong?" Elsbeth was instantly concerned.

"This is my aunt."

"The woman with Jonas is his nanny, Mrs. Margaret Ferguson."

"My aunt's name was Margaret Ferguson. Isla was her middle name. Her family had always called her Isla. I have this same exact photo. My aunt sent it to my father, her brother, all of those years ago."

"The red hair, the color of your eyes, your petite frame, the vintage Claddagh ring, I almost feel like I already knew you were Nanny's niece. It all makes sense now. You have some of your aunt's mannerisms ... and you definitely have her spirited nature. Now here *you* are ... in our lives and in our home."

"It's not by chance, Elsbeth." They turned to look at Ela ... all except for Isla. "The lavender roses ... do you order those often?"

"This is the first time. I do a fair amount of gardening, but I was not aware that lavender roses existed. The idea just popped into my head. I must have seen them in a decor magazine or maybe a gardening magazine. On impulse, I telephoned my florist, ordering lavender roses. He had to make quite the effort to locate some. They're lovely, though. I was told that they symbolized love at first sight. I thought it was romantic and doubled my initial order."

"Isla, tell everyone the title of your next book." When Isla couldn't find her voice, Ela spoke in her stead, "Isla's next book will be titled *Lavender Roses*."

"So ... if everyone doesn't have goose bumps by now ... Elsbeth, is there a pond on your property with a wood and wrought iron bench that overlooks it?"

"Yes, there is. It's where Mrs. Ferguson spent time reading to Jonas and helping him with his homework. Sometimes they would have a picnic there. It was their special place. How do you know about the pond and bench?"

"Isla told me … reluctantly, I might add." Isla was still speechless and appeared to be in a trance-like state.

"Isla had a dream a few weeks ago about her aunt. They were at a place exactly like this photo, but in color. We only see the corner of the house in the picture, but Isla saw the pond, the bench, the house in its entirety, and the long driveway. The driveway was gravel in her dream though."

"It was gravel. We had it paved eventually, because of how dusty the cars got," Elsbeth was compelled to explain.

Ela nodded. No discrepancy there, then. "Isla described everything to me in great detail. In the dream, Isla's aunt looked right at her, as if she knew who she was, though she would not have been born yet. She beckoned for Isla to join her and the little boy, who we now know is Jonas. In the dream, Isla recognized the vintage Claddagh ring on her aunt's hand. It was the one she had inherited. I should mention that this was the first time that Isla had fallen asleep while still wearing the ring. She simply forgot to take it off after an exhausting day of promotional appearances. In sleep the mind is unguarded."

Jonas re-entered the family room pleased with himself because he had transferred the two perfectly chilled flacons of Champagne de Venoge Louis XV Brut 1996 into one easy to carry extra-large ice bucket.

Silence greeted him. Everyone was sitting except for Isla. She was standing by the fireplace. All except Isla, turned to look in his direction wearing an odd expression he could not read. Isla remained transfixed by the photograph on the mantel.

"What did I miss?"

ACKNOWLEDGEMENTS

Thank you to:

My husband and the family and friends who encouraged me in my career as a wine agent to begin with.

The people who helped me to reach higher professionally and go farther in the world of luxury wine than I could have ever imagined.

The hardworking wine producers who continue to hone their craft so that we may find pleasure in every glass.

The colorful people in the world of luxury wine that lent texture to the characters on the pages of this book. My hope is that you never give in to convention and continue to live life on your own terms. You are so much more interesting the way you are.

The *special* person who ignited my imagination. Our paths crossed for a reason. When I drink white wine in the summertime, I think of you and smile.

The family and friends who encouraged me in my career as a novelist and shared my vision. I loved it when you demanded updates and that I sign your copies. It was very motivating.

SPECIAL THANKS

Gilles, you have always impressed me with your *out of the box* thinking; I am convinced this is the reason you are so successful. Your suggestion to do a series is why there is a series.

Kristine, you are so talented in your own right. You nurtured my writer's soul and gave me some good advice along the way.

Alex, Tomi and Angela, your support was precious.

Celeste, you are such an accomplished woman. Seeing *my* characters through *your* eyes was invaluable.

Donna, you are so creative yourself, and you have faced and overcome huge challenges. You showed me that a strong will can take us were we need to be.

Jayne, my pen pal from across the pond since sixth grade. It started with letter writing, and now look.

Sue, I'm so glad you got me hooked on historical romance novels when we were in our teens.

Al, when I walked into your office and announced that I was writing this series, you took me seriously and immediately offered to help. You gave my work that professional touch. Jannike, outstanding job.

Madeline, you definitely know the genre and the pointers you gave me were great.

Michel, sharing your knowledge about web design and construction to promote author and series put me on the right path.

Robert, the way you were thinking "big" for me was inspiring.

Alain, your quote is priceless, "It's all fiction … except for the facts." I love your wicked sense of humor.

Everyone at the salon, the way you shared in my excitement was uplifting.

Avid readers and next-door neighbors, for your perspective on what's entertaining.

All of my readers. You are the ones that *really* bring the characters to life.

Professional Credits:
Al Stavro and Jannike Hess: Layout, design and production.
Vin Par Vin: Wine expertise
Madeline Hopkins: Editing services

 DIANA SOBOLEWSKI leads a double life: wine agent and author of provocative contemporary fiction.

Diana, who resides in Montreal with her husband and two dogs, has a B.A., Marketing Communications from Concordia University, was President of the Montreal Chapter of the Business/Professional Advertising Association and has worked in marketing communications on the corporate and agency side.

Passionate about fine wine, it was only natural that she would combine her education, skills and work experience with her knowledge and appreciation of luxury wine.

In 2004 Diana established Les Vins Aldi, an agency specializing in the sale and promotion of such wines in the province of Quebec. She sought a Champagne house of historical significance with a wide range of styles to represent, which did happen eventually, but her big break came the same year; when she turned her attention to the prestigious and rare wines of Bordeaux. In 2007 she was inducted into *La Jurade de Saint Émilion* and became an ambassador for the wines of Saint-Émilion in her part of the world.

As an insider, Diana was afforded a front row seat to this fascinating world and the *bigger than life* individuals that pass through it.

Luxury wine is therefore the underlying theme of this provocative work of contemporary fiction celebrating characters and readers over thirty. Like her main female character, the author believes that great wine can take you on a hedonistic voyage outside of yourself.

The author is still working actively as a wine agent, though her portfolio has been streamlined to accommodate the dual careers. Diana fulfills a long time dream with the upmarket DESIRE & LUXURY WINE series in which she introduces readers to a world of flamboyant seductive characters that dedicate themselves to the pursuit of pleasure. At the center of each story are two compelling individuals destined to be together.

www.dianasobolewski.com
facebook.com/diana.sobolewski

Printed in Great Britain
by Amazon